SIX FOOT UNDER

Also by Katherine John

Without Trace

SIX FOOT UNDER

Katherine John

St. Martin's Press ☎ New York

A THOMAS DUNNE BOOK.
An imprint of St. Martin's Press.

ISBN 0-312-14416-4

First published in Great Britain by Headline Book
Publishing PLC

First U.S. Edition: May 1996

10   9   8   7   6   5   4   3   2   1

To Ralph Spencer Watkins

Prologue

The clouds hid the moon. The only light that reflected in the garden came from the muted orange glow of the street lamps just above and outside the high walls that enclosed the grounds. Their rays cast an eerie, pyrotechnical tinge on to the tips of the Victorian iron spears that crowned the brickwork. A cool night breeze rustled the newly unfurled summer buds on the trees, and rattled the skeletons of the dead leaves that had escaped the gardener's rake by piling deep in the undergrowth.

Buildings loomed: a massive Gothic silhouette surrounded by rectangular blocks of ebony; black cutouts in a world of grey shadows. Occasionally a pencil thin line of light glimmered from beneath a blind and, at the end of long rows of gleaming blank panes, squares of soft amber shone in kitchens, bathrooms and ward offices, mute testimony to those unfortunates who had to work through the hours of darkness.

A phantom rippled through the garden. Softly, stealthily it floated within the shadows that fell from the trees and the high, encircling wall. Occasionally it paused, but always close to a tree trunk, or deep in the shelter of thick, tall bushes that masked its presence. Its spine was bowed, curved into a hunchback. The shade it cast was huge, malformed, an enormous swollen mass crowning thin, gangly legs.

It continued to drift, bush to bush, tree to tree, the pauses when it was motionless were filled with silences when ears strained and senses stretched to their utmost.

A clock struck, its ringing chimes crashing raucously, disturbing the rustles of fieldmice and voles. A barn owl swooped low, screeching when it missed its prey. A dog barked somewhere on the suburban estate outside the wall, which sprawled on what, until recently, had been hospital land.

1

On the main road outside the front wall a car engine roared, closely followed by an angry squealing of brakes. Then came the monotonous, unmelodic siren of a police car. The phantom crouched low in the undergrowth, waiting until the clamour passed.

Later, much later, it inched forward, faltering on the skirts of a patch of gleaming lawn. A low hill of soil loomed to the left of the clearing. In front of it the lip of a large puddle, blacker than any ink, wavered with the wind blown trees that swayed above it.

Hesitation, caution, then a quick scurrying movement, sideways like a crab. The hunchback stood poised for a moment. It leaned forward, bent double, and was hunchback no longer. It stood tall, broad and straight on the skyline. The hard stencil of a shovel protruded from the mound of earth. The phantom stooped, took it, and began to transfer the earth from the hill into the pit, with steady, rhythmic movements, spadeful by spadeful.

A silver light bathed the scene in frigid wintry beauty as the moon edged its way out from behind the soft, grey billowing clouds. The phantom worked faster, faster, stopping only to pass its left arm across its brow. The mound began to diminish at the right-hand edge, and still the figure worked on. Ever alert, ever watchful. Pausing momentarily between each load, listening and waiting.

The bottom of the pit was dark, damp, and colder than ice. The air stank with the mouldy reek of rot and decay. A figure bound rigidly in a sheet, resembling more giant chrysalis than anything human, stared relentlessly upwards. Only its eyes remained within control. It was a strain to keep them unblinkingly open, gazing at the oblong of textured blue night sky, misted by clouds and punctured by the pinpricks of a million tiny stars. In the left-hand corner shone a small, brilliant segment of silver light. Pitted and scarred it had to be the moon. To the left Orion shone down, recognised from schooldays and the one astronomy lesson that had graced the entire geography course.

Cold and – something else – paralysed. No matter how strenuously the brain willed limbs to move, they remained limp and leaden; log-like appendages to a lifeless body where only the mind roamed free, painfully and acutely active. All strength and power that remained was focused, concentrated desperately but vainly. The paralysis that reigned supreme denied the body even the dubious comfort of shivering.

What prevailed was the infinite depth of the segment of night sky. The mind worked feverishly as the eyes stared upwards, collecting thoughts, attempting to arrange them in logical, coherent order. The last memory was of walking – walking from the consulting room to the gate. Feet sinking into fresh, glutinous tarmacadam; the smell had come too late to give warning. Newly laid, and softened by the warm spring sunshine, the sticky black substance had ruined brand new green leather shoes. But, as well as fury over the spoiled shoes, there had been a feeling of exhilaration. Exhilaration because the last appointment was over. The gate symbolised freedom. The walk ahead was towards liberty and independence. The depression that had resulted in incarceration, if not totally cured, could at least be dealt with while one's life was lived in the outside world.

Walking – walking towards the gate. Then – then a shout, a cry . . . an iron-tanged, bitter, icy darkness. Confinement by something other than paralysis and constricting cloth. Blazes of light, pinpricks that hurt overly sensitive skin, darkness . . . more darkness . . . then sky. Exquisitely beautiful, crystal-clear night sky.

A shower of earth fell, dry, dusty, powdery, rattling against the taut, drawn cloth. The sound triggered a single, devastating flash of realisation – and panic. Another shower came. There was a fierce struggle to force open glued lips, to formulate a scream; but the lips gummed tightly shut refused to obey, and no sound was born in the throat, not even a whimper.

The frantic effort, conceived in the mind, withered and died from lack of strength. Terror crawled, dry, insidious, and foul-tasting in the mouth. Snakes of fear slithered from the spine, saturated with the certainty of impending death.

This pit had to be *somewhere*! Perhaps people were close by! People who couldn't see the hole, but would hear a cry.

3

Force, concentration – skin ripping noisily, painfully from raw lips. They hurt so much, but the anguish dissipated with the realisation that the body had finally succeeded in its goal of effective movement. The mouth opened. A large damp clod fell in, weighing heavy on the tongue. There was no more thought of cries or sounds, only a frenzied struggle to draw breath. Tongue and teeth heaving to spit out chunks of earth. Lungs burning, bursting, with the need to ingest air. But dirt lay crushing, choking, against the back of the throat.

Had to remain calm – had to fight – stay calm – to live. Hysteria subsided as air inflated scorching lungs: air that travelled in through the dirt beginning to pack the nostrils. But another shower of fine dust was followed by yet more moisture-laden clods, they blanketed one eye, stinging, searing – filled the nose, dry, choking . . .

Someone would come. They had to. If only they would hurry. There was no air, no breath . . . couldn't breathe . . . couldn't . . .

Then a silhouette. Tall, wide, wielding a spade, it blocked out the light and the stars. A blackness hovered in the pit, darker than any night; its depths wavering with a rich red glow, smouldering with an intensity that scoured ineffective lungs.

The figure moved back. Another shower followed, and another . . . and another . . .

For the first time since that walk along the newly tarmacadamed path, there came warmth. Warmth and comfort. There was no more fight for air – for anything. Only a quiet drifting. Floating on a soft grey cloud of down that gently caressed and enveloped. Carrying the whole body downwards into deep, relaxing sleep.

The spade once again stood upright in the earth. The mound had diminished, but not so much that a careless glance would notice, particularly the glance of a disinterested YTS trainee. A few scuffs of the shoe, a few pats to loosen and spread the drier top soil over the whole mound. One more studied glance down into the pit. There was only darkness, stillness and silence. No gleam of white betrayed the sheet that lay hidden beneath the earth.

4

The phantom flowed back towards the trees. A triangle of light shone briefly across the lawn, dimming suddenly as the door that had been opened closed again – in a room in the nearest block. Its glow burned for only an instant, but long enough to outline the figure of a woman. A woman who stood stiff and straight, hands planted firmly on the glass pane before her, one on either side of her head. The phantom in the garden looked up, and saw. As did the woman. And even when the light faded behind her, the white lace nightgown could still be seen by someone who realised she was there.

An unseen hand pulled down the blind. It was easy to imagine the nurse gently leading the protesting patient back to bed. A patient who had seen – how much? All? Enough to talk? Enough to . . . but then the phantom smiled as it once again retreated into the shadows. Who'd believe her? Or any other patient who reported seeing strange happenings in the night.

Psychiatric nurses and doctors were obliged to listen to their patients. They were paid to. But sooner or later they learned to ignore the chatterings of the inmates. Patients who resided in Compton Castle frequently had difficulty in distinguishing between reality and fantasy.

Even if that particular woman hadn't claimed to have seen visions and apparitions before, there was always a first time. After all she was mad. And who'd believe anything a mad woman had to say?

Chapter One

Peter Collins thumped his horn furiously and impatiently at an old man who was dithering between the left and right turns at the entrance to the hospital visitors' car park. Hearing the horn, the elderly man panicked, pressed his foot down too hard on the clutch and stalled his family saloon. Cursing loudly through the open window of his sports car, Peter accelerated swiftly. Mounting the kerb, he drove straight across a neatly trimmed bank of lawn and did a fast, furious and perfect three-point turn, which landed him in prime position to make a quick getaway the minute visiting was over.

Picking up two plastic carrier bags from the passenger seat of his car, he slammed the door, locked it, and stormed off in the direction of the main building, noting with grim satisfaction the queue of irate motorists already building up behind the old man. Short-tempered at the best of times, Peter was now seething, and not only because of the aged driver. Despite his loathing of the place, here he was visiting Compton Castle psychiatric hospital – again.

He'd always detested hospitals and sickness, because they brought a sharp reminder of his own mortality. And, as he'd discovered during the past few weeks, he had a particularly strong aversion to psychiatric wards. But a nagging sense of guilt and loyalty to his colleague Trevor Joseph drove him to this place whenever his free time coincided with visiting hours.

As a result, he'd been dragging himself to and from various hospitals for a long time. 'Too bloody long,' he cursed as he jumped over a low wall that edged the path, in order to take advantage of a short cut across the lawns. He'd earlier held vigil at Trevor's bed while his friend had hovered close to death, during three interminable weeks of dedicated care and superhuman nursing in the intensive care ward of the General Hospital. He'd then visited daily while Trevor had spent four and a half months on the neuro ward, with pretty smiling nurses all too willing and able to care for his every whim, let alone his needs. And despite regular visits from a very shapely blonde physiotherapist, and a pretty brunette psychologist, Trevor had still failed to pull himself sufficiently together to avoid a transfer from the General to what Bill Mulcahy, their superior in the police force, insisted on tactlessly referring to as the 'funny farm.'

Granted it wasn't Trevor's fault that he'd had his head hammered to a pulp by an insane lunatic, who also happened to be a murderer, but if it had been Collins instead of Trevor who'd faced the nut-case, he was confident that he would have handled himself very differently. But, then, even discounting the 'how' of Trevor's injuries, fractures – even skull fractures, multiple leg fractures, and infected wrist fractures – do heal, given time and expert medical care. And Trevor had already had more than his fair share of both. Most injuries could be recovered from if the person concerned made a determined effort to pull himself together. Which in Peter's considered opinion, Trevor Joseph was most certainly not doing.

The cans of beer he'd bought clanked against one another in the carrier bag. He wound his fingers tightly around the plastic in an effort to stop their noise, while damning his partner yet again for not even trying to recover.

Collins continued past a newly-dug flowerbed decked out with trays of stumpy clipped rose-bushes waiting to be planted. The surrounding lawns were thick with soil, and he recalled a crumbling but strangely attractive stone cupid that had stood there when he had first come to visit Trevor. Was that really only three weeks ago? He wondered where the cupid was now. It was the sort of decoration he wouldn't mind putting into his own garden – that's if he had one. Home, when he remembered to go there, was a flat in a crumbling Edwardian terrace next to the sea.

'Well, if it isn't my favourite man. Sergeant Collins, how lovely

8

to see you.' Jean Marshall, the sister in charge of Trevor's ward, greeted him with the same hearty voice she used for everyone in the hospital: patient, visitor and doctor alike. It was a voice that reminded him of all-girls' schools, netball, and brisk Girl Guiders, and it invariably set his teeth on edge.

'How is he today?' he demanded brusquely, jerking his head towards the door of the private room which Trevor occupied, courtesy of his status as injured policeman rather than just another clinically ill patient.

'Fine.' Sister Marshall nudged his ribs, and he caught a heady whiff of Estée Lauder. 'He attended Spencer's art class this morning,' she divulged in a confidential whisper, omitting the word "therapy". 'Perhaps he'll show you what he's done.'

'I could die waiting.'

'Is that a clanking of tins I hear, Sergeant Collins?' she raised her eyebrows.

'Non-alcoholic beer and crisps. Trevor needs some decent nourishment to counteract the effects of the junk you feed him in here.'

'Just as long as it *is* non-alcoholic,' she warned.

'Do you want to check?' He gave her the benefit of his most winning smile.

'And if I say yes?'

'I'll owe you one if you say no.'

'I'm still waiting for you to buy me that drink in the Green Monkey – the one you promised me the last time I turned a blind eye.'

'One day I'll surprise you.'

'Just be sure you take the empties away with you,' she whispered, as she glimpsed a woman wandering down the corridor, dressed in a scarlet silk negligée. Vanessa Hedley, one of the ward's more 'difficult' patients, was apt to act out the oddest bedroom fantasies at a moment's notice.

Glad of the distraction that had diverted Sister's attention away from his carrier bag, Peter moved on. Jean Marshall was a smart, imposing woman; tall, and well built, with a majestic figure, red hair and green eyes. She'd once mentioned a son at university, so he put her age at roughly forty to forty-five, though she looked younger. He could not deny she was

9

extremely attractive and, what was more to the point, she'd already made it abundantly clear that she was willing to put her attractions at his disposal. Divorced and frequently lonely for female company, Collins rarely turned down the kind of signal she was transmitting, but there was something about her that put him off. Possibly her over-efficient manner coupled, with a whiff of hospital antiseptic that invariably overpowered whatever perfume she was wearing. Or, what was more likely, her overwhelming confidence in her own power to attract, which killed any temptation to chase and conquer.

Either way, though he flirted mildly with her whenever he came to visit Trevor, he would never go near the Green Monkey, the pub where the Compton Castle staff congregated during their off-duty hours, unless he was absolutely certain she was safely on shift.

Ignoring the pantomime about to begin in the corridor, Peter pushed open the door to Trevor's room. To his dismay he found Trevor seemingly slumped in exactly the same position he'd left him in two days ago. In fact, if Sister Marshall hadn't mentioned that Trevor had attended art therapy that morning, he could easily believe that Trevor had remained seated in the same chair for two days and nights. His growth of beard certainly suggested it.

Trevor looked painfully, almost skeletally thin. He was still wearing the crumpled pair of once black, but now faded grey cotton slacks that he had worn every day since he'd been urged to dress in something other than his pyjamas. His navy sweatshirt was unravelling at the neck and cuffs, and would have been rejected by any self-respecting jumble-sale committee. Peter couldn't recall Trevor ever dressing quite so down-at-heel before, even when they'd worked undercover in the vagrants' and junkies' paradise of Jubilee Street.

'Brought you some beer,' he barked, dumping his carrier bags unceremoniously in Trevor's lap. 'It's old traditional, and cold. Straight from my fridge.'

'Thanks,' Trevor murmured mechanically.

'Well, go on. Open the bag,' Collins badgered. 'There's crisps in there too. Smoky bacon.' Trevor obediently fumbled with the plastic carrier.

10

'Not that one.' Peter snatched away the bag irritably. 'That's your clean washing. I got my cleaner to do it for you.'

'Thank you.' Trevor didn't even look up as Peter opened the wardrobe door and threw the bag on to the floor.

In the end it was left to Peter to reach for two of the set of four cans he'd thrown on to Trevor's lap. He ripped open a ring-pull, and put his lips to the froth that gushed out. 'Can you open your own, or do you want me to do that for you, too?' he demanded belligerently.

'I can manage.'

'Can I watch?' Peter questioned caustically, sitting down heavily on Trevor's bed, the only other place in the room to sit.

'Can you what?' Trevor asked blankly.

'For God's sake, man, I've come to visit. I've brought you a goody bag.'

'I've said thank you.' Even his voice sounded distant.

'It's not your bloody thanks I want. It's your company.'

'I'm sorry. I'm not very sociable these days.'

'I can see that,' Peter retorted heartlessly. He polished off half of his can in one long, thirsty gulp. 'So, don't you want to hear what's been happening down at the station?'

'Not really.'

'What's the matter? Doesn't the thought of rejoining the Drug Squad excite you?'

'Frankly no.' Trevor showed the first sign of any real animation that Peter had witnessed since he'd regained consciousness. He even ripped back the ring pull on his beer can. Perhaps threats of returning to work were the key to getting him roused.

'We're doing the nightclubs this month. Good beer, good whisky, good entertainment, sex-starved over-eager divorcees throwing themselves at you, music that'll deafen your ears, and all on expenses. What more could a man want?'

'A quiet life.' Trevor's eyes flicked involuntarily towards a sketchpad that lay face down on the cabinet next to his bed. Collins leant over and picked it up.

'Florence Nightingale out there' – he glanced towards the door – 'told me that you'd been to art therapy and done something good.'

11

'That doesn't mean I want *you* to see it!' Trevor snapped.

It was too late. Peter had already peeled back the cover. He let out a long, low whistle as he stared at a sketch of a woman with large sad eyes and long hair that tumbled romantically around her face.

'The girl of your dreams, Joseph?' He tossed the book contemptuously back on to the cabinet. 'Isn't it time you grew up and started looking at real-life women that can kiss back?'

'Always got to reduce life to the lowest common denominator, haven't you, Collins?' Trevor retorted savagely.

Peter was elated, but he was careful not to show it. After months of trying, he'd actually elicited some responses. Maybe not quite the ones he wanted, but responses nevertheless.

'And the lowest common denominator is the pub,' he rejoined unabashed. 'How about I persuade your warden out there to let you off long enough to enjoy a quick one with me.'

'No thanks.'

There was a firmness in this refusal that Peter hadn't detected before either.

'Everyone in the station sends you their regards. Bill told me to warn you he's saving all the best jobs for when you get back.'

'I just might not come back,' Trevor threatened.

'Haven't you heard, there's a recession on? That means there aren't enough jobs to go round for well-qualified, intelligent people, let alone ex-coppers who've been stupid enough to get themselves mangled in the line of duty. Here, drink up,' he commanded briskly, after finishing his own can. 'So what's new around here?'

'Not a lot.'

'I spoke to Harry Goldman about you.'

'Why?' Trevor demanded suspiciously, his open can, still untouched, held upright in his hand.

'Because your brother and your mother are stuck in Devon with a farm to run, so they haven't time to come up and check on you every weekend. And also because they asked me to,' Peter replied in exasperation. 'Whether you like it or not, Joseph, doctors do not assume total responsibility for their patients. They like to discuss their charges with *someone*: family, friends or, unfortunately for you, in the absence of anyone better, me.'

12

'What did he say?' For the first time since Collins had entered the room, Trevor raised his head, and met his gaze steadily.

'He told me you're a fraud. That you're quite fit enough to go out *now*. All you need is a push in the right direction.'

'And you volunteered to do the pushing?'

'You can't hide in here forever, with' – Peter jerked his thumb towards the sketchpad – 'memories of what might have been.'

'I still get headaches. I feel weak . . .' Trevor instinctively repeated the same catalogue of excuses he'd been reciting for months. But as far as Collins was concerned, they'd long lost any validity they might have once had.

'When was the last time you left this room?' Ignoring Trevor's flinching, he walked across to the window and yanked the curtains wide, flooding the gloomy little cell with bright afternoon sunlight.

'You know I went to Spencer's class this morning,' Trevor mumbled, screwing his eyes into narrow slits.

'Big deal. You walked down two corridors and a tunnel to attend art therapy,' Peter mocked. 'Come on, you and me are going out, mate.'

'I don't feel up to it.'

'Now!' He took one look at Trevor's worn and pitted carpet slippers, opened the wardrobe door, and extracted a pair of equally shabby canvas trainers. 'Put them on,' he ordered.

Trevor looked at them, but didn't make a move.

'I'm not taking you to the pub – only for a turn around the grounds. There's no one out there now,' he lied, eyeing a procession of patients and visitors walking down the centre path that bisected the main lawn.

'I can't stand strong sunlight any more.'

'Then borrow these.' Peter pulled a pair of dark glasses from the top pocket of his blazer and pushed them on Trevor's nose. They hung there crookedly, one lens considerably lower than the other. He yanked the door of the room wide open.

'Come on, Joseph. Either you walk out of here, or I carry you out,' he threatened. 'And in your present state of health, I could do it with one hand tied behind my back.'

Trevor stared at him for a moment. Collins almost thought

he'd lost yet another battle, when Trevor slowly kicked off his slippers and reached for the trainers. What Peter didn't realise was that this reaction was anything but a positive one. Lacking the energy to fight his partner's bullying tactics, Trevor had opted to take the easy way out: to capitulate. After all, Collins never stayed very long. And after he'd gone, he'd be able to return to his room, his chair, his sketchpad, and – most comforting of all – 'his memories of what had never been', as his colleague had so scathingly put it.

'That's it, boy. One more step and you'll actually be somewhere other than this hallowed cell.' Peter laid a firm arm across Trevor's shoulders and propelled him sharply out of the door.

'I need my stick?' Trevor cried out, staggering precariously on legs that had fractured, then healed, but were still weak from lack of exercise.

Collins took a sturdy cane from its resting place behind the door, and shoved it into Trevor's hand. Much to his annoyance, he then stepped into the corridor only to find that he had propelled Trevor into the centre of a fierce physical altercation between Jean Marshall and the petite, sharp-featured female patient who had been swanning around earlier in the red negligée, and whom he chiefly remembered for her constantly changing hair colour. Today it was black, but had been auburn on his previous visit, blonde the time before, and grey the week before that. Sister Marshall was lecturing the woman in that firm matronly voice she employed whenever one of the patients was being 'difficult', which, if his earlier visits were anything to go by, was more often than not.

'Come on, Vanessa, you don't really want to go outside until you've changed your clothes. If you walk down to the ward with me, I'll help you choose something . . .'

'No!' Vanessa hissed vehemently, slithering eel-like out of her clutches. Before the Sister could stop her, she slammed backwards, pushing open the door into a long, narrow, shelved storeroom where at that moment a drugs trolley was being re-stocked by Lyn Sullivan, a rather gorgeous, black-haired, dark-eyed, six-foot, slim student nurse whom Collins had frequently lusted after but had regretfully left alone on the premise that teenagers, even those heading into their twenties, were too young for men who'd hit the wrong side of thirty.

'Come on, Vanessa, out of there,' Jean Marshall commanded authoritatively.

'Who do you think you are? You can't order me around, you bitch!' Vanessa hissed vehemently.

'No one is ordering you around, Mrs Hedley,' Lyn Sullivan murmured, gently clasping Vanessa's arm.

'I know you.' Vanessa shrugged off her hand. 'You think I'm stupid.' She peered into the girl's face. 'You think I don't know about you and my Ian. You're all the same. Bitches!' Vanessa's eyes rolled alarmingly in her head as her final words pitched higher, ending in a screech. She flailed her arms wide. Catching the edge of the trolley, she flung it back hard against a shelf, forcing the nurse into a corner. Sweeping her hands wildly, Vanessa picked up and hurled everything she could reach. Bottles and jars flew through the air, landing on the tiled floor and scattering in a crescendo of splintering glass, rattling, skidding pills, and the splash and gurgles of potions. Lyn Sullivan tried to duck past her and out through the door, but wasn't quick enough. An enormous jar filled with small white pills thumped between her shoulderblades, and she fell heavily, crying out in pain as she landed on the carpet of broken glass.

Laughing crazily, Vanessa grabbed a set of cast-iron scales. Long since obsolete, they'd been relegated to a back corner of the store-room shelves. She brandished them high, poising them precariously above Lyn's head. Peter and Jean Marshall both ran towards the cupboard and, like a bad comedy sketch, jammed against each other in the doorway.

It was left to Trevor to crawl between their legs and offer the girl a helping hand. She tried to grasp his fingers, but instinctively he gripped her wrist and heaved her forward, ignoring her cries of distress as broken glass sliced into the flesh of her legs through her thin trousers.

As Sister Marshall stepped back to allow Lyn through the doorway, Vanessa miraculously quietened. For a moment she stood in the midst of the wreckage, surveying the havoc she'd created.

Collins seized the opportunity to make a move towards her.

'I know what I saw,' Vanessa whispered, staring at him.

'I don't doubt you do,' he concurred evenly, reaching out to take the scales from her.

'Come along, Vanessa,' Jean Marshall crooned soothingly, easing her way into the doorway again. 'You're just tired. A rest will set you up fine. You'll feel much better after a lie-down.'

'I don't want a lie-down,' Vanessa protested, lifting the scales higher. 'She's there, I tell you. In the flowerbed. Planted like a tulip bulb. All of that earth on top of her. Shovelful after shovelful. She can't move, you know,' she assured Peter gravely, lowering her voice to a whisper. Her eyes grew rounder, the whites more prominent. 'Do you think she'll grow into a people tree?' She burst into a cacophony of mirthless laughter as she stared at Peter again. 'She's dead,' she said finally, with a sudden eerie calm. 'She would be, with all that earth on top of her. Dead as mutton. She's dead, and not one of you cares enough to move her to the cemetery. That's where they put dead people. I know. I've been there.' She lunged towards Peter, but he succeeded in sliding one hand on to the scales. 'I wanted to put my Ian there, but they . . .' She glared furiously at Jean Marshall and Lyn, who'd now been helped to her feet by Trevor. 'They stopped me. If I'd put him there' – she moved closer to Collins and he took advantage of her proximity to lay a second hand on the scales – 'he'd still be mine. He'd have to stay there. Wait for me to visit him with flowers. He wouldn't be able do anything else, would he?'

She drew her hands back, as if intending to hurl the scales at Sister Marshall's head, but Peter quickly wrenched them from her grasp.

'You're in league with those bitches,' she snarled. Snatching the one remaining pill bottle from the trolley, she flung it full in his face. Still clutching the heavy scales, he ducked, but not low enough. The bottle connected painfully with his cheekbone, splitting open the skin.

'He's probably still with some whore . . . but not the whore I found him with,' Vanessa rambled. 'She wouldn't be pretty enough for him. Not any more. Not after what I did . . .'

'Vanessa! Mrs Hedley!' Collins commanded in a voice that carried authority. 'Look at me.' Staring into her eyes in an effort to attract her attention, he fumbled blindly for the shelf at his side, and deposited the scales there. The second his hands were free, he moved like lightning. Grasping Vanessa's wrists he hauled them high behind her back.

'Where do you want her?' he asked the Sister.

'Out of that damned dispensary for a start,' Jean said hollowly, sickened by the chaos that Vanessa had made of the once secure drug cupboard.

'You should have locked it,' the policeman observed laconically as he yanked Vanessa out into the corridor.

'The lock jammed three months back. When we asked for it to be repaired, they put a padlock on the outside, which is a lot of damned good when you're working inside. I've complained every day for three months, and got nowhere,' Jean Marshall responded angrily.

'I've phoned security. They're on their way. I've also asked for a couple of porters and an extra nurse,' Lyn murmured weakly from the open door of the ward office. Trevor had helped her into a chair, and there she was sitting, trouser legs and sleeves rolled up, dabbing ineffectually with a tissue at the mass of small cuts on her arms and legs.

The Sister gazed at her. 'You'd better phone for an ambulance to take you to casualty in the General,' she said with unintentional harshness, shocked by Lyn's appearance.

'I'm all right,' the girl murmured unconvincingly, taking a sip of water from the beaker Trevor had brought from his own room.

'No arguments. Telephone them, now. I'll be back to check on you as soon as I've dealt with this. Can you keep a grip on Mrs Hedley for the moment, Sergeant Collins?'

'I think I can manage,' Peter replied cynically.

'Come on now, Vanessa. There's a good girl. We'll soon get you to bed.' At the mention of bed, Vanessa thrashed around and screamed like a demented dervish.

Keeping his hold on her, Peter watched as a security guard, two porters, and a male and female nurse entered the reception area of the ward. He tightened his grasp when Vanessa, also seeing them, tried to kick his shins with her slippered feet.

'I thought everyone was safely out in the garden,' Lyn apologised weakly, as her superior picked up the key to the drug cupboard's padlock and hared back down the corridor. They heard her cursing and swearing as she and the porters struggled to close the door over the scattered debris.

'Looks like everyone was out there, except us and this lady.' Collins smiled coldly at Vanessa.

'I dread to think what could have happened if any of the other patients had been here – or if you hadn't.' Lyn returned the beaker to Trevor then slumped back into her chair.

When the door to the cupboard was finally secure, Jean Marshall signalled to the female nurse. Collins followed them, pushing Vanessa ahead of him into a treatment room.

'I tell you, I saw him,' Vanessa screeched, thrusting her red face very close to his as they entered the room. 'He buried her right there, right in the middle . . .' she stopped abruptly mid-sentence, and stared into space.

'In the middle of what, Vanessa? Peter probed with more tact than he would usually display down at the police station.

'Why should I tell you anything?' she demanded slyly. 'For all I know, you could be the one.' She turned to the Sister and whispered, 'It could be him . . .'

'I'm a policeman, Vanessa,' he interrupted.

'I don't believe you,' she said flatly.

'If you promise not to move, I can show you my identification. Then I'll investigate whatever you want me to,' he added slowly, giving his words time to sink in. 'That's my job. Now, would you like to sit down quietly and tell me all about it?'

'You promise to catch him?' she screeched.

'I promise to try.'

He kept his fingers securely around her wrist as she sat in the chair that Jean Marshall pushed behind her. Moving his left hand steadily into his inside pocket, he withdrew his wallet. Flicking it open, he displayed his identification card. 'There you are, Vanessa, colour photograph and all. Now will you tell me all about it?'

Vanessa looked around the room. The recently arrived nurse – cool, blonde and beautiful, Peter noted appreciatively – had primed a syringe. She hid it hurriedly behind her back.

'*She* wouldn't believe me!' Vanessa shouted furiously, glaring at Jean.

18

'You're wrong, Vanessa. Sister Marshall knew you were upset. That's why she sent for me.' Still holding her wrist, Peter knelt in front of her, giving her all his attention in the hope that she would reciprocate, but he was careful to keep his body primed for action. 'Now's your chance. Come on, tell me all about it. From the beginning.'

'He must be a murderer,' she whispered confidentially, visibly relaxing back against the chair.

'Let's start from the beginning,' Peter continued calmly. 'What exactly did you see?'

Her eyes suddenly grew wild again. The sleeve of her wide-necked negligée slipped low, exposing one shoulder. 'It was late,' she whispered. 'Really late. Everyone was asleep . . .'

'Except you?' Out of the corner of his eye, Peter caught a glimpse of the blonde nurse drawing closer.

'Except me,' she giggled childishly. 'He thought I'd be asleep. Only I wasn't.'

'Who, Vanessa?' Peter probed, automatically slipping into the interrogation routine used in police procedures.

'Him, of course,' she snapped irritably. 'He was carrying her over his shoulder like a sack of potatoes.'

'How did you know it wasn't a sack of potatoes?' Collins asked absently, watching as the nurse reached for Vanessa's arm.

'Because of the feet, silly.' She giggled again. 'They didn't have shoes on, and they were dangling down in front of him.'

'Time for your medication, Mrs Hedley,' Jean Marshall said smoothly.

'Later!' Vanessa screamed. 'I'm talking to this policeman.'

'You can still talk to me while you receive your medication. You need to be well, so you can tell me everything you remember. What did he do with the body he was carrying?'

'He took it over to that pile of earth. The big mound of earth.' Carried away by her story Vanessa extended her arm over to the Sister. Jean slapped it, and the nurse inserted the needle. On this occasion, familiarity really did breed contempt, and Vanessa ignored what was being done to her. 'He went over to the edge of the pit . . . the big pit . . . the big pit and . . . and . . .'

'And what, Vanessa?' Collins allowed himself to relax as her eyelids drooped. '*And*,' he persisted. 'Come on, what happened then?'

'She's gone,' the nurse announced. 'Want a hand to put her to bed Jean?'

'Yes please,' Jean Marshall answered. She turned to Peter, 'Nurse Ashford. Sergeant Collins.'

'Pleased to meet you,' the nurse said formally.

'And you,' Peter smiled, then he noticed the gleaming wedding ring, and the smile died on his lips.

'Thanks for helping us,' Jean said gratefully. 'It's always easier to sedate them when they're not struggling against you.'

'Any time,' he said carelessly as he rose from his knees.

'You do realise, don't you, that from now on every time she sees you, she'll want to give you more grisly details of this phantom burial,' Jean said.

'Crazy witnesses and their confessions go with the territory. Last night a junkie told me he'd smuggled heroin in from Mars. After listening to that rubbish, Vanessa's story sounds almost plausible.' He opened the door and left them to carry their patient away. For a moment he pondered that, although he frequently considered his own job a swine, theirs was infinitely worse.

Sister Marshall caught up with him as he was returning to the ward office.

'If you come back to the treatment room, I'll put something on that cut,' she offered.

'Shouldn't you see to Nurse Sullivan first?' he asked, reluctant to allow Jean too near him.

'She needs more attention than we can give her here. Besides, I wouldn't dare encroach on Karl's territory.'

Peter saw a male nurse taking charge in the office where Trevor was still sitting close to Lyn. He felt his left cheekbone, and when he withdrew his fingers he was surprised to find them covered with blood.

'It always looks and feels worse than it is, when it's a cut on the face,' she commented, confident in her medical knowledge.

'I've found that out the hard way,' Peter agreed drily, following her to the treatment room. There he allowed her to clean up the cut, and cover it with a plaster.

'Vanessa *would* have to choose Sunday afternoon visiting hours to go berserk,' Jean complained, as she washed her hands. 'Weekend cover is barely two-thirds of normal, and a quarter of the pathetic few staff we do have here are on teabreak at this time.'

'Sod's law,' he commented briefly, as the cut stung viciously.

'Do me a favour? she asked plaintively.

'I didn't see or hear anything. I wasn't even around,' he replied astutely.

'It's not that I want to deny you the role of hero, but I'll never see the end of the paperwork if they find out I allowed a visitor to manhandle one of our patients.'

'What visitor?' Peter responded blankly – but he wasn't slow in demanding a return favour. 'How about I come back later with a take-away for Trevor? He looks as though he hasn't eaten for months, and he used to enjoy them.'

'It will be a miracle if you get him to eat it.'

'You don't mind me trying?'

'On the contrary.' She led the way out, locking up the treatment room with one of the keys that hung from her belt. They walked briskly up the ward towards the corridor, where the porters were still clearing away the mess of broken glass and spilt drugs, under the supervision of the security guard. 'I probably shouldn't be saying this to you,' she muttered, 'but there's really nothing we can do for Trevor. He has to help himself. He's depressed, but not clinically so – at least no more than anyone who's suffered what he has is entitled to be. Part of his trouble is that he's become institutionalised. Hospital can seem a nice cosy place. Too cosy. It's long past the time when he *should* have made his break back into the real world. Doctor Goldman's been recommending short, solitary afternoon outings ever since Trevor's second day here. As far as the front gate would be a start, but if Trevor doesn't make an effort soon, we'll have to put a boot behind him.'

'We were on the way out just then, when you distracted us.'

'I appreciate you trying to help, but the effort has to be *his*, not yours.' She smiled in an attempt to mitigate her reproof.

'On the other hand,' Collins halted thoughtfully in front of the office door, 'he did drag Nurse Sullivan out of that cupboard.'

21

'So he did.' The Sister stared through the open door, where Trevor was still hovering at Lyn Sullivan's elbow while Karl bandaged her legs. 'It could be the first small step,' she admitted cautiously.

'I'll give him the hand, or the shove, he needs to make the second,' Peter said confidently, feeling better about his friend than he had done since the day intensive care had told him Trevor was going to survive.

'Make sure you're back with that take-away before I clock off at eight,' Jean warned him artfully. 'The night sister isn't quite as accommodating as me.'

'I promise,' Peter said flatly. 'I'm on duty myself at nine, so I'll probably make it back around seven.'

His reply dampened the glow in her eyes. If he'd come right at the end of her shift, she might have finally succeeded in inveigling him into the Green Monkey.

It had been almost four years since her husband, a scrap-metal dealer, had left her for a beauty queen less than half her age. She'd picked her lawyer well and paid him enough to ensure that she'd come out of the divorce financially sound. Her share of her husband's assets included their luxurious four-bedroomed apartment on the Marina, a five berth yacht, and enough gilt-edged securities to make work a pastime she could relinquish any time she chose to. But she had long since discovered that money was no substitute for emotional and sexual satisfaction. She was tired of singles groups, of the bridge club that was dominated by obscenely happily married couples, and of sleeping alone. Peter Collins was undoubtedly a hard man, but he was physically fit, more than passably good-looking in a clean-cut, military sort of way, and she had a shrewd suspicion that if she ever succeeded in enticing him into her bed she'd find his soft centre.

She never doubted for an instant that he had one. In her opinion all men did. It was just a question of the right handling. All she had to do was make that crucial, initial breech through the defences he had erected around himself.

Chapter Two

'Right, you take this wheelbarrow and shovel,' Jimmy Herne, chief gardener of Compton Castle, thrust the said implements at Dean Smith his YTS trainee. 'Then you proceed to that point over there, beneath the willow tree, where I've marked out the turf with white chalk,' he continued, labouring his directives. 'You listening to me, boy?' he bellowed irately.

Dean Smith shrugged his shoulders, which irritated Jimmy even further. Dean was used to being shouted and screamed at, and not only by Jimmy Herne. His parents had done so for as long as he could remember, and as soon as he was old enough to go to school, the teachers had continued where his parents had left off. As a result he was now completely immune to any display of anger, impatience or temper from anyone who held a position of authority over him.

Sixteen years of age, he lived for the hours he spent shooting aliens and outwitting commandos in the gaming machine palaces, and ogling girls while downing pints of illicit beer with his mates in the pub affectionately known as the 'Little Albert' – the only bar in town that catered for the needs of under-age drinkers.

'I'll be over to check on you in ten minutes,' Jimmy droned on; but Dean took as little notice of Jimmy's threats as he did of the tuneless Muzak that played in the supermarket his mother dragged him to every Friday night. 'And if you haven't finished lifting the turf, and digging out a good couple of inches by then, you can look out.' Jimmy stopped to regain his breath. 'You hear me, boy?' he bawled.

'Yes, Mr Herne.' Dean threw his spade into the barrow and trundled in slow motion over to the willow tree. He poked the spade halfheartedly into the grass, and gingerly lifted the piece of turf he'd cut. If he didn't trim the edges neatly, it would only set the old geezer off again, and that would mean sweeping leaves and clearing gutters for the rest of the week. He and Jason Canning, the other YTS trainee assigned by the council's horticulture department to Compton Castle, constantly vied with one another for the dubious privilege of being the lowest common denominator in Jimmy Herne's bad books. Fortunately for him, today was Jason's turn. Jimmy had caught him chatting up Mandy Smith in the kitchen when he should have been bedding out geraniums, so it was Jason who was doing the dirty work for a change.

He lifted out about four square inches of turf, and laid the tiny sod down gently in the centre of the barrow, then he leant on the shovel and took a short rest before digging and lifting the next section. After his break, he managed six inches. He stared at the rich, black earth he'd uncovered. An enormous, fat, pink worm was oozing its body away from the bright sunlight back into the darkness of the soil. It didn't ooze quite quickly enough. Dean took great delight in chopping it in two with his spade, and watching both ends writhe.

'Here, boy! Here, boy, this minute! Can't you hear me? Are you deaf?' A sharp prod in the back with the pointed end of an umbrella diverted Dean's attention away from the worm. 'I want you to dig over there.' The umbrella swung in the direction of the new flowerbeds that he'd only dug out the week before. 'And I want you to dig *now*.'

The woman was short, rounded, with a beaky face that reminded him of a particularly officious teacher who'd taught him in primary school. But she was wearing a white jacket. And that was enough to put him on his guard. Only doctors wore white jackets, and even Jimmy Herne listened to doctors.

'But I dug out those beds last week, miss,' he protested, unconsciously lapsing into the pupil-teacher jargon of his recent schooldays.

'I don't care when you dug them out. You will dig that one out now!' she insisted uncompromisingly.

The 'now' coupled with the white jacket did it. Dean jumped to it. Throwing his spade into his barrow, he wheeled it reluctantly over to the flowerbed.

'Right here!' The woman was at the spot before him. She ground the heel of her shoe into the loose earth, and pinpointed the place where she wanted him to dig. 'That's it, boy,' she said, as he lifted his spade out of the barrow. 'Come on, put your back into it.'

He pushed the spade into the earth. It slid in easily. The soil was loose, crumbly and, fortunately for him, fairly dry.

'Don't put what you take out in the barrow, you idiot. A deep hole's needed here, for a . . . for a tree,' she said suddenly, as though the idea had only just occurred to her. 'There'll never be room for everything you take out in there, and I don't want you wasting valuable working time carting it around. Pile it up here on the grass.'

'It won't be easy to clean up afterwards,' he complained. 'And Mr Herne . . .'

'Mr Herne nothing.' She dismissed his superior arbitrarily. 'All you'll need to clean it up is a good stiff brush. Come on now, pile it up. Quickly. I want to see a hole deep enough for a mature beech here in ten minutes.'

Dean wanted to ask why the rush, when he couldn't even see a tree waiting, but he didn't dare. The woman hovered around, staring at the ground like a fretful chicken searching for grubs, while he dug slowly, methodically, but steadily downwards. Occasionally she looked over her shoulder, scanning the garden as though she was expecting someone. He presumed it was the someone with the tree. And, in-between, she chivvied him as though her life depended on his progress.

'Come on, boy. An old man of ninety could dig faster than you. Move it. Come on, put more swing into it. Come on, there's no time for that.' She clouted him smartly on the arm with her umbrella when he rested momentarily on his shovel. He glared at her angrily. Not even Jimmy Herne had ever dared to hit him, but he pushed the shovel back into the hole, which in his opinion was already deep enough for any normal tree.

'What the hell do you think you're doing, lad?' It was a voice he recognised only too well. Jimmy Herne was thundering over the grass towards them, a look of pure fury darkening his wizened monkey face.

'He's working for me.'

Dean continued to dig, only too happy to delegate the explanations to the officious lady.

'A deep hole needs to be dug here,' she stated coldly. 'For a tree. And it needs to be dug this minute.'

'First I've heard of it, and this is my garden,' Jimmy asserted dogmatically, stating the truth as he saw it. 'This here is a flowerbed, not a tree site, and it's been dug out enough. All it needs is a barrow or two of manure and it will be right to plant out the roses.'

'Not before I've had this hole dug out.'

Something in her manner rang warning bells in Jimmy's mind. 'You're one of *them*, aren't you?' he asked cryptically. 'You're no bleeding official. You're one of them.' He laughed and slapped his thigh with glee. 'Boy, have you been had. Had good and proper.' He grinned at Dean, who was staring white-faced down into the hole he'd dug.

'Mr Herne, you'd better come and take a look at this.' Dean gawked at Jimmy through dark, frightened eyes. The gardener stepped forward, and peered cautiously into the hole.

Locks of dirty, straggly, blonde hair clumped and bunched around a single eye set in a small, uncovered portion of grey-white face. It stared upwards from the earthy debris, its expression one of blank, blind terror. Jimmy gripped Dean's shoulder.

'Inside, boy. Tell them to call the police. Tell them I said so,' he commanded in an unnaturally loud voice.

The woman in the white jacket was beside herself with joy. Dancing and skipping around the pile of earth heaped on the grass, she chanted triumphantly.

'I told them so – I told them so – I told them all, but they wouldn't listen.' She clutched at Dean's shirt collar as he passed. 'But you listened, didn't you, boy? You listened, and you found her. You . . .' Her face loomed close to his. He could see hairline veins of red in her eyes, the wide deep pores that pockmarked her skin, her make-up caked into creases that lined the valleys of her wrinkles. 'You hit the jackpot, boy.' Her cackling laughter followed him as he ran headlong into the main building.

26

* * *

Spencer Jordan, the resident art therapist at Compton Castle was well respected and liked by both patients and staff, but they all admitted that, on first sight, he took some getting used to. New patients were invariably intimidated by the sheer size of him. Six foot seven inches, with the slim, strongly muscled frame of a basketball player, a physique he'd put to good use during the year he'd spent, after art college, studying textiles in a Californian university. He simply didn't fit most people's stereotype of an artist. Although his hair was long, it was always neatly trimmed, as were his beard and moustache. He was quiet, softly spoken, and usually he dressed casually in jeans or plain black trousers with sweaters – and his sweaters were generally the first thing that people noticed about him.

They were wild, colourful affairs that depicted scenes of every type and variety. The more subdued ones mirrored vivid, abstract modern art; others, were illustrated with animals and scenery. The one he'd chosen to wear that Monday morning was adorned with ferocious-looking black and white rabbits gambolling over a background of improbably bright-red grass, liberally sprinkled with green and purple daisies. And the most amazing thing about Spencer Jordan's sweaters was that he knitted them himself, occasionally between his art classes.

'You're putting a lot of work into that sketch, Trevor,' Spencer commented, looking over Trevor's shoulder as he stood silently rubbing pastels on to a piece of paper pinned to an easel propped in the darkest corner of the room. 'I like the background colours, and I take it, that's the same lady we've seen before. Long dark hair, grey eyes. Am I allowed to know who she is?'

'She's a figment of my imagination,' Trevor replied harshly, picking up a grey pastel to darken the clouds above her head.

'Pity. She has the kind of face I'd like to know more about.'

He stood behind Trevor for a few moments more, inviting further conversation. When none was forthcoming, Spencer moved on to the next easel, where his youngest male patient, Michael Carpenter was working on a chocolate-box picture of that idyllic country cottage of lacklustre poets' imagination.

27

Straw-thatched roof, roses climbing around a peaked wooden porch, small leaded-glass windows and, sitting dead centre of the picture, a pretty auburn-haired girl who was clutching a bunch of bluebells on her Laura Ashley clad lap.

Just as Trevor Joseph always sketched dark-haired women, so Michael Carpenter always painted girls with short auburn curls. All Spencer knew about Trevor was that he was a policeman suffering from understandable depression after receiving devastating, life-threatening injuries. He had no idea where the dark-haired lady fitted into his past, if indeed she did, but he knew all about Michael's lady.

Carpenter's sole topic of conversation was Angela – and Angela was the underlying reason why he was here in Compton Castle. He had previously been a quiet, studious bank clerk with no noticeable interests other than work, or spending time with his girlfriend Angela, and building his model railway. When Angela told him there was someone else in her life, so she wanted out of their relationship, he just couldn't take it. He took to spending all his evenings watching her; following Angela and her new boyfriend whenever they went out. Camping out all night in her parents' garden, gazing at her bedroom window whenever she stayed in. Threats and warnings from her family, the police, the supportive and very real concern of his own family, none of it had any effect until that particular night when he had sat in Angela's garden waiting for her family to go to bed.

An hour after the last light was switched off, he had calmly and deliberately cut a hole in the dining-room window, at the back of the house, set fire to rolls of newspaper he had brought for the purpose, and pushed them through the hole so they'd landed on the carpet close to the drapes. The room had been ablaze in a matter of minutes and, if it hadn't been for the timely intervention of a retired police officer who had seen the flames through the open curtains of the living-room window, the family would probably have been burnt in their beds.

So Michael had arrived at Compton Castle, via the courts, prison, and a directive that he undergo therapy. But Spencer was beginning to seriously doubt whether the treatment this patient was undergoing in hospital offered any real solution to his problems. Carpenter had been attending his art class now for six months, and he was still only drawing idyllic cottages with his ex-girlfriend sitting in the garden. Sooner or later someone, or something, had to force him to digest the unpalatable fact that Angela was no longer part of his life – and wouldn't be, ever again. While he continued to reject that notion, he may as well resign himself to living out the rest of his existence in an institution.

'Spencer, would you take a look at my work please?' Alison Bevan – a professional mother suffering postnatal depression after the birth of her ninth child, the result of her fourteenth 'serious' relationship in as many years – fluttered her sparse eyelashes at him and smiled. He returned her smile and walked over to her easel. She'd drawn a touching, childlike picture of children at play. No figure had arms or legs of the same proportion as any others, and all their mouths were fixed in determinedly upturned happy grins. Standing at the bottom of the left-hand corner were the tall solicitous figures of a man and a woman. The woman's face bore the same determinedly bright smile as the children, but the man's face was blank, devoid of features.

'Isn't he happy, Ali?' Spencer probed sensitively, pointing to the suited, matchstick-like figure.

'He wouldn't be, would he?' Alison retorted. 'He's a man, and everyone knows that men have to do all the work and bring in all the money.'

'I see. So he carries all the responsibility.'

'Isn't that what it's like for you, Spencer?' she questioned artfully.

'No, Alison, it's not.' A warning note crept into Spencer's voice. 'I've only myself to consider.'

'You must get lonely sometimes,' she persisted suggestively. 'Just like the rest of us.'

'Your picture's coming on,' he said firmly, ignoring her final comment. 'I particularly like this touch of the flowers on the ground matching those in the children's hands.'

He moved on to Lucy Craig, a plump, nervous seventeen-year-old who had cracked under the pressure of studying for her A-Levels.

'Look, Mr Jordan.' Despite all his prompting to the contrary, she could never bring herself to use his Christian name. 'There's a police car driving on to the lawn. It's churning up all Mr Herne's turf. He won't be very pleased, will he?' She glanced at Spencer, but he was now watching Trevor. Head down, Trevor was still diligently smudging pastels, evincing no interest whatsoever in what was happening outside. Spencer scratched his beard thoughtfully and wondered about the truth that lay behind the old maxim: 'Once a policeman always a policeman'.

Constable Michelle Grady stood awkwardly on the lawn, a carefully measured twenty yards from the hole that the YTS trainee had dug out. The stubby heels of her walking shoes had sunk into the turf, and her uniform was hot, prickly and stuffy in the warm spring sunshine, but she didn't move an inch from her self-appointed sentry post. She'd heard a number of horror stories in police college about rookies allowing crucial evidence to be destroyed at the scenes of crimes, and she intended to make sure that no one would be able to accuse her of negligence.

Already her carefully trained eye had spotted flecks of earth amongst the blades of grass, some distance away from the pile of earth that Dean Smith had heaped up. She smiled in self-satisfaction at the thought of pointing this out to her superiors, then she blanched as she heard Sergeant Peter Collins' voice, loud in contempt, echo across her imagination.

'Of course the hole must have been dug out more than once, you stupid woman. If it hadn't been, the damned body couldn't have been buried there in the first place.'

She rocked back on her heels. She must be careful not to state the obvious. Sergeant Collins wasn't the only man in the station with a sharp tongue. Sometimes, just sometimes, she wished she'd chosen to make her way in a career dominated by women, not by male chauvinists only too ready to make her the butt of all their jokes.

She wrenched her heels out of the soil and stamped up and down impatiently, just for the sake of doing something. This waiting was horrible; waiting for superior officers – waiting for the serious crimes squad – waiting for the pathologist from the General. Didn't *anyone* care about the poor woman now lying at the bottom of the hole?

'Whoever or whatever's down there can wait, Constable. It isn't going to complain.' Dan Evans, the inspector in the town's serious crimes squad, appeared from behind her.

'Inspector.' She nodded briefly and correctly, as she'd seen the men do.

'Impatience was written all over your face,' he explained slowly. 'When you've dealt with as many peculiar anomalies as I have, you learn to take your time. Move quickly, and you're apt to make mistakes.'

'Anomalies!' she exclaimed warmly. 'That poor woman . . .'

'How do you know there's a woman down there?' he asked. His slow speech, coupled with his probing, nitpicking method of questioning, irritated her intensely.

Dan Evans was a mountain of a man who'd once been an international weightlifter. A good six-foot-four, and a heavily-built twenty stone, he towered over everyone in the station. Before he'd joined the force he'd been a farmer, and she knew that his family still worked land around Carmarthen, which explained his lilting Welsh accent and his exasperatingly languorous speech.

'I know it's a woman, because she has long hair. Blonde hair,' she emphasised, glancing into his hooded and enigmatic blue eyes. 'She's also wearing eye shadow, bright blue,' she added knowledgeably.

'Could be a gay,' Evans commented sleepily.

'Doesn't look like a gay. Looks like a woman, and as she's been murdered . . .'

'Murdered? That's quite a diagnosis. How did you come to that conclusion?' he persisted softly.

'Because she's buried here, in the hospital grounds. Someone evidently wanted to hide the body from the authorities.'

'Or someone couldn't afford to pay for a funeral.' He smiled. 'They're getting pricier every day. Would you like a mint?' he asked incongruously, thrusting a crumpled paper bag under her nose.

'No, thank you,' she refused stiffly.

31

'You really should learn to relax, Constable . . . Constable . . . ?'

'Grady. Michelle Grady.' She drew herself up to her full height of five foot six inches, but she still felt like a child standing next to him.

He pushed his fingers through his fair, thinning hair and studied a battered blue estate car edging its way through the gates.

'Here's the pathologist now. Ever meet Patrick O'Kelly?'

'Not to talk to,' she replied warily. She'd heard a lot of stories down at the station about Patrick O'Kelly, and all of them had been reinforced by the compulsory postmortem that she, along with every other rookie, had been forced to attend.

'You're in for a treat.' Dan Evans pushed another mint between his lips, before stepping forward to open O'Kelly's car door, as it drew to a halt on the lawn.

'What have you got for me today?' Patrick asked, as he heaved a battered wooden case out of the back of the estate car.

'So far, only a face, partially uncovered in fresh-dug earth.' Dan winked at Michelle. 'Although our constable here thinks it could be murder.'

'Could be someone wanting to avoid funeral costs,' O'Kelly ventured.

'That's what I told her.'

'Police ambulance here yet?'

'No.'

'I'll make a start anyway.' He glanced from the hole to the stretch of grass around them. 'Who's been tramping all over this site?' he asked, peering suspiciously at Michelle.

'The YTS boy who dug out the hole. The patient who ordered him to do it. The gardener. And myself.'

'What patient ordered him to do *what*?' Evans interrupted. Constable Grady pulled out her notebook and flicked through the pages to prove that he wasn't the only one who could be pettifoggingly correct.

'A Mrs . . . Hedley, Vanessa Hedley, insisted that she saw someone bury a body in the garden the night before last. When she told the staff on her ward about it, they wouldn't believe her; and when she persisted in repeating her allegations, they sedated her. According to the Hospital Administrator, Mr Tony Waters, they had good cause to ignore her. She did get fairly agitated just before that. She threatened two nurses, and smashed up a drugs trolley. Anyway she says that her first opportunity to investigate the matter came this morning. She dressed herself in a white jacket that she just happened to find lying around, in the hope that she would be taken for a doctor. Then she came out and ordered one of the YTS trainees to start digging . . .'

'And he was dull enough to do what an *inmate* told him?' O'Kelly questioned incredulously.

'Fortunately for us, yes,' Michelle countered primly.

'I'm confused,' Evans murmured, 'as to who exactly is in charge of this place.'

'You and me both.' Patrick pushed his glasses further up his nose, and snapped on a pair of rubber gloves.

'As you can see, I walked towards the site alongside that pile of earth, following the footprints of Mrs Hedley and Dean Smith the trainee,' Michelle continued bravely. 'Since then I've kept everyone back.'

'Good girl.'

Michelle was still rookie enough to bask in the approbation implied in Patrick's absentminded comment.

'Coming with me, Dan?' he asked, as he stepped across the lawn.

'As far as the edge.' Evans followed Patrick to the lip of the hole. A few seconds later he shouted for a spade and Michelle took him the one that Dean had abandoned next to the barrow. As she returned to her post, she stared disapprovingly at the crowd of patients, and domestic staff on teabreak, who were teetering on the edge of the lawn, and she began to shoo them back. She found she enjoyed wielding the authority that came with her uniform. When she'd forced them all to retreat a couple of token inches, Michelle returned to her own spot on the grass. Standing stiffly to attention, she strained her ears, trying to listen in on Evans' conversation with O'Kelly. But all she could make out was a succession of 'Steady's', 'There she goes', and 'Look at that'. None of them proved to be in the least enlightening.

33

Another police car arrived with Sergeant Peter Collins, her immediate superior, and anything but her favourite colleague. As he began to direct the erection of green canvas screens all around the site, she continued to stand her ground, though getting in the way of the men, and not quite knowing whether to offer help or not. Soon the entire area was shrouded off, much to the disappointment of the crowd of onlookers.

Peter Collins stepped back to join the sightseers, stood amongst them for a few moments to test the efficiency of the screens, then walked over to her.

'I hear you were first on the scene,' he commented.

'I was,' she admitted brightly.

'What's the run-down?' he demanded gruffly.

'A YTS gardener uncovered part of the face in the flowerbed . . .' She sounded like an eager pupil being tested in an oral examination, preparing herself to repeat the whole of what little she knew yet again.

'Just a face, or is it attached to a body?' he questioned acidly.

'I think it's attached to a body.'

'Stupid place to put a body,' he observed, 'where a gardener's going to dig it up.'

'He wouldn't have dug it up if a female patient hadn't ordered him to . . .'

'Have you thought to ask that patient how she knew there was someone buried here?' he enquired coldly.

'She claims she saw someone burying a body in the garden the night before last.'

'Saturday night,' Collins murmured, recalling Vanessa's ramblings during the rumpus in Trevor's ward. Instinctively he fingered the cut on his cheek. What had Sister Marshall called her? Hedley . . . that was it. 'Vanessa Hedley,' he said out loud.

'You know about her, then?' Michelle was crestfallen at relinquishing her edge on the case.

Collins didn't hear her. 'Well I'll be damned,' he muttered under his breath. 'Some lunatics aren't so mad after all.'

For the first time since Spencer Jordan had taken over the art therapy classes, the patients were growing restless before the

34

end of their allotted time. They were abandoning their sketchpads, pastels and easels for the greater attraction of the police cars and the mysteriously veiled area on the lawn. Only Trevor remained incurious, apparently indifferent to the drama being played out in the grounds.

Unable to proceed with any useful work, Spencer allowed his group to disperse ten minutes before time. Vanessa Hedley, eyes glowing, nerves at fever pitch, was first out through the door. Once everyone, except Trevor, had left, Spencer moved quietly around the room, collecting portfolios, picking up the odd pencil that had rolled on the floor. The whole of the time he was clearing up, Trevor continued to work diligently and silently in his corner. The hands on the clock crept slowly around to one o'clock, and still Trevor remained engrossed in his sketch.

At five minutes past one, Spencer lifted down a rucksack from a peg behind the door. Picking up a chair, he carried it over to a table close to where Trevor was working.

'Sandwich?' Spencer asked, opening a large packet neatly wrapped in greaseproof paper.

'No, thank you,' Trevor replied distantly, without glancing up from his drawing.

'They're salad and goat's cheese. A friend of mine made the cheese, and I mixed the salad myself. Guaranteed organic, no chemical, no fertilisers – unnatural fertilisers, that is.' He smiled, pushing the packet closer to Trevor.

Trevor looked up, stared at the sandwiches for a moment, then, after dusting off his hands on his sweatshirt, he finally took one. 'Thank you.' His voice sounded strange, rusty from disuse. He opened the sandwich and peered inside the twin slices of rye bread.

'No butter, I'm afraid,' Spencer apologised. 'I try to eat healthy.'

Trevor closed up the sandwich and took a small bite.

Spencer produced a bottle of mineral water from his rucksack, and a paper cup. He filled the cup and took the bottle for himself.

'Drink?' He handed Trevor the cup, forcing him to take it.

'Thank you.'

'Harry Goldman told me you're allowed out now. For short periods anyway. Would you like to have a drink with me in the Green Monkey this afternoon? They do a nice line in non-alcoholic wines that don't interfere with any medication.'

'No, thank you.'

Spencer took a sandwich himself, and bit a huge chunk out of it. 'You're going to have to make that first move sometime soon,' he cautioned, through a full mouth. He finished off his sandwich and took another. 'You don't realise what you're missing until you go outside,' he continued casually. 'I know. It's not that long since I was sitting where you are now.'

Trevor stared at him, the barely touched sandwich trembling in his hand. 'You were a patient?' The question was timidly phrased, but it was still a question, and Spencer understood what a profound step forward that represented for someone in Trevor's depressed state of indifference.

'Yes I was a patient. In America first, then here.' He ran his fingers over the scars that radiated from the glass eye in his right socket. 'I'll tell you about it sometime.' He hoped Trevor wouldn't press him further. If he had to put him off, it might close the chink he'd just made in Trevor's defensive armour, and that could prove disastrous to a man teetering on the brink of re-establishing communication with the rest of the world. But . . .

That 'but' was the agony that Spencer had tried and not always succeeded in living with, for nearly three years. The agony Harry Goldman had warned him he might never fully come to terms with. The present – and Trevor – faded as he remembered California. A sun-drenched sidewalk in the pedestrian-only area of Main Street. The beat of popular music echoing from the fashionable boutiques that catered for the young and well-heeled, drowning out the more temperate classical music that enhanced a suitably elegant atmosphere for the art-lovers who were crowding into the gallery behind him. He saw again the discreetly splendid window that held a varied selection of his originals, and the walls inside that were hung with limited – very limited, and very exclusive – signed editions of his prints.

The smart set – the rich smart set. Alfredo, who owned the

gallery, and always checked the bank balances of his clients before their professional titles and social standing, smiled at him as they elbowed their way into the gallery. Spencer smiled back. He had reason to be grateful to his patrons. His house was Californian redwood built on stilts on a fashionable hillside that commanded a sweeping view of a breathtakingly beautiful wooded bay. Enormous windows: vast expanses of glass which he'd designed to frame the scenery outside. Designer Italian furniture, designer suits of raw silk and fine linen, designer crystal – everything he owned was the best that new and up and coming talent had to offer. Everything! It would have been churlish and miserly of him to stint himself and his family, when the world's wealthy were queuing to buy his signed prints at five thousand dollars a time, and his originals at anything from fifty thousand dollars upwards. He had everything a man could possibly want. Everything! The sun, the lifestyle to go with it, a sweet beautiful wife, sweet beautiful babies . . .

'Spencer Jordan, isn't it?'

Still back in California, Spencer stared blankly at the cropped hair and steel grey eyes of the man who appeared suddenly in front of him.

'Spencer Jordan?' the man repeated tersely. 'I'm Peter Collins. Sergeant Peter Collins,' he emphasised sternly. 'I'd like a word with Trevor Joseph.'

Spencer wrenched himself painfully out of the past. He'd already promised himself that he would never allow himself to drift back. Not any more. It was too raw, too painful. And here he was again, only this time in broad daylight. He didn't even have the excuse of insomnia, loneliness and darkness. What had prompted it? Of course, Trevor – he'd told Trevor that he himself had been a patient.

'Use this room, Sergeant Collins.' He rose from his seat. 'I have things to do in the staff room.' He turned to Trevor. 'See you later?'

'I'd like that. Thank you for the sandwich.'

It was difficult to judge who was more astounded by Trevor's animated response; Peter Collins or Spencer Jordan.

Chapter Three

While Jordan retrieved his rucksack and left the room, Trevor moved from his position behind the easel and sat in the chair Spencer had vacated. Collins pushed aside a mess of paint pots, jars and brushes crowding on a table, laid a sheet of paper over the area he'd cleared, then perched on it, facing Trevor.

He studied Trevor critically as he waited for the door to close, making no allowance for sentiment or friendship. Depression was etched into every inch of Trevor's sagging body, from the lank greasy hair that straggled, badly in need of a cut, over his forehead and collar, to the limp colourless hands that lay inert and lifeless in his lap. Thin at the best of times, Trevor was now gaunt. His pale sunken cheeks were covered with black stubble, and he was dressed in the same faded, threadbare clothes of yesterday.

'I looked in on your flat,' Peter said abruptly. 'After I dropped in the take-away yesterday evening. Did you eat it?'

'Yes.'

'Good fish and chips?'

'It was curry,' Trevor contradicted flatly.

'Just testing. It's the same mess as usual – your flat,' Collins explained. 'No burglar's been in yet to tidy up. Frank was locking up his shop down below. He'll be glad to see you back; the local kids have been giving him hell for the last couple of months. It didn't take them long to realise no one was sleeping over the shop any more. Frank's display window has been smashed in three times since Christmas, and his cigarette and chocolate machines have been vandalised so often he's had to take them down.' Peter continued to study Trevor as he extricated a packet of small cigars from his shirt pocket. 'Anyway, Frank said to tell you he'll call in here one of these

39

days. Probably late on a Sunday afternoon, because that's the only time he shuts the shop.' He lit the cigar and puffed a cloud of smoke Trevor's way. A year ago Trevor would have protested mildly or strongly, depending on his mood. Now he sat apparently oblivious, passively wreathed in cigar smoke.

'Your mother phoned me,' Collins proceeded. 'I said you were okay, making good progress, and that you'd write or phone as soon as you had a chance. Do you think you could manage that?' he added harshly.

'Yes,' Trevor answered.

'You've noticed the rumpus outside?' Peter asked.

'Yes.'

'Aren't you interested in what's happening?'

'No.'

Peter rose, turned his back, and walked over to the window. After witnessing Trevor's earlier animation, it was as much as he could do to curb his instinct to pick him up and shake him like a rat. Despite the doctors' explanations, he still ascribed Trevor's continuing depression and monumental indifference to simple lack of effort on his part.

If Trevor had reacted violently, ranting and raving against the injustice of fate that had broken his arm, legs and head, he could have sympathised with him. But Trevor hadn't ranted and raved; instead he'd withdrawn deeper and deeper into a monosyllabic melancholy that had totally erased the personality of the old Trevor, replacing him with a stranger he no longer knew or liked.

Joseph's frigid responses, hung between them; a dense, dividing curtain that threatened to smother what little remained of their once warm, if fraught, relationship. Peter contemplated the human wreckage hunched before him. Trevor had been a good friend; probably the only real friend he'd ever had. He couldn't just sit back and take this! For the first time since Trevor had been attacked, he really let rip, allowing emotions usually tightly reined, to erupt to the surface.

'I never thought I'd say this, but work is a swine without you,' he muttered savagely. 'That damned girl guide Mulcahy's dumped on the squad is bloody useless. She's got a degree in anthropology,' he added inconsequentially. 'Do you mind telling me what bloody good a degree in anthropology is to the Drug Squad? A degree in fortune telling would be better. God only knows, it's difficult enough to cover your own bloody arse in this filthy business without having to watch out for a useless female as well.' He turned uneasily from the window and paced back to the table. 'So, the sooner you get off your backside and out of here, the better it will be for all of us. Then Bill can push Mary Poppins into a quiet corner where she can sit behind a desk and anthropologise – or whatever it is that females like her do. And you and I can get on with the job.' He confronted Trevor. 'What do you say to that?'

'I told you, I might not be coming back,' Trevor reiterated.

There was a sharp rap at the door, and Michelle Grady stuck her head into the room.

'Sergeant Collins, Inspector Evans is asking if you'd go to the main administration office, to check if there are any plans or maps of this place.' She spoke with the bright, determined enthusiasm that was her one defence against Collins' biting cynicism.

'I'll be there in a few minutes,' Peter barked at her.

She shut the door quickly.

All Trevor wanted was for Collins to go, so he could be left alone with his portrait.

'But,' Peter continued his harangue, 'a body is buried in the grounds, right under your nose, and you saw bloody nothing! Christ, man, even the craziest female nut on your ward saw it happen. Where *were* you – that's what I'd like to know? Dead, or off this planet!' He walked away in disgust, slamming the door behind him.

Trevor continued to sit still on his chair. After five minutes, he raised his eyes so he could once again look at his portrait.

'What's the verdict, Dan?' Superintendent Bill Mulcahy had been on site for less than five minutes, and already the constables and rookies were acting more alert, snapping to attention whenever he passed, trying to look as busy as any policeman can who has nothing more to do than control a passive crowd.

'O'Kelly's still down there. We'll know more later.' Evans pulled a crumpled linen handkerchief from his pocket and wiped his hands with it. 'But, for the moment, I can tell you she's young. Early twenties, Patrick thinks, fairly pretty, and she was probably buried alive.'

'Alive?' Even the Superintendent's calloused mind was repelled by the thought.

'Her mouth had been glued shut. Probably with one of those bonding-in-seconds, stick-anything jobs, and both her nose and her throat were jammed tight with earth. Patrick thinks that's because she was struggling for breath until the very last minute.'

'Poor bitch.'

Dan inspected his fingernails. 'It couldn't have been very pleasant for her,' he murmured, the master of the understatement.

Mulcahy yanked himself back into the present. 'Right, where shall we start?' he asked, as though he had not already made up his mind. 'Routine enquiries and interviews all around the hospital?'

'You never know your luck. We might pick up something useful. I need to draft some good coppers on to the team.' He looked inquiringly at his boss. 'Do you have any to spare?'

'Do I ever. There isn't a section that isn't pushed to the limit at the moment.' Mulcahy studied the sky, as though he hoped to find a solution in the heavens. 'You can have Constable Grady,' he glanced around. 'That's her over there.'

'The one with brown hair?'

'She's only a rookie,' the Superintendent apologised, 'but she's keen. And you'd be doing me a favour by taking her. Collins has become downright impossible since I transferred her to the Drug Squad as a short-term replacement for Trevor Joseph.'

'Is he still sick?'

'Sick, *and* in here.' Mulcahy didn't even try to keep the contempt from his voice.

'Is he, now?' Evans rubbed his chin reflectively. 'That could prove useful. Very useful indeed.'

'Don't pin any hopes there,' Bill dismissed the notion flatly. 'The man's cracked; nutty as a fruitcake.'

'I thought he just had depression?'

'Depression or nuts: it amounts to the same thing, doesn't it?' Evans debated whether it was worth arguing the point, and decided against. 'I'll take Grady, and anyone else you can spare,' he said finally. 'I'd like to see at least twenty men working on this by the end of the day.'

'You'll be lucky, but I'll look around and see who I can come up with. I might be able to lend you Collins for a while.'

'I thought the whole idea was to separate him from Grady?'

'It is. But he really needs separating from all the rest of humanity. Trevor Joseph was the only one who could ever put up with his bloody moods.'

'I've a feeling there'll be enough leg-work on this one even for the prima donnas,' Dan returned his handkerchief to his pocket.

Collins sat in the office of Tony Waters, Compton Castle's chief administrator, and groaned. Dan Evans had asked him to check the layout of the building, while Evans was conferring with Patrick O'Kelly, the pathologist, at the crime scene, but five minutes' study of the plans had told him everything he needed to know. The place was an absolute nightmare from a policing and security point of view.

'As you can see, Sergeant Collins' – Tony Waters waved his manicured hand over the papers on his desk; he was a tall man, six foot one or two, in Peter's estimation, with startlingly white-blond hair and pale blue eyes – 'the whole place is a mishmash of bits and pieces from every building that's been erected on this site since Norman times.'

'It looks that way,' Collins agreed sourly, noting the ruins of the outer wall of the Norman castle on the southern boundary of the plan, and the sketched-in blob of masonry marked 'Folly'. He jabbed his finger on it, with a questioning look at Waters.

'It's down as Victorian, but if you want my opinion the foundations are Norman, like the name of this place. I think it was easier for the Victorian architect to dovetail the more solid

Norman bits into the subsequent building than to demolish them.'

'You sound as though you know what you're talking about,' Collins muttered grudgingly.

'I try to take an interest in my surroundings, Sergeant,' Waters smiled without warmth. 'If you look at these contours,' he ran his thumbnail over the plan, 'you'll see what remains of the old moat.'

Collins noted a steep-sided depression on the northern edge of the old hospital, then he turned his attention to the main building.

The mid-Victorian edifice was a prime example of Gothic architecture at its most ornate and, in Peter's eye, most horrendous, housing a vast network of narrow passages and steep staircases that led to communal wards the size of ballrooms and servants' attics that were mouseholes by comparison. There were cavernous storerooms, towers and turrets that seemed about as useful as the stone gargoyles that decorated the main facade of the building, and endless hallways, foyers and offices. This rabbit warren of rooms extended from a vast cellar, which had been partitioned off to hold the incoming electrical supplies and central-heating boiler, to the fourth floor attics originally designed as accommodation units for live-in skivvies.

From what Peter had seen on his way to the administrator's office, via three-quarters of the present hospital, only a few cosmetic changes had been made in the old building itself since Queen Victoria had sat on the throne. Scratched and stained vinyl tiles lay over whatever flooring the Victorians had walked on, but the walls were still covered to shoulder height by brick-shaped white tiles topped by a strip of dark-stained oak dado; and if the green paint that darkened the walls from the dado up to the ceiling wasn't the original, it deserved to be.

The greatest change that had been made was in the use of the building. The first, second and third floor corridors were still partitioned off by huge sets of solid-oak double doors that sported massive brass and iron locks, now rusty with disuse, but these doors no longer led to locked wards. The old patient areas had been taken over by the administration department of

44

the local Health Authority. The dusty corridors and huge echoing rooms now reverberated to the sounds of printers and telephones, and the clicking stiletto heels of clerks as they walked from one office area to another. The therapy units were housed in a collection of thirty-year-old demountable buildings that had been erected close to the back of the Victorian building as a short-term, temporary measure, and had never been dismantled; but the wards themselves had been moved out in the early 1980s to modern, purpose-built, four-storey blocks erected further behind the old hospital. Of soulless box-type construction, they were connected to the old building by long winding tunnels of opaque perspex. And, as if the buildings themselves weren't headache enough, the grounds beyond were vast. Laid out in a parkland of lawns, wooded areas and shrubberies, they could have comfortably concealed an entire battalion of enemy, let alone a solitary killer carrying one single warm, living body.

'These gates . . .' Collins indicated openings marked in the external wall that surrounded the grounds. 'They locked at night?'

'All but the main gates fronting on to Hanover Street. We have to leave those open in case of emergencies.'

'They manned?'

'They used to be, but our security budget was halved in the second lot of cutbacks two years ago.'

'So *anyone* can walk in and out?'

'The grounds are patrolled by a guard with a radio transmitter, and the entrances to the hospital blocks are manned at their individual reception areas. *This* building is locked at night.'

'Have a lot of problems with prowlers?' Collins asked sardonically.

'Frankly, yes,' Waters replied.

Collins looked up from the plans. 'I'm not surprised. Tell me, now we've established that any lunatic can just walk right in here off the streets, what about the ones already here?'

'I presume you mean our patients?'

Collins sensed Waters' hackles rising, but that didn't stop him from pressing the point. 'Could they easily walk out of their wards at night and take a stroll around the grounds?'

45

'I told you, the reception areas in the ward blocks are manned.'

'Continuously? By more than one man?'

'Obviously not by more than one. The hospital budget . . .'

'The hospital budget doesn't stretch to cover him when he goes for a pee, or to fix himself a cup of coffee.' Collins pushed the plans aside in disgust. 'What you've got there, Mr Waters, is a bomb waiting to explode. The only wonder is it didn't go off any sooner.'

The administrator insisted on accompanying Collins when he finally left the office. Side by side they walked through the long corridors and out of the back entrance, entering one of the perspex tunnels that connected the administration block with the wards. Neither spoke. Waters was clearly offended by Collins' criticism of the hospital administration, and the Sergeant was too busy mentally filing his initial impressions of the place to make polite small talk.

Collins was not a sensitive man. He had always relied on cold logic to take him through life, but even he had felt uneasy as they entered the perspex tunnel. Its floor and walls were white. No image penetrated the opaque, arched walls, though light did. It was intense, blinding; he felt as though he had stumbled into a surrealist painting. Almost as soon as they entered the tunnel, it curved sharply. He turned his head and looked back. All he could see behind him was the tunnel disappearing into itself. Ahead, the same thing. He was beset by the most peculiar sensation, of being disembodied in time and space.

'If you're not nuts when you come into this place, you could well be nuts by the time you leave,' he muttered.

'You don't like these tunnels, Sergeant Collins?'

'Do you?'

'They're cheap, they serve their purpose, and they're ideal from the security viewpoint. No one can get into them from the outside, except by the exit and entry points, which have been kept to a minimum; and they provide a dry, direct route from the wards to the therapy blocks. The staff can send patients through them with confidence, knowing they will turn up safely at the other end.'

'Always supposing they aren't blinded before they get there.'

'The company that installed them are now experimenting with other colours, possibly a pale green or a mottled effect.' Peter noticed how the strong white light drained away what little colour there was in Tony Waters' pale face and white-blond hair, and he reflected that a mottled green face might look even more bizarre.

Ten minutes later, as they exited the tunnel and walked into the foyer of the building housing the one secure psychiatric ward, he could breathe a little easier.

'Collins,' Bill Mulcahy nodded, as the two men strode over the lawn towards him. 'And you are?'

'Waters. Tony Waters, of hospital administration.' He extended his hand in a way that instantly conveyed that he *was* hospital administration.

'Glad you're here. We need to set up a system for interviewing your staff and patients as soon as possible, particularly this . . .' Bill flicked through his notebook, 'Vanessa Hedley, who ordered the gardener's lad to dig here.'

'I can organise a rota for you to interview the staff, but I'm afraid you're going to have to consult Harry Goldman before you interview any of the patients. He's the chief psychiatrist here, and patients' welfare is his responsibility.'

'Where can I find him?'

'Unfortunately not here at the moment. He's in court.'

Mulcahy raised his eyebrows.

'He's giving evidence in a case involving one of our patients.'

'I see. In that case we'd better begin with the staff.' He could see Evans' and O'Kelly's shadows moving around behind the screens. 'If you make out a list, Collins, then you and Grady can begin with the nursing staff working on this Vanessa Hedley's ward. You've no objections Mr Waters?'

'None at all, Inspector . . .'

'Superintendent Mulcahy,' Bill informed him coldly.

Collins shafted an evil look at Mulcahy as he pulled his notebook out of his pocket. Not even attempting to conceal his ill humour, he strode across the lawn towards Michelle Grady.

At that moment Dan Evans and Patrick O'Kelly emerged, deep in conversation, from behind the screens. O'Kelly peeled a pair of rubber gloves from his hands, as he studied a sheaf of polaroid photographs that Evans was holding in front of him.

'We're ready to move her out, Bill,' Evans divulged softly. 'If you could get this crowd shifted back, and the ambulance up . . .'

'I'll see it's organised right away.'

Dan looked questioningly at Tony.

'This is Mr Waters, hospital administration.'

'In that case, perhaps you can help us,' Dan suggested.

'I'd be only too delighted to, in any way I can. But, as I've already explained to Superintendent Mulcahy, I can't author- ise you access to any of the patients. I'm afraid you'll have to wait for Dr Goldman's permission.'

Ignoring his apologies, Dan lifted his hand and offered Waters a selection of the Polaroid photographs.

'I realise this is a long shot, but I don't suppose you recognise her?'

Waters accepted the photographs gingerly, as though they were contaminated. He held the first one high and squinted at it.

'Blonde hair, blue eyes five foot six inches tall, well nourished – could even say plump I suppose,' O'Kelly supplemented. 'No distinguishing marks that I can make out at the moment, but I may uncover some in the lab. Probably early twenties. Strike a chord?'

'Difficult to say. We have over four hundred nurses here, between the day and night shifts, and that's without the auxiliaries, administrative and domestic staff. Not to mention the patients. But, then, I'm probably not the best one to ask. I spend very little time out of my office. Could I make a suggestion?' he ventured as he handed the photographs back.

'You could,' Mulcahy agreed drily.

'If you intend showing these to any of the nursing staff, would you please make sure that there aren't any patients around? Some of their minds are very delicately balanced.'

'I think we can safely promise that. We'll also try to arrange a better photograph back in the lab.' Dan studied the picture of the contorted face. Patrick O'Kelly had done his best to scrape the earth away, but the features were still smudged with dirt, and the skin was grey, heavily disfigured by livid blotches.

'She doesn't look her best,' Mulcahy commented. 'We'll check out her description with our missing persons files and put out an appeal to the media. Hopefully we shouldn't be too long in identifying her. I don't suppose you'd know if you have any nurses or patients missing at the moment, Mr Waters? Any that haven't turned up for work during the last couple of days, perhaps?'

'All of our nurses are extremely reliable. If they're sick for a day, they're meticulous about phoning in, because they're well aware of the strain any absence will place on colleagues who work on the wards. Patients,' Waters shook his head, 'now they're quite another matter. The voluntary patients are forever coming and going, because whatever the doctors' diagnosis, we have no real authority to keep them here. In any given week, at least half a dozen discharge themselves.'

'And disappear?' Evans asked.

'Certainly, as far as our records go. Some don't even bother to go through the formal procedure of discharging themselves from the wards, and that's not to mention those in the halfway houses—'

'What are those?' Dan interrupted.

'We have three halfway houses nearby,' the administrator explained forbearingly. 'Six bedroomed units that we use to accommodate and support patients the psychiatrists consider fit enough to be returned to the community. They're located just outside the walls, on the west side. Each patient has their own room, but they share kitchen and bathroom facilities. Some have even been found sheltered job placements, or positions on Employment Training, by their social workers.'

'Is any check kept on their movements?' Mulcahy demanded.

'There's a warden in charge of each hostel, and the staff sleep in on a rota basis, so we're aware if any patient stays out all night. They also have to keep an appointment with their own psychiatrist once a week.'

'Let me see if I've understood this right,' Evans said slowly. 'These hostels, you did say they were *outside* the grounds?'

'They are.'

'So there's no way that the people living there could enter the hospital area at night?'

'I suppose they could come through the main gate, if they wanted to,' Waters conceded reluctantly.

Mulcahy looked at Collins, who shook his head in despair.

'You haven't heard the half of it yet,' he grimaced. 'I've a nasty feeling about this one. But then, whoever said it was going to be easy to find one murderous nut in a nuthouse full of cracked shells?' Oblivious to Tony Waters' angry glare, he summoned Michelle Grady and they walked back towards the wards.

Collins had worked on the Drug Squad for ten out of the fifteen years he'd spent on the force. Drug-squad work was dirty, occasionally dangerous, often boring, wet and cold; but at least he operated in familiar territory. So he generally had a good idea of what he was up against, and what he was looking for. Most of the time, interviewing people was comparatively straightforward. His questions were centred around *what*, *when*, *how*, and *where*, they'd seen, sold or handled illegal substances.

A murder enquiry was an entirely different affair. This wasn't the first time he'd been drafted into the Serious Crimes squad, but even moderate prior knowledge of what would be required of him didn't make the task any easier. He hated having to interview people without really knowing what he was looking for. At best, all he could hope for was a few scraps of information that might prove useful. Scraps that probably wouldn't even be identifiable as useful until they were carefully pieced together back at the Station, along with fragments and crumbs of gossip that other officers had picked up. And that piecing together rarely took place until late in the evening, when everyone on the team was exhausted, tired, hungry and too irritable to co-operate peacefully with one another.

He sat back on a hard wooden chair in Sister Marshall's office, and spooned around a peculiar beige-coloured substance that the domestic on duty had assured him was coffee. He was due to interview Jean Marshall in five minutes. Constable Grady sat across the desk from him, nervously crossing and uncrossing her legs. They weren't wonderful legs, too thin for his taste, but at least she was another body; and he hoped her presence would protect him from the Sister's more blatant overtures.

In the event he needn't have worried. When Jean Marshall finally arrived, she had Nurse Lyn Sullivan in tow, and both were carrying iced bottles of mineral water.

'You are brave.' Lyn's smile lit up her entire face, and Collins found himself smiling back, in spite of the frustration burning inside him.

'I know,' he answered amiably, 'but I didn't think it showed.'

'I mean, not many people will drink that.' She pointed at the coffee. 'Heaven only knows what Josie puts into it. The latest theory included powdered laxatives.'

'Now you tell me,' he complained. He glanced across the desk to see Michelle Grady studying him intently, and changed the subject abruptly. 'Run the events of Sunday past me one more time?' he said to Jean Marshall.

'You yourself were there,' she pointed out quietly, lighting a cigarette.

'Not in the early stages. When exactly did Vanessa Hedley start talking about bodies buried in the garden?'

'She was already well into that theme when I came on duty at eight on Sunday morning,' Lyn Sullivan chipped in helpfully.

Peter found himself staring at the expanse of thigh the girl was showing beneath her short skirt. He hadn't seen a pair of legs as good as hers in a long time.

'Didn't you think to question the night staff about her story?' Constable Grady questioned her testily, while looking daggers at Collins.

'None of the staff would consider a patient's ramblings worth discussing.' Sister Marshall blew smoke in Michelle's face. 'It may have escaped your notice, Constable, but this is a psychiatric hospital. Most of our patients, including Mrs Hedley, have great difficulty in differentiating between reality and fantasy.'

'They would, wouldn't they,' Collins observed sarcastically, returning Michelle's hard glare with interest.

'Has she said anything since?' Michelle persevered, in the face of open hostility from all quarters.

'Only "I told you so" – with as many variations as she can fit in. I thought the questioning would best be left to you people,' Jean smiled broadly at Collins.

'Apparently we have to wait for the psychiatrist's permission,' he said flatly, without returning her smile.

'Do you think she really did see something?' Grady asked sceptically.

'It's bloody obvious she did,' Collins snapped. 'She must have done, to be able to pinpoint the exact spot where the body was found.'

An uneasy silence fell over the room.

'Sorry we can't be any more help.' Sister Marshall poured some water into a glass, 'but you know what this place is like. Or you should do after the time you've spent visiting here. Trevor's a simple depressive, which is understandable considering the physical injuries he's had to cope with, but some of the other cases on his ward are a great deal more complicated. Vanessa, for instance. And then there's Lucy Craig; she convinced herself that she didn't need to bother about her A-levels because she's married to Jason Donovan. Paranoid delusion is all very easy to laugh at, but to her, the delusions and fantasies are as real as these four walls.'

'I hear what you're saying,' Michelle Grady's use of psychologist's jargon irritated Collins intensely. 'Anyone else reported odd happenings in the night lately?'

'Lyn's the one who works two weeks on, two weeks off, on night shift. I'm days regular.' Jean stubbed her cigarette out in the ashtray. 'If there's nothing more, I really should be getting back to the ward. You know where to find me if you want me.'

'Patients are always imagining they've seen something at night. Only last week we had to physically restrain and sedate Vanessa to keep her from running outside,' Lyn Sullivan said thoughtfully. 'She was convinced that her lover was waiting for her out in the grounds.'

'Has she ever managed to get out?' Collins queried, pricking up his ears.

'No, I don't think so. At least not since I've been here. To be honest, at night she's usually too heavily sedated to move one foot in front of the other.'

'We try to keep the more difficult ones under control,' Jean Marshall explained moving towards the door.

Michelle raised her eyebrows. 'By knocking them out with drugs?' she enquired tactlessly.

'No, by tranquillising them so they can't leave the safety of the ward and harm themselves in any way,' Lyn retorted defensively.

'Was she tranquillised on Saturday night?' Peter finally gave up on his coffee and pushed it away in disgust.

'I assume so. There's nothing in her notes to suggest the contrary.'

'Then how do you explain her being up and awake in the small hours?' he persevered.

'Patients can generally develop an immunity to most drugs after they've been using them for a while,' the Sister lectured knowledgeably.

'Then you need to increase the dosage to gain the desired effect?'

'That's right.'

'I see. And Vanessa hasn't had her dosage *increased* lately?'

'There's nothing indicating that on her record card.'

Lyn Sullivan glanced at him guiltily. 'We halved Mrs Hedley's medication last Saturday,' she admitted in embarrassment. 'The pharmacy was closed, and we'd run out of the type of sleeping pills she's written up for.'

Collins smiled. 'Lucky for us that you did.' He now had his first piece of concrete evidence; the reason for Vanessa's wakeful night. It wasn't much, but it was a beginning. And all investigations had to start somewhere.

Chapter Four

'I'm Harry Goldman. Inspector Evans, isn't it?'

'It is.' Dan examined the diminutive man in front of him. Dr Harry Goldman was the caricaturist's dream of a psychiatrist: short, just over five feet two inches, with a mop of unruly brown hair, weak eyes half hidden behind gold-rimmed glasses, and a scrawny inadequate body that looked far too fragile to support his oversized head.

'I'm sorry I wasn't here this morning when all of this happened,' Goldman apologised. He looked across the gardens to the screened-off area of lawn. 'I was in court. One of our patient's applied for access to his children,' he explained in a high pitched, squeaky voice.

'No matter,' Evans said lightly. 'However, we would like to question all of your patients, and one in particular, as soon as possible.'

'Of course. Tony Waters has already filled me in. Met me in the car park,' he replied in answer to Dan's inquisitive look. And I have no objection to you questioning Vanessa Hedley, or any of our patients, as long as the questioning is done in a considerate and sympathetic manner and either myself or one of my senior colleagues is present, preferably my chief assistant, Dotty Clyne. However, I feel I must caution you that any information you gather must be treated with the utmost caution, and subjected to the closest scrutiny. Because of the nature of their illnesses, some of our patients are bound to make the most unreliable witnesses.'

'Contrary to general belief, there's as many disturbed people wandering around outside this hospital as there are inside, Dr Goldman, and a fair proportion seem to find their way down to the Station sooner or later. We're aware of the drawbacks, and

we have skilled people waiting, to interpret and piece together any information we glean. However that's not to
say that we'd turn down any help that you're prepared to
give us.'

'I'd be only too delighted,' Harry mumbled indistinctly,
wondering if he'd over-stressed the difficult nature of his
patients. Presumably Dan Evans was a professional too – of
sorts.

'Right, if you don't mind Dr Goldman, I think the sooner we
make a start, the better,' Dan directed briskly.

'Before we do, Inspector Evans, Tony Waters also mentioned
that you've requested a tour of the hospital. If you've no
objections, I'd like to take you round myself. If I can explain the
layout, the areas you can have free access to, the areas where
the patients' interests and welfare are paramount, the areas
that need to be approached with particular caution, and the
areas which are completely out of bounds for good reason,
perhaps it would make life a little easier for both hospital staff
and police while you carry out your investigations.'

'I appreciate your co-operation, Dr Goldman.'

The doctor looked for a trace of sarcasm in Evans' face and
found none.

'Shall we start by interviewing Vanessa?' Dan proceeded
across the grass, leaving Goldman no choice but to follow.

They made a detour to pick up Collins from the room where he
was interviewing staff, assisted by Michelle Grady. Aware of
Collins' reputation, both as an extremely competent detective
and one who generally didn't bother to even pay lip-service to
the rules, Evans asked him tactfully to sit in on his session with
Vanessa, but nothing more. In the absence of anyone better, he
had little choice but to use Collins as a deputy, but Evans
intended to make it clear from the outset that he himself would
be the one setting the terms and conditions of the investigation. There was more than one copper down at the Station who
blamed Peter Collins, rightly or wrongly, for Trevor Joseph's
injuries, and Dan was determined to ensure that any notions
Peter entertained of schoolboy heroics remained firmly off his
beat.

Harry Goldman's office was a large, square room decorated in warm shades of yellow and orange, its couch and chairs upholstered in restful shades of pale green. Typical psychologist's decor, Evans reflected cynically, as Harry graciously offered him the use of his desk and chair. Without voicing the slightest protest, Collins sat himself in the most unobtrusive corner of the room, behind the door. Goldman picked up a hard, uncomfortable chair, acquired by the hospital more for its stacking abilities than for comfort, and sat down alongside Collins.

Vanessa Hedley was brought to the door in a wheelchair pushed by a porter. She was escorted by Nurse Lyn Sullivan, and Harry's assistant Dotty Clyne, a large, fair-haired, masculine woman whom people chiefly remembered for her moustache. The porter helped Vanessa to stand upright, then she tottered into the office, leaning heavily on Lyn's and Dotty's arms. She wore the dazed, disorientated look of the heavily sedated, but, unlike the day before, she was dressed in a blue floral frock that would have looked more at home at a Buckingham Palace garden party.

'Mrs Hedley . . . Vanessa, you remember Sergeant Peter Collins, don't you?' Lyn asked tentatively.

'I do,' Vanessa snapped with surprising vehemence, considering her heavy eyes.

'And here's Dr Goldman.' The young nurse guided her swiftly away from Collins towards safer introductions.

'And I'm Dan Evans. Inspector Dan Evans.' Dan held out his hand in an attempt to break the ice – an attempt which backfired quite spectacularly. As he rose from his chair behind the desk, Vanessa shrank back through the door and screamed.

'It's him. It's him!' Intimidated by the sheer size of Dan Evans, she clearly equated him with the shadow she'd seen in the garden.

'This isn't the man you saw in the garden, Vanessa. This is a policeman,' Lyn Sullivan protested.

'Did he look like me, Vanessa?' Dan demanded, cutting in. 'Was he big? Was his hair thinning like mine? Was it fair?'

'You're him,' Vanessa hissed, fighting Lyn's grip as the girl tried to prevent her leaving the room. 'I know you're him.'

57

'How do you know, Vanessa?' Dan asked, less urgently this time, in response to warning looks from Goldman and Dotty.

'Because I know . . . Because I do . . .'

One of the joys of being a copper in a smallish town, Dan reflected, is knowing the life history of most of the 'characters' that town had to offer. He'd been around the Station the same night they'd brought Vanessa Hedley in. It must have been all of eight, maybe more years ago, but he had known about her long before that. Who didn't? Her husband had owned and run the biggest, plushest and most popular hotel on the seafront, and Vanessa had been the right person to help build it up, with her attractive, sharp-featured face, trim five-foot-two figure, smart designer clothes, and a memory like a seasoned CID officer for people's names, faces, likes and dislikes.

Earlier that night she'd decided to find out for herself whether something she'd long suspected was true or not, and that decision was to have repercussions on more lives than her own. When her husband drove the staff home at the end of a long Christmas shift, she'd set out to follow the hotel minibus in her Porsche. At a discreet distance, of course. Not that her husband could have been looking out for it. He'd been too busy dropping off all his staff but one at record speed. She'd followed his minibus, with its single remaining passenger, to a deserted car park on the cliff above Lovers' Leap, sat in the car and waited, presumably watching while her husband and his passenger had their fun and games. When they'd done what they'd set out to do, and were about to turn back, Vanessa had revved her engine and crashed her car into the minibus at full speed.

The first coppers on the scene almost cried. Some of them talked about nothing else for months. The spectacle of a two-month-old Porsche turned into a lump of written-off scrap metal was more than most grown men could bear. But by some miracle, or the intervention of the fates that look after wronged women, Vanessa Hedley walked away from the wreckage without a scratch. Her husband and his lover weren't so lucky. Neither had bothered to fasten their seatbelts, and the barmaid, who was fixing her lipstick at the time in order to

58

allay any suspicions that her extremely new husband might have about her unusually late finishing hours, plunged straight through the windscreen. To quote the duty sergeant who'd tried to interview her in casualty, 'her face had looked like a jigsaw Picasso'. And if the sight Dan had seen a couple of months later in court, had been anything to go by, it hadn't healed too well either. Mr Hedley's case had been even sadder. He still ran the hotel – from a wheelchair. And it hadn't been just his legs that had gone. Vanessa had laughed so much when she'd found out the full extent of his injuries, she'd had to be tranquillised.

But, then, Dan reflected, sooner or later most prisoners are released. Only if they continue to behave like lunatics *after* their release, they end up in places like Compton Castle. On the other hand, perhaps they were better off there. Psychiatric hospitals might smell funny, but hospital aromas are a whole lot more wholesome than prison stench.

'You're him!' Vanessa's screech brought Dan Evans sharply back into the present. 'I know.' Her glance darted from Lyn Sullivan to Dan, taking in the two men sitting behind the door. Realising she had quite an audience, she began to play the scene for all it was worth. 'You didn't believe me yesterday,' she screamed at Collins. 'You patronised me!' She tossed her head haughtily. 'Not one of you,' her gaze lingered on Lyn, 'has ever been interested in anything I had to say. And it was *true*,' her voice dropped menacingly. 'Every word. Now you know it's true, you want to talk to me. Well I don't want to talk to you. Not now. Not after the way you treated me.'

'I can understand that Vanessa.' His tone was muted, apologetic. Dan stared at Collins dumbfounded. He'd never heard him speak softly before.

'I know what I saw,' Vanessa repeated, her voice climbing high with hysteria. 'You buried her. – *You* . . .' she pointed at Dan.

'Not Inspector Evans, Vanessa – but someone else. And we know about it because, thanks to you, we found her. You were right, and we were wrong. But she's found now, and we'd like you to tell us what you saw. Will you, please?'

'He buried her right there, right in the middle . . .' She began to repeat the sentences of yesterday word for word. Peter Collins sat back, preparing himself for boredom, but then she said something that galvanised his attention. 'It wasn't like last time.'

'What last time?' They asked the question in unison.

'Last time he buried one.'

'Where, Vanessa? Where did he bury another one?' Collins' voice hardened with urgency.

'Not telling you.' She clammed her lips shut, and turned her back on him.

Harry Goldman shook his head in warning as Evans half rose from his seat.

'Vanessa?' Collins left his chair and offered it to her. 'Won't you sit down?'

'No.'

'Please, take my chair,' he repeated lightly.

She hesitated for what seemed like forever to the apprehensive audience in the room, before finally sitting down. Harry Goldman eased himself out of his seat, and left it for Peter. Everyone's attention now fixed on Vanessa and Collins as they sat facing one another in the corner by the door.

'Vanessa, you told me yesterday that I didn't care enough to give the body in the garden a decent burial. I promise you, I do care. And I care about the other one as well. Won't you tell us where we can find it, so we can bury that one too?'

'It's out in the garden,' she replied irritatingly.

'It's a big garden Vanessa. Can't you be any more specific?'

She whirled around and pointed at Dan again. 'He knows. He buried them. You ask *him*.'

'Vanessa, that's Inspector Evans. He's a policeman,' Collins explained testily, his patience wearing thin.

'He did it. And I'm not going to talk no more.'

She turned her face to the wall, and sat in obdurate silence.

Goldman touched Peter on the shoulder and shook his head. Collins reluctantly left his chair.

'I'm going now, Vanessa.' Though he stood in front of her, she refused to look at him. 'But I'll come back and see you later.'

'Sergeant Collins is going now Vanessa, but will you stay and have a little chat with me?' Goldman asked. 'I can send for tea and biscuits.'

'I'm tired.' She closed her eyes.

'Later perhaps?' he pressed.

'Want to go to bed.'

'Just five minutes.'

'*Bed*!'

Lyn Sullivan nodded to the porter, who wheeled the chair forward. Dan followed Collins towards the door.

'Get through to the Station and tell them to call out the helicopter and heat-seeking cameras. I want every inch of the grounds photographed as quickly as possible,' Dan ordered tersely. 'And that means today.' He stood watching as the porter pushed Vanessa's wheelchair up the corridor.

'What Mrs Hedley said about there being another body buried in the garden,' Harry Goldman said briskly. 'Well, she's had so much attention lavished on her since this morning, I suspect it's simply attention-seeking. She's drip-feeding you false information in the hope that it will give her even more importance in your eyes. You really wouldn't be doing her any favours by paying credence to what she says. This syndrome is well known in cases like hers.'

'The problem is, Dr Goldman,' Dan turned his round, tired face to Harry. 'That after what we've uncovered, following her last bout of "attention seeking", we dare not ignore *any* information she volunteers. I'm afraid the risk of not "doing her any favours" is one we're simply going to have to take.'

Trevor Joseph stood poised in the doorway that separated the warm familiar, secure world of his ward from the cold, frightening and unknown world of the gardens. He closed his eyes, took a deep breath, and put one foot on the doorstep. Leaning heavily on his stick he dragged his other foot forward. Finally, stepping down on to the path, he opened his eyes again.

He swayed, overwhelmed by the noise and the people rushing around. He shrank back, afraid they were set on a collision course with him, although in fact the nearest of them was a good ten yards away. Fighting giddiness and nausea, he

61

struggled to take another step, sideways this time, so he could remain near to the building. A man rushed past him from behind, so close Trevor could smell the sweat soaked into his serge uniform. A group of curious patients walked towards him, heading for the screened-off area on the lawn. Panic stricken, he froze where he stood.

He shuddered, feeling as though he were surrounded by uniformed police and lab assistants in white coats – although there were less than a dozen within sight. A screech resounded in his ears. He whirled around wanting to know who was laughing at him, and saw that Alison Bevan was leaning out of a window in the therapy block, cackling at one of the porters who'd dropped a sandwich into a flowerbed.

He took another deep breath, forcing himself to remain motionless for a moment. He told himself that if he managed to look away from all the police activity towards the rest of the garden, he would be able to cope. But there were no tranquil scenes anywhere for him to gaze upon. Everywhere were long lines of police, beating the bushes, combing the lawns, standing guard over green-canvas shrouded areas. The drive he'd intended walking down was dotted with vehicles, police cars, ambulances, and overflow from the car parks which were jam-packed with television journalists' and reporters' cars.

The scene grew grey, dim, fading alarmingly from view as his panic turned to hysteria. Reaching blindly, he groped for the door handle; as soon as it was safely within his fingers, he turned on his heel, swung his stick and, in his eagerness to return to the cocooned security of the ward, slammed the whole length of his body painfully against the edge of the door.

Bile rose into his mouth as he fought to push the door open, so he could retreat from the threatening, alien world of the outside. But all he succeeded in doing was thumping the full weight of the metal-framed UVPC door in his face; painfully hitting the bridge of his nose, and almost knocking himself out in the process. He reeled backwards, dropping his stick, falling to his knees, but still retaining his grip on the door handle.

'Trying to get in, Trevor? Here, let me help you.' Spencer Jordan's strong hands supported his elbows. Easing Trevor to his feet, and backwards at the same time, he opened the door, and helped him in. 'Your stick.' Spencer retrieved and handed it to him. 'First time is always a bitch,' he murmured, unconsciously lapsing into American jargon. 'I remember it well.'

'I . . . I was going to . . .' Trevor only just made it to his room in time to vomit the goat's cheese sandwich into the toilet bowl of his private bathroom. Spencer held his head and sponged his face with cold water; and Trevor, now used to nurses ministering to his needs, saw nothing odd in Spencer's actions. When he had finally finished retching, Spencer helped him back into his room, steering him away from the bed and into the chair.

'As I was saying, the first time out is a bitch.' Spencer smiled. 'But you can be proud of yourself. You did it. And you did it on your own.'

'I couldn't face it. I turned and ran,' Trevor muttered dejectedly.

'You wouldn't have if there had been fewer people around.' Spencer pulled a packet of cigarettes from his pocket. 'Smoke?'

'I don't, but thank you.'

'Neither do I,' Spencer returned them to his top pocket. 'I keep them for patients who do.' He fingered the packet ruefully. 'Sometimes I wish I did smoke. It gives you something to do with your hands.'

Trevor looked down at his fingers, fidgeting nervously with a will of their own in his lap, and managed a small smile.

'Feel better?'

'Yes. Yes, thanks,' Trevor said diffidently. 'I don't want to keep you if you've got a class or something,' he said awkwardly.

Spencer walked over to the window, moved the curtains, and looked outside. 'I haven't a class for another hour and a half, but if you'd rather be left alone, I'll go.'

'I don't want to be a bore and monopolise your time, when you have something better to do.'

'I've nothing better to do, and you're not a bore.'

'Just one more job in your crowded day,' Trevor said drily.

'No,' Spencer replied. 'You're not a job, either.' He turned to face him. 'You remind me of myself, of where I was at until recently. In fact, until you came along, I was beginning to wonder if I'd made any progress at all.' A ghost of a smile hovered at the corners of his mouth. 'Then, when I saw you, I realised I *had* moved on.'

'So, I'm good as a progress indicator, if nothing else.'

'You're different from the others,' Spencer said slowly. 'Your depression stems directly from the devastating effect your injuries have had on your body. Sometimes doctors are all too ready to dismiss the havoc that severe physical damage can do to the mind, as well as to the body. It's all very well for them to tell you you're fit now, and you can get on with your life. Pick yourself up, dust yourself down, and start again where you left off, as though nothing had ever happened. You and I have both found out the hard way that it's not that easy. First you're weak as a kitten because you've done nothing except lie around hospitals for months. Second, while you've been gone, the whole world has turned around and changed, become suddenly bigger, noisier and more threatening. Even the simple everyday things like getting up in the morning, washing, dressing, talking, walking out through one door and in through another, take more effort than they ever did; and that's without taking into account the pains that cripple parts of you that never hurt before.'

'You really have been through it, haven't you?' Trevor challenged.

'Yes.' Spencer left the window and went to the door. 'But today *you* took your first and biggest step. You opened the door and went outside of your own accord. Nothing will ever take as much effort as that did again. Believe me, I know.'

'But I panicked . . .'

'So what? Next time you pick your time better, when there are fewer people around. You walk . . .' He thought carefully for a moment not wanting to set Trevor impossible goals. '. . . say two steps further than you did today before you turned back. You have to start somewhere. The day after, it'll be further. One day you'll reach the gate. And sometime after that you'll get on a bus.'

'You really think it's that simple?'

'I know it's not that simple, because every step and every move will take enormous effort. But as I just said, you took the biggest step today. Keep reminding yourself of that, not the panic that drove you back.' He opened the door, 'But that's enough of me lecturing. Want to come down to my room, and finish the drawing of the mysterious lady with the dark hair?'

'No,' Trevor said thoughtfully. 'No I don't think so.'

Spencer didn't try to coax or coerce him. 'Perhaps later. I'll be there all afternoon.'

'Perhaps,' Trevor murmured vaguely, as Spencer closed the door behind him.

You took the biggest step today. Nothing will ever take as much effort again.

Trevor wanted to believe Spencer, really believe him, but at that moment all he wanted to do was crawl into his bed, close his eyes, pull the sheet over his head, curl up, and never emerge again.

'There are six modern blocks, all built to a very simple, functional architectural plan. As you can see, there are staircases at either end, corridors straight down the centre linking with both sets of stairs, and rooms on either side. Toilets, bathrooms and sluice rooms, at the far end. Kitchens, linen cupboards and day rooms at this end; patients' double, single and four-bedded rooms in the centre. The single rooms tend to be reserved for difficult patients.'

Collins listened carefully to Harry Goldman, remembered Trevor's single room, and suppressed an urge to thump the diminutive psychiatrist.

'This particular block is for people suffering from Alzheimer's Disease . . .' The roar of a helicopter hovering overhead drowned out Goldman's words. Dan looked at Collins and nodded. Headquarters hadn't wasted any time. '. . . we have only elderly patients in this particular block. They're very confused . . .'

Collins peered through the glass walls that fronted the day room. About twenty elderly men and women were sitting in a carefully arranged circle. The room itself was neat, clean, and sterile, the furniture upholstered in green vinyl, the walls decorated in the same psychologically-correct shades of warm yellow as Goldman's office, and hung with a series of bland pastel landscapes. Two nurses were engaged in trying to evoke the patients' interest in books of old photographs that they were valiantly attempting to balance in hands that refused to clasp them.

'I hope they shoot me before I get to that stage,' Peter muttered to Dan under his breath.

'Something I can help you with, Sergeant Collins?' Goldman enquired.

'I hope not,' he replied flatly.

'As I was saying,' the psychiatrist continued, 'each block provides a home to people of varying degrees of illness. Some are severe, some mild – although we try to treat most of the mild cases as outpatients. We do, however, try to group like with like, it simplifies the arrangements for therapy. The ward that your friend Trevor Joseph is on, for instance, mainly houses those who have been admitted for observation, alongside those who are clinically depressed. The block across the way,' Goldman pointed out of the window to a parallel block, 'is where we try to place the majority of our phobia cases. The one directly in front of us caters for the manias. The block behind us has been utilised by the drug and alcohol dependency units. We even have a block for mothers suffering from postnatal depression, unfortunately an increasing syndrome in today's world. That block is slightly larger than the rest, as it also incorporates a nursery for the children.'

'If you group like with like, how come Vanessa Hedley is on Joseph's ward?' Collins demanded.

'I did say we *try* to organise things that way, Sergeant Collins. Unfortunately, in a less than ideal world, we don't always succeed in housing our patients, or arranging their therapy, the way we would like to. Because of the nature of depression, and because we try to keep most of our patients *in* the community, and treat them as outpatients, your friend's ward tends to be the one with the least pressure on its resources. Mrs Hedley is still being evaluated, and as there was a bed available on that particular ward . . .'

'How long has she been here?' Dan interrupted.

'On the ward or in the hospital?' Goldman asked.

'Both.'

66

'I'd have to check the records. But if my memory serves me correctly, I'd say that she's been on that ward about two months.'

'And in the hospital?'

'Longer.'

'Did she come here directly from prison?'

'I really shouldn't be discussing . . .'

'It doesn't matter.' Dan Evans knew he could find out all he needed from the records down at the Station. He glanced at the plan he was carrying folded over his diary. 'All six blocks are connected to the main block by perspex tunnels, am I right?'

'You are,' Dr Goldman asserted gravely.

'But not with one another?'

'Not directly, no. You'd have to walk to the main block then retrace your steps down one of the other tunnels to reach a separate block.'

'And all the therapy units lie in this area here.' Evans jabbed his massive index finger over a large space set behind the old hospital building, but in front of the modern blocks. It was dotted with the narrow outlines of demountables.

'Not any longer, I'm afraid. We're in the process of relocating one or two of the therapy units in the old hospital alongside the administration offices. You see those particular blocks were purpose-built in the sixties.' Goldman shook his head, 'And, like most buildings of that era, they're sadly lacking. Their roofs are flat and leaking, there's damp patches on most of the walls, the windows are metal-framed, warped . . .'

'In short, they are all cold, draughty and soaking wet with rotting fabric. There isn't much you can tell Sergeant Collins or me about buildings built in the sixties Dr Goldman,' Dan said wryly. 'Our station is one of them.'

'We all have our crosses to bear, Inspector Evans. As I was saying, all of these blocks, apart from the postnatal depression ward, are identical, and our staff man them at all times. If there was anything untoward happening in any of them, we'd find out about it immediately. There's really little point in you looking over all of them. It would gain you nothing, and the advent of any outsider might disturb the patients. I really would appreciate it if you and your men only visited these

67

wards accompanied by a senior member of my staff, and with my or Miss Dorothy Clyne's express permission.'

'And where do we find you in an emergency?'

'The switchboard can always reach one or other of us, if necessary by using the pager.'

'I'm afraid we *will* have to visit them, if only to interview the patients, but I'll bear your directives in mind, Dr Goldman. As long as *you* also remember that we are here to conduct a murder investigation.'

'Where would you like to go next?' Goldman asked abruptly.

'The therapy units, then the old hospital.'

'The therapy units, like the wards, are the province of the patients. I would appreciate it if you used the same discretion when entering them. Always and only with a staff escort.'

'You mentioned earlier that there were *some* areas of the hospital to which we could have free access Dr Goldman,' Dan said with a trace of irony. 'Perhaps now would be a good time to tell us exactly where they are.'

'Those would be the floors of the old hospital which have been taken over by the Health Authority's administration unit. Few patients have any cause to go there. You may have free access there, but it might still be as well if you cleared your needs and movements with our administrator, Tony Waters.' He looked pointedly at his watch. 'Now, if you'll excuse me, I have an appointment with a patient. If you'd be kind enough to wait here, I'll get a nurse to take you to Tony's office.'

He left them standing in the corridor and disappeared into the ward office. Through the open door Collins saw a male nurse talking to the cool, attractive blonde who'd helped Jean Marshall sedate Vanessa Hedley the day before.

'That sod doesn't trust us,' Collins informed Dan coldly.

'He has a hospital to run,' Evans said calmly.

'Or something to hide.'

'That's what I like to see, Collins, coppers assuming everyone guilty until proven innocent.'

Harry Goldman returned with the blonde.

'Nurse Ashford, here, has very kindly volunteered to give up a few minutes of her free time to take you to Mr Waters' office.'

'Sergeant Collins.' She nodded to Peter.

'You know each other?' Goldman looked surprised.

'I met Sergeant Collins in A ward yesterday afternoon.'

'Ah yes, of course. Our unfortunate incident. Well, if you'll excuse me, gentlemen.' Goldman walked away down the corridor, then, as an afterthought he turned back. 'You will keep me up to date with your progress, Inspector?'

'If we make any,' Evans assured him drily, 'you'll be the first to know.'

Chapter Five

'Dirt's clogging the sink again!' Patrick O'Kelly shouted to his assistant as he peered through the magnifying glass that he was moving slowly, centimetre by centimetre, along the thighs of the body laid out on the slab.

'I thought I'd got rid of it all,' his assistant grumbled as he left the earth he was sifting, from one side of a body-bag to the other, through a fine-meshed sieve.

'Amazing how it clings,' O'Kelly murmured absently, inching the glass upwards on to the torso. 'Superintendent,' he acknowledged Bill Mulcahy who just then walked in through the double doors.

'Anything for us yet?' Bill asked, surveying the postmortem-scarred body stretched out on the slab in front of O'Kelly, and the body-bag opened out on the slab next to it.

'I haven't even finished examining the body,' the pathologist retorted irritably.

'Sorry to press you, but at the moment we know absolutely nothing.' Mulcahy trod warily. The mortuary was very much Patrick's reserve. Here he reigned supreme, and both police and hospital authority had learned diplomacy the hard way. 'A few basic facts would go a long way towards kicking off our investigation,' he added quietly.

'Like?' O'Kelly asked, although he already had a very good idea what Mulcahy was looking for.

'Like who she was, and how and why she died?'

'The *who* I can't help you with. The *how* I told you on site.' Patrick straightened up, discarded his magnifying glass, and walked to the head of the corpse. Pushing back the eyelids with his thumb and forefinger, he prodded at the burst blood-vessels that had flooded the whites with scarlet. 'And again here,' he indicated evidence of several smaller haemorrhages on the forehead. And those are just the ones you can see. I found a lot more in the internal organs. Asphyxiation, without a doubt.'

'Then she was buried alive?'

'Yes, even without the haemorrhages the build up of dirt in the nostrils and lungs confirms it.' O'Kelly pushed aside the bone-cutter he'd used to open the ribcage, and removed the square of tissue he'd used to cover the slit in the skin, not out of any finer feelings for the corpse but rather from a desire to keep contamination of the other body parts down to a minimum. 'Judging by the amount of earth and debris in the bronchial tubes,' he palpated a tube he'd slit open, and a crumb of black dirt fell into his hand, 'she must have struggled for breath until the very last second.'

'How long would that have taken?' Mulcahy was a seasoned, hardened policeman, but even he recoiled at the thought of the young girl stretched out dead and naked before him, as she battled and fought for air, while being slowly smothered by shovelful after shovelful of earth.

'Impossible to put a time on it. A lot depends on whether he worked quickly or slowly. And, then again, he might have dumped her at the bottom of the pit some time before he actually started to bury her.'

'All right, let's look at it another way. How long would it have taken from the first breath that was more dirt than air, to the last?' Mulcahy pressed, refusing to allow O'Kelly to fob him off.

'Going by what I've dug out of her tubes and lungs, I'd say somewhere between five and ten minutes; but she probably wouldn't have been fully conscious towards the end.' Patrick retrieved his magnifying glass and resumed his minute study of her skin. 'I was right about the lips, too. They had been superglued together. She managed to tear them apart, but not that long before she died, judging by the bleeding. Bingo!' he shouted gleefully.

'You've found something.' It wasn't a question.

'Puncture marks, upper right arm. A whole beautiful series of them.' O'Kelly smiled grimly. 'Some bruised and old, some fresher, and one *very* fresh.' He switched on and spoke into the dictaphone tucked into the top pocket of his laboratory coat, before marking the sites with a blue pen. 'I've taken blood samples, so if it's anything detectable, we'll soon know about it.'

'How long has she been dead?'

'You know I hate questions like that.' Patrick glared.

'And you know I have to ask,' Bill replied, summoning what remained of his patience.

'Body temperature that of the surroundings when I examined her in the pit, so that puts death at least eighteen to twenty-four hours before, taking into account that asphyxiation usually causes body temperature to rise, not fall, immediately after death. No rigor mortis present, little deterioration – that means your guess would be as good as mine.'

'I hate it when you say that.'

'Flattery will get you nowhere.' O'Kelly tore off his rubber gloves and threw them in the bin by the head of the table. He switched off the water that was rippling around the inert, lifeless body, folded his arms, and leant back against the tiled wall. 'But there is something that might interest you. The stomach was completely empty, and the body dehydrated.'

'So?'

'I'd say she'd been starved before death. No food or water.'

'For how long?'

'After examining the small intestines, I'd say at least forty-eight hours – possibly longer.'

'Then she could have been taken and kept somewhere?' Mulcahy mused, talking to himself more than to O'Kelly.

'That's for you to find out. Pretty thing, wasn't she?' the pathologist murmured, staring at the girl's face.

Bill looked at the corpse, really looked at it for the first time. O'Kelly's assistant had washed the body and hair, and combed the shoulder-length curls back away from the face.

'Taken new photographs?' Bill asked shortly, attempting to mask his emotion by immersing himself in the practicalities of the situation.

'Polaroids are in the office. You'll have to wait for the others to be developed.'

'Anything on her?'

'Nothing that identifies her, but, then, is there ever? Rings, one gold set with a cheap red onyx stone, one silver in the shape of a wishbone, a gold chain, crucifix and Saint Nicholas, all nine-carat, and a lot of good they did her. The patron saint of travellers must have been on tea-break when she was being buried.' O'Kelly nodded towards the two pathetic piles; a small one of jewellery and a larger one of clothes, heaped on to a side table. 'Oh, and there's a key-ring with two Yale keys on it, which we found in the pocket of her skirt. Everything that could be has been dusted for prints, so they're safe to handle.'

Bill picked up the key ring and fingered the tab, a miniature rubber troll with his thumbs in his ears and his fingers extended.

'The clothes won't tell you much, I'm afraid,' O'Kelly continued. 'Usual chain-store labels, no name tags, no markings, and nothing except the keys in the pockets, but I've taken dental X-rays. There's fourteen fillings, so she should be on someone's records. No strange or foreign fibres on the skin or the clothes. Can't tell you about the dirt; as you can see it's still being sifted.'

'Sexual assault?'

'No outward signs of it. Clothes are soiled but they appear to be undisturbed. Vaginal swabs tested negative for semen. Oh, there *is* a tattoo.' He took a small rubber sheet, wrapped it around the right leg and rolled the corpse on to its side. The back, thighs and calves were livid, dark with stagnant blood. 'Butterfly high on right thigh. Nice work,' he commented. 'Better than some I've seen.'

'Age?'

'I'd say twenty to twenty-four, no more. Blue eyes, dyed blonde hair; the rest you can see for yourself. I've told you just about everything, but if you want to listen to the tape in my office you can. Typing facilities being what they are in this place, it won't get done until tomorrow.'

'I can wait.'

'Coffee?'

'No thanks,' Bill refused, catching a glimpse of Patrick's assistant coming out of the office with three specimen jars filled with murky beige liquid.

'Bring us a chocolate biscuit, Alan,' Patrick called.

Alan dumped the jars on to an empty slab and opened one of the refrigerated body drawers, extracting a packet of chocolate wafers.

Bill had met O'Kelly the man after hearing a great deal about O'Kelly the legend. The first time he'd visited the mortuary it had been lunchtime. He had walked in on Patrick, his assistant, and the senior surgeon from the staff of the General, sitting in a row on one of the slabs, facing a laid-out, opened-up body while eating pasties and drinking cans of lager. It was what O'Kelly termed a 'working lunch'. They were trying to determine cause of death in the case confronting them. They had, as Patrick had delighted in telling him, been spoilt for choice. The man had lung cancer, heart disease and liver failure. At first he'd thought that O'Kelly had set out to deliberately shock him, or any other copper or doctor who happened to wander in unannounced and trespass on his domain. Ten years on, he knew better. The pathologist had lived with dead bodies for so long, he simply treated them as things; inanimate objects there to be examined, studied and treated with the same careful unemotional regard he bestowed on his instruments or the laboratory furniture.

'If you don't want to wait, I'll let you know if we find anything in the dirt,' Patrick offered as he jumped up and sat on a spare slab.

'I'd appreciate it.'

'We'll carry on as soon as we've finished this.' He held up his coffee and biscuit.

Bill knew O'Kelly was dismissing him, but the knowledge didn't prevent him from lingering in the formaldehyde-ridden atmosphere. 'Lot of work on at the moment?' he ventured, glancing around the mortuary. There were no other bodies in sight, and apart from the slabs that the body bag and victim were laid on, they were all clean and scrubbed, but Mulcahy was detective enough to notice that a good three-quarters of the mortuary drawers were tagged. And that either meant there'd been a rush for the pathologist's services, or one was about to start.

'Same as usual.' O'Kelly shrugged his shoulders as he peeled the silver paper from his biscuit. 'Why do you ask?'

'We photographed the grounds of Compton Castle an hour ago,' Bill pushed his hands deep into the pockets of his raincoat.

'Heat-seeking cameras?' Patrick looked warily at Bill. 'Come on, tell me the worst.'

'We can't be sure yet.'

'How many sites have you earmarked to dig?'

'Three. But they may mean nothing; like buried compost rotting and generating heat.'

'Close to the kitchens?'

'No, back and side flowerbeds.'

'That's it, then.' Patrick looked to his assistant. 'Better clean up and repack my site kit as soon as you've finished your break.'

'It's probably nothing,' Mulcahy said uneasily, afraid that he'd said too much and made a fool of himself.

'I'm no detective, but even I noticed the compost bin outside the kitchen door.'

'The spots are in the flowerbeds.'

'Concentrated spots? Not a thin spread?'

Mulcahy nodded. Patrick pushed the remainder of his wafer between his lips and finished his coffee in a single gulp.

'Get moving, boy. We've got work to do,' he mumbled, his mouth full.

'As you can see Sergeant, Constable.' Tony Waters smiled warmly at Michelle Grady, who'd been called in from outside duty by Dan, and foisted on Collins yet again, much to the Sergeant's disgust. 'These attics haven't been used for years.'

Waters, irritated by Collins' insistence on starting his tour at the top of the building, halted on a landing above a steep, narrow staircase, and opened identical opposing doors, on to opposing long, low-ceilinged galleries. Both of these were strewn with dust balls and decorated by spiders webs. Nonplussed by Waters' obvious vexation, Collins walked along the right-hand gallery and opened the door at the far end. Box upon cardboard box, all covered with dense layers of grey dust, were piled up in a long narrow room that boasted only a single small, narrow window.

'Old records?' Collins asked.

'I presume. I've only opened one of them. They were here when my department moved into this building,' Waters cast his cold blue eyes around the dilapidated attic.

'It seems bizarre to build new blocks out in the grounds while all this space remains available and rotting,' Collins commented.

'The stairs are steep, and leave a lot to be desired,' Waters rejoined coolly. 'The bannisters have dry rot, and compliance with the spirit of our equal opportunities policy would have meant ripping the fabric of the building apart to put in lifts. And, even supposing we found the money to spend in the first place, every penny spent here would be good money gone to waste. Compton Castle was put on the list for eventual demolition in the 1980s. We've been trying to run it down for the past ten years. If it hadn't been for the cutbacks that held up the building of new psychiatric wards in the General, it would have been a pile of rubble years ago – except for the new blocks, of course. The Health Authority administration offices will be moved into them. They're not purpose-built, or ideal for the job, by any means, but at least the buildings will be relatively new and sound, unlike the one we have at present.'

'I didn't know they were opening a psychiatric unit in the General?' Peter commented.

'Thirty-five beds.'

'How many do you have here?' Peter asked.

'We've run down to three hundred and sixty.'

'You're the main psychiatric facility for the County, right?'

'That's correct.'

'So the Health Authority intends to attach psychiatric beds to every local hospital?'

'No,' Waters replied abruptly. 'The present Government policy is to rehouse all psychiatric patients who can be moved, including those previously considered long-term, out in the general community.'

'And the poor devils who can't cope, or the ones who are a danger to the public?' Peter asked sharply.

'Will be catered for in that unit in the General.'

'Thirty-five beds!' Collins exclaimed incredulously. 'Against three hundred and sixty here.'

'The Victorian idea of removing large sections of the

community into institutions, where they can be held incarcerated out of sight and out of mind of the rest of the population, is as brutal as it is outmoded,' Waters declared firmly. 'The vast majority of our patients here could easily be accommodated in the community at large,' he continued smoothly, voicing the official line. 'And, in the opinion of most professionals, both patients and community would benefit greatly by that amalgamation. Patients would learn to care for themselves and to cope with day-to-day living, and ordinary members of the community would learn additional tolerance for those not quite as fortunate as themselves.'

'Do you really believe that people are ready and willing to welcome geriatrics, junkies, depressives and maniacs into their neighbourhoods with open arms?' Collins asked sceptically.

'I think they can be educated to do so, certainly.'

'Even when their children are shouted at on their way home from school and accosted by drunks or maniacs, who cannot differentiate between reality and fantasy. Or their houses are broken into by junkies looking for money for their next fix. Or they are faced with the sight of depressives who've killed themselves in public places because no one has time to talk to them, or remind them to take their next pill.' He stared at Tony Waters in disgust. 'Take a walk around the real world, and take a good long look at what is already happening to the people you turn away from this place now because of lack of beds. You can't discard people who've never fended for themselves in the whole of their lives, and suddenly thrust them into a world they can neither understand nor cope with. They'll end up sleeping on skid row, or dead in some canal or river, or as yet more fodder for the down-and-out statisticians who visit Jubilee Street . . .'

'Jubilee Street?' Waters looked blank.

'It's down the dock end of town. The *unfashionable* end,' Collins emphasised. 'You won't find any smart restaurants there. Only doss houses run by priests and Salvation Army people who've learned to tolerate the lice and the smell.'

'I don't think you appreciate the practical problems raised by a building the age and condition of this one, Sergeant Collins. If you've any experience of surveying old buildings, you'll see ample evidence of both dry and damp rot on this floor. The roof's perished, not only the tiles but also the timbers. The surveyor's report of twenty years ago recommended that it would be cheaper in the long run to replace the structure than repair it.'

'That's exactly the point I'm making,' Collins said brusquely. 'Replace it.'

'And we are. A great deal of money is being put into the community care programme . . .'

'Which will provide jobs for a lot of fat cat administrators, and dewy-eyed social workers who've never in their lives had to squash a louse, clean up a junkie after cold turkey, arrest a violent lunatic who's beaten in an entirely innocent bystander, or cope with a raving lunatic who thinks he's being eaten alive by rats. And all of which are, unfortunately, too common everyday events in the life of a policeman.'

Angry with Waters for trying to push Government policy down his throat, simply because it was expedient to do so, and with himself for climbing too readily on one of his hobby horses, Collins turned his back on both Michelle Grady and Waters and walked off down the gallery, opening various doors on to similar-sized cell-like rooms, until he found another even steeper and narrower staircase than the one they'd just ascended.

'There are four staircases on this floor,' Waters briskly reverted to practicalities. 'The central one we came up by, another like this that serves the left-hand side of the building, and one metal fire escape outside at the back.'

'Does each floor have access to the fire escape?' Collins asked, noticing for the first time that Michelle was religiously writing down in her notebook everything the administrator was telling them.

'Yes, there's an outside landing on every floor except the ground floor.'

'You do realise this is only a quick once over,' Collins informed him curtly as he turned back, 'before we bring in teams to conduct a complete and thorough search of the entire complex.'

'As far as this building is concerned, you can search away. But I'd be grateful if you searched the ground-floor rooms that are used for therapy either late or early in the evening, when they're not being used by patients.'

'We'll bear your request in mind,' Collins replied cryptically.

'The only thing you're likely to find on this floor is spiders,' Waters said, eying an enormous web that spread almost six feet from the windowframe to the door.

'And the mice,' Peter observed, noticing a pile of mouse droppings by the cardboard boxes.

With Waters leading the way, they descended the small staircase Collins had located.

'Built for the maids,' Tony informed them, reaching out to support Michelle's arm as she caught her heel in a stair tread.

'Miniature maids,' Peter grumbled, as his shoulders brushed both the left and right hand walls at the same time.

When they reached the floor below, Waters opened a door directly in front of them, and led them through a series of enormous, high-ceilinged, wooden-floored old wards packed with expensive displays of modern office technology.

'This looks strange,' Michelle mumbled nervously, intimidated by the strained silence between the two men.

'What?' Peter demanded.

'Modern office furniture, computers, printers, faxes, in these surroundings.'

'The furniture was bought for the new County Hall offices. We had to move out last year because of pressure on accommodation.'

'God bless civil servants and local authorities,' Collins remarked irreverently. 'You can always trust them to expand to fill every available inch of space.

'This is the general office and typing pool,' Waters ignored his barbed comment, as he again headed towards the centre of the building. Nodding briefly to the clerks and typists, mostly middle-aged women, with a sprinkling of young girls and boys. 'Most of the assistant administrators are on the floor below; reception and my own office on the ground floor, as you know.'

'Lucky, lucky you. No stairs to climb.'

'The layout was decided before I took this post,' Waters countered stiffly.

The administrators' offices were housed directly below the typing pool, in what had once been one single vast ward. But this area had been subdivided by plasterboard and glass partitions to provided separate cubicles.

'These rooms are kept locked, simply because they're disused. We try to save as much as we can on cleaning bills; they're astronomical enough as it is.' He extracted a key from a massive ring that he was carrying loosely in his right hand, and opened a door set across the landing. 'Old ward kitchens,' he explained as they walked past a series of small rooms still containing stone sinks and zinc-covered cupboards and tables. 'Pantries and storerooms.'

'These rooms lie empty, while the attic ones are full of boxes? Didn't anyone think to tell the removal men that they could have stopped off halfway?' Collins stared at the film of dust that blanketed the heavily scarred floorboards.

'Those boxes contain records that were put away in the fifties, when this area was still being used as a ward. When I first got here, I opened one box and the papers inside dated back to the turn of the century.'

'They could be worth a fortune.'

'I doubt it – but the town archivist has been notified. When they find time, they'll get round to examining them. That's about it, on this floor. Shall we head down to the ground floor?'

At the foot of the stairs Collins noticed a narrow passage that wound behind the staircase, ending abruptly in a locked door facing the rear of the building. He raised his eyebrows at Waters.

'That leads to the old padded cells. They were ripped out twenty years ago, but they hadn't been in use for a while before that.'

'Can we take a look?' Collins went over to the door and examined it.

'There isn't much to see.' Waters had to try four keys in the lock before coming up with the right one. They proceeded along a long dark passage lit by widely-spaced weak lightbulbs. After twenty yards the corridor began to slope steeply downwards. There Waters switched on another string of lights. 'As you can see, they were ripped out.' He halted before a row of six identical concrete cells.

'Not even doors,' Collins agreed, staring at the open eight-foot-square, grey concrete boxes.

'Like a lot of common practices in the old mental hospitals, they were illegal, both in concept and law, and that's without bringing human rights and morality into it,' Waters said firmly taking this opportunity to counter Collins' earlier criticism of new mental health policies.

'And this door?' Peter pointed to a plain steel door at the far end of the corridor.

'Leads into the old laundry and mortuary areas. You can also get to them from the main corridor, but seeing as we're here, we may as well go this way. He fumbled with the keys again. After five minutes of trial and error, the rusty lock finally gave way. He switched on the lights ahead.

'Are we at ground-floor level or basement?' Collins asked. There had been no windows in the old padded cell area, nor had he expected to find any. But the corridor ahead also loomed dark and forbidding, totally devoid of any sign of natural light.

'Somewhere between the two,' Tony flicked on another light. 'It's a half-level floor, built into a mound at the back. You can see it quite clearly on the plan. Michelle Grady obediently unfolded the drawing she was carrying. 'This has to be the first time in ten years that anyone's walked through to this area from that end. 'As you can see, we use it for storing rubbish before it gets burnt in the incinerator.' He opened a door on to a concrete storeroom stacked with neat rows of bulging bright pink plastic bags, boldly imprinted DANGER MEDICAL WASTE. 'And this,' he selected another key and opened a wooden door, 'is the male mortuary.'

'The what?' Michelle echoed disbelievingly.

'The male mortuary. The female mortuary is down there.' Waters pointed further along the corridor, to the left.

'You separate male and female dead?' Collins laughed mirthlessly. 'What's the problem? You afraid they'll get up to something they shouldn't?

'Not me,' he replied humourlessly. 'The Victorians built this place.' He opened the door on a surprisingly large, light and airy room, although all the illumination came from bubbled glass panes set close to the ceiling. Fully tiled in white wall tiles and black floor tiles, it contained two zinc-covered tables, the most enormous stone sink Collins had ever seen and, facing them, a bank of twelve body-sized steel drawers.

'Tin-lined.' Waters pulled one drawer out after another. They moved stiffly, their runners warped and rusty.

'I take it you don't use this place any more, either?'

'Yes, we do, as a matter of fact. But only for routine deaths that don't require a postmortem. If there's any problem with diagnosis or death certificates, we have to telephone the General for an ambulance to convey the body to their mortuary.'

'And Patrick O'Kelly?'

'I beg your pardon.' Waters stared blankly at Peter.

'Patrick O'Kelly, the pathologist in the General. I thought, as you worked for the Health Authority, you might have heard of him.'

'Afraid not.'

'So these are still used?'

'More often than not, particularly when someone dies on the geriatric ward.'

'You have a high patient turnover on the geriatric ward?'

'There's a heavy demand for the beds there, yes.'

'And are the geriatrics also going to be housed in this thirty-five bed unit in the General?' Collins raised his eyebrows again.

'Of course not,' Waters replied testily.

'Then where?'

'They will be rehoused in the private sector . . .'

'Ah, yes, of course. How silly of me. The private sector. Tell me, do you have a mortuary attendant?'

'Not full time no.'

'Since when?'

'Not since we made the last one redundant two years ago.'

'Then who lays out the bodies?'

'Usually a nurse. One or two of the porters can do it at a push.'

'Can we see the female mortuary?' Michelle Grady asked brightly.

'Want to find out if they're going to lay you out behind flowered curtains?' Collins enquired derisively.

Michelle seethed in feminist indignation as she followed the administrator into the room. It was identical in every respect to the male mortuary: damp, musty, rank with disuse.

'The laundry.' As they emerged from the half-level Tony

Waters pointed out a vast hall dotted with sinks and enormous round boilers.

'Disused.' Collins didn't even phrase it as a question.

'Laundry was put out to tender years ago. Kitchens,' Tony opened another door, this time on an area that was bustling with noisy activity – and people.

'Not put out to tender?' Collins whistled in amazement as he gazed at the white-overalled staff who were flitting between modern cookers and stainless-steel work surfaces.

'Our premises, contractors' staff.'

'Might have known.'

They descended, via the back staircase, to the cellars and a boiler-room that was fed on gas, the sub-station that housed the cables for the incoming electricity supplies and the generator back-up. Remembering another case he'd worked on, Collins lifted the iron plates that covered the incoming supply, but there were only thick black cables to be seen.

'The incinerator was installed only last year.' Waters pushed back a heavy sliding door and nodded to a man who was fiddling with rows of dials. Collins stood back and looked up at the mass of pipes, cables, and small tunnels leading off into darkened spaces.

'We've seen the whole of the old building?'

'More or less.'

'It's a paradise for someone who wants to conceal a body,' Collins muttered between clenched teeth. 'And bloody murder for a policeman looking for clues. Absolute bloody murder.'

Chapter Six

'Anything interesting?' Dan Evans asked as Collins and Michelle Grady appeared in the doorway of the administrator's office.

'Nothing obvious,' Peter replied. 'Only a nightmare of a building to search. Who's organising that?'

Dan studied his fingernails and said nothing.

'You can't do this to me?' Peter protested.

'Everyone knows that Drug Squad officers organise the most thorough searches,' Evans flattered.

Waters said something to his secretary in the outer office before joining them. His face creased in open annoyance when he saw Evans sitting thoroughly at home in his comfortably-padded executive chair, behind his desk, a notepad covered with scribbles in front of him, the telephone conveniently placed at his elbow.

'Can I get you anything, Inspector?' he enquired heavily.

'No thank you,' Dan replied pleasantly. 'Your secretary has been most helpful. She's provided me with everything I need, and more.' He moved his empty coffee mug to the edge of the desk. 'And now,' he rose from the chair and walked around to the desk, surprisingly light-footed for someone of his size. 'I think we've prevailed on your hospitality quite long enough. If it's all right with you, we'll move a mobile headquarters into the grounds.'

'A demountable building?' Waters asked warily.

'Sort of,' Dan hedged. 'Perhaps you can advise us on the most unobtrusive site.'

'I doubt that there is such a place in the grounds.'

'If it's space you're looking for, there's rooms the size of football pitches going begging up above us in this very building,' Collins interrupted.

'Our mobile HQ would be better. It contains all we need, and we won't get under anyone's feet,' Evans countered. 'Where do you suggest we put it, Mr Waters?'

Tony Waters was first and foremost a bureaucrat; he also knew when to bow down to pressure that he didn't have the weapons to fight. Police investigating a murder case were bound to have access to bigger guns than he could call on. 'I'll think about it,' he compromised, putting off the time when he'd have to make a decision.

'It'll be here in an hour.'

'In that case, perhaps you could site it close to the main gate, that way we can keep police traffic in and out of the hospital buildings to a minimum.'

'I don't think that will suit at all,' Dan said thoughtfully stroking his well rounded chin. 'Too public. It will attract too many sightseers. I thought somewhere at the back of this building. Behind the tunnels perhaps?'

'As you wish,' Waters agreed ungraciously, wondering why Dan had bothered to ask his advice when he'd already made up his mind as to where he was going to locate the makeshift station.

'I'm also expecting two teams of police,' Evans continued.

'To search the building?'

'Not exactly, although they may do so later. First I want them to do some digging.'

'Digging!' Waters stared at Dan.

'The heat-seeking cameras came up with a few spots. They're probably nothing, but just to be on the safe side we're going to be doing some further investigating in your flowerbeds.'

'I see. May I ask how long this "further digging" is likely to take?' Waters was beginning to wonder if the day was ever going to end for him.

'There's two hours of daylight left, so we'll start as soon as they get here.'

'Which will be?'

'With luck,' Evans lifted his left arm to peer at his watch, 'in the next ten minutes. I have to warn you, though, that if we do find anything unusual, we may have to work through the night.'

'In the dark?'

'We'll use floodlights.'

'I must protest. Lights would definitely disturb the patients.'

'I apologise, but we may have no choice in the matter. And don't forget, at the moment there's still a strong possibility that we'll find nothing. Oh, just one more thing before we go,' Dan pulled a sheet of typed paper from his pad, and a photograph. 'These came up from the Station half an hour ago. Full description and new photograph of the victim. Perhaps you'd be kind enough to circulate it to your staff.'

'I'll do that.' Waters picked up the photograph, and blanched.

'You knew her Mr Waters?' Dan asked.

'I don't know. I think so. It looks like . . . like . . .'

'Like who?' Dan pressed.

'Rosie. Rosie Twyford,' Waters gripped the edge of his desk until his knuckles stood proud and white, but there was no further trace of the shock he'd just experienced left in his voice. 'The hair's right,' he faltered, 'but the face is all wrong. The skin's too dark.'

'The complexion would be dark, Mr Waters. She's been smothered,' Dan explained. 'There's a description; five foot six, dyed blonde hair, blue eyes, no distinguishing marks other than a butterfly tattooed on her rear end.'

'I wouldn't know about the butterfly Inspector Evans.' Waters dropped the photograph down on the desk. 'But everything else fits.'

'Who was she?' Peter demanded, watching as the administrator took possession of his chair.

'She worked in this department as a clerk, then she had a complete breakdown and became a patient here. That's how I came to know her. She was the first staff member since I took up my position to be admitted into Compton Castle as an inmate.'

'And?' Peter asked.

'And? It might not even be her. I could be mistaken.'

'When was the last time you saw her?' Dan demanded.

'I can't remember.'

'Think!'

'It's probably not her.'

'Think!' Peter Collins repeated abruptly.

'It must have been sometime last week. Harry Goldman told me that she was being discharged as an outpatient. She'd been discharged from the ward weeks ago. He said that she was thinking of going home – home was Cornwall – for a break. Afterwards she intended to return to work.'

'If home was Cornwall, where did she live when she was here?' Collins pressed.

'How should I know?' Tony replied irritably. 'A rented room, or flat I suppose. I only spoke to the girl once or twice. If you want to find out more, I suggest you ask Harry Goldman, or the Personnel Manager here.'

'I'll do that,' Evans said calmly. 'I'll do just that. Thank you very much for your assistance, Mr Waters. No doubt we'll come into contact again soon.'

'Where to, now?' Collins asked as they left the administrator's office.

'First Personnel, then Dr Goldman,' Dan suggested. 'Here.' He handed Michelle the photograph and sheet of paper detailing the victim's description.

'You want me to do it, sir?' she asked, bristling with pride at the trust he was placing in her.

'May as well, but better be quick. I've a feeling these offices shut early, and it's four now.' He watched as she hurried down the corridor, her long-legged stride hampered by her narrow skirt.

'Were any of us ever that keen, Collins?' he asked in a tired voice.

'I can't remember,' Peter replied flatly.

'Tell me,' Dan led the way into a perspex tunnel, 'what did you think of our friend the administrator?'

'He's a stuffed shirt who might know a bit more about that girl than he let on – that is, if she is the victim.'

'Yes, well we can't build walls until we have a few foundations to lay them on,' Evans mused, keeping his own thoughts to himself. 'I want you to oversee all the staff interviews.'

'Must I?' Peter groaned inwardly.

'I said "oversee". That doesn't mean you have to do them all yourself.'

'But it means I have to co-ordinate the resulting information.'

'As well as supervise the complete search of these buildings, but I'll see to it that you have plenty of help. Bill's bringing in a couple of teams . . .'

'Shouldn't we go and check if they've arrived?' Collins prompted, hoping to find something to occupy Evans' mind, before the Inspector thought of anything else that he could unload.

'They can start without us,' Dan murmured philosophically. 'You do know that if they don't find anything else, we're going to have to scour every inch of garden that can be seen from Vanessa Hedley's window?'

'With what?' Collins asked warily.

'Probes.'

'Probes?' Peter echoed.

'Into every single centimetre of ground,' Evans said firmly.

'But that could take weeks.'

'Which is why I'm half hoping that Bill will come up with something *now*.' Dan turned the corner, and once more he and Peter were locked into that strange, disembodied white world of the tunnel. 'But right now I intend doing something I've been trying to find time for all day. I'm going to visit Trevor Joseph. And as I never knew him that well, I'd like you to re-introduce me.'

'He's a hopeless case,' Collins snapped.

'I'd like to see how hopeless for myself. That's if you don't mind,' Dan replied calmly. 'You do know where to find him, don't you?'

Trevor was in his usual position, slumped in the chair in his room, but to Collins' surprise he had a book on his lap, and as it was the right way up, Peter had no reason to suspect that he hadn't been reading it.

'You remember Inspector Evans?' he effected the introduction as he sank down on to Trevor's bed.

'Dan Evans.' Dan held out his hand and Trevor lifted his own, but he refused to meet Dan's steady gaze, and continued to stare down at his book.

'May I come in?' Dan asked.

'If you want to,' Trevor replied ungraciously, moving his legs so he could sit alongside Collins on the bed.

'You've heard that we found a body buried in the grounds here?'

'Yes.'

'You don't seem very interested?'

'Why should I be?'

'It's murder. A young girl, early twenties. She was buried alive, a rather horrible way to go,' Evans informed him impassively.

Trevor shrugged his shoulders, but said nothing.

'I was hoping you could help us.'

'I'm ill.'

'Yes,' Dan agreed patiently. 'You're ill, and you're also actually *in* this place.'

'As a patient,' Trevor reminded him sharply.

'Patient or not, you're a trained detective,' Dan persisted. 'I don't have to tell you what a murder case can mean.'

'No, you don't.' Trevor rose from his chair and walked over to the window. Pushing aside the curtain he looked out into the garden. It was the first time Collins had seen him as much as glance at the outside world since he'd been injured, but he rightly suspected that Trevor had resorted to this gesture in preference to acknowledging Dan's request.

'What happened to you on that last case . . .' Dan paused awkwardly. 'It could have happened to any one of us,' he said quietly.

'But it didn't happen to just any one. Only to me.'

Peter had to strain his ears to catch what he was saying.

'It was tough luck. I know what you must be feeling,' Dan continued tentatively.

'You can have no possible idea what I'm feeling,' Trevor broke in.

'You're quite right,' Dan braved the silence that followed Trevor's outburst. 'That was presumptuous of me. I can't even begin to imagine what you've been through.'

'Or what I'm still going through,' Trevor added savagely.

'I wouldn't be sitting here if I could think of someone else I could turn to who has your qualifications and some inside knowledge of this place. We need your help,' Evans declared simply.

'I'm sick. I'm not fit enough to work.'

'I'm not asking you to work. All I want is for you to sit down with us now, and tell us about some of the people here. You've a trained eye; you know what we're looking for.'

'These people have been taking care of me,' Trevor protested. 'I haven't been watching them with a suspicious eye.'

'But you know them?' Dan persevered.

'Not as well as they know me, and not well enough to know if any one of them is a murderer.'

'Won't you at least talk to us?'

'I wouldn't be any help.' Trevor still kept his back firmly turned to Evans.

'You must know something. This Vanessa Hedley, for instance.'

'She's disturbed. She rarely sleeps. She's always wandering around the place creating problems.'

'And Sister Marshall – Jean Marshall?' Trevor hadn't said anything new or useful, but Dan felt elated. At least he was holding a conversation with him, and that was heading down the right track.

'She's capable enough,' Trevor said succinctly.

'Nurse Sullivan – Lyn Sullivan?'

Collins thought he saw a flicker of interest in Trevor's eyes, but the glow died before he could be certain.

'She's young, pretty, far too vulnerable for a place like this.'

'Spencer Jordan?'

'He's a good therapist. Look, I'm not stupid. I know what you're trying to do here, but I'm really not in a position to help you. Not now.'

As silence reigned in the room once more, Trevor watched

squads of blue-coated men move into the grounds. A police dog-handler's van pulled up in the DOCTORS ONLY parking bay. Bill Mulcahy stood in the centre of the lawn, next to the largest flowerbed, alternately consulting a large sheet of paper in his hand, and talking to an officer who stood at his elbow.

'How many more are there buried in the grounds?' Trevor asked abruptly.

'Who said there were any more?' Dan asked.

'It doesn't take much detective work to fathom what's happening out there.' He continued to stare out of the window.

'Time you and I went to work, Collins.' Dan rose from the bed. 'All right if we call in and see you tomorrow, Trevor?'

'I can't stop you,' Trevor dropped the curtain, but he didn't turn around to look as they left.

'Is he always like that?' Dan Evans whispered to Collins as they headed down the corridor towards the main door of the ward.

'You caught him on one of his good days,' Peter said acidly. 'Today he actually answered your questions.'

'Have you thought that it might be him?'

'Trevor?' Peter stared at him in disbelief.

'Why not? He's in here. And he had the opportunity.'

'And what bloody motive?' Collins said angrily.

'He's depressed, disturbed. He's in here . . .' Dan repeated.

'As the result of being thumped on the head,' Peter broke in defensively.

'I heard that he became obsessed with one of the witnesses on his last case. A woman, with long dark hair.' Dan looked at Collins. 'And besides the rumours, I saw that drawing on his bedside cabinet.'

'They knew one another before the case . . . he . . . they . . . Damn it all, this is Trevor Joseph you're talking about!' Peter exploded.

'I shouldn't have to remind you of the first rule of detection; keeping an open mind in all cases.'

'Even where one of our own is concerned!'

'Especially where one of our own is concerned,' Dan reiterated firmly.

* * *

Neither Evans nor Collins returned to Trevor's room that evening. If they had, they would have found him, head in hands, hunched in his chair, paralysed with fear; trembling at his own incapacity to face up to reality and the harsh, hostile, frightening place that the world had suddenly become.

'We've pinpointed the sites with markers, and surrounded them with screens,' Bill Mulcahy announced as the two men walked across the lawn towards him.

'O'Kelly?' Dan asked.

'Standing by the telephone down in the General. He can be here within ten minutes of us finding anything. Collins, you work with the group closest to the building. Dan take this one . . .'

Peter walked slowly across the soft green turf towards the group that Mulcahy had entrusted to his care. It was a beautiful early spring evening. For the first time in months he actually took time to listen to the birds singing. The sun was low on the horizon, a blazing golden ball; the air was redolent with the smell of magnolia and cherry blossom.

'I joined this force to catch criminals, not to pass out parking tickets and shovel bloody shit!'

Collins recognised the eternal lament of the rookie. He stepped behind the green canvas screens. 'What's your name, boy?' he enquired.

'Brooke. Chris Brooke,' the rookie snapped smartly to attention, after handing his jacket over to one of his colleagues.

'Shovelling shit is all you're likely to do while you continue to moan.' Collins thrust a spade into his hands, and stood watching while Brooke pushed it into six inches of heavily manured soil.

'You,' he shouted to a female constable standing on the public side of the canvas, 'Take those plants he digs up and lay them next to that tree will you?'

'I haven't worked in this garden, man and boy for forty years, to have a lot of flatfooted coppers come along and wreck it in one night!' Jimmy Herne strode purposefully across the grass and grabbed the rose-bush that Brooke was handing over the

93

canvas wall. 'These were only planted last week. You're disturbing the roots. One hard surface frost and they'll all be . . .'

'How deep did you dig down last week?' Peter interrupted curtly.

'The right depth for rose-bushes,' the old man retorted angrily. He barged behind the low canvas screen and thrust his face aggressively close to Collins'.

'One foot? Two?' Peter demanded.

'Three foot. Always three foot,' Herne snarled impatiently. 'And then lace the digging generously with well rotted manure. Any fool can tell you that.'

'Thank you,' Collins replied drily.

'But that doesn't help what you're doing here. It's hard enough to keep this garden going – you've no idea how hard – when all you've got is your own two hands and two dumb boys no one else will give house-room to, and now . . .'

'I'm sorry, grandpa,' Peter apologised condescendingly, 'but it can't be helped. We'll put everything back the way we found it.'

'As if you'd be able to,' Jimmy scorned. 'I've yet to meet anyone these days who can tell a daffodil bulb from a bloody onion. Look at her!' He turned on the hapless female constable. 'Just look at her, setting that rose down roots up. You stupid woman, you haven't got a bloody . . .'

'See that man over there?' Collins pointed across the lawn. 'He's in charge.' He whispered it softly close to Jimmy's ear. Jimmy Herne stormed off towards Bill Mulcahy. Soon his screeches of indignation could be heard all over the garden, vying creditably with the hospital clock as it chimed the half-hour.

Collins looked down at the rookie. The mound of earth was growing in height, but the lad's pace was slackening.

'Change-over!' he shouted.

'Thanks, sir.' Brooke climbed out of the four-foot hole, mud clinging to his shirtsleeves and uniform trousers. He passed a grubby hand over his damp forehead.

'You were bloody well slowing up. I've no intention of spending the whole night here,' Collins commented.

Humiliated, Brooke retreated beyond the canvas screen, where he passed the shovel to Andrew Murphy. Murphy was that rarity on the force; a constable close to retiring age. He had joined the police a good many years before either Collins or Joseph, but he had neither sought nor received promotion, preferring the comparatively responsibility-free life of an ordinary constable to the hassle that comes with command. Hanging his jacket on one of the posts supporting the canvas screen, he stepped athletically down into the hole. Collins crouched on his heels to watch while Murphy dug steadily downwards.

'Anything yet?' he ventured after ten minutes of hard, sweating silence.

'A bloody awful stench.' Being older than Peter, with a memory that encompassed the days when he himself had taught not only Peter but also Dan Evans the ropes, he did not hold Sergeant Collins in the same awe as the rookies did.

'In that case you'd better proceed carefully.'

'Too royal,' Murphy agreed. 'Damn!'

Peter looked down to see a seething whirl of maggots shoot off the edge of Murphy's spade. He then reeled backwards as the stench hit him; the foul, sickly-sweet, instantly recognisable reek of death.

'I've sliced the leg off a dog,' Murphy's voice floated up from the bottom of the pit. 'A great big bloody hairy dog. And there's . . .'

'What?' Peter demanded urgently.

'A suitcase.'

'A what?' Collins didn't trust his ears.

'A bloody suitcase. Filthy dirty, damp, the top's cracked, but it's still a bloody suitcase.'

Head held high, oblivious to the wolf-whistles of the junior police who had nothing better to do than eye the nurses as they walked up and down the drive, Carol Ashford moved swiftly and directly to the staff car park. Shaking her keys from her purse, she opened the door of her green, open-topped sports car and threw her handbag inside. Starting the engine, she drove slowly down the drive, to join the flow of traffic wending its way along the main thoroughfare through the suburbs. Turning right at the foot of the hill, she left the mainstream that was heading from the town centre, and raced out along the coast road.

It had been a long hard shift on the geriatric ward, and sometimes, just occasionally like now, she regretted attending that recruitment presentation that had led her to specialise in geriatric psychiatric nursing. Not that the promises hadn't materialised. She had indeed received rapid promotion; there weren't many fully-fledged sisters under twenty-eight years of age, but she was one. And that was a promotion she could be proud of, confident she had been awarded it for her own merits, and not through her husband's influence.

It was just that today had seemed worse than usual. Probably because the patients had been so unsettled by all those police crawling around Compton Castle. God only knew why Harry Goldman had decided to use her ward as a base to describe the layout of the ward units to the police. As a result, Mrs Hobley had whined repeatedly that she wanted to go home; and not even to the home she had shared with her husband for fifty years, but back to her childhood home that had been bombed by the Luftwaffe during the war. Mr Greenway was so fascinated by the events in the garden, that he hadn't made any effort to recognise his son and daughter-in-law when they came to visit, refusing to glance at them for more than a second. Mrs Adams, excelling herself, had managed to wet herself four times in as many hours.

So, not for the first time, Carol Ashford found herself wondering what she, or any of the nurses who worked under her, were accomplishing by keeping the old dears warm and fed, when most of them barely realised they were alive.

She turned off the road and into the lane that led to the farmhouse she and her husband had bought and refurbished with money inherited from her parents-in-law. Slowing the car to a crawl, she pressed the button that lowered the window, so she could hear the birds and smell the new blossom on the trees. She turned a sharp corner behind the high wall of an outbuilding, then drove into the farmyard and savoured the scene spread out before her. The old barn, its grey stone walls scraped clean and repointed, and one wall entirely replaced by glass, now housed their indoor swimming pool. Behind the house they'd had a tennis court built within the walls of the old kitchen garden; and in front of her waited the house itself, its arched windows handcrafted in hardwood, framing her carefully chosen William Morris print curtains.

This house was very special, something she and her husband had dreamt of the day they had married, and had worked towards afterwards, never really believing that they'd be able to afford anything like it until they were well into their fifties. But here she was, not yet thirty, the proud possessor of everything she'd ever wanted – including, and especially, her man.

She pulled up on the hard-standing at the side of the house, next to the kitchen door. There was no sign of her husband's car, nor did she expect to see it. She was used to being the first to arrive home. Although she would never have admitted it to anyone, especially her husband, she didn't like walking into an empty house, even this one. It was so isolated. If anything happened to her she could scream until her lungs burst, but no one would hear. Even the burglar alarms and the two trained guard dogs offered little comfort. Burglar alarms could be cut, and dogs poisoned. It did happen; she read about it weekly in the national newspapers.

Opening the back door, she walked through the long porch that they'd built specifically to hold their boots, walking and working coats, and the dogs, before she unlocked the kitchen door. The dogs greeted her enthusiastically, before she let them into the main house. Warm air belched out into the fresh spring atmosphere. No matter what the weather outside, the kitchen was always warm and cosy, sometimes oppressively so. The Aga stove saw to that. There was a welcoming smell of food, as she lifted the lid of the pot warming on the slow-burner plate on top. The chicken casserole prepared the night before had now cooked to perfection. She opened the oven door and pushed the pot inside, keeping an ear open for any unusual noise the dogs might make. They were quiet, so no intruders had broken in today.

Breathing a little easier, she looked around her. It was the help's day for cleaning the brasses and oak cupboards. She could still smell the polish. Dropping her handbag on to one of the cushioned bentwood rockers that stood either side of the massive open hearth which now housed the Aga, she kicked off her shoes and padded barefoot around the whole of the ground floor, checking every room as she always did when she came home after a day at work. The sitting-room, more elegant than cosy with its handwoven Brussels tapestries decorating the grey, unplastered stonework and its richly upholstered Parker Knoll chairs and sofas, seemed cold, exquisite and untouched. No body imprint disturbed the cushions, neatly balanced on their points, just as the daily had left them. The study, with its built-in shelves, desks and book-lined walls, was a bit dusty. It wouldn't get cleaned until Wednesday.

The dining-room, cool, elegant and Regency in style, with a massive period sideboard, striped upholstery, burnished silverware and a polished mahogany table that could seat twelve in comfort, yawned vacantly back at her. The den, her husband's favourite room, with its television, video recorder, and pool table, was tidier than they'd left it; the litter of newspapers and circulars had been gathered up by their daily and returned to the magazine rack. And finally the morning room – the room she had claimed as her own, and furnished with pine bookcases, dressers, pretty chintz-covered sofas, and round occasional tables. She stopped to pet her two Siamese cats, who divided their time equally between this room and the outside, before brushing back past the dogs who had chosen to lie on the Persian rug at the foot of the stairs in the galleried hall. Finally after one last look round, she climbed the solid oak staircase her husband had bought from a builder who'd salvaged it from one of the town's seaside mansions, demolished to make way for the marina.

Ripping off her nurse's cap and unbuttoning her uniform as she moved, she opened in turn the doors to the four unused bedrooms, each with its own ensuite bathroom. All were furnished in solid Victorian pine furniture. Their floorboards were polished, the rugs that covered them handmade Turkish. Although she could see into the bathrooms from the bedroom doors, she made a point of checking each unit individually and carefully before stepping into the master bedroom that she'd had papered in that same beautiful Morris print that she'd fallen in love with as a child, when visiting her grandmother's house.

She sank down on the chaise-longue in the corner of the large room, and began to unroll her stockings. The massive fourposter bed, handmade to her husband's exacting specifications, hung with thick, crunchy lace curtains, and covered with a matching bedspread, dominated the area beneath the largest window. In the corner opposite to where she was sitting stood an antique roll-top desk and captain's chair. This one room alone had cost an absolute fortune, but it was worth every penny she reflected as she thrust back the sliding door of her walk-in wardrobe.

She stripped off her uniform and underclothes and threw them, together with her stockings, into the linen bin that was emptied daily by their cleaner. Naked, she returned to the bedroom, and studied herself in the cheval mirror. Was that a pad of fat forming over her hips? She turned her back to the mirror, and twisted her head, trying to assess it over her shoulder. She couldn't be sure, but she resolved to eat less and exercise more, just in case. Her husband abhorred anything less than perfect, including the female figure. She touched her toes with the flat of her hands ten times, before heading into her bathroom. Her husband had his own mahogany-lined dressing-room and bathroom, leading off the other side of the room. She turned on the taps of the huge Victorian bath, another product of her husband's expeditions to the salvage yard, and tossed a handful of bathsalts into the water.

Humming a tuneless ditty, she pulled the pins from her long blonde hair. It swung heavily to her waist, before she caught and rolled it up, pinning it securely on top of her head with a stick. Testing the water with her hand, she found it exactly as she liked it; stinging hot. Stepping in, she held her breath as the water burned her skin and turned it a bright rosy pink. She submerged her body slowly, inch by inch, then, closing her eyes, she emptied her mind, lay back and soaked, surrendering her senses to the idle pleasure of the moment.

The strains of a Brahms lullaby lilted sweetly into the

atmosphere, as suddenly, without warning, the bathroom door flew open.

'Tony, is that you?' she called out, fearfully turning around, fighting the terror that rose in her throat. Her heartbeat quietened and fear turned to a smile when she saw him framed in the doorway, his blue eyes and white-blond hair half hidden by the curls of steam that filled the air.

'I brought you a martini, and I'd hand it to you if I could find you,' he murmured languidly.

'If I speak, can you follow my voice?' she joked.

He walked across to the bath and handed her an ice-cold champagne glass filled to the brim and decorated with an olive. 'You look extremely inviting in there,' he murmured into her ear, pink and . . .' he touched one of her exposed breasts lightly and surely, teasing the nipple to a hard peak.

'And?' She sipped her martini and looked at him over the rim of her glass.

'And how about you get out of this bath?'

She obediently rose from the water, and he handed her a towel. She wrapped herself in it before stepping out on to the Indian cotton bathmat. He took the martini she'd picked up again and placed it together with his own on the windowsill.

'The bed or the floor?' he asked bluntly.

'The floor's wet?'

'We could play at fishes,' he stripped the towel away and flung it aside, before pushing her down on to her back.

Carol was used to Tony's lovemaking, hard, abrasive, totally devoid of any gentleness or tenderness. When they made love during daylight hours, as they often did, he rarely even bothered to undress. She suspected that he never gave either her or her enjoyment a single thought; that he was single-mindedly concerned only with the gratification of his own needs. But as she lay back, acquiescing to his sexual whims, and acting out the fantasies he had taken care to acquaint her with, the knowledge that he took pleasure in her body was enough for her.

She loved him passionately, deeply, with every fibre of her being, although she was careful never to allow the depth of her obsession to show, lest he see it as a smothering emotion to be

100

avoided. Sometimes she felt as though she existed only as an extension of his being. But, then, she had to be so much to him; wife, lover, friend – and child. For when the tests following her failure to conceive had resulted in the disclosure of Tony's negative sperm count, he had been devastated. She knew how much it had hurt, not only his pride and fragile masculine ego, but his whole philosophy. He had built everything, the house, his career, even their friends, around the life he had wanted to provide for his children. And she also knew that if it had been herself who had proved infertile, he would have left her and sought to conceive children with another partner, without giving her a second thought. She knew it, because he had told her so, bitterly and frequently during that first uneasy year when they had struggled to come to terms with their misfortune.

'You can return to your bath now.' He left her abruptly, standing up to button his trousers. Reaching over he picked up his martini and drained it. Trembling, her breasts, thighs and buttocks stinging with pain where he had hurt her, she returned to the bath and began to soap herself.

'As soon as I finish, we can eat. It's chicken casserole,' she ventured timorously, hoping he'd be pleased with her choice of meal. Tony's moods were often aggressive, and always unpredictable after they'd had sex.

'I know. If you don't mind I'll eat now and not wait for you.' He wasn't really asking her permission, and she knew it. 'I have to get back.'

'To the hospital?' She failed to keep the disappointment from her voice. Mondays were special; the one night a week they kept for themselves, when neither of them attended any of the committee meetings or clubs they belonged to, or visited or entertained their wide circle of colleagues and friends.

'The police are still there,' he informed her tersely.

'I saw them,' she said briefly, trying to remain cool and detached, but angry with herself for allowing her emotions to show, knowing how he hated anything resembling 'a scene'.

'They're searching for more bodies.'

'More?' she stared at him. 'Have they found any yet?'

'That's what I'm going back to find out.' He picked up his

empty glass. 'I may be late, so don't wait up for me,' he said casually as he left the room.

Pain twisted in her heart like a knife. Every time he said those words, she had visions of a flat, a mistress – someone young, angelic and beautiful like Lyn Sullivan; but again she knew better than to allow her fears and suspicions to show on the surface. Their inability to procreate had driven enough of a wedge between them, without her voicing the insecurities that had begun to plague her since she had first detected another woman's perfume on his clothes.

Instead she must strive to be charming, amiable, attractive, compliant and obliging at all times. She knew that was the only way to hold him; to make him want her enough to return to her, no matter what amatory escapades he indulged in.

Thus she loved him enough to allow him free rein to hurt her. And she would continue to do so, no matter what it cost her, simply because life without him was unthinkable.

'I'll be down as soon as I'm dressed, darling,' she called out pleasantly. 'Perhaps we can have coffee together?'

He didn't hear her. He had already gone.

Chapter Seven

Peter Collins supervised the lifting of the almost liquid remains of the dog – which unfortunately for both him and his team had, as Murphy'd said, been a large and hairy one – on to a canvas stretcher and out of the pit. Once on the grass the carcass was packed, stretcher and all, into a body-bag with the same meticulous care that would have been bestowed on a human corpse. As soon as the dog was disposed of, Collins returned to the hole, where Murphy was still ensconced, digging out the suitcase, which was damp, mouldy and foul-smelling as a result of being buried beneath the dog.

It was a good twenty minutes before Murphy managed to scoop the case on to another canvas stretcher that Brooke had brought up, and even then Collins wasn't satisfied that the hole had been properly excavated. He checked out the crater carefully for himself, crumbling the earth between his fingers, before switching Brooke and Murphy again, ordering Brooke to dig down another three foot.

He heaved himself out of the pit, and stood on the grass, brushing clumps of mud from his trousers and breathing in great gulps of clean, sweet-smelling evening air. There was intense activity around the other sites. As soon as the light had begun to fade, Bill Mulcahy had ordered portable lamps brought up, and they were dotted around the lawns, shining bright spotlights into the dark, puddled depressions hidden behind the canvas screens, and casting silver shadows over the newly-mown carpet of grass.

'Anything?' Collins mouthed silently to Dan Evans as he stepped over his canvas screen and walked towards Dan's site.

'Other than loose earth, all the way down to five foot, no.'

'Sounds ominous. What about the Super?'

'Same problem as here; the deeper they dig, the softer the earth, and the more often it caves in.'

A whistle blew, and two constables from Mulcahy's team raced forward. Evans and Collins ran towards the site, just as Bill's bald head emerged from behind the screens.

'Phone O'Kelly,' Bill ordered abruptly. He didn't have to say any more. Dan moved, as quickly as his bulk would allow to the mobile HQ that had been hauled to the back of the main hospital building.

'Another body?' Collins ventured.

'Looks like it,' Bill replied. 'Call off the late meeting down the Station, and have it rescheduled here, tomorrow afternoon. And you'd better supervise Dan's site as well as your own for the moment.' Mulcahy disappeared back behind the screen. Collins could hear him screaming at the hapless constable who was still down in the hole.

'Out, right now, this minute, before you do any more damage. Leave it – I said leave it for the pathologist, boy.'

Peter turned and smiled wryly to himself, recalling all the times that he and Trevor had taken Mulcahy's flak. But before he had time to take a second step, another whistle blew. He whirled to the right, just as a young constable surfaced from behind the canvas screens that shrouded Dan Evans' site, green-faced and retching. He watched the lad withdraw into a thick copse of shrubs. Once again the calm, clear twilight and the perfume of the tree blossoms were overshadowed by the pervasive, sickly-sweet stench of death.

'Patrick'll be here in ten minutes.' Dan ran towards him, puffing, his round face bright red from the unaccustomed exertion.

'I hope he brings a nightcap with him. Something tells me we're going to see in the dawn on this one,' Collins murmured, as he pulled two cigars out of his pocket and offered one to Evans.

Spencer Jordan noticed the lights and the commotion in the hospital grounds from the kitchen window of his flat as he was

104

preparing his evening meal. The flat was located on the third floor of a halfway house, and was jocularly referred to as the 'penthouse' by the inmates inhabiting the bedroom units on the floor below.

Pronounced fit and ready to live in the community, after two years as a patient in psychiatric wards both in America and Britain, and then six months in a halfway house attached to Compton Castle, the thought of returning to anything remotely resembling a 'normal' domestic existence had made Spencer's blood run cold. Thanks to Harry Goldman's influence, he'd been given an art therapist's post at Compton Castle, so when the question of accommodation had come up, he'd tried to solve his problem by volunteering to act as warden to the same halfway unit in which he himself was an inmate. The Health Authority, wary of his recent illness, had turned him down with the excuse that he already had his work cut out just to run the art therapy classes.

He guessed the real reason, but had no choice but to accept their decision. When a letter had finally come which asked him to vacate his room in the hostel, he had begun to panic, and regress – losing the considerable ground he'd won under Harry Goldman's caring eye.

Harry intervened yet again, and the Health Authority compromised. Spencer was given the post of assistant warden, which carried a rent-free flat, in return for two nights 'sleep in' duty when he was required to supervise the residents and ensure that none of them stayed out later than midnight without permission from their psychiatrists. Not that any of them ever did. Recovering from phobias and depressions, their problem was being persuaded to relinquish the familiar security of their unit for more than ten minutes at a time, not getting them to return to it afterwards.

Although officially he was on duty only two nights a week, staff shortages, and absences frequently stretched these two nights to four and sometimes even six. Spencer didn't mind; he, like the residents he supervised, rarely went out in the evenings. He knew no one in the town other than the staff members and a few ex-patients, and there was nowhere

105

particular he wanted to go. Art exhibitions, the theatre, even the cinema invariably conjured up the painful memories he continually struggled to keep submerged.

Spencer's social and family life had come to an end in America; not even Harry Goldman could persuade him otherwise. Most evenings he was content to return to the soulless utility-furnished flat, to sit in an uncomfortable, gold-moquette institution armchair, and stare at his bare cream-painted walls. The hospital authority had provided him with pictures but, unable to bear the chocolate box prints, he had soon taken them down. He doubted that he'd ever produce his own art again, but remained sensitive enough to reject what was bad whenever he saw it.

He mixed himself a salad, breaking a few ounces of the same white goat's cheese that he had used in his sandwiches amongst the lettuce, cucumber, grapes, peppers and tomatoes. Taking this, and a bottle of mineral water, he went into the living-room and switched on the television. He sat watching the news that catalogued the current series of global human disasters. They stretched from the starving in Africa, to war orphans in the Balkans, finally ending with the battered and murdered victims of a series of race riots in inner-city America. The mention of America, and the pictures of devastated city streets, their familiar shop-signs torn down and trodden into the gutters, hit too close to home. He changed channels with the remote control and ate his salad to the shrill accompaniment of a forty-year-old Hollywood musical.

Spencer had finished his meal and cleared up by six-thirty. The evening stretched ahead of him, an empty void to be filled – with what? He flicked through the local evening paper that he bought every day for its television page, and studied the options available on the small screen. A documentary on the break-up of the Eastern Bloc, the third episode of a detective series he'd never got into, a half-hour situation comedy, a film he'd enjoyed the first time around – and absolutely hated the fifth time. He switched off the television and went to the window. Night had fallen, dusky, velvet-hued, but still the lights continued to flicker in the hospital grounds, casting eerie shadows over the distant blurred, blue-suited figures that

106

scurried between the lawns and the police cars. An ambulance had been driven up over the grass, and parked close to one of the canvas screens. Two men walked around to its back doors, and began to unload body-bags. Spencer recognised these instantly for what they were, and shuddered as he drew his curtains to shut the scene from view. He paced uneasily from the small living-room to the tiny kitchen, the box-sized bedroom, the bathroom, and back.

He stared at the cheap, teak veneered sideboard, summoning every inch of willpower he possessed, fighting an urge to open the doors. He knew he wasn't strong enough to look at its contents – not yet. If he opened them, he'd suffer. A few moments – moments of what? Not happiness certainly, that was far too strong a word, and afterwards there'd be so much pain . . .

The temptation proved too strong. Dropping to his knees, he wrenched open the sideboard door, and tenderly removed a box of photograph albums. Stroking the scars that radiated from his glass eye, he sat at the table to open the box, gently taking the top album into his large hands. He turned its cover and stared at the first page. A wedding group outside a registry office in London. Himself, smiling broadly, wearing an outrageous scarlet silk suit, navy-blue shirt, and red and purple tie; his arm wrapped around Danielle, four months pregnant, in bright green and blue cotton voile.

The reception . . . friends . . . he could taste the wine and strawberries, hear the toast: *Long Life and Happiness!*

The house in California . . . a naked, fat, pink gurgling baby in his arms . . . then in Danielle's. More friends, gallery openings, another baby – and another – he slammed the album shut. Blinded by unshed tears, he stumbled to the sideboard and returned it to the shelf.

He then sat with his back to the sideboard, but after only a moment's hesitation, he turned to wrench open the drinks compartment. He wasn't on duty tonight, so it didn't matter what state he got himself into. He took out a full whisky bottle, unscrewed the top and poured himself a tumblerful. He drank half of it without even bothering to go into the kitchen to fetch ice. Holding the glass in one hand and the bottle by the neck in the other, he returned to his chair and switched on the television again. He'd watch the film for the sixth time. It was easier to cope with what he knew, with what was undemandingly, comfortingly familiar, than to try and face the past, the future – or worst of all – the present.

Mulcahy, Evans and Collins were leaning lethargically against the bonnet of a police car when O'Kelly surfaced from the last pit, and walked wearily towards them. Collins had the inevitable cigar in hand, Evans was chewing a mouthful of peppermints, and Mulcahy was amusing himself by shouting at each and every rookie foolhardy enough to stray within his sights.

'I've done what I can here. They're all in body bags. I'll continue in the lab tomorrow morning.' O'Kelly tore off his rubber gloves and stuffed them into the pocket of his coat.

'Thanks, Patrick. Appreciate you coming out,' Bill said shortly, helping himself to one of the cigars that protruded from Collins' pocket.

'I know you're dying to ask,' O'Kelly said wryly, 'so I'll tell you what I can be sure of, so far, but I'd appreciate you keeping the serious questions until after the PMs tomorrow.'

'You've got it.' Evans yawned, glancing up at the hospital clock as it struck four.

'They're both female, both young; one in an advanced stage of decomposition, the other little more than skeletal, with a few rags of dried organs attached. Both have soil in the mouths, nose and as far as I can make out, air passages.'

'Buried alive?' Mulcahy ventured.

'I should be able to answer that tomorrow. Both were brunette, one had long hair, the other short.'

'We found another suitcase and two handbags buried beneath the dog,' Collins divulged abruptly. 'They're all bagged, and in the ambulance.'

'Will you take a look at the dog, as well?' Mulcahy asked. 'As a favour,' he pressed, seeing the distaste on Patrick's face.

'As a favour, I'll take a quick look before I send it on with the suitcases to the police lab. But don't make a habit of it,' O'Kelly conceded reluctantly.

'I won't.' Both Bill and Patrick knew the value of Bill's assertion.

'See you in a couple of hours,' O'Kelly muttered as he stumbled towards his car.

'Right, let's clear this place up,' Mulcahy announced briskly.

Collins looked over to the blocks housing the patients. Apart from the ward office and the bathroom windows, the buildings were in total darkness. He imagined Trevor curled up warm and comfortable in his bed.

'Lucky sod!' he swore as he stared at the battlefield of trenches and mounds that had been yesterday's neat lawns and flowerbeds.

Collins didn't reach the flat he called home until six in the morning. The rays of dawn had transformed the sky from deep rich navy to cold steel grey. He switched on his car alarm, locked the vehicle securely, and walked up the short red-tiled path that led to the front door of a five-storey Edwardian building. Originally built as a comfortable middle-class home for family and servants, it now housed six flats and four bedsits. His flat, chosen primarily for its view and its proximity to the town centre, was on the third floor.

He turned the key and stepped into a hall that was still as large and spacious as when the house was first built. Its air of spaciousness was the only thing that hadn't changed. Unconcerned with period authenticity the landlord had replaced the old mahogany panelled staircase and ornate, mouldering plasterwork with unimaginative modern substitutes that were neither cheap nor expensive, merely functional.

Collins took the stairs two at a time, and opened the door to his flat. He walked straight into a beautifully proportioned, high-ceilinged living-room. The bedroom and bathroom were minute. The kitchen was built into what had once been a fairly commodious airing cupboard, and it had an air-vent instead of a window. But he forgave the flat its other failings for the one handsome room, poorly furnished as it was.

Moving across the rough brown cord carpet to the window, he opened it and stepped out on to a fire-escape that looked out over the sea. Leaving the window open, he went back inside to the kitchen, ground a handful of fresh beans in the electric coffee-grinder, and made himself a pot of filter coffee. His stomach told him he was hungry, the problem was for what? He looked into his bread bin. There was half a loaf of green mouldy wholemeal bread that he had bought over a week ago. He opened the small fridge that sat beneath the work surface. A six-pack of beer, a tub of low-fat spread, a carton of long-life milk, two eggs and a stale corner of cheese. The small freezer compartment wasn't much more inspiring; he found a ready-made lasagna for one, a pizza, half a pack of sausages, but no bread. He had more luck in the cupboard, where he discovered a packet of melba toasts of uncertain age.

Scrambling the eggs, he spread low-fat spread on to ten of the tiny toasts. When the meal was ready, he filled a tray and carried it out on to the fire-escape. Leaving the tray on the metal platform, he returned to pull a cushion off one of the chairs in the living-room. He sat down, leaning forward on the safety railings, dangling his legs in space while he ate. In front of him lay the eternal, perpetually-moving vista of the sea. He could hear the slurp of the waves as they reclaimed rivulets of foam from amongst the pebbles scattered along the foreshore, the cry of the gulls as they scavenged along the shoreline. Ahead, the sun rose, casting its glittering rays in shimmering streaks that lit up the grey surface of the vast undulating expanse of water.

He shivered, but still sat and ate; the cold carried in its chill an antiseptic property that cleansed away the cloying stench and aftertaste of unnatural death that had fouled his long night. And there was still so much to be done. Three victims to identify, a murderer to find – and Trevor Joseph to wrench back into the world of the living. In the meantime another perfect spring day was about to begin, and all he wanted was his bed.

He finished his meal without really tasting it, threw the cushion back on to the chair, carried the tray into the kitchen, dumped the dirty dishes in the sink for his daily, wiped over the work surfaces, and went into his bedroom. His trousers were filthy, caked with mud. He took them and his jacket off, fling-ing both into the linen basket, before crawling beneath the duvet in his shirt and underpants. He looked at his alarm, debated whether to set it or not, before finally deciding against making the effort. Bill or Dan would want him soon enough, and both unfortunately knew where to find him. Two minutes later all that could be heard was his quiet snoring as he slept the heavy dreamless sleep of the truly exhausted.

'Trevor.' Nurse Sullivan knocked at his door before tentatively opening it. 'Time to get up. As soon as you're dressed, you can lay the table.'

'It's *my* turn?' Trevor asked from the depths of his bed.

'It's your turn,' she agreed, returning to her trolley and pouring out his tea the way he liked it. She set it on his bedside table, before moving on down the corridor.

Trevor leant on his elbow and sipped the tea. His head ached from the sleeping tablets he had taken the night before in the hope that even a drugged sleep would be preferable to sitting up all night afraid to close his eyes lest bloody spectres from his last case should haunt his dreams. The face of the clown – bloody knife in hand – make-up running down its cheeks . . .

Pushing the image firmly from his mind he stumbled out of bed and into the bathroom, stripped off his pyjamas and climbed into the shower. The morning-after of sleeping pills was more deadly than that of too much drink, he decided miserably, as he held his head under the cool jet for two full minutes, in the hope that, the water would galvanise his tired, aching body and numbed brain back to a semblance of life. On an impulse he began to wash his hair. Rubbing the strands, he discovered they were longer now than he'd ever remembered them. Could he do what Spencer had suggested; take another step outside today? How long before he'd make it as far as the front gate? And how long before he actually travelled into town to have his hair cut?

He rinsed the lather from his body and hair, wrapped a towel around his waist, and stepped back into his bedroom absently trying to drink the cup of now cold tea that Lyn Sullivan had laid on his bedside table.

Then he picked up his threadbare tracksuit top from the chair where he had dumped his clothes the night before, and stared at the faded cotton trousers underneath it. He reached

111

for the trousers and screwed them, together with the top, into a ball before thrusting them into his dirty linen bag. He opened the wardrobe door and studied the selection of clothes that Peter had brought from his flat when he had been moved here from the General Hospital. There wasn't much choice. Two pairs of jeans, as faded as the trousers, but even more threadbare. A hand-knitted woollen jumper his mother had sent him last Christmas which had gone drastically out of shape after he had taken it to the launderette. An anorak that stubbornly remained grubby no matter how often he flung it into a washing-machine, and a couple of white shirts. He settled on one of the white shirts and a pair of jeans. The jeans sagged a good three inches around his now slender waist. He looked for a belt, eventually finding one in a bag of underclothes and socks that Collins had brought and he had never even bothered to open.

He pushed the belt through the loops at the waist of his jeans, but even when the prong was hooked into the last available hole, the belt hung slack and ineffective. He pulled it tighter and marked the spot where another hole was needed, then he looked around for something to make one with.

'Trevor?' Lyn Sullivan knocked at the door again.

'Come in,' he shouted.

'Oh, you are up. It's just that breakfast will be ready in ten minutes, and you haven't laid the table yet, but now I can see why.' She smiled. 'You do look smart.'

'Smart?' he stared at her blankly, suspecting her of teasing him. 'These are just a pair of old jeans.'

'Old jeans and white shirts are the latest fashion,' she assured him. 'What's the problem? Belt needs another hole?'

'I was just looking for something to make one with.'

'Here give it to me. I'll use scissors.' She grabbed hold of the buckle and pulled the belt from his trousers. 'I'll bring it back in a moment.' She closed the door behind her.

Trevor brushed his damp hair away from his face with his fingers and stared at himself in the full-length mirror fixed to the wall beside the wardrobe. His clothes might be clean but they were worn, and he looked thin, tired and incredibly old. Like his father had done just before he died. Was that where he was headed; an early grave, dying young before his time, like his father? But then his father'd had cancer, and he'd only been injured in the line of duty.

It was probably just as Peter told him so often; lack of effort on his part. Sitting around all day doing nothing. He'd put action off long enough; always tomorrow. If he went out today, took another step forward . . .

He opened the bedside table and extricated his wallet. It held fifty pounds cash, and his credit cards. He was still getting paid, so he had no money worries, and Peter had checked that the couple renting the flat he owned, but hadn't lived in for years, were paying their rent into his bank account. Today he would take one more step forward. If he forced himself, he could make as far as the gate. Once at the gate it would only be a small step to board a bus into town. Then he could have his hair cut, and perhaps even buy some clothes. Possibly even take another bus out to see his flat. Check on both his flat and his car – pick up the threads. It would be a beginning; and after he made a beginning he could decide on the rest of his life.

He felt sick to the pit of his stomach at the prospect of leaving the hospital, but he also felt a sense of exhilaration. For the first time since he'd been injured, he was going to take responsibility for himself and his own actions. To do something positive that would lead him back into the bustle of real life.

The phone began to ring in Peter Collins' bedroom in what seemed like less than five minutes after he fell asleep. He rolled on to his side and stretched out his arm.

'Collins,' he muttered automatically.

'Mortuary, ten minutes.' The line went dead, but not before he recognised Bill Mulcahy's dulcet tones. He lay back and closed his eyes, recognising even as he began to succumb to temptation that it was a deadly thing to do. If he didn't move now, right away, he wouldn't wake up again for another eight hours, and nothing, not even eight hours of blissful sleep, was worth incurring the total wrath of Bill Mulcahy.

He jerked himself abruptly out of bed and headed for the shower. Five minutes later, still damp but dressed, he walked out to his car. He glanced at his watch it was just after ten.

113

O'Kelly must have worked right through for there to be sufficient information already to justify calling a meeting. A peculiar feeling in his stomach identified itself as hunger. The scrambled eggs and melba toast hadn't filled much of a hole. After this little session he'd see about breakfast. He knew better than to eat anything *before* he visited a mortuary, particularly one that Patrick O'Kelly was in charge of.

'We're carrying out further tests, but the brand name doesn't matter. It could even be a cocktail of several different drugs. We've identified an anti-depressant, a tranquilliser, and a muscle-relaxant that's effective to the point of paralysis. I found definite traces of curare in the bloodstream, but the effects of the drug were probably wearing off at the time of her death, because she managed to tear her glued-up mouth open. We know that much from the considerable fresh damage done to the skin on her lips,' O'Kelly dropped his scalpel on to the slab where his assistant had laid out Rosie Twyford again.

'Are you saying she would have been paralysed up until that moment?' Dan Evans asked.

'Collins, how nice of you to visit us,' Mulcahy called out with elaborate sarcasm. 'Do come and join us.'

Peter entered the room, and closed the doors behind him while valiantly fighting the smell of putrefaction that not even the strong odour of formaldehyde could kill.

'The degree of paralysis suffered would relate to the amount of drug ingested,' O'Kelly tried to answer Dan's question as best he could. 'Curare undoubtedly causes paralysis, and there was a significant amount in her bloodstream at the time of death, but there is other evidence, and other factors to consider.'

'For instance?' Mulcahy asked tersely.

'For instance the torn lips, the open eyes, the amount of soil in her air passages. That girl fought for her life as no unconscious person would have done. The conclusion I'd draw is that if she had been administered a high enough dose to cause total paralysis, it was wearing off at the time of her death. She was either conscious, or regained consciousness, shortly after she was put into the hole,' Patrick continued.

'We're talking about the first victim,' Dan explained to a bewildered Collins.

'Then this villain, whoever he is, likes to see his victims' eyes as he shovels dirt on top of them?' Mulcahy suggested angrily.

'You could argue that, although I've come up with no evidence to support it other than the fact that she was still alive when she was buried, and both her eyes were open when she was uncovered,' O'Kelly corrected carefully.

'Michelle Grady came up trumps. We think the first victim is one Rosie Twyford,' Evans revealed in his slow, lilting Welsh drawl. 'She was discharged from Compton Castle six months ago, but she returned for twice-weekly outpatient sessions with Dorothy Clyne, one of the senior psychiatrists on Dr Goldman's team. I rang Tony Waters early this morning, got him out of bed, and had him check her file. She was discharged as an outpatient a week ago. Her last appointment was a week yesterday.'

'Grady also checked Rosie Twyford's bedsit last night,' Mulcahy chipped in. 'The keys we found fit the front door, and Rosie's bedsit inner door. Grady spoke to a neighbour who occupies the next room. The last time he saw her was the morning she left for her final hospital visit, exactly one week ago yesterday. When she didn't return, he assumed she'd been kept in again. He did say that she appeared unusually nervous.'

'He didn't think to ring the hospital and check?' Collins asked cynically.

'Apparently they didn't have that kind of relationship. It was more of a "good morning, nice weather, good evening" acquaintance.'

'If she's the same one Waters was talking about yesterday, she has a family in Cornwall. Weren't they in touch with her either?' Collins walked over to the tiled wall and leant against it. The combination of the smell and the sight of the corpses was proving too much for him. He felt sick, dizzy and faint – and not just from lack of sleep.

'Cornish police notified them of her death this morning. There's a mother, stepfather and two stepbrothers. Apparently they'd frequently go for weeks at a time without hearing from her.'

'Then if she went missing a week ago . . .' Collins began.

'If she went missing a week ago, someone kept her alive until last Saturday night, when Vanessa Hedley saw her being buried in the grounds of Compton Castle.'

'And Vanessa Hedley's story fits in with what I've got,' O'Kelly said casually, reaching for one of the beakers of strong black coffee that his assistant had prepared. Peter and Dan balked at the coffee, but Mulcahy took one.

'I'm sorry, gentlemen, but if I don't sit down soon I'm going to fall down.' O'Kelly turned and led the way into his office where he sank into the huge vinyl-padded swivel-chair behind his desk.

'Then the way I see it . . .' Bill dumped his own coffee on to the desk, flicked back the pages of a notebook until he found a clean sheet, pulled a pen from his pocket and started to scribble.

Victim one, Rosie Twyford, keeps appointment in Compton Castle last Monday.

'And after Monday, that's it. She disappears into a void. Nothing is heard or seen of her until Vanessa goes into the garden a week later. On Saturday night Vanessa Hedley saw a bulky shadow burying a body in the grounds, and no one,' he glanced wryly at Collins, 'took any notice of her until Monday morning, when she bullied the YTS lad into digging up the flowerbed. Then we find Rosie Twyford.'

'And Saturday/Sunday fits in with my calculations,' O'Kelly interrupted, resting his head in his hands. 'I'd say she died twelve hours either side of midnight Saturday.'

'Closer?' Mulcahy demanded.

'Can't make it any closer, sorry.' He didn't sound in the least apologetic.

'OK then. That will have to do. Which means . . .'

'Which means that Rosie Twyford was kept alive somewhere around Compton Castle from Monday afternoon to midnight on Saturday,' Dan said thoughtfully.

'Not necessarily,' Collins played Devil's Advocate. 'She could have gone to stay with someone – a boyfriend perhaps.'

116

'If she'd been abducted, it would fit in with her physical state; the dehydration, the starvation.' O'Kelly opened his eyes.

'Waters took us round the whole of the old building.' Collins offered his pack of cigars.

'Was there *anywhere* that could be used to hide a body?' Bill asked.

Peter recalled the rambling corridors, the empty attic rooms blanketed with undisturbed layers of dust, the cellar walls lined with pipes. 'If you knew the building well, I dare say you could come up with a thousand and one places,' he said drily. 'There's corners of that place that haven't seen people or daylight in years.'

'There were twenty-five needle sized holes in Rosie's arm,' O'Kelly commented flatly. 'You need comparative privacy to inject twenty-five doses of muscle-relaxant, tranquilliser and anti-depressant over a period of days; that's if you don't want to be noticed.'

'Exactly. Which proves my point that she'd been held captive before she was buried,' Mulcahy crowed.

'Unless she was a junkie,' Collins countered.

'Nothing on her record card. Dan already checked with Tony Waters.'

'Or in her bloodstream,' Patrick added.

'Then if she was held captive and tranquillised, what's the motive? Sexual?' Collins questioned.

'No signs of a struggle . . .' O'Kelly began.

'There wouldn't have been if she was tranquillised.'

'I said no signs of struggle,' O'Kelly repeated sternly. 'No signs of forced rape, no tearing of tissues, no traces of semen, but I can't rule out sexual intercourse. Just no signs, no stray hairs, no fibres, no nothing.'

'The other two victims?' Mulcahy asked.

'No semen in either of the vaginas, but the soft tissue has decayed in both bodies. One had been buried, I'd say, on the first rough calculations, for six to eight weeks, the second for four months. But please, bear in mind those are rough calculations based on condition and depth of the burials. I may have something more exact for you later.' He finished his coffee and took another from the tray. He looked grey, drained and exhausted.

'You didn't sleep last night?' Evans asked.

'I snatched an hour on one of the slabs between PMs.'

'I managed three,' Peter said unthinkingly.

'Glad to hear you're set up for the next twenty-hour shift, then Collins,' Mulcahy barked.

'You get anything from the suitcase or handbags, Patrick?' Dan asked.

'I sent them and the dog to the police laboratory for further tests.'

'Right, Collins, that's your next stop. Then afterwards you can liaise with Grady, see what she's come up with on Rosie Twyford's last movements. And I want you to be there when she starts interviewing everyone in that bedsitter block at six.'

'Yes, sir.'

Patrick rose from his chair and pulled off his lab coat. 'I'm for home and bed,' he yawned.

'Just one more question before you go,' Dan Evans murmured. 'Supposing we're right, that the killer does pick his victims a week ahead, that he drugs them and keeps them somewhere in the hospital before burying them.' Dan eyed Patrick. 'What can you tell us about such a man?'

'That's one for the police psychiatrist. I'm a scientist, not a shrink.'

'But you've seen dozens if not hundreds of murder victims. Surely you're interested in the outcome. You must have an opinion?' Dan Evans pressed.

'Off the top of my head, and going by information gleaned from past cases, he could be an impotent male who is dominated by a female, possibly a mother or a wife, even a sister. Someone who wants to be in control, but isn't. But then,' he said firmly, 'that is pure and absolute speculation, with no basis in fact.'

'But it does give us one more thing to consider and get to work on,' Mulcahy said shortly. 'And that's where we're all going now, gentlemen. To work.'

118

Chapter Eight

'I *saw* him.' Vanessa Hedley glanced theatrically over her shoulder and around the room before moving her head close to Alison Bevan's and lowering her voice. Trevor, who was sitting across the breakfast table from them, found himself straining his ears to catch what Vanessa was saying.

'It was dark,' Ali Bevan, her fellow patient, pointed out logically, 'so how could you see anything?'

'There was a moon,' Vanessa snapped. 'I saw his features quite clearly. He was huge . . . massive. I knew straight away that he was evil. It's the eyes.' She lowered her voice again. 'They always give the character away. The eyes and the mouth, and he had a cruel, vicious mouth.' She embellished her story until Trevor felt it had the same credibility as a badly made horror film.

'If you saw that much of him, and he saw you, aren't you terrified?' Ali asked, her eyes now round with fear.

'Of what?' Vanessa retorted sharply

'Of him coming after you.'

'She's right.' Roland Williams an alcohol dependent lecher leered suggestively. 'The murderer could be here, right now, in this room, listening to every word you're saying.' He glanced around the dining-room, which was crowded with patients, domestic staff and nurses. 'You're the only one who can identify him,' he emphasised; 'who knows who he is. He could be watching you, waiting his chance to grab you, rape you . . .'

'That's enough, Roland,' Nurse Carol Ashford ordered, catching the tail end of his conversation as she passed their table.

'Sorry, Nurse,' Roland apologised insincerely as he eyed the full, rounded breasts beneath her thin dress.

119

'Rape?' Ali hissed as soon as the nurse had disappeared through the door. 'I didn't know any of the victims had been raped?' Her voice quivered with emotion. It had been bad enough to learn that the police had found more dead women buried in the grounds, without hearing that they'd been violated.

'Of course he raped his victims. Why else would he kill them, and try to hide the bodies? Like the Neanderthals, he probably stripped them first, then—'

'The murderer isn't here,' Vanessa interrupted quickly, cutting him short. The one topic of conversation guaranteed to excite Roland's interest, and keep him pontificating for hours, was perverted sexual activity – usually as practised by primitive tribes that only he seemed to have heard of. And if he started lecturing on that subject now, he'd succeed in diverting everyone's attention from her, and her story, which was where she wanted to keep it.

'All I'm trying to do is warn you ladies.' Roland slurped his tea noisily, and his double chin wobbled as he licked beige drops from his fat, wet lips. 'I'd hate to think of anyone kidnapping one of you, tying you up, stripping you – and playing with you at his leisure.' He bent his head close to Ali's. 'Stroking your breast, putting his fingers in . . .'

Trevor dipped his spoon into his uneaten porridge and stirred it around, mixing the crust of sugar into the glutinous mass of oats. Once a detective, always a detective, he reflected fatalistically. He hadn't wanted to get involved with this case, or hear a single word about it, but he hadn't been able to stop himself from listening to Vanessa Hedley, or coming to the conclusion that, for all her boasting, she didn't have much if any idea what the killer really looked like. Shadows in moonlit gardens were easily distorted. They merged with bushes and trees, wavered with the wind, contorting any figures that walked in the darkness, making them appear larger and wider, or taller and wispier than they really were. Vanessa's 'massive killer' could simply have been a small man wearing a padded anorak. And he seriously doubted that the killer, whoever he was, had come close enough to Vanessa's window for her to see any details, such as the eyes.

He'd looked out of his ground-floor bedroom window that morning, watching while a raw young constable pointed out the first burial site to a colleague. Though it had been clear, sunny daylight, he hadn't been able to discern either of the constables' features beneath their helmets. So what chance had Vanessa of seeing and committing to memory the murderer's features as he'd shovelled earth on top of his helpless victim? But if the killer was somewhere around, and listening to Vanessa's prattling, would he actually realise that fact?

Trevor lifted his spoon to his lips and peered cautiously around the room for signs of someone actively watching Vanessa. Apart from Lucy Craig, Roland Williams and Alison Bevan, who were listening enthralled to her narrative, everyone else appeared to be quietly minding their own business.

He recalled quite a few of the tall stories forced on him by his fellow patients, even when he hadn't wanted to listen. Roland Williams, for instance. If a quarter of his stories could be believed, Roland had done some very peculiar things with both men and women, singly and in groups, and not only under the influence of drink. Last week he had caught sight of Roland's rotund figure retreating into the shrubbery with a bulging brown paper bag under his arm. He had assumed the bag contained alcohol, which was banned in Compton Castle. Had it contained something more sinister?

Then there was Michael Carpenter. Michael's sole topic of conversation was his ex-girlfriend, Angela, who had jilted him. It was common knowledge that he was incarcerated in Compton Castle because he'd set fire to her house, and almost succeeded in burning her entire family to death. What if Michael had decided in his mania that the only way to hold on to a girl of his own, was to kill her and bury her in a grave known to no one except himself – where she could be kept, his forever more? That wasn't so far-fetched when one recalled Vanessa's railings against those who had prevented her from putting her husband in a grave where she would have had total and absolute control over him.

'Go on, Vanessa,' Lucy Craig pestered childishly. 'Go on, tell us what he *really* looked like?'

'I've told you,' Vanessa replied irritably. 'Big – huge – with thick black hair, and a mouthful of white teeth. Enormous arms packed with muscles, like those wrestlers you see on television on a Sunday afternoon. He picked up this huge, heavy spade as though it was a toy, and brandished it above his head . . .'

'Not hungry, Trevor?' Nurse Sullivan, neat and clean in a smart red-polo neck sweater and black jeans, and smelling of fresh magnolias, took the empty chair beside him, making him suddenly and painfully aware of the shabbiness of his own clothes.

'Not for porridge, no,' he admitted, tentatively returning her smile with a small one of his own.

'Do you want some toast then?' she asked.

He thought about that for a moment.

'Fresh toast,' she coaxed. 'Not those cold rubbery slices laid out on the table ten minutes before anyone gets to eat them.'

'Sounds good,' he admitted.

'I'll help you make some in the ward kitchen. You know where it is?'

'Yes,' he muttered between clenched teeth. If Lyn had simply brought him the toast, he would have eaten it, but he hated going into the ward kitchen. It was always full of people, staff as well as patients.

'Come on, then.' She left her chair and waited for him.

'Lyn,' he asked as he followed her out into the corridor. 'Can you get hold of Peter Collins for me?'

'I could try,' she replied doubtfully. 'But he warned us yesterday that with everything that's going on he'd be extremely busy. If you want to see him that urgently, why don't you walk down the tunnel to the main hospital? The police have set up their mobile headquarters just outside the back door.' She paused outside the ward kitchen, allowing Trevor to precede her. She smiled, pleased with herself. If Trevor Joseph wanted to see Sergeant Collins badly enough, he'd have to make his own effort to leave the block, and that was the moment she'd been waiting for ever since he'd been transferred to her ward.

'I didn't expect to see you at work for a few days. Have your cuts healed?' Nurse Carol Ashford asked as Lyn entered the kitchen.

'They weren't as bad as they looked.' Lyn glanced down at the crisscross of lines on her palm that weren't even covered by plasters. She turned to Trevor. 'There's the toaster. Bread's in the enamel bin next to it. Be an angel and pop a piece in for me.' She took the electric kettle from the work surface behind Carol, and filled it, effectively blocking Trevor's exit from the narrow galley kitchen.

'Ladies.' Karl Lane, the male nurse, stood in the doorway and nodded to them. 'Any tea going?' He smiled at Lyn. Trevor saw the smile and was amazed at being stung by a sudden painful, bitter pang of jealousy. Not jealousy because Karl Lane was looking at Lyn Sullivan in such a proprietary way, but because the glances they'd exchanged had reminded him that there were people who had fulfilling private relationships away from the public eye. A phenomenon he hadn't himself experienced in years.

He felt suddenly angry; angry and empty because his own private life consisted only of his mother, married brother, sister-in-law, nieces and nephews – and Peter Collins. And fond as he was of all of them, not one of them could act as a substitute for a loving girlfriend – or wife. If only . . . he pushed the thought savagely from his mind. There were far too many *if onlys* in his life for comfort.

'Toast's burning,' Carol Ashford called out to Trevor. She finished her tea. 'It's time I was back on my ward to check that none of my little darlings have gone a-wandering.'

'What do you make of all this, Carol?' Karl asked casually.

'All what?'

'All these bodies,' he said in exasperation.

'Oh, yes, they've found even more haven't they? Well, what do you want me to make of them?' She turned the question neatly back on him.

'What does Tony think?' he pressed.

'The last time I saw Tony,' she said, recalling her husband's white face as he stumbled into their bed just as she was getting out of it earlier that morning, 'he was too tired to think.'

'Do you reckon the killer's a patient or a member of staff?' he persisted irritatingly.

'It has to be a patient,' Lyn said quickly. The other two turned and stared at her. 'Well it does, doesn't it? It's obvious. After all, this is a psychiatric hospital.'

'So they tell me.' Karl took the tea that she handed him.

'In my opinion we should stop trying to play guessing games, and leave it to the police to find out,' Nurse Ashford said. 'I've more than enough on my plate just running my ward and my house. I couldn't cope with a murder hunt as well. See you later.'

Trevor's hand trembled as he offered Lyn a plate of toast that he'd buttered and cut into triangles.

'Thank you,' she smiled. 'You know Karl, don't you, Trevor?'

'We met last Sunday.' Karl held out his hand to Trevor. 'But we weren't introduced. You're a policeman, aren't you?'

'I used to be a policeman,' Trevor corrected.

'There's nothing preventing you from being one again. That's if you want to rejoin the force.' Lyn bit into her piece of toast.

'I'm not sure what I want any more.' Trevor picked up his own toast, which was singed and black around the edges. He'd kept the burnt pieces for himself, and made some fresh for Lyn.

'I can understand that,' Karl murmured. 'Police duty must be almost as bad as working here; no let up, all the hours God sends, and—'

'And also dealing with the dregs of society,' Trevor supplied succinctly, intuitively knowing what he was about to say.

'Present company excepted,' Karl interrupted hastily. 'But then you must forgive me; I don't work on this ward. I'm on manias, and they're very different to depressions. Much more loopy,' he added wryly. 'See you, Lyn.'

'He didn't mean that. It's just that this job can get to you,' Lyn apologised to Trevor afterwards.

'I can imagine.' He dropped the barely nibbled toast back on to his plate.

124

* * *

'It's one of those terraced houses on the hill leading up to the heights,' Constable Michelle Grady explained laboriously to Collins' blank impassive face. 'You know the ones, just outside the town centre? From the outside they look quite small, door in the middle, bay windows either side, and three windows above, but they're surprisingly big inside. There's six bedsits in there, and they all share the bathroom and kitchen. There might even be an extra toilet downstairs.'

'I don't think that recommendation is sufficient for me to want to uproot myself there, even with the extra toilet,' he said caustically, weary of listening to her witterings.

The main police laboratory was attached to the forensic science unit of the university in the neighbouring town, forty miles away. Normally he would have enjoyed this drive; he always regarded driving time as quiet thinking time. But he refused to enjoy anything in Michelle Grady's company.

'I only spoke to the man who lives in the bedsit next-door to Rosie Twyford's,' Michelle continued courageously, refusing to be intimidated by his response. 'But, as he said, the walls are quite thin, so if she'd returned *after* last Monday he would have heard her.'

'Did you think to ask him if she had any friends she might have been staying with?' he demanded abruptly.

'Not exactly,' she answered hesitantly. 'Well he did say, that Rosie'd only moved in three months ago, I checked the date,' she digressed, 'and it ties in with her discharge from Compton Castle.'

'And in all of three months she never once stayed out all night?'

'I didn't think to ask him that.'

'You wouldn't,' Collins snapped unkindly.

She fell silent, and he caught sight of her bottom lip quivering as he turned a sharp corner, but he felt no remorse for giving her a hard time. Quite the contrary. If she wanted to be a copper, then she had to get used to everything her superior officers were likely to throw at her. If she couldn't cut it along with the rest of them, then she'd have to find another career; one more suited to a girl who needed nannying.

He slowed down, signalled and took a slip-road off the motorway, turning into the network of narrow suburban streets that surrounded the town centre. Mindful that she may be asked to visit this place alone sometime, Michelle tried to follow his route, but he took turning after turning, delving deeper and deeper into a mixture of 1930s and 1950s housing, until she began to wonder if he was deliberately following an unnecessarily complicated route in order to confuse her.

Eventually he pulled up in a car park that fronted a huge red-brick, flat-fronted block set with steel casement windows. A sign outside declared it to be UNIVERSITY ANNEX B.

'We're here,' Collins announced gruffly. 'As soon as you step out, I'll lock the car and put the alarm on.'

Michelle jumped out so quickly she jarred her ankle, but she would have sooner died than admit to feeling pain in front of Peter Collins. Then she stood back, allowing him to lead the way through the double doors and into the lobby. As she'd expected he made no concessions to her sex, not even checking to see if she was behind him as he pressed the lift button.

The police laboratory was situated on the top floor and, like in the mortuary, the smell of rotting flesh was overwhelming. They noticed it the moment the lift doors opened. Collins made no comment as he pressed the bell for attention, but he took grim pleasure in the sight of Michelle O'Grady fumbling in her handbag. For one brief, luxurious moment the heady smell of musky perfume overcame all the other odours, but its supremacy was short-lived. As soon as the door to the laboratory opened, a foul stench – choking, breath-taking – engulfed his senses once more.

The first thing he noticed was the dog laid out in all its putrefying glory on a steel-topped table, which was strategic-ally placed beneath a window in the far wall. On two other tables were the suitcases and the handbags. All the hard surfaces were covered with a thin grey film of fingerprint powder.

'Collins, isn't it?' A white-coated, grey-haired man nodded to Peter. 'Recognise you from that last drugs haul. You may not remember me. Thomas is the name. Phil Thomas.'

'I remember you.' Collins looked carefully at Thomas's hand before shaking it. With so much muck around these laboratories, you never could be too careful.

'How's life on the Drug Squad?' Thomas continued.

'Wish I knew,' Collins moaned. 'Been seconded to Serious Crimes.'

'Dan Evans' lot?'

'That's the one.'

'And this is?' Thomas turned and smiled at Michelle.

'Grady,' she held out her hand awkwardly, wondering how long she could last without breathing. She was certain that the moment she took a deep breath, she'd throw up. 'Michelle Grady,' she shook his hand, but without subjecting it to the same scrutiny that Collins had.

'New I take it?' Phil Thomas asked her.

She nodded. 'Does it show?'

'Only the eagerness,' he smiled. 'Old hands like Sergeant Collins here are never eager about anything, even their days off.'

'Seen it all before,' Peter muttered laconically, wishing the old bore would spare a thought to those who hadn't grown accustomed to the foul atmosphere around him, and get on with it.

'Well I've not come up with anything that's going to startle you.' Thomas walked over to the tables holding the handbags and suitcases. We've been through this little lot with a fine-tooth comb; got all the prints we could find. Only two sets I'm afraid; one matches one case and handbag, and the other matches the second set, so the chances are these belong to the two victims. Here's a list of contents found in both sets of cases and handbags. Nothing that a girl wouldn't take with her on holiday. Selection of under and top clothes – hairdrier in one, so she couldn't have been about to fly off anywhere . . .'

'Of course,' Michelle said brightly, 'no electrical goods are allowed in the luggage holds of aircraft.' Collins gave her a tired look and she fell silent.

'There's a nurse's uniform, belt with silver buckle, and a couple of nurses' textbooks in one of the cases. There's a driving licence in the better of the two handbags, for an Elizabeth

Moore, twenty-four years old. Also a couple of certificates carefully rolled into a tube at the bottom of the bag; they identify her as a State Registered Nurse. Prescription in the second handbag for tranquillisers made out to a C. Moon. No address, but there's a Compton Castle stamp. If she was an inmate, you should be able to track her down through hospital records.'

'I'll get to work on it right away.' Collins felt as though another minute in this close, fetid atmosphere would suffocate him.

'Feel free to take away whatever you want. I'll get one of the lads to help you with the suitcases. And here . . .' he handed Peter a sheet of paper.

'What's this?' Collins asked, squinting at the almost illegible scribble that covered the page.

'Report on the dog. Sorry, our typist's sick and we don't rate a replacement. I thought you'd rather have it as it is, and get someone to type it up in the Station. Nostrils, upper part of the lungs and air passages filled with dirt. Traces of curare in the bloodstream. I'd say it had been drugged and buried alive.'

Peter paused in the doorway. 'You sure about that.'

'You questioning my professionalism?'

'No, it's just that . . .'

'What, Sergeant Collins?' Phil Thomas demanded, suddenly icy.

'I wonder why the hell someone would go to all the trouble of killing a dog in exactly the same way they've murdered women.'

'That's for you to find out,' Thomas said with a glimmer of a smile. 'I've done my bit. Now it's your turn.'

Trevor hesitated at the entrance to the long perspex tunnel that connected his ward to the main hospital building. He paced up and down a few times, debating whether to turn around and go out into the garden. The grounds might have been a pleasant option if there weren't so many people there he knew; rookies and older colleagues that he'd worked with . . .

He turned on his heel and walked quickly back to the security of his own room. Panting, out of breath, he fumbled with the door handle while he pondered for an excuse to cover his actions. His wallet – that was it. If he was going as far as the old hospital, he might as well keep going. Walk to the main gate, and wait for a bus. Go into town get his hair cut. And if he took his wallet and his credit cards, maybe even buy some clothes.

He opened the bedside cabinet drawer and extricated his wallet, then he pulled opened his wardrobe door and removed his grubby anorak. Slipping it on over his shirt, he stuffed the wallet into his inside pocket. He stood before the closed door leading into the corridor, and held his breath. It was simple; all he had to do was open it, walk down the tunnel and he'd be right in the main building, close to the police HQ. It was that simple.

He jerked the door open, hitting his thumb painfully as the handle sprang back into his hand. Looking neither left nor right, he walked straight ahead, to the end of the corridor and, like a diver plunging recklessly into a deep pool, he set foot in the tunnel. He took one step, then another, then another . . . until he merely walked on blindly and mechanically.

As the white walls and floor closed around him, he fought a sensation of panic that threatened to overwhelm him. Wiping clammy hands down the sides of his jeans, he took a deep breath. Letting the air out of his lungs slowly, he forced another breath. Provided he kept going, one step at a time, it wouldn't take him that long. Patients and nurses walked this way every day, without thinking anything of it. Closing his eyes to narrow slits against the blinding white glare, he drove himself forwards. He heard footsteps echoing behind him, and jumped to the side of the tunnel, his heart juddering loudly, painfully, in his chest.

'Hi, Trevor.' Karl Lane walked past, a bundle of files tucked beneath his arm.

'Hi,' Trevor managed to whisper, what seemed like an eternity after Karl had moved on. He stood pressed against the side of the tunnel, his eyes closed, until he could no longer hear Karl's footsteps. Only then did he move hesitantly into the centre of the tunnel again. One step, then another, then another. Repeated again and again and again . . .

'Sergeant Joseph,' Sarah Merchant, a constable who usually

worked in the computer room at the Station, greeted him as he emerged into the grand hall of the main building.

Trevor wiped sticky hands over his sweating brow and looked at her.

'It's good to see you up and around, sir,' she said quietly, keeping any thoughts she might have about his sickly, emaciated appearance to herself.

'Thank you, Constable Merchant,' Trevor said, attempting to conceal his panic behind a brusque, businesslike facade. 'Is Sergeant Collins around?'

'I haven't seen him this morning, sir, but Inspector Evans and Superintendent Mulcahy are in the mobile HQ. Would you like me to fetch them?'

Before she had a chance to walk over and knock at the door of the makeshift unit, Dan Evans jumped down from the van and called out to Trevor.

'You've saved us a trip,' he called heartily. 'We were just on our way to see you. Come in.'

He opened the door wide and ushered Trevor into the mobile unit. Trevor immediately recognised his surroundings. The overflowing ashtrays, the scattering of dirty coffee mugs, the bins crammed full of takeaway food wrappings; typewritten papers and reports strewn from one end of the van to the other, and piles of tabloid newspapers badly folded and stacked in the corner, all with their page-three girls uppermost.

'Coffee?' Dan thrust a mug at him, and Trevor took it, not because he wanted a drink but because it gave him something to do with his hands.

'You look better today, Joseph,' Bill Mulcahy commented tactlessly.

It was on the tip of Trevor's tongue to say he didn't feel any better, but then he realised that whining would get him nowhere with Mulcahy, especially when everyone else on the force was working flat-out to solve a difficult case. Instead he said the first thing that came into his head.

'Thought I'd go into town and get my hair cut.' He could have kicked himself. Now he was committed to going into the town, when it had already taken all the strength and effort he possessed to get him this far.

'Good idea. You look like a stray sheepdog,' Bill agreed.

'I wanted to see you,' Trevor began hesitantly, 'because something occurred to me when I was eating breakfast this morning.' Realising just how ridiculous he must sound, he paused and looked at the others, but they were all clearly waiting for him to continue. 'It's Vanessa Hedley; she's been telling all the other patients that she managed to get a good long look at the killer.'

'Has she now?' Mulcahy stroked his stubbled chin pensively.

'And I thought . . . I thought,' Trevor stammered, succumbing to yet another panic attack. He was now back where he had been before his accident; working with Serious Crimes, mixed up in a murder investigation he wanted no part of. He could get hurt again – killed even this time. Feeling faint and nauseous, he slumped forward and stared at the floor.

'Being a detective you thought that, if the killer was anywhere within earshot, Vanessa Hedley's not going to live very much longer,' Dan Evans finished for him, following his thought.

'That's about the size of it.' Trevor was grateful that he didn't have to say more.

'Thank you for warning us.'

'What exactly did she say?'

'She gave no useful description,' Trevor said. 'Certainly nothing you could use. She said it was a huge, enormous figure. Black hair . . .'

'Which could have been a hood, or even a balaclava if he'd been wearing a coat,' Evans broke in.

'And evil eyes.'

'Evil eyes?' Dan exchanged glances with Mulcahy. 'That's a new one.'

'I was watching two policemen from my bedroom window this morning as they walked around the flowerbed where the first body was found,' Trevor murmured. 'I couldn't even make out their features let alone see their eyes.'

'Are you saying that she didn't see anything?'

'No.' Trevor gripped the edge of the padded bench. He was finding it a tremendous strain to talk to Evans and Mulcahy. He'd forgotten just how cynical policemen were. And he was left with the uncomfortable feeling that neither believed a single word he was telling them. 'She must have seen something; the finding of the body confirms that. All I'm saying is that I doubt she could have seen his features from that distance.'

'Unless he walked right up to her window?' Mulcahy suggested.

'Or, unless she already knew who he was,' Dan suggested softly.

Chapter Nine

Vanessa Hedley's attentive audience did not desert her that morning. Roland Williams, Michael Carpenter, Lucy Craig and Alison Bevan dogged her shadow from breakfast onwards, to therapy classes, then outside into the garden during the staff coffee break. Their excursion into the garden was the most noticeable deviation from normal behaviour. Spencer Jordan watched from his room as they followed Vanessa in gabbling, single file, as she guided them on a tour of the flowerbeds. These were now being painstakingly reinstated to their former glory by an angry, noisy Jimmy Herne, who was commanding his two YTS boys as though he were directing opposing army battalions through a series of complicated military manoeuvres.

'I know Harry's always on to us to get our charges interested in something, dear boy,' Adam Hayter lisped as he left his therapy unit to stand next to Spencer. 'But I think he'd draw the line at gruesome murder, don't you?'

'Probably,' Spencer murmured, not really listening to what Adam was burbling on about. He was nursing the foulest, most dreadful hangover within the realms of memory, and had already promised himself seven times that morning that he would never, never, allow alcohol in any shape or form to pass his lips again.

'I must say though,' Adam Hayter chattered on, cheerfully ignoring Spencer's uncommunicative silences, 'it's certainly made the little darlings a lot easier to deal with. They're far too busy gossiping and whispering amongst themselves to even think of going bonzo bananas. And I actually found the time to make a nice lamb stew for Dotty and me tonight in my first class this morning. And that, darling, simply isn't normal.'

133

'What isn't normal?' Nurse Sullivan asked, as she walked into the room.

'It isn't normal for our sweeties to be so quiet,' Hayter purred, eyeing her lasciviously. 'Look at the little angels! Just look at them hanging on to Vanessa's every gory word. What is it about murder that excites everyone so?'

'I'm damned if I know!' Spencer exploded savagely, turning his back to the window. 'Is there anything I can do for you, Adam?' he enquired harshly.

'I came to borrow the tinsiest, tiniest choccy biccy,' Adam smirked sheepishly, his diffident smile carefully calculated to bring out his dimples.

'Help yourself. You know where I keep them.' Spencer nodded towards the top drawer of his desk.

'Thank you, darling. And you won't tell Dotty, will you?' When Spencer didn't answer his question, Adam helped himself to three of the biscuits, and skipped quickly out the door.

'It isn't often the wind blows you down here, Lyn. Can I do something for you?' Spencer asked bluntly.

'I came down to beg a favour,' she began warily. Spencer was generally more even-tempered than any of the other staff in Compton Castle, including Harry Goldman, who saw it as part of his duty to remain calm through everything fate, the authorities or the patients threw at him. She'd never seen Spencer Jordan in this mood before, so instinctively she trod carefully. 'They've finally fitted a bolt to the inside of the drug cupboard. Trouble is, somehow or other they managed to strip most of the paint from the outside of the door at the same time, and it draws attention to the one place we'd like to keep low-profile. So I wondered if you had any white paint to spare. It doesn't have to be gloss. Anything will do to patch it in, until maintenance gets around to re-painting it. You know how long they take.'

'I do,' he commented drily. 'If you can wait, I'll take a look for you at lunch time.'

'I'm on split shift today, but if I'm not there, Jean will be around.'

'Fine,' he murmured absently, picking up his coffee and returning to his window.

* * *

134

Boycotting the perspex tunnels, Lyn Sullivan walked the long way round from the therapy units as she returned to her ward. She noted that Spencer Jordan wasn't the only one watching the patients take their unaccustomed constitutionals in the hospital grounds. Dotty Clyne and Harry Goldman were also studying the group gathered around Vanessa, from the psychiatrist's office window. And she saw Tony Waters glance their way as he talked to one of the senior police officers in the drive. She only hoped that all this attention wouldn't send Vanessa Hedley over the edge again.

Vanessa finished her tour of the gardens, and returned to the therapy block. Basking in the unfamiliar glow of attention and flattery, she even began to flirt mildly with Roland Williams. As she continued to wander through the corridors and rooms of Compton Castle, she was totally unaware of all but the most obvious of glances and comments that came her way.

But amongst those watching was someone who did not seek to cajole more information out of Vanessa. Someone who walked discreetly down the corridors, someone who stood outside the open door of the therapy rooms as Vanessa continued to excite her audience with gripping first-hand stories of the live burial in the grounds.

A frown creased a previously smooth forehead. It didn't matter that Vanessa's story owed more to horror-film dialogue than to reality. Too much was being said, and submerged in the ramblings lay the kernels of truths that could not be allowed to take root and sprout. But what needed doing could not be done immediately. Now was daylight, people – far too many people. Later, when darkness fell, when there were fewer staff on duty, when the wards were quieter – and Vanessa was sleepy from the increased prescription of tranquillisers she'd proudly announced to all and sundry that were to be administered to help her recover from her traumatic experiences. Later – no one would notice anyone slipping from one quiet room to another . . . later . . . it would have to be later . . . but not too late to prevent Vanessa Hedley from spending yet another day saying far too much.

*   *   *

Trevor Joseph stood outside the mobile police headquarters. He leant heavily on his stick and shivered, as the fresh spring breeze penetrated the thin denim of his worn jeans and his totally inadequate, shabby anorak. He wanted to rush back up the drive as fast as his shaky legs would carry him, to the safe, warm, familiar confines of his own room. But Dan Evans was standing next to him, prolonging his leave-taking, making it obvious that he had no intention, yet, of leaving him alone.

'I'll walk with you to the gate,' Dan offered, as he again sensed Trevor's attention wandering.

'That's not necessary,' Trevor replied abruptly, sensitive to the hint that he wasn't capable of getting anywhere by himself.

'I know,' Dan laughed shortly. 'But I want to see the officer on gate duty, to check the names of everyone who visited this morning. We're trying to establish a pattern for the whole hospital. To find out exactly who –'

'Comes in, and who goes out, at certain times of the day. In other words, the people we can expect to find within these walls at any given time,' Trevor finished for him.

'That's about the size of it,' Dan said good-temperedly. 'I'd forgotten you'd worked with Serious Crimes before.'

'Not often,' Trevor conceded.

'You didn't enjoy the experience?'

'I was used to the Drugs Squad.'

It was close to the staff lunchtime, and the first shift of nurses, doctors and therapists were walking through the gardens towards the staff dining-room in the old hospital.

'*That's* interesting,' Dan mused as he stood monitoring the groups as they walked through the side door of the main building.

'What?' Trevor demanded, irritably.

'The staff. If you look at them, they're all walking through the grounds. Every one I've spoken to, doctors, nurses, even Tony Waters, they all say how useful those tunnels are, yet not one of them appears to ever use them.'

'Can you blame them?'

'No,' Evans smiled. 'I don't know about you, but those shiny white corridors give me the creeps. It's like a poor man's film version of the road to heaven.'

* * *

'Inspector!' The young constable manning the gate jumped stiffly to attention.

'You've met Sergeant Joseph?' Evans introduced Trevor.

'Haven't had the pleasure, sir.' The rookie nodded to Trevor.

'I'll be on my way then, Dan,' Trevor said awkwardly, moving slowly on. If Dan hadn't been right behind him, he would have turned round there and then. But as he limped past the barrier and through the enormous main gates, he sensed Evans' eyes boring into the back of his head, just waiting for him to turn and run.

Fortunately the bus stop was just outside, and when he reached its dubious, single-sided shelter, he rested on his stick and turned, glancing back at Evans. He realised then that the eyes had existed only in his imagination. Dan was standing with his back to him, and it was the constable who now faced him, but even his attention was fixed solely on Dan. Neither of them evinced the slightest interest in him, or his doings.

He stared ahead at the grey expanse of road and pavement, at the trees fringing the small park across from the hospital, their delicate new leaves wavering in the wind. An old man walked towards him, leading a tired old spaniel. The man touched his hat and nodded to Trevor as he passed, his manners a relic from another, politer age.

He'd made it! He was outside the gates. The enormity of this suddenly hit Trevor full force. Spencer Jordan had warned him that it might take days, if not weeks, before he got this far. Yet here he was at the bus stop, only one day away from the shivering panic attack that had driven him back into his room from the door leading out of his block. He glanced at his watch; it was nearly two o'clock. He stared down the road. Cars were streaming past with noisy regularity, but no buses. How long had it been since he'd last sat on a bus? Ten years? Maybe longer? He hadn't even thought to ask how often they passed by the hospital, and there wasn't a timetable in sight. Perhaps he should walk back? At least as far as the porter on gate duty.

A small, bright red car drove out of the gates and pulled up in front of the bus stop. Nurse Sullivan reached over and opened the passenger door.

137

'Going into town?'

'I was thinking of it,' he admitted uneasily.

'Hop in. I'll give you a lift.'

'There's no need . . .'

'Don't be silly. The buses only run every half-hour, and you've just missed one. Can't you tell? You're the only one waiting here.'

Trevor hobbled hesitantly forward. Pushing his stick into the back seat of the car, he held on to the door and climbed clumsily into the passenger seat.

'I'm working a split shift today,' she explained. 'And I really hate split shifts. So I thought I'd go into town and spend some money to cheer myself up.' She slammed the car into gear and pulled off sharply, cutting in behind a fast-moving Mercedes.

'Won the pools?' he asked, after racking his brains for something to say. Had he always found making light conversation this difficult? He tried to remember the people he'd talked to regularly before his accident – and what he'd said to them.

'No,' she smiled. 'My twenty-first birthday.'

'Congratulations.'

'You're a bit late; it was last week. And my parents, not knowing what else to give me, sent me a cheque. I intend to buy a whole new wardrobe,' she beamed. 'An utterly extravagant and up-to-the-minute wardrobe,' she stressed. 'It hasn't been much fun trying to live on a student nurse's money for the last three years.'

'It couldn't have been,' he agreed mechanically.

'But hopefully all that struggling will soon be over with.'

'You've sat your finals?'

'Three weeks ago.' She held up her hand, fingers crossed.

'You'll pass,' Trevor said firmly.

'I wish I had your confidence. But tell me, where are you off to? To buy a new wardrobe as well?'

'I was just thinking of getting my hair cut,' he murmured. 'But you're right, I do need a whole new wardrobe. From the state of what I'm wearing, desperately.'

'I'm sorry, I didn't mean it that way,' she blushed. 'It must have sounded dreadful; really patronising. I really am sorry . . .'

'Forget it.' It was most peculiar, but her embarrassment only served to put him at his ease, and increase his confidence.

'After searching through the selection of clothes that Peter brought up from my flat, I've come to the conclusion that either he rummaged through my ragbag, or all of my clothes should be relegated to one.'

'He probably just didn't want to bring your best clothes into hospital.'

'I've never had best clothes,' he admitted wryly. 'Undercover work for the Drug Squad called for the jumble sale reject variety, and I don't think I ever used to go to any place that called for much else.'

'I can't imagine someone not taking any interest in their clothes.'

He stared out of the car window, and checked off the familiar landmarks as they passed by. They were travelling through the east side of town, eventually reaching the suburb where he had bought his flat. Was that really only eight years ago? Somehow it seemed much longer, almost as if it had taken place in another lifetime. Someone else's, not his own. He and his one time girlfriend Mags had bought the place together, although he had paid for it. She had always balked at anything that wasn't frivolous; entertainments, clothes, relationships – especially relationships. But, then, he and Mags had been over and done with for a long time. Strange, he'd been completely devastated when she'd left his flat and his life, to move in with a married man who'd deserted his wife. Now he could barely remember what she'd looked like. Yet they'd been together for six years; longer than some marriages, and long enough for him to come to hate the flat, the decor, the furniture, the fitted kitchen and even the fancy Persian cat, all chosen by Mags and all abandoned by her when she'd moved on.

He'd been lucky in managing to rent out the place, furniture, fittings, cat and all, to another copper. He could see it now; set high on the hill that towered above the town. That had been its major attraction; the magnificent view over the whole of the town, and the bay, beyond.

Trevor envisaged the flat he'd lived in since; its scruffy, poky collection of small rooms over Frank's minimarket in the old, neglected Victorian dock area. The unfashionable end that the town planners hadn't even considered when they'd designed and built the new Marina.

'Where do you want to be dropped off?'

Confused, he turned and looked sideways at Lyn. Lost in thought, he'd completely forgotten that she was driving him.

'Sorry, I was miles away. Did you say something?'

'I was asking where you wanted to be dropped off.'

'Anywhere. It really doesn't matter.'

'Of course it does. If you want to get your hair cut, then the only possible place is that new unisex salon on the Marina. *They* really have some idea of style there.'

'Your family own it?'

'No.' She laughed. 'But I approve of the results that walk out of there. And, incidentally, my brother does patronise the place. But he's not a hairdresser; he's an accountant. Like my father.'

'Then you have your hair cut there?'

'No. There's no point. Mine's so long, all I do is trim the ends once a month with my nail scissors.'

'Well, as I have nowhere else in mind, I'll take you up on that suggestion.'

'And if it really is clothes you're after, then you'll want to go to one of the men's shops in Main Arcade.'

'I will?'

'I'm sorry, I should have warned you, shopping is something of a passion with me.'

'I'm beginning to find that out.'

'I must sound terribly shallow.'

'No?' He smiled at her, and she smiled back. Seeing her outside the hospital environment for the first time, she looked a lot younger than her twenty-one years. Perhaps it was the change of scene. Driving into town, and chatting casually, had put their relationship on a different footing to that of nurse and patient. Somehow, somewhere on the journey she had lost whatever authority she held over him. Her appearance helped. Her clean, clear skin was devoid of make-up, she was wearing the same jeans and sweater she had worn at breakfast, and she now looked about sixteen.

140

'My mother's a complete shopaholic,' she continued apologetically. 'As a child she taught me that daddys make the money and the women in the family spend it. I'm afraid she ingrained some pretty bad habits into me from an early age, but now I curb my shopping expeditions to splurges at birthdays and Christmas. And I always buy my father and brother clothes in those small shops in the arcade. The cut on their trousers and jeans are always superb, and the sweaters, especially the hand-knitted ones, are very good. Here I go rabbiting on again.' She smiled defensively.

'I don't mind. Really.'

'Really?'

'At the moment I find it easier to listen than make the effort to talk.'

'That will soon change, believe me. Look, if you really are intent on shopping, why don't I at least show you where those shops are. I don't want to be pushy, but . . .'

'I look like a scarecrow.'

'I didn't say that.'

'No, I did,' he said easily. 'And if you show me where the shops are, then at least I'll know where to look.'

She parked her car in the multi-storey car park on the fringes of the pedestrianised area, and waited while he lugged first his stick, then himself out of the car. She slowed her pace to his as they walked towards the town centre.

'Here's the arcade.' She paused outside its entrance, sandwiched between two large department stores. 'And those are the boutiques. That one with the purple sign is the best. But whatever you do,' she lowered her voice to a whisper, 'don't go to the hairdresser here. It has to be the one on the Marina.'

'I'll remember.'

'See you.'

She disappeared into the nearest boutique. It had a window display of feminine lingerie that brought a burst of colour to his cheeks and made him step away quickly the minute he realised what he was staring at. He could almost hear Collins' jeering laugh, the one he reserved for pathetic old men reduced to ogling women's underclothes in shop windows.

Feeling rather lost and forlorn, he gazed up and down the

arcade. One of the better things about a midweek afternoon was a half empty town. Taking Lyn's advice, he steeled himself and passed through the doorway of the shop she'd recommended.

Inside he was faced with a bewildering array of racks all crammed with clothing. That closest to him held jeans, above it hung sweaters, and beyond were rows of trousers and shirts.

'Can I be of any assistance, sir?' The boy was young and anxious to please. No owner, Trevor guessed, but an employee working on commission.

'I'm just looking,' he murmured diffidently.

'If there's anything I can do to help, please ask.' The boy retreated behind a counter.

Trevor flicked through the jeans rack. They were cut differently to the ones he remembered, and they all had buttons instead of zips. He held up a pair, chosen at random, realising he didn't even know any more what size he was.

'They won't fit you, sir. Those are a thirty-six waist. I'd say you were a thirty or thirty-two,' the boy hazarded. Trevor replaced them on the rack. He'd been a thirty-six inch waist before he'd been injured. He realised he'd lost weight; but that much?

'If you'd like to try these, sir? They're the same style, but more in your size.'

In the event, buying a new wardrobe was simpler than he had expected. The shop remained quiet, and he was the only customer, so he had the undivided attention of the assistant, who managed to tread the difficult line between helpfulness and pushiness without ever coming down on the latter side. Trevor found that the jeans fitted, so he picked up a second pair. He flicked through the sweaters and found two he liked. He wandered over to the racks of trousers, and bought two pairs of those, a couple of casual shirts, a new jacket to replace the worn-out grubby antique he was wearing. An hour and a half later, the dust had been blown off one of his credit cards, he had a bundle of carrier bags to manage, and the clothes he had worn into the shop were stuffed in a bin at the back of the arcade. As he limped out, the handles of the bags cut into the fingers of one hand, while he gripped his stick in the other.

Outside the shop, he paused and looked down at his ragged fabric trainers. Two doors up the arcade he spotted a shoe shop. There he picked out two pairs of smart, designer trainers, and two pairs of good leather shoes. Unable to decide between their various merits, he bought all four pairs and, discarding the shoes he was wearing, left the shop wearing a pair of new trainers.

Feeling totally and utterly exhausted, he spent a few moments assessing exactly where he was in the town. Remembering a taxi rank at the end of a cul-de-sac, he took a short cut through one of the stores. He hobbled slowly forward, smiling at the memory of chasing a drug dealer through the same store's crowded aisles one Saturday afternoon. At that precise moment he wasn't even capable of chasing a small child up a blind alley.

The department store, like the arcade, was blessedly free from crowds. But as he staggered along between the aisles, he bumped into an old woman who put her head down and scuttled away warily. As he glanced after her, he realised that he wasn't alone in feeling afraid. There were others, like that old woman, who felt terrified every time they set about the simple everyday tasks of life: shopping, walking down the street to pay the paper bill, even opening the front door to the milkman. So perhaps he wasn't so different from the rest of humanity after all.

He stopped at the menswear counter and examined some boxer shorts and socks. Juggling with his bags and his stick, he tried to pick up a pair of shorts, but only succeeded in dropping everything he was holding. A young assistant came to his rescue. She picked up his stick, returned his carrier bags to his numbed fingers, and packed the garments that he chose. He almost fell into the cab when he reached the taxi rank.

The hairdresser that Lyn had recommended proved easy to find. He left his parcels gratefully at the desk as he asked for an appointment. Luckily George was free. George who turned out to be huge, and burly, was covered in tattoos and proved incredibly camp, and chatty. Too tired to cope with his banter, Trevor was content to relinquish himself into George's care, close his eyes and listen to an ongoing diatribe against the town councillors, who apparently had an unjustified prejudice against bikers.

His hair, according to George, when he interrupted his railings, was out of shape, out of condition, and would disgrace the head of a shaggy sheepdog. If nothing else, George certainly knew how to take his time over cutting and shaping. A gopher brought Trevor coffee, strong and black, the way he used to drink it before hospitals had regulated his life.

'There you are, sir.' Trevor opened his eyes and scarcely recognised the face that stared back from the mirror. With his hair cut fashionably short at the back and sides, and long at the top, he was seeing himself in an entirely new light. One that he wasn't too sure he liked.

'I've left it a bit longer here,' George pulled on a few strands above Trevor's left ear, 'to hide the scars. They look rather nasty. Accident?'

'Sort of,' Trevor replied brusquely. But it wasn't just the sight of the scars that wound their way up as far as his left temple; it was the bloodless lips, the thin face, the sunken cheeks.

'Will there be anything else, sir? We do a nice range of toiletries and aftershave.'

'I'll take a look.' He was beginning to understand Lyn Sullivan's comments about shopaholics. There was something comforting about spending money; as if the new image he was buying for himself was sufficient in itself to change his entire life.

He added a carrier bag of cologne and toiletries to his collection, and limped outside. The clock on the bell-tower of the Marina struck five. A pub loomed enticingly before him; a blackboard outside bore the inviting slogan: HOME-COOKED PUB FOOD AVAILABLE ALL DAY. He realised he hadn't eaten anything since the toast he'd shared with Lyn Sullivan early that morning.

Trevor stumbled across the cobblestones and went into the pub. It was nearly empty; just a couple of middle-aged women who were sitting as far away as possible from an old man who was the only other customer.

He ordered himself a pint, and a large steak with chips and

salad. It had been a long time since he'd tasted steak. And Spencer Jordan was right; it had been the first step that was the hardest to take. But now he'd actually got going, he felt capable of tackling almost anything.

His mouth watered at the prospect of the steak. He downed his pint and ordered another. Life wasn't so bad after all. Why had he waited this long to pick up the threads?

Chapter Ten

'Does the name Elizabeth Moore mean anything to you?' Walking past two upright stacking chairs, Inspector Dan Evans sat in the one comfortable seat Tony Waters' office offered apart from the administrator's own. Dan looked up expectantly, waiting for an answer.

'She used to be a staff nurse here.'

Dan thought he saw the same flicker of interest in Waters' eyes that he had noticed when Rosie Twyford's name was first mentioned. He decided it was just as well that Peter Collins was away delving through the staff records.

'When and why did she leave?'

'She left about ...' Waters thought for a moment, 'three months ago, but that is only a guess, I'd have to check the records for a precise date. She'd accepted a nursing post in America. We were sorry to see her go, but that's life in British hospitals at the moment, I'm afraid. Pay and conditions, particularly for psychiatric nurses, are much better in the States than here. Why do you ask?'

'Because we have reason to believe that one of the bodies we dug up last night was Elizabeth Moore.'

'No!'

The cry carried more than the shock or surprise Dan would have expected from an administrator learning the tragic fate of a staff member. There was something deeper in it ... something personal. Dan looked forward to hearing what Collins would have to say. The sergeant had a reputation for uncovering dirt on people.

'We have reason to believe that the other victim dug up last night was ...' Evans consulted the information Constable Michelle Grady had so carefully written out. 'Claire Moon.

And we believe that she was once a patient here.'

Just then Tony Waters' secretary, Angela Morgan, walked into the room and laid a tray of coffee, milk and sugar on his desk.

'We also found the corpse of a dog,' Dan revealed, glancing at Michelle's list while still watching Waters carefully over the edge of the page. 'Large, hairy, breed unknown. Grey dog with white at the tips of its fur . . .'

The secretary jerked her hand just as she was spooning sugar into Evans' cup, and knocked it over. 'I'm sorry,' she cried, rushing into the outer office in search of paper towels. 'But that sounds just like Honey Boy – doesn't it, Mr Waters?'

Evans glanced from the secretary to her boss. There was a pained expression on Waters' face, but it was difficult to determine whether it had been prompted by the spilled coffee that had soaked the papers in his in-tray, or the news of two more girls found buried in the grounds, or the dog.

'May I ask who owned Honey Boy?' Evans asked the secretary.

'No one. That was the problem. You must remember Honey Boy, Mr Waters?'

'Of course I do,' he answered irritably.

'He practically lived in this office last winter, Inspector Evans,' Angela prattled nervously. 'He was a stray, and turned up in the grounds starving, without a collar. We rang the pound, but they said if they took him in and he wasn't claimed within a few days, they'd put him down. Well it isn't as if this is a proper hospital that needs to be sterile or anything, so we kept him for a while. We all chipped in with food, and . . .' She dissolved into tears.

'And I'd just decided to take him home with me.'

'Home?' Dan eyed Waters quizzically.

'I live on a farm. I already own two large dogs, so another one wouldn't have made that much difference.'

'Then he disappeared.' Tears were trickling down Angela's cheeks. 'We searched everywhere for him, but assumed that he'd gone back to wherever he came from. It was a shame, because Mr Waters would have given him such a good home. I tried to persuade my husband to take him in, but we live in a flat on the Marina. It's not very big, and he was such a large dog. We also have two cats . . .'

'Angela, could you go down to personnel and pull Elizabeth Moore's file for me. Then could you give Patients' Records a ring and ask them to send up the file of someone called Claire Moon. You shouldn't have any problem. I doubt we get that many Moons.'

'I'll do that, sir.' She dabbed her eyes with a crumpled tissue that she pulled from her pocket, and left the room.

'Efficient secretary but a bit overemotional,' Waters declared. Dan almost expected him to add "It's her time of life."

'You must have hundreds of patients passing through here in a year,' he commented.

'Somewhere in the region of five thousand,' Waters admitted. 'The numbers are about average for a town of this size.'

'And you remember Claire Moon?'

'Yes.'

'I wasn't aware that you had much contact with the patients, Mr Waters.'

'Normally I don't. But the colour supplement of one of the better Sunday papers did a feature on her while she was here, and I monitored the interviews at the request of the Health Authority.'

'Worried about adverse publicity?'

'Concerned about misrepresentation,' Waters rectified precisely. 'Claire's father is Arnold Moon.'

'The businessman?'

'If you can call a multi-millionaire a businessman. Yes. She came to this town to go to university, went off the rails and discovered drugs. She was in here for drug and alcohol addiction, and if I remember rightly she made quite spectacular progress.'

'And where did she go when she left here?'

'She intended to visit her mother's home in Spain. Her parents divorced some years ago, and her mother remarried a Spanish hotelier.'

'No one contacted you to say that she never arrived there?'

149

'I'd have to check on that with Angela. We frequently have letters from the families of ex-patients, trying to get in touch with them. It's quite common for voluntary psychiatric patients to discharge themselves and then go missing. You of all people should know that, Inspector. Some of them must end up on police missing-persons files.'

'Was Claire Moon a voluntary patient?' Evans meant to keep the line of questioning firmly on his own track, not on Waters.

'Possibly. I'd have to check. The chances are, with drug addiction, that she would have been.'

Evans rose from his chair. 'When the files arrive, would you be good enough to send them over to our mobile HQ? And I'd be grateful if you'd keep the identities of the victims a secret for the moment. Not Rosie Twyford, of course. Her mother is coming up this afternoon to identify the corpse. But Elizabeth Moore and Claire Moon. We're in the process of contacting their families now.'

'Of course.'

Dan hesitated in the doorway for a moment. 'I don't suppose *you'd* be able to identify them for us?' he asked casually.

'I don't think I'd be the best person,' Waters answered quickly. 'I met Claire Moon only a few times, and I can barely remember Elizabeth Moore.'

'On second thoughts, perhaps identification is best left to their families,' Evans said quietly as he closed the door behind him.

Superintendent Bill Mulcahy stood in front of an enormous white board which was pinned to the rear wall of the mobile headquarters. He glanced around at the twenty or so men and women crammed into the tiny space around him.

'Everyone here?' he barked. No one dared to comment on the absurdity of the question. 'Right, we'll start with the victims. Constable Grady?'

He relinquished the centre spot to Michelle, who stood stiffly to attention in her immaculately brushed uniform, and ostentatiously consulted her notes.

'First victim we found, and the last in chronological order of death, was Rosie Twyford.' She pointed to a large blown-up photograph of Rosie that had been printed off one found in the hospital files. It was pinned to the top of the board.

'Blonde hair, blue eyes, five foot six inches tall, heavily built, twelve stone, attractive and twenty-five years old. She suffered from clinical depression. She had previously worked in the old hospital, in the administration department, but after a particularly severe bout of illness was admitted as an in-patient. Rosie was discharged as an inmate six weeks ago, but continued to attend an out patient clinic. Her psychiatrist was Dorothy Clyne. Rosie was discharged from the clinic last Monday, and as yet we haven't found anyone who remembers seeing her between the time she left Ms Clyne's office on Monday afternoon and the time she was dug out of the flowerbed this Monday morning by the assistant gardener.'

'You and Sergeant Collins are returning to her bedsit tonight to interview her neighbours?' Mulcahy interposed.

'We are, sir,' Michelle agreed smartly.

'Continue,' he ordered abruptly, as she hesitated, in case he intended saying something else.

'We believe the second victim was killed approximately two months ago,' Michelle looked over to Bill Mulcahy, who nodded confirmation. 'We think she was Elizabeth Moore, who had worked here as a staff nurse. But as she hasn't been formally identified as yet, we have no picture, and we're waiting for hospital administration to send us her file.' She glanced at Dan Evans who gave her an encouraging smile. 'We think the last victim found, and the killer's first, was a patient by the name of Claire Moon, but as her body hasn't been formally identified either, we can't be certain of her identity.'

'Thank you, Constable Grady,' Mulcahy took over again as she sat down. 'I called this meeting because I want to save time on individual briefings.' He rested his hands on the conference table in front of him. 'I don't need to tell you that we appear to be dealing with a dangerous psychopath here. I've got a psychologist working on the profile right now . . .' Peter Collins groaned audibly. 'Sergeant Collins,' Mulcahy turned towards him with a face like thunder. 'Don't keep your contribution to yourself. Share your thoughts with all of us.'

'Police psychologists are often proved wrong—'

'And on occasions are proved right,' Mulcahy contradicted testily. 'Have you any better suggestions on how to catch this killer?'

'Police work.'

'This *is* police work, Sergeant. Modern style. At this very moment the psychologist's feeding all the information we have, into a computer that holds data on all known serial killers. And in case it's escaped your attention, that's what we clearly have here. A serial killer who's likely to strike again at any moment. We can't even be sure whether he picks out his victims beforehand, or merely kidnaps them at random. All we can be certain of, is that they all had connections with this hospital. Our villain seems to know the grounds inside out, and it's fair to assume that he's a cunning devil. We probably wouldn't have found *any* of the bodies if a patient hadn't spotted him burying his last victim in the garden. Our villain also knows how to pick his time,' Mulcahy continued. 'If we have our victims tabbed right, they were all on the point of leaving this hospital, or else they were voluntary patients whose absence wouldn't be missed. Because none of them, as far as yet ascertained, was ever reported missing.'

He paused for breath before pointing out a series of sentences scribbled on the far right of the board in red ink.

'The pathologist confirmed this morning that all the victims were drugged before death. It's also possible that they were kept alive for some time before burial, because Rosie Twyford and one of the others had needle marks in the upper arms. In Twyford's case, twenty five separate syringe punctures have been identified. In the other victim the pathologist found only twelve, but not for the want of looking. The reason why he can't be more specific is because the last two corpses disinterred are, to put it mildly, somewhat ripe, and one of them has very little skin left. What he can confirm, however, is traces of drugs in the organs of all three victims, including tranquillisers and the drug curare, which has a paralysing effect on the body. However, in Twyford's case their effect must have been wearing off by the time of burial, because she managed to tear apart her lips which had been superglued . . .'

Michelle Grady shuddered at the thought.

'So it's fair to assume from the timescale of Twyford's disappearance, that our villain abducts his victims, hides them somewhere secret, probably within the hospital or its grounds, and keeps them drugged until such time as he can safely bury them in the garden. While still alive. All three corpses had earth in their air passages. So what can we deduce from that?'

'He has a good knowledge of this hospital, and a working knowledge of drugs and how to administer them,' Collins diagnosed quickly.

Mulcahy handed a marker to Evans, who noted Collins' observations under the heading of KILLER PROFILE.

'Anyone think of anything else?'

'The killer has to be either a doctor or a nurse,' a young Constable chipped in.

'What's your name, son?' Mulcahy demanded.

'Constable Pike, sir.'

'Why does the killer have to be a doctor or nurse, Pike?' Bill enquired in an ominously calm voice.

'Because he knows how to administer injections. And, he must have easy access to drugs . . .'

'Hasn't it occurred to you that there are patients here that can also gain access to drugs? Not to mention the pharmacists, or the porters who unload and stack the stuff. And as for administering it, any diabetic or first-aid course will give you the rudimentary knowledge needed.'

'Yes, sir.' Suitably chastened, Pike shrank back into his chair.

'Anyone else?'

'The dog, sir?'

'As you know more about that than me, tell them, Collins,' Mulcahy ordered brusquely.

'The dog we dug up last night was also drugged with curare – and also buried alive. As far as we can ascertain from the lab report approximately three to four months ago.'

'Could it have been a practice run?'

'Nice try Grady,' Evans said briskly. 'But timing places it between the first victim and the last two.'

'Right, that's it for now,' Mulcahy roared. 'Until further notice we'll have debriefing sessions every night at eleven-thirty sharp either here or in the Station.' He dismissed the groans that met his announcement. 'I don't care how much overtime you put in, or what it costs you, your family or your social life. I want this villain caught. And I want him caught yesterday, before he has the chance to turn another young woman into garden fertiliser. Right, gentlemen and ladies. We all have work to do. I suggest we all go out there and do it.'

Trevor was comfortable in the pub on the Marina. The chairs were padded and cosily upholstered in thick tapestry, and a log fire blazed warmly at his feet. He stared into the flames, taking his time over eating his meal, but he barely managed half the salad and steak, and less than a quarter of the chips. His stomach must have shrunk, he reflected dismally, surveying the food that he hadn't managed to eat.

'There isn't anything wrong with your meal, is there, sir?' the waitress asked, as she came to clear his plate.

'Nothing,' Trevor replied apologetically. 'The food was fine. Just a lot more than I've been used to eating lately.'

'Would you like to see the dessert menu, sir?'

'I don't think I could face it, but thank you for asking.' He felt as though he was learning to live again. Simple conversation wasn't that difficult after all, he decided, as he returned the waitress's smile.

He bought himself his third pint and continued to sit in front of the fire, watching as the bar filled with office workers who'd stopped for a quick one on their way home. His three pints became four, and he was beginning to feel distinctly fuzzy around the edges when a familiar voice greeted him.

'Sergeant Joseph? You're the last person I expected to see in here.' Jean Marshall stood in front of his table, a double gin in one hand, and a bottle of tonic water in the other.

'Sister Marshall.'

'For pity's sake don't call me that outside. It makes me sound like a militant nun. It's Jean. May I join you?'

'Of course,' he moved his chair closer to the fire, to make room for her.

'I almost walked past you. I didn't recognise you at first.' She sat down in the chair opposite him. 'I like your haircut, and the

154

clothes. They're a great improvement,' she complimented, as he moved his assortment of carrier bags out from under her feet.

'I've lost so much weight, that nothing I own fits me.'

'I wish I could say the same, but my clothes don't fit me for a very different reason.' She poured half of the tonic water into her glass. 'I haven't even been home yet,' she confided. 'Thought I'd treat myself to a pick-me-up first.'

'Hard day?'

'No more than usual.' She kicked off her shoes and toasted her toes before the fire. 'It's good to see you out and about. You look . . . different,' she finished decisively.

'How?' he asked.

'Different,' she teased. 'Not just the clothes and the hair, but something else. Something . . .'

'I must admit I do feel different.' He smiled.

'See what I mean. A smile even.'

'I don't know why I put off going outside for so long.' He began to cough. He glanced over his shoulder, and saw a girl blowing cigarette smoke in his direction. 'But then again, perhaps I do.' He grimaced.

'I take it you don't like cigarette smoke?'

'Can't stand it. Never could.'

'Then how did you work with Peter Collins? Every time I see him, he has a cigar in his mouth?'

'I used to complain non-stop.' Trevor grinned, recalling some of the wilder arguments with his partner. 'And I'd open windows wide in the office or the car, even in the middle of winter. It's a wonder we didn't drive each other mad.' He finished his pint and looked at Jean's empty glass. 'Same again?'

'I'd love to, but if I drink on an empty stomach I'm going to get plastered. I need to eat.'

'It's probably time I was going anyway,' Trevor said, taking her refusal as a rebuff.

'I was going to ask if you fancied a meal and a drink at my place.' She slipped her shoes back on. 'It's just around the corner.'

'I'd like to, but I've just eaten.'

'OK how about cheese and biscuits and a beer. I've got some first-class Dutch lager in the fridge that a friend brought back from Holland.'

'Sure I won't be imposing?' Trevor asked.

'Quite sure. I live alone because I like it that way, but that's not to say I don't enjoy company from time to time. Besides,' she grinned wickedly, 'there's nothing on the TV tonight. I checked in the paper.'

Jean led the way out of the pub, and over a bridge spanning the yacht berths. 'I live on the far side.' She pointed out one of the most expensive blocks that fronted the open sea on one side and the Marina on the other.

'Nice view?'

'You'll see just how nice in a moment,' she promised, waving to the porter as they walked through the foyer. She went into the lift and pressed the button for the top floor.

'Penthouse, no less.'

'Of course, what else,' she joked. The lift halted. There was only one door in the lobby. Jean scrabbled in her handbag for her keys, finally tipping its contents on the doormat in exasperation. When she managed to extricate them, she opened the door.

Trevor stepped in behind her and found himself in a large, square, windowless hall with mahogany wall panelling, carpeted with a blue and red Persian rug, and hung with what turned out to be, on close inspection, *very* suggestive Persian prints.

'I like the Orient,' she announced, pretending not to see his blushes as she opened one of the panels to reveal a cupboard. 'Can I take your jacket?'

Trevor handed it over as he looked for somewhere to drop his bags.

'Put those out of the way in the corner,' she suggested.

He followed her into a living-room that could have swallowed the whole of his own flat four times over. Two walls, were of glass, one overlooking the sea, the other the Marina, and he felt as though he had wandered into a people-sized fish-tank.

'The view is spectacular,' he complimented.

'Then you must like the sea, too?'

'I love it,' he said. 'I can just about see the dirty corner next to the sewage works from my kitchen window.'

The other two walls were painted in blending, contrasting streaks of shades of blue. The ceiling was pale grey, and the floor was carpeted in navy-blue Wilton. Even the sofas were upholstered in deep blue leather; the only softening touch lay in the Persian tapestry cushions on the sofas, and handwoven Persian silk hangings on the walls.

'Orient again?' He raised his eyebrows. Jean smiled as she brushed her hand across one of the hangings, which was almost but not quite as suggestive as the pictures in the hall. The colours were perfect for the room; predominantly blue and grey, with just a few touches of white and burgundy.

'You certainly know how to put a home together,' Trevor complimented, staring at the grey-washed, limed-oak glass cupboards that held a selection of pale blue Turkish glass and Chinese porcelain.

'Thank you. Take a seat, and I'll mix us a salad and fetch the drinks.'

'I'd rather help.' He followed her out of the living-room into another inner hallway.

'Cloakroom,' she pointed to a door ahead of them. 'Bedrooms, bathrooms, kitchen, dining-room and study,' she indicated the doors. 'It's not vast, but it's comfortable. Take a look around if you like.'

'I wouldn't dream of it.'

'Don't be so polite. People are always curious about other people's living space, especially when it's in these apartments. Adam Hayter asked me straight out if I had gold-plated baths and loos when he found out where I lived. I'm afraid the publicity campaign the builder ran when he tried to sell these places has backfired. People expected rock musicians and film stars to move in, not the local scrap merchant.'

'Scrap merchant?' Trevor looked at her quizzically.

'My husband,' Jean explained briefly. 'Or at least he was before he ran off with a eighteen-year-old tart.'

'I'm sorry.'

'There's no need to be. He did me an enormous favour. I was getting extremely tired of hearing him crow day and night

157

about his face-lifts and lipo suction. Mind you it was fairly alarming to wake up next to him after the last face-lift. Something went wrong and he couldn't close his eyes properly. Let's hope his dolly bird doesn't mind sleeping next to a wide-open stare all night. In the meantime, I most certainly am "All right Jack", thank you very much. My share of our divorce settlement gave me this apartment, the first boat you see in the row if you look out the study window, and enough money to tempt all the toyboys I want into my bed when the mood takes me.'

She moved into the kitchen and, unable to resist his curiosity, Trevor walked into the study and looked out of its huge picture window. A large ocean going cruiser was berthed in front of a line of yachts.

'That's your boat?' he called into the kitchen.

'*The Turkish Queen.*' she called back. 'It's five-berth. Comfortable berths too. He had it specially built, and christened it after we holidayed in Turkey. At the time I thought he named it after me; now I'm not so sure. I'd like to rename it, but that's supposed to be unlucky.'

He turned around to look over the rest of the study. Books lined the white-painted oak shelves from floor to ceiling, all Everyman editions, all matching, and all in mint condition, as though they'd never been opened, let alone read. A huge bleached oak desk dominated the centre of the room its surface clear apart from a covered electric typewriter. The room looked strangely empty and characterless, like a display in a museum or a furniture shop.

He went into the cloakroom and washed his hands and face in a large Victorian-style sink. The tiles on the wall were Minton, the thick fluffy towels American. Resisting the temptation to peer into the bedrooms, he headed into the kitchen where he found Jean mixing a salad in between sips of gin.

'This room's far too big for someone like me, who never cooks,' she waved her hand around the expanse of ultramodern black and grey units. 'I've never switched on one of the fridge-freezers, and I don't think I've ever used the large oven in the cooker, but then I'm too idle to move house, and I suppose it's better to have too much space and too many gadgets than too few. Here.' She handed him a tray with the salad and a can of lager on it. 'I'll bring in the chicken pie and cheese. Sure you won't have some salad, too?'

'Perhaps just a little?' Trevor's appetite was sharpened by all the beer he'd drunk and the tempting appearance of the pie.

'Good man.' She loaded pie, cheese, biscuits and fruit on to another tray, then led the way back into the living room. To Trevor's amazement she opened the patio doors.

'We'll freeze,' he protested.

'In a centrally-heated conservatory? It's quite cleverly designed; you have to look hard to see where the glass ends and the balcony itself begins. The balcony was so huge, and the winters always so damned long, it seemed a silly waste of space until I had the idea of glassing half of it in.' She turned a corner and set her tray down on a cane table positioned in a trellised alcove sheltered by plants. Returning to the living-room she picked up two beautiful glass plates, silver cutlery, and a silver box of paper napkins. 'Sorry about these disposable napkins, but I hate washing things. In fact I hate all housework.'

'This is absolutely marvellous.' Trevor sat across the table from her, facing both the open sea and the Marina. 'I'd forgotten life could be this good,' he murmured, resolving to do something about his shabby little flat at the first chance he got.

Life was short, very short. It had taken a close brush with death for him to realise just how quickly the flame of existence could be snuffed out; and now he'd learned that no one, least of all himself, was immortal, perhaps it might be just as well if he continued to remember his mortality for whatever time was left to him. Jean Marshall was showing him a glimpse of the good life, and he resolved to enjoy it to the full; and, if he could, carry something of its beauty forward into whatever time remained. He'd seen so much of ugliness, perhaps now was the moment to look for something better that offered, if not the certainty of happiness, at least the chance.

They ate and drank, quietly, companionably. Dusk fell; one by one the harbour lights flickered on. First the lights in the pubs and restaurants that glittered over the cobblestones of the quayside, then the lamps that sprinkled slivers of silver on the waves along the water's edge. Finally the mast lights of the boats berthed in endless lines along the Marina, wavering unpredictably, buffeted by the wind and waves that rocked the dark shadows of the crafts.

'You don't need any gold-plated baths,' he said. 'This view is worth every penny you paid for it.'

'I didn't pay for it. I earned it as a reward for twenty years of marriage to a boorish lout who couldn't even spell his own name. But then again.' She chuckled throatily. 'I think the compensation was worth every second of the sentence. Don't you?'

Chapter Eleven

'Vanessa Hedley's gone missing?'

'What?' Karl Lane looked up from the pile of forms he was filling in and stared in disbelief at Lyn Sullivan. She was standing in the doorway of his ward office.

'I said Vanessa Hedley's missing.' She was white-faced from a combination of panic and shock. 'I can't find her anywhere . . .'

'Calm down,' he said sternly, exercising his authority as senior nursing officer on duty. 'You've checked the ward thoroughly?'

'Yes.'

'What about the therapy units?'

'All the therapists left two hours ago.'

'Spencer Jordan sometimes runs an evening class.'

'Not tonight. I checked his room.'

'Have you telephoned security?'

'Yes. I asked them to search the grounds.'

Good,' he replied, trying to forget the forms he'd been engrossed in. 'Have you informed Tony Waters?'

'It's nearly nine o'clock. I assumed that he'd have gone home by now.'

'He rarely leaves his office before eight on any normal evening, and what's happening around here at the moment is anything but normal. I'll try him.' He picked up the telephone and dialled an internal number. 'Look, you'd better get back to your ward. She probably just wandered off through the gates when the porter wasn't looking. You know what she's like. Wherever she is, I don't doubt she's safe. Our patients have the luck of the devil when it comes to surviving. Besides, what could happen to her with every

161

inch of this place crawling with police? How long has she been gone?'

'I saw her myself at the evening meal. She went off somewhere with Roland Williams . . .'

'Williams? She was with *him*?'

'They only went into the dayroom,' Lyn replied shortly, knowing full well what he was thinking. 'According to Lucy Craig, Vanessa then left the dayroom to go to the toilet. She never returned. And that was just after seven o'clock.'

'Did you ask if Roland followed her?'

'No,' she admitted slowly, 'but he's on his own ward now. I saw him there just ten minutes ago.'

'That means nothing where Roland is concerned. They could have gone out together earlier, and then he returned without her. He spends half his life skulking in the gardens. I rather suspect he has a whole bar hidden there behind the bushes. In fact I think we'd better get security to trawl the shrubberies Roland's probably had her in there, and she's got lost searching for her knickers in the dark.'

'Karl, this is no time to joke,' Lyn complained, annoyed with his flippant attitude.

'Who says I'm joking? Well Tony isn't in his office, or anywhere near.' He finally hung up the telephone that he had allowed to ring until it cut off.

'Shouldn't we tell the police?' she pressed.

'Whatever for?'

'Vanessa Hedley's missing,' she repeated in exasperation. 'She's the only one who claims to have seen the killer . . .'

'Come on, Lyn, you're allowing your emotions to run away with you. Vanessa Hedley's a psychiatric patient. Psychiatric patients go missing all the time. If we rang the police every time one decided to go walkabout, we'd be the laughing stock of the Health Authority.'

'I think in this case we should alert them,' she asserted firmly.

'I'm senior nursing officer on duty.' He folded his arms, pushed back his chair, and glared at her. 'And I say any decision to contact the police has to be made by the senior admin officer. That means it's Tony Waters' baby not ours. Can you imagine what the local press will make of this, if it leaks out. Think of the headlines? *Compton Castle staff ask murder squad to find crazy lady they misplaced.* They'll have a field-day, particularly when they find out who she is. And, believe you me, someone's bound to recognise her name. They'll dig up all those headlines from the time she tried her best to kill her husband and his mistress. And then there'll be a hue and cry from all those wealthy locals who bought luxury executive homes just outside the hospital walls, and who don't want a potential murderer living in the same square mile as their beloved offspring.'

'I can imagine the more serious headlines this incident will make if she *has* been snatched by the killer,' Lyn said acidly. *'Vanessa Hedley murdered by psychopathic serial killer while hospital authorities see fit to stay mum.'*

'I think you'd better return to your ward, Nurse Sullivan,' Karl Lane said icily. 'You've done the right thing; you've reported Mrs Hedley's absence to your senior. I'll take it from here.'

'Karl . . .'

He looked at her, remembering the previous night spent together, when they'd both been off duty. She was beautiful, even with her long dark hair gathered into a loose knot at the nape of neck. Probably the most beautiful girlfriend he'd ever had, and the best bedmate he'd found in a long time. He rose from his chair and laid his hands lightly on her shoulders.

'I understand your concern,' he said gently, stroking her earlobes. 'But it *will* be all right. No one's going to blame you. Everyone's aware that just two trained staff and two auxiliaries can't supervise twenty-four patients every single minute of their day and night. Unfortunately for them, the authorities have already been forced to accept that nurses are only human, and they weren't born with eyes in the backs of their heads.'

Quite a few things about Karl had began to annoy Lyn lately, not least his occasionally grand, and patronising attitudes.

'I'm not concerned with being hauled over the coals by the authorities, you stupid man,' she countered furiously, 'but with what might have happened to Vanessa. She's a significant witness . . .'

'Back to your ward, Nurse Sullivan,' he ordered sternly.

'Damn you, Karl Lane,' she hissed. 'For all our sakes I just hope that you're right and nothing's happened to her.'

'Been out, mate?' Peter Collins slowed his car in the drive of Compton Castle, and wound down his window.

'To town,' Trevor replied, stopping to lean heavily on his stick. 'You wouldn't give me a lift up to my ward, would you?' he asked. 'I'm whacked.'

'Bill received a directive from Tony Waters that all police vehicles were to keep to the first hundred yards of the main drive, and well away from all wards, but you know me and rules. Jump in.' Collins opened both back and front doors, and Trevor offloaded his carrier bags into the rear seat, flinging his stick on top of them, before he clambered awkwardly into the passenger seat.

'Been shopping?' Peter enquired mildly.

'Yes.'

'Until now?'

'No, I had a meal.'

'You what?' He stared at Trevor in amazement. Even in the darkness he could sense a change. A subtle increase in confidence, a rebirth of humour, even.

'Steak and chips.'

'And beer, by the smell of you.' Collins waved a hand in front of his face. '*Lots* of beer.'

'Four or five,' Trevor admitted with a grin.

'And you're obviously feeling very proud of yourself, even if you're now on the road to alcoholism. Welcome back to the land of the living, mate.' Collins masked the emotion he felt behind a show of heartiness. 'It's about bloody time, even if I am jealous as hell at the thought of you munching steak and chips in town, when I'm confined to a diet of takeaway grease eaten at ungodly hours in mobile HQ.'

'I thought I could smell something.'

'Something rapidly getting cold.' He halted outside the ward block. 'Here you are. Home. Does mother know you've been out?'

Trevor pulled a pass from his jacket pocket. 'Allowed out until nine-thirty,' he read, with difficulty in the poor light.

'Well you've made it with a minute to spare. No ticking-off for you today. Here, I'll give you a hand with your bags. Bloody hell!' he exclaimed, as he picked up the one containing the shoes. 'What have you been buying?'

'A new image,' Trevor retrieved his stick, and limped towards the front door.

'Good Lord, so you have.' Peter noticed Trevor's clothes for the first time as he stood beneath the light and rang the bell. 'And you've had your hair cut, too. Well, that settles it.'

'Settles what?' Trevor was mystified by Peter's train of thought.

'You really have left the Drugs Squad haven't you? Just look at you; you're too damned clean and neat even for the CID.'

Collins watched the door open, and Trevor walked inside. Returning to his car, he almost tripped over a security guard who was shining a torch beneath it.

'I'd like to ask what you are doing here at this time of night?' the man demanded officiously.

Collins looked him up and down. Ex-forces by his build, and carriage, young, and probably working for under two quid an hour, he decided cynically. He moved a hand swiftly inside his jacket pocket and brought out his wallet, flashing his badge, before the man had time to challenge him again.

'Hospital Authorities have declared this area out of bounds to the police, sir,' the guard pointed out in a marginally politer tone.

'Returning an injured suspect,' Collins replied disarmingly. He returned to his car. The smell of fish and chips reminded him that his supper wouldn't be getting any warmer. And there was nothing worse than cold fish and chips. They inevitably reverted to blocks of solid, tasteless grease. But as he drove away from the wards, and down towards the mobile head-quarters, he couldn't help feeling uneasy. Something was wrong; he could feel it in his bones. He just couldn't put his finger on whatever that something was.

'Anything new on Rosie Twyford?' Dan Evans asked as Peter walked into the core room of the headquarters.

'Just what I expected; absolutely bloody nothing.' Collins

165

handed over one of the two paper-wrapped bundles. 'Thought you might be hungry,' he replied to Dan's enquiring look.

'That's kind of you.' The more Dan saw and worked with Collins, the more he found himself genuinely amazed by his generosity and thoughtfulness, which often came directly after a bout of particularly belligerent behaviour.

'I came back because I'd rather sit out the night here, than listen to Mary Poppins regurgitate the blanks we drew in Rosie Twyford's bedsit.'

'It was that bad?' Dan picked up a handful of chips and squashed them into his mouth.

'The only one who even admitted to ever seeing her was the guy in the next bedsitter, and he claimed he had only met her twice in the hallway. But at least four of the other residents have been hauled in by us for pushing, and three for soliciting. It's not exactly the kind of friendly household where you invite your neighbour in for a cup of tea and a chat.'

'It's the kind of household the social workers look to when they want to offload their difficult charges?'

'You got it in one,' Peter mumbled, his mouth full.

'Well, I'm certainly not going to object to extra help. After we've eaten, you can give me a hand with this lot.'

'What is it?' Collins asked warily, staring at the enormous, grey cardboard box deposited on Dan's desk.'

'All the current staff files of personnel employed in this hospital.'

'Official files.' Peter grinned. 'They never tell you anything you want to know. I've already done some work on the staff myself. Friend of mine works in an agency, the kind that deals in press cuttings. I gave him a staff list yesterday afternoon and, as usual, he came up trumps. They're out in my car.' He cornered the last of his soggy chips in the blind end of the greaseproof paper bag, then crammed them into his mouth. Screwing the bits of greasy paper into a ball, he flicked it into the bin. 'Let's see what he found, shall we?' He walked out of the door.

'The personnel files are little more than a collection of CVs, medical histories, and job descriptions. If I hadn't been assured otherwise by our Mr Waters, I'd say the whole lot had been personally sanitised for our benefit,' Dan Evans complained an hour later, as he pushed the fourth file aside and reached for the coffee pot warming on its stand. He poured himself an unappetising paper cup full, and looked inquiringly at Collins.

'May as well,' Peter muttered. 'Ah, now this looks a bit more like it.' He extracted a pile of national press cuttings from the mass of local paper's wedding photographs and details of charity cheque handovers. 'My friend is nothing if not thorough. Here we are.' He spread out a large photocopied double sheet, taken from the *Sunday Times* arts supplement.

'"Darling of the art set makes his first million",' he read. '"Spencer Jordan has added to his phenomenal success by selling his current Californian exhibition to the Metropolitan Museum of Modern Art . . ."'

'You sure that's the same Spencer Jordan?' Evans asked.

'Want to see the picture?' Collins passed it over. 'He looks younger, better dressed and hairier, but it's the same man. What have you got there on his CV?'

Evans rummaged through his files until he found Spencer Jordan's.

'It says he was a successful commercial artist. Exhibitions, lots of exhibitions, art college here, then in America .. taken on to the staff of Compton Castle as a therapist two years ago. A note on his medical file says he had an eye removed, as if we couldn't see that much; and that he also made a good recovery from severe clinical depression. Isn't that what Trevor Joseph has too?'

'Yes,' Collins replied briefly. He suddenly let out a low whistle. 'Look at this,' he pushed a paper across the table. Lurid headlines blazed above a gruesome photograph that covered almost the entire front page of a tabloid paper.

'Has to be American press,' Evans commented. 'Not even a hardened jackal of the British press corps would sink this low.

Four bodies laid out on a lawn. Only the faces were covered, inadequately, with tiny squares of cloth that barely obscured their features. The hair and ears were in plain view. Two were small, one a tiny baby. All the corpses were bloodied, clothes and skin slashed to shreds.

'"Artist's entire family slain by bizarre sect in ritual killing,"' Evans read slowly. He turned the page of the newspaper. '"Spencer Jordan, the well-known British artist returned to his Californian home after hosting an exhibition in New York, to find his entire family slain and their murderers still occupying his house."'

There was another photograph, lower down the second page, and smaller this time, of Jordan being led out of the house by a uniformed ambulance man. Blood poured down his right cheek, and a gauze bandage covered both his eyes.

'"One of the sect viciously attacked him tearing out his eye, but despite his horrific injuries Mr Jordan managed to fight his way to the front door and raise the alarm."'

'Which explains why he might suffer from depression,' Collins observed gravely.

'The eldest child was four, and the youngest only two months,' Dan murmured, sickened by the account. 'Poor bastard. No wonder he started his career here as an inmate. Something like that would make anyone go over the top.'

'Is his medical history detailed in his personal record?' Collins asked.

'No, Waters' secretary let it slip.'

'It's probably worth buying her a drink or two in the Green Monkey.'

'I thought so too,' Evans replied. 'I took her there earlier this evening. Find the local gossip, ply her with drink, pump her, and you'll save yourself a lot of leg work.'

'Police College motto?' Collins smiled tightly.

'Pays every time. What do you think? The man obviously suffered?'

'But did he suffer enough to lose his marbles and turn into a killer? When did he first take up his post here?'

'A year ago. But when did all this happen.' Dan rammed his finger down on the newspaper.

'Three years ago. Two years missing.' Collins pushed a smaller article covering the trial towards Dan. 'There's a footnote here saying Spencer Jordan could not be called to give evidence because he was incarcerated in a state mental institution. The killers were convicted on forensic evidence, and sentenced to life.'

'What's life in California?' Evans asked.

'Probably the same as here,' Collins replied cynically. 'Ten years off for every six months of good behaviour, a pat on the head and a directive never to be a naughty boy again when they're released?'

'I think that man's been's through a lot,' Evans said evenly, turning the front page picture away so he didn't have to look at it.

'He could be our man,' Peter suggested. 'He obviously went bananas, to end up in a state mental institution and then in this place.'

'I'd end up here too, if I saw my own family butchered like this.'

'The question is, did he go sufficiently bananas to feel compelled to bury innocent people alive?' Peter mused, 'And then again, have you thought that the killer could actually be Vanessa Hedley?'

Dan merely laughed.

'Vanessa,' Peter mused. 'Let's just look at the facts as they stand. She tried to kill both her old man and his mistress, and damn near succeeded. She spent six years in Broadmoor before coming here. And just about everyone's heard her fantasy of wanting to bury her old man so she could keep an eye on him. She's been a patient here long enough to realise how to give injections. Security in this place is a joke, so if she really wanted to, she could gain access to drugs. And with only one guard on at night, it's easy enough to dodge your way around the hospital grounds.'

'Your theory's fine until you take into account Vanessa's size,' Dan said slowly. 'She's tiny, five foot two, and what – seven stone?'

'About that,' Collins agreed reluctantly. 'But that's not to say she isn't strong,' he protested.

'Can you really see her carrying a twelve-stone woman out of this place, then dumping her in a hole and burying her?'

'She's the only one who knew where the body was buried,' Peter persisted.

169

'Then why did she ask the gardener to dig it up?'

'Because she's nuts, and nutty people do nutty things.'

'OK, then, where's the dirt on her clothes,' Dan asked. 'I got Grady to check out her wardrobe. We found nothing at all. What else have you got?'

'Adam Hayter.'

'The therapist?'

'Needlework and cookery.'

'It takes all sorts,' Dan smiled wearily. 'What about him?'

'Soliciting with intent in a men's toilet, *and* indecent exposure. Nabbed last Christmas,' Collins pushed the half-inch of column across the table.

'Found guilty, and fined. So what?'

'So he's a sexual deviant?'

'We already knew that. You do know who he's shacked up with, don't you?'

'Enlighten me.' Collins finished his coffee and made a face, but he still reached for the jug again. He needed something to keep him awake. The hours between two and three in the morning were always the worst.

'Dotty Clyne?'

'Our female impersonator,' Peter said scathingly. 'Have you seen her moustache?'

'Yes, but she's a female all right. Says so on her medical record.'

'I don't believe it.'

'OK, let's move on to Harry Goldman. Anything on him?' Dan followed Peter's example, and poured himself another coffee. He rubbed his hands through his thinning hair until it stood on end.

Collins put aside the cutting he was looking at and shuffled through those that remained on the table. 'There's something here about possessing and distributing pornographic material.'

'A psychiatrist? And he's still in work?'

'Says here it was for his PHD thesis. He did one on sexual deviants.'

'He should know about those, with all the obvious examples floating around this place.' Dan began stamping his feet to bring the circulation back to a numb leg. 'Anything else?'

'Only the usual stuff about the nurses; wedding photographs, charity photographs, that sort of thing.'

'Nothing on Tony Waters? Dan asked.

'A nice photograph of him taken on his appointment. A photograph of him and his wife outside the church when they got married. Good Lord, he's married to that nurse . . . Nurse what's-her-name?'

'Try Carol Ashford?' Evans said.

'You knew?'

'I've just about finished reading all the files. Why are you so surprised? Hospital staff marry each other all the time. Doctors, nurses. Administrators, nurses. What's the difference?'

'None, I suppose. It's just the name.'

'A lot of women stick to their maiden names after marriage these days.'

'I know. It's just that she's fanciable, and he's so weird.'

'You can't charge a woman because you fancy her, or a man because he's a cold fish.'

'Pity. We'd solve this case in five minutes, if we could.'

'Look, I suggest we make a start by opening a file on every single member of staff. Then get one of the girls to enter their details into the computer, and as soon as we get the killer profile from the psychologist we can do a cross check.'

Collins rested his head on his arms and stared at the papers littering the desk. 'You know what the problem is here, don't you?'

'I've a feeling you're going to tell me,' Dan said unenthusiastically.

'We've a dozen or more good suspects on the staff, and we haven't even started on the patients,' he moaned.

'We start on *their* files tomorrow,' Evans said cheerfully. 'And then the fish and chips are on me.'

'What's the matter? Can't sleep?' Lyn Sullivan snapped, as Trevor crept out of his room at three in the morning.

'I don't know why. I should be exhausted,' he apologised

contritely. 'Sorry, I didn't mean to startle you.' He pushed his hands into the pockets of his shabby paisley polyester dressing-gown and shivered.

'Did you want to get yourself a drink?' she asked.

'No, a book. I've just finished the one I borrowed from the hospital library.'

'There's plenty of magazines in the office.' Her anger dissipated as she felt suddenly sorry for him. He looked so exposed and vulnerable in his shabby nightwear, and his fashionable new haircut didn't help, contrasting strongly with his pale, thin, sickly-white face. 'I was just going to make myself a cup of tea. Do you want one?'

'Thank you. Yes, I would.' He followed her into the cold and deserted ward kitchen. 'No one else around?'

'They've had trouble down on geriatric, so we sent our auxiliaries to help, and the other nurse is on meal break.'

'You mean you're superintending this ward all by yourself?' Trevor asked in a shocked voice.

'Locked in with all you crazy people?' Lyn laughed. 'Yes, but don't worry, I'm used to it. It happens quite often at night, and once you realise that the reality of life on the wards isn't at all like the advert in the *Sunday Times* colour supplement that enticed me into becoming a psychiatric nurse in the first place, then it's not that bad really. Beats nine-till-five shorthand typing and word-processing.'

She put the kettle on, and turned to Trevor. 'Toast?'

'No, thank you. I don't think I could face it.'

'Too many pints?' she asked intuitively.

'How did you guess?'

'It happens to everyone, first time out.'

'I hate being *everyone.*'

The phone rang, and she was out of the room and down the ward before Trevor realised what was happening. He took over making the tea, and had a plate of toast made and buttered before she returned.

'Anything important?' he asked.

'It was only geriatric asking if they could keep our auxiliaries for another hour,' she muttered.

'Expecting more trouble?'

'Not really.'

'You sure?' he asked.

She eyed him over the rim of her cup. 'You really have come a long way, haven't you? Now you're over the worst, you want to take up amateur psychiatry?'

'Sorry.'

'You seem to have switched from depression to . . .'

'Elation!'

'Not elation. If that was the case, you'd be in real trouble,' she said. 'Try normality.'

'Whatever that might mean.'

'If Goldman sees you behaving like this, he'll throw you out of this hospital tomorrow.'

'I hope so.' Trevor smiled. 'I really hope so. I feel now that I'm ready for it. I've actually begun to make plans . . .'

'Such as?' she interrupted.

'To change the way I live,' he said lightly, not wanting to say too much in case he sounded ridiculous or naive. He watched her pick halfheartedly at her toast. Instead of trying to make conversation with him, as she usually did with her patients, she glanced constantly over his shoulder and out of the window, as though expecting something or someone to appear.

'Something really is wrong, isn't it?' he pressed.

'Yes. But I've been ordered by my superior to keep my mouth shut, so I can't tell you what it is.'

'Tell me?'

'No.'

'Tell me off the record then,' Trevor suggested. 'If I discover anything, I promise not to implicate you.'

She stared at him.

'I promise,' he repeated, sensing her hesitation.

'Vanessa Hedley's disappeared,' Lyn divulged. The words tumbled out in an almost indecipherable surge, as relief percolated through her veins. 'And we can't find her anywhere.'

Chapter Twelve

'What are you going to do?' Lyn Sullivan asked warily.

'Inform the police so they can organise a search,' Trevor replied flatly.

'You organise a search and I'll lose my job.' She bit her lip nervously. 'When I told Karl earlier . . .'

'Karl Lane?' Trevor asked, remembering the goodlooking male nurse who had tended Lyn's cuts after Vanessa went berserk.

'Yes. He's senior duty officer tonight. When I told him Vanessa was missing, he warned me not to tell anyone until he contacted Tony Waters.'

'Did he now,' Trevor said thoughtfully. 'That's interesting.'

'Not in the way you think,' Lyn countered sharply. 'Karl's no murderer, he's just obsessed with always saying and doing the right thing, lest it adversely affect his promotion prospects. He doesn't want anyone berating him for kicking up a fuss which could lead to press headlines telling the world what a load of incompetents run this hospital.' She paused and fell silent for a moment. 'Damn!' she exclaimed angrily. 'This is one situation where I can't win no matter what.'

'I wouldn't say that,' Trevor smiled. 'You mentioned that your junior nurse was on meal break. Have you had yours yet?'

'No.'

'When do you go?'

'When she gets back, which should be,' she glanced up at the clock on the wall. 'In about twenty minutes. Why?'

'Where's Michael Carpenter?'

'Sleeping I hope. . . Trevor . . .'

'The bed to the left of the door of the four-bedded ward?'

175

'But . . .'

He held a finger to his lips and smiled.

'He who asks no questions need tell no lies afterwards. Good coffee, this,' he added innocently.

'What the hell was that?' Dan Evans jumped up from the table where he'd been dozing over the last of the files, upsetting coffee dregs from his paper cup over his trousers.

'Fire alarm by the sound of it.' Collins hurried out of the room and into the outer office, where the two female constables were trying to peer through a tiny window. He pushed past them and opened the door. The cool, fragrant night air came as an invigorating, bracing surprise after the smoke-laden stuffiness inside the van.

Two security guards came running out of the main building and headed over the lawns towards the wards. Once they had passed he stepped down on to the gravel and proceeded up the drive.

'Isn't that the ward Trevor Joseph is in?' Evans caught up with him, and pointed to a group crowding the doorway in their nightclothes.

Collins ran the last hundred yards though he was overtaken by Karl Lane, who began shouting unintelligible orders at the patients who were stumbling sleepily, in drugged and tranquillised confusion out of the building. A junior nurse, close to panic, was trying to call out names off a list. A cloud of black smoke billowed from an open window at the far end of the same block.

A security guard pushed his way past the bewildered patients and into the porch of the building, ignoring several bewildered nurses who'd left their own wards to see if they could help.

'Very clever. I've never seen a guard without breathing apparatus or protective clothing run into a burning building before. What training school did he go to?' Dan murmured scathingly.

'Pyromaniac's been at it again,' Collins muttered.

'First I've heard of a pyromaniac,' Dan stared at him closely. 'Tell me more?'

176

'Remember a Michael Carpenter being brought into the Station?'

'Who set fires, and tried to kill his girlfriend and her family?'

Collins nodded.

'The sooner we start examining those patient files the better.'

Karl Lane continued to scream commands at the dazed patients who, despite his efforts, refused to remain still for a moment. The junior nurse had to run after Alison Bevan, to retrieve her from the rear of the block, where she'd wandered off in the hope of getting a better view of the conflagration.

'I was in the staff dining-room on break.' Lyn Sullivan ran up, breathlessly and grabbed Karl Lane by the arm. 'Are they all out?'

'How in hell should I know?' he snarled viciously. 'Your junior is bloody useless.'

Lyn grabbed the list from the girl's shaking fingers. 'Everyone over here,' she called out coolly. 'Come on now. Over here, or you won't be allowed back into your beds.' This threat seemed to do the trick. The dressing gowned, and slippered figures shuffled slowly towards her.

'Alison Bevan?'

'Here.'

'John Carter?'

'Present, miss.'

Everyone laughed except Karl Lane, and some of the tension dissipated. Peter scanned the ranks of patients carefully, then shrugged his arms out of his coat sleeves.

'What do you think you're doing?' Dan asked, as Peter began to move towards the building.

'I can't see any sign of Joseph. Stupid fool's probably trying to play the hero. Will he never learn?'

The security guard had moved no further than the porch.

'You can't go in there,' he snapped at Collins, blocking the inner doorway.

'You going to stop me, mate?' Peter squared up threateningly.

At that moment a fire-engine came racing up the drive, siren

177

blaring, its wheels scattering gravel over the adjacent flowerbeds. Before it even drew to a halt, Trevor stumbled, hunched and coughing, out through the inner doorway of the building.

'You bloody fool!' Collins threw his jacket over Trevor's thin dressing-gown. 'Where the hell have you been?'

'Checking to see no one was left behind,' he whispered in a hoarse voice, leaving the porch and walking out into the fresh air. 'It's not as bad as it looks,' he informed the first firemen to leap from the engine. 'Just some old magazines, cotton wool and a blanket bundled into the sink and set alight. I turned the tap on them.'

'Trying to roast us in our beds again, darling?' Alison Bevan glared at Michael Carpenter, who sat shivering on a bench, a sleep-numbed expression on his face.

'I didn't ... I didn't ... I didn't,' he chattered like a monkey.

'That's what you always say,' Ali snapped savagely.

'Is anyone missing?' A fireman asked Lyn, seeing the list in her hand.

'Yes,' she answered, giving Karl Lane a defiant look. Female, five foot three ...' she hesitated, trying to remember what colour Vanessa's hair had been dyed that morning.

'She's a blonde today, darling,' Roland Williams chipped in from the crowd that had gathered outside the drug and alcohol dependency unit. 'But there's no use looking for her,' he said blandly to the fireman. 'She's been missing for hours.'

'She's been missing for hours and you didn't think to inform us?' Collins turned furiously on Nurse Lyn Sullivan.

'I reported her disappearance to the senior nursing officer on duty at eight o'clock this evening,' she retorted defensively.

'And what pen-pushing moron ... ?'

'Karl Lane, meet Sergeant Collins and Inspector Evans,' Lyn effected the introductions.

'A material witness in one of the most callous murder cases I've ever had the misfortune to deal with just disappears, and you didn't think to inform us?' Evans turned angrily on Karl Lane.

'She's gone missing before,' he offered lamely.

'For God's sake man . . .' Collins began.

Evans interrupted urgently, 'Has she ever gone missing all night before?'

'Not that I can remember.' Karl Lane squirmed uneasily, looking around for Lyn. This had to be her fault, and tomorrow morning he'd see that she was well and truly hauled over the coals.

'I want to see whoever's in charge of this apology for a hospital – and I don't mean you,' Dan Evans raged at Karl. 'If they're not in our HQ in ten minutes, I'm going to the press. And not *just* the press either; television, radio – the full works.'

'It's three o'clock in the morning,' Lane protested feebly.

'I couldn't give a single sweet damn what time it is,' Evans' voice dropped ominously low.

'I'll telephone Mr Waters.'

'In our HQ in ten minutes,' Evans repeated firmly. 'And in the meantime I'm instigating a full search of the whole hospital and all the grounds.'

'You can't do that. Not without authority . . .'

'I have all the authority I need. Collins, ring the Station. Get as many coppers here as you can. Now!'

Trevor turned back to the ward, intending to get dressed.

'You can't go in there.' The security guard tried to block his path.

'Those the only words you learnt in school?' Collins roared at him, before making his way back to headquarters.

Leaving her patients in the care of a staff nurse, Lyn sought out Karl Lane.

'It's freezing out here. Where do you want me to put my patients?'

'Wherever you like!' he growled.

She stared furiously after his retreating figure. 'Right, every one of you into the main hall,' she shouted. Turning to the nurses standing by she called out, 'I have twenty-four patients here who need temporary housing overnight. See how many spare beds you can find in each block, make a note of the bed number and the ward, and report back to me as quickly as you can in the main hall.'

179

'That's what I call initiative,' Dan Evans murmured to Trevor as he emerged again, dressed in the clothes he'd worn back from town.

'I need to talk to you, in private,' Trevor croaked.

'Then you'd better follow me back to HQ. Perhaps you'd like to help out,' he added dryly. 'We're going to need every man we can lay our hands on. Even sick ones.'

Dan poured out three fresh paper cups of coffee, and handed them around. 'If you don't mind me saying so Trevor, you appear to be a whole lot fitter than the last time I saw you.'

'I don't mind you saying so, but that doesn't mean I'm in any hurry to get back to work. In fact I'd like to take some time off . . .'

'What's going on here?' Bill Mulcahy stormed into the office, knocking over the overflowing waste-paper basket and sending greasy chip papers and empty cans shooting across the floor. 'I was woken up by some idiot gabbling on about Vanessa Hedley—'

'She's gone missing,' Evans interrupted.

'Oh Christ, that's all we need!' Mulcahy sat down and shook a cigarette from a packet he kept in the top pocket of his suit jacket. 'Can't you just hear the screams upstairs when they find out that we didn't give her round-the-clock protection. She was our only witness.'

'Who was incarcerated in what is supposed to be a secure ward in a mental institution,' Peter grumbled, as he lit one of his cigars.

'Seems to me that those wards are anything but secure.' Mulcahy stared at Trevor. 'If they were, *he* wouldn't be here.'

'We wouldn't even know she was missing if it wasn't for him,' Collins rounded on Bill defensively. 'He only found out by chance, from one of the nurses.'

'She told him before she told us?'

'Vanessa Hedley was first missed early this evening, but the hospital authorities decided to keep her disappearance quiet.' Peter blew smoke in Bill's direction.

'Let me get this straight. She went missing early this evening and they told *no one*?'

'The nurse in charge of the ward informed the senior duty nurse, but he tried to hush it up.'

'Why on earth would he do that?' Bill demanded sharply.

'Usual bureaucracy. He wouldn't do anything without the admin officer's say-so, and Waters wasn't available.'

'Then how did you find out?'

'Let's say, when a fire broke out in Vanessa Hedley's ward block and the head-count was one short.'

'What fire?' Mulcahy looked suspiciously from Dan to Peter, and then to Trevor, and back.

'I wouldn't bother to investigate that one too closely,' Dan murmured.

'Are you saying that one of you set a fire?'

'There's a well-known pyromaniac on the ward,' Trevor murmured softly.

'I still haven't worked out what *you're* doing here, Joseph?'

'Assisting us with our enquiries,' Evans said shortly. 'If we're going to search this place thoroughly, we'll need all the help we can get.'

'Not from the mentally sick.'

'I was hoping to be discharged tomorrow.'

Bill looked at him through narrowed eyes. 'Then you really are feeling better?'

'I believe so,' Trevor repeated firmly, refusing to let Mulcahy intimidate him.

'If you're as fit as you say you are, you could be more use to us inside than out.'

'What do you mean?' Trevor asked, although he already had his suspicions.

'If we had someone on the inside . . . a good detective, which you used to be, Joseph, we might, just make some headway with this case.'

'You're asking me to stay on this hospital just so you can have another pair of eyes on the case?'

'A pair of *inmate's* eyes,' Mulcahy qualified. 'And they see a lot more than any copper who only comes in to interview witnesses. Come on, Joseph. Even a few days more might make all the difference. I'll see that you're put back on full pay immediately.'

181

'I'm very happy with sick pay.'

'Look, we've got nothing concrete as yet. If this Hedley woman really has been abducted by our villain, then the chances are she's still somewhere around the hospital. And still alive! You could be her only chance.'

'I thought you were planning to search the whole place thoroughly?'

'We will, but even if we do eventually find her, there's no guarantee that we'll get to her in time.'

'Mr Waters is here now Superintendent.' A female constable knocked sharply on the door and put her head round.

'I'm off to bed,' Trevor seized the opportunity to rise from his seat.

'Lucky, lucky you,' Collins moaned.

'You'll think about what I just said?' Mulcahy asked.

'I'll think about it, but I'm promising nothing.'

Trevor stepped outside and shivered. All the lights were on in his ward block. Without thinking he entered the perspex tunnel and began to walk. There was nothing inside, ahead or behind him. He knew because he stopped dead several times and looked quickly around. But he was still left with an uneasy feeling that he was being followed.

Quickening his pace, he hurried on, hammering the locked door of his block as soon as he reached it at the other end.

Lyn Sullivan opened up, holding a carton of scouring powder in rubber-gloved hands.

'You've been with the police all this time?'

'Gossiping, that's all,' he dismissed lightly.

'They started searching yet?'

'Just getting started.' He stepped inside and bolted the door behind him. 'Want some tea?'

'Is that your way of asking me to make you a cup?'

'No,' he replied. 'I've just drunk more coffee in an hour than I've drunk in the last month. But tea would be a way of getting you to sit down for five minutes. You look about all in.'

'I am,' she admitted wearily.

As he followed her down the corridor, the ward seemed eerily silent without its patients, the rumpled beds and hastily thrown-back sheets and blankets adding to the air of ghostly

182

desertion. Their footsteps echoed disconcertingly across the tiled floor as they entered the kitchen.

'The patients have all been split up between the five other wards. When the fire service finished here, I thought I may as well come back and clear up, so everyone could move back in first thing in the morning.'

She peeled off her rubber gloves and sank down in a chair. Trevor filled the electric kettle and switched it on. There was a strong smell of cleaning fluid and bleach in the kitchen, and every surface shone, free of the grime and smuts deposited earlier.

'You really do look done in,' he commented, as she passed her hand over her forehead. 'I'm sorry.'

'For what?'

'For causing a mess that you had to clean up.'

'I'd rather clean up a mess than be haunted for the rest of my life by something I didn't do, and should have.'

'And I'm also sorry for making trouble between you and Karl Lane,' he ventured tentatively.

'You can hardly hold yourself responsible for that.'

'I hope it will soon blow over.'

'What will soon blow over?' Was she being deliberately obtuse?

'I thought there was something between you.'

'There *was*,' she said emphatically. 'And *was* is where it will stay after tonight.'

He opened the caddy and removed a tea bag. Putting it into a cup he poured boiling water on top. 'How do you like it?'

'Milk, no sugar.'

The atmosphere between them felt suddenly strained. He had to say something.

'If *you* were going to hide a body in this hospital, where would you put it?' he asked.

'Difficult to say,' she mused. 'A hundred and one places could spring to mind.'

'Try naming ten.'

'There's hundreds of odd corners in the original old building. Last Christmas some bright spark at the staff party came up with the idea of playing hide-and-seek. We found all sorts of

183

staircases, towers, and lots of little rooms. Most of them were locked, but not all. And there are odd doors in odd corners at the rear of the building that don't even have locks, and some of those lead back into other nooks and crannies.' She smiled.

'Something funny?'

'Not really. That was when Karl, Kelly, myself and the staff nurse from manias, caught out the great Mr Waters. If he'd ever found out who we were, I'm sure he'd have sacked the lot of us.'

'What do you mean "caught him out",' Trevor frowned.

'Karl barged into a room at the top of the building, God only knows where. I doubt any of us could find our way there again. Well, there was a mattress in the corner, and a half-naked couple going hammer-and-tongs on top of it. We stayed just long enough to register what they were doing, then we beat a hasty retreat.'

'You sure it was Waters?'

'No other man around here has that colour hair. The woman saw us, I'm sure. But if she recognised us, she couldn't have said anything. If she had, he'd have followed it up. He can be a vindictive bastard.'

'What makes you say that?'

'Oh, nothing he's done to me. Just what I've heard from some of the other nurses. Written warnings when they've booked in two minutes late for a shift, when all the traffic in the town's been ground to a standstill. Like last month, when there was that mammoth pile-up in the middle of town. Remember it?'

'I don't remember anything that happened last month – or the three before that,' he said with a wry smile.

'I'm sorry. Stupid of me.'

'You're not stupid. Tell me, has Waters got a reputation for that sort of thing?'

'Womanising?'

'Yes.' He boiled up the kettle again, rinsed out her cup and prepared more tea; two cups this time.

'According to Angela Morgan his secretary, yes. She says that strange women are always phoning him up. I'd feel sorry for his wife but . . .'

'Sister Ashford?'

184

'Yes, she's a first-class nurse, but she's also a bit of a cold fish. Always gives me the impression that she couldn't give a damn about anything except herself. But, then, I suppose that comes with the job; concealing your feelings, I mean. You get hard-bitten doing work like this, whether you intend to or not. And, then again, Karl told me that he's occasionally seen her about town with some fellow . . . Look, this is all very well, but it's hospital gossip. You're not interrogating me, are you?' she sounded suddenly suspicious.

'Absolutely not.' He handed her a mug. 'I'm sick – unfit for duty.'

'But you still spend hours talking to your work mates.'

'Policing is a funny job. You can go months without seeing a real civilian – outside of the villains that get booked into the Station – and when a big case needs cracking like now, you eat sleep and drink nothing but the case. You live with coppers, eat with coppers, but you can't even socialise with coppers because there's no time for social life for the duration.'

'So I take it you don't sleep with coppers?'

'I've had to share a room with Peter on occasion.' He made a peculiar face. 'And twelve down-and-outs once, when we went undercover in Jubilee Street.'

'That must have been fun.'

'Police work can be funny, but not for coppers' girlfriends, family or wives. It all takes its toll. None of us are married now. Peter's divorce is being finalised later this year. The super's wife walked out on him during our last big case, the one I got mangled on. And Dan Evans is a widower.'

'And you?'

'I was never married,' he said shortly.

'But there was someone.'

'Just a girl I lived with for a while. She got tired of spending nights on her own, and found someone else.'

'And she had long dark hair.'

'Short blonde actually. Why do you ask?'

'The girl you keep sketching.'

Trevor drank his tea in silence.

'I'm sorry I didn't mean to pry.'

'You're not, really. After all, you told me about Karl and

yourself. It's just that I'd probably find it easier to talk about her if something *had* happened between us. But it didn't.'

'You wanted it to?'

'Yes. But whenever we met, it was always the wrong time and the wrong place.'

'And now?'

'She isn't even in the country. I couldn't get hold of her, even if I wanted to. Which I don't,' he added firmly. 'Dreams are best left where they are.'

He wondered if he really meant what he'd just said. He'd carried a torch for Daisy for so long now, he couldn't even begin to imagine what life would be like if he actually relinquished it. He'd have nothing left – nothing at all except mundane, soul-crushing, bleak reality. All the time he'd lain in intensive care, he'd dreamt of her returning to him. Visiting his bedside with a smile on her beautiful curved mouth.

'I've come back, Sergeant Joseph . . .'

He couldn't be sure, really sure, what he'd feel for Daisy if she walked back into his life now. So much had happened, so much of his life – and hers – had been destroyed.

He jerked himself out of his imaginings, and turned to look at Lyn, remembering their current conversation.

'Then, if you wanted to hide someone's body you'd aim for the old hospital?'

'And hope I didn't stumble across Tony Waters indulging in extra-marital activities.' She laughed. 'Or else I'd consider the grounds. There's supposed to be passages down in the cellars that come up outside in the bushes. But if they exist, I've never seen any evidence – only heard the older staff like Jimmy Herne talk about them.'

'Does *he* know where they are?' Trevor realised that if such a passage did exist, it could signify a lot.

'According to Tony, who knows more than anyone about this place, they were all blocked up years ago. I think that's probably true. Jimmy did show us the beginnings of one once, down by the folly, but the earth had caved in? She paused for an instant, and frowned. 'Knowing what I do about the way this place is run, there'd be no need to hide a body anywhere secretive.'

'What do you mean?'

'One extra drugged zombie wouldn't be noticed, or, even counted on most wards from one week to the next. Especially on geriatric.'

Chapter Thirteen

Vanessa was cold. Freezing! Not shivering. There was no feeling in her body other than *cold*. Nothing – no sensation at all. Not the slightest tingle, the slightest pain – only numbness, as though her mind was floating, disembodied in a turgid, icy, black void. She strained her eyes and stared intensely into the darkness. She knew her eyes were open because she could actually hear the whisper of her eyelashes moving. This solitary, single, alarming sound in a vacuum of silence. All around was frosty, black, enveloping darkness unpunctuated by the slightest glimmer of grey shadow. She wondered if perhaps the air itself had changed colour?

Her body had to be somewhere. She tried to move, but there seemed to be no physical form for her brain to command. Her mind sent messages to nerves that dissipated into an intangible, insensitive void. There were no limbs to react, simply nothing at all. She heard the murmur of her eyelashes again, and concentrated on her facial muscles. She screamed, but the piercing screech resounded only in her imagination. Her lips refused to open, and the only sound born in the back of her throat was a tiny grunt that startled her, conveying blind terror and panic in its wake. She forced herself to remain calm, to think – to remember!

A grisly memory from her childhood, a scene from an almost forgotten horror film, flooded unbidden and undirected into her mind. A brain in a jar? No she had to be more than a brain in jar. A whole head! But a head without a body. Or was she already dead? Was this what death was like? Cold black nothingness!

Vanessa screamed and screamed her silent cries, again and

again. Eventually worn out, exhausted, she tried to rid herself of that repulsive image of a disembodied head, by concentrating on her more immediate past.

She had been . . . where? The day-room. Roland Williams, disgusting, fat lecherous Roland, who put his damp sweaty hands on her knees and tried to move them higher every chance he got. She saw again the small half-moon slivers of skin she'd gouged out of the back of his hand with her fingernails when he'd tried to maul her thighs.

Lucy, sweet naive Lucy, her eyes wide open, agog with a mixture of wonder, terror, delicious fascination and morbid curiosity as she'd related the story – the embroidered and embellished version, of the phantom burying the body. The phantom! The phantom who buried live women, after – if Roland was to be believed – gross violation of their bodies. She was where? In the earth? Was that why she couldn't feel anything?

No. She breathed! She could hear her own breath. Soft, quiet, but still there; in – out – in – out. If she was buried in the earth, she wouldn't be breathing. She would be suffocated. Dead! Was this hell? No, she was cold, and hell was hot; devils hammering red hot spears of metal. She listened for the blacksmith sounds, her eardrums straining to breaking point. But the only noise that rang in her consciousness was a droning that came from inside her own fevered brain. Then faintly in the background the tired jingle of an old pop song. *Bop, bop, bop, be bop* – as incessant and irritating as a dripping tap. Was that also a product of her imagination? She could no longer fathom what was real and what was not.

Then came panic again. Hysteria as she remembered the woman at the bottom of the pit! Was she the woman? Planted! Dead! A people tree – she had said something about a people tree. But there was no such thing as a people tree! Dead people didn't grow into anything. They rotted. Decayed and rotted! And Ian – he wouldn't know where she was. But then he wouldn't have wanted to visit her anyway. He hadn't visited her ever. Not once. Not here. Not in any of the other places she'd been taken to before this. It wasn't fair. If he'd tried to kill *her*, she would have visited him.

190

She pictured her husband as he'd been when she had first met him. When he'd loved her and truly worshipped the ground she walked on. Slowly, tenderly she recreated every detail she could recall of his features. The lock of rich brown hair that insisted on falling over one eyebrow. His smile, lopsided, cynical. His eyes, deep dark brown, mirroring – yet at the same time concealing – so many of his thoughts in their gleaming depths. The feel of the skin on his back, smooth, silky beneath her fingers as they'd made love in their king-sized bed in the best bedroom suite in their hotel. No point in stinting themselves when life was so good. If the guests lived in luxury, why not they?

And afterwards, when she was alone, and Ian was no longer part of her life. Horrid little cells with nasty iron bedsteads covered by ugly, grey, itchy blankets and darned cotton sheets, not the silk or satin she'd slept on with Ian. Odious little cells with chamberpots in the corners. Ugly, foul-smelling, not even clean. But then neither had she been clean, as she was allowed only one bath a week.

A noise came from outside her head. The sharp, rasping grate of metal scraping against metal. A light, intense, blinding, shone directly into her eyes, forcing her to close them. She tried to speak, but again managed only small animal grunts. Something came towards and over her, blanketing, smothering. It touched her face, fell over her nose, but she still breathed, then it went away. The light grew dim. There was a quick, sharp pain in her arm. Despite the hurt she marvelled that she felt it. She still had a body after all!

Warmth came. A pleasant glow that stole up from her arm and enveloped her consciousness. A radiation that rapidly transformed itself into a burning agony of scorching pain. She tried to cry out, but all she heard was a succession of the same, small bestial whimpers as before. Metal on metal. Darkness. No light. Only agony, absolute agony; she could only feel pain. Total consuming, absolute suffering. She *was* pain.

The torment continued without respite. Continued for all eternity. Pain! Absolute pain. Burning, searing, raging – nothing else existed. Nothing at all!

191

* * *

'Right, all of you to the attic. Station one man at the top of every staircase, radios at the ready The rest of you, comb every inch of the building. I want everything up there moved and searched; boxes, files, rubbish sacks, furniture. I don't care how thick the dust is, or how small the space. I want every door unlocked, every room scrutinised, every cupboard emptied, all the walls tapped, and anything that rings hollow ripped apart. This place is condemned, and if we have to, we'll raze it to the ground and worry about the inconvenience and cost later. When you've finished the top floor, you leave a man on each staircase and check all the routes down to the next floor, then you repeat the whole procedure again, until you've worked your way down to the cellar. I want men left on every floor. The split second you see anything vaguely suspicious, you scream down your radios for me. Don't forget to check for possible gaps between ceilings and floorboards, and do remember to use the floor plans and the measuring tapes you've been given.' Collins knew he was labouring the point, but weariness had set in, making him apprehensive and unwilling to trust anyone's work but his own.

'Sergeant Collins,' Michelle Grady was at his elbow again, bright-eyed, sharp as a button. Didn't the damned woman ever get tired like the rest of them? 'Superintendent Mulcahy and Inspector Evans would like to see you in the mobile HQ as soon as possible, sir.'

'Tell them I'll join them when I can,' he barked irritably.

'There's a man from the Home Office with them, sir,' she informed him with a smug smile.

'I've given you my reply, Constable.' He turned away and faced the team of men and women lined up in the shabby echoing hallway of the old hospital. 'Right, go to it. I'll be with you as soon as I can get away. Remember, note any and every little thing that's remotely out of the ordinary, and call me the minute you find anything suspicious. Constable Grady will go with you, she knows where we disturbed the dust the last time we took a look around,' he said, pleased with himself for getting her off his hands again so quickly.

192

Reluctantly turning his back on the search parties, he left the hall and walked through the back door towards the mobile headquarters. He passed through the outer office ignoring the two women who manned the telephones, but acknowledging Constable Sarah Merchant, who was operating the computer, with a curt nod, before he opened the door into the inner sanctum that Evans and Mulcahy had virtually claimed as their own territory.

Harry Goldman and an enormous, burly, red-headed man he'd never seen before were sitting sweltering in the close, sticky atmosphere that reeked of stale coffee, cigarette smoke and greasy food.

'Collins,' Mulcahy muttered wearily. He and Evans, like Peter himself were looking the worse for wear. The bags under their eyes wouldn't shift or lighten in a month of regular early nights; all three were clearly living on the fag-end of their reserves, yet they were barely three days into the case 'This is Professor Crabbe,' Mulcahy introduced the stranger.

'John Crabbe, Home Office,' he extended a massive, square and very hairy hand to Collins. 'I've come down here with a psychological profile of your chap.'

'I thought it best if we three run through it with Professor Crabbe first, before revealing it to the full team.'

'Good idea.' Collins pulled a chair up to the table and sat alongside Dan Evans. Mulcahy banged on the door and shouted in a voice calculated to carry through the thin walls. 'Fresh coffee for five.'

'Yes, sir,' came a surly reply from one of the two women constables. Collins sensed the resentment in her voice.

'Right, with another woman missing, we've no time to waste, so let's get down to business.'

Collins detected the strain in Mulcahy's demeanour. The investigation hadn't been going well even before Vanessa's disappearance had brought a new and keener edge to the proceedings, and Collins knew his colleague well enough to read his thoughts. Here they were, the three most senior and experienced officers in the investigation, sitting idly on their arses listening to two shrinks, instead of getting out there and on with catching the warped individual who had already claimed three innocent lives and was probably now claiming a fourth.

'We've taken all the data you've accumulated and fed it into a computer that holds everything we know about all documented serial killers convicted during the past thirty years, both here and in America—'

'Why America?' Collins interrupted.

'You know the saying,' the Home Office psychologist smiled insincerely. 'What America does today, we'll be doing in twenty years time. When it comes to crime, I'm afraid that maxim appears to be true; the Americans seem to have cornered the market on serial killers. Rather spectacularly.'

Collins remembered Spencer Jordan and his American connections, but said nothing. That was something to mention later, when Harry Goldman and this Home Office chap with his condescending manner were elsewhere.

'Shall I begin?' John Crabbe lifted his steel-coated briefcase on to the desk and manipulated the combination lock. He clicked it open and extracted a thick file, bulging with loose papers. 'We're looking for a man, the computer says anything between twenty-five and forty, but I'd be inclined to lower the upper limit to thirty-five. He's a loner, finds it difficult to form relationships with either men or women, but the lack of women in his life upsets him more than the lack of male friends. He's impotent . . .'

'Impotent?' Dan Evans broke in.

'There's no sign of sperm,' Crabbe declared emphatically.

'I thought there was no evidence of rape?' Evans corrected.

'Without sperm, or physical signs such as tissue tearing, it's not always possible to determine if entry has been forced or not. But whether the victims were in fact raped isn't crucial to this profile.'

'It isn't?' Collins asked with an assumed air of innocence.

'Psychologists now agree that rape itself is not a sexual crime.'

'Try telling that to some of the women I've interviewed after the event,' Collins muttered mutinously.

'Rape is a crime of violence that delineates power over the helpless victim. Our man takes women, holds them, and whether he attempts rape or not – and I'm inclined to the latter opinion – he's certainly unable to consummate any kind of lasting meaningful relationship with his victim, physical or otherwise. He's a loner who gets his kicks, if you'll forgive me for putting it that way, in asserting his power over another being.' Crabbe continued talking briskly to discourage further interruptions. 'Possibly from a small family, probably an only child. Unused to living with, or relating to others in what we'd consider a "normal" fashion, although I use that word, as always, with caution. He lives either alone or with a single domineering female relative – mother, grandmother, aunt or older sister. He has no friends, as we'd define them. In fact, as I've already said, he finds it difficult to form any kind of relationships at all. It's ninety per cent certain that he comes from the lower socio-economic group. Blue collar worker or unemployed, either way he's a low achiever.'

'Except in the case of murder,' Peter murmured caustically. 'What I'd like to know is whether we're looking at a patient here or a member of the hospital staff?'

'Difficult to say,' John Crabbe hedged. 'Could be either. As a rough guideline I'd say your man will fit at least fifty per cent of this profile, possibly more.' He patted his file fondly. 'But on the other hand, I must caution you; do use this computer profile with circumspection. On occasions, we have been proved wrong.' He laughed mirthlessly. 'This is not yet an exact science, but in most cases it has been proved extremely helpful.'

'We're aware of the possibility of error.' The irony of Mulcahy's reply wasn't lost on Crabbe.

'According to our profiles, if the killer has a police record at all, it will only be for minor, unrelated offences.' Crabbe determinedly ignored Bill's hostility. 'We have discounted the kidnapping-for-profit theory. I'm right in saying there have been no ransom demands?' he looked inquiringly at Bill.

'You are,' Mulcahy agreed. 'And, apart from Claire Moon, the victims have hardly been the wealthy type that any self-respecting kidnapper would want to snatch.'

'Have you considered that this man may be a collector,' Harry Goldman made his first contribution to the proceedings.

'A collector?' Evans stared at the psychiatrist. 'Would you

195

please explain?' he continued in his slow, deceptively sleepy drawl.

'A collector,' Crabbe repeated, 'is someone who accumulates a number of related, generally useless, decorative objects purely for his own personal gratification, because they give him pleasure of ownership.'

'Like those people who get their kicks out of poring over a book of stamps?' Collins suggested.

'Exactly,' Goldman twittered excitedly. 'Or butterflies, or china frogs, or photographs, and memorabilia connected with a certain personality, sports or film stars.'

'Let's get this straight,' Mulcahy laid his hands flat on the table. 'Are you saying our man could be a collector of marbles who's moved on to collecting women?'

'Could be. Tell me, have your people worked out any significance in where you found the bodies, or the way they were laid out?'

'Laid out?' Evans leant forward over the table, and propped his head upon his hands.

'Well, were the bodies buried in any precise or significant pattern? For example, were their feet pointing north? Is he planting them at the four corners of the hospital grounds, or in the shape of something recognisable; a star perhaps?'

Evans left his seat and walked over to the wall behind the desk. He retracted a roller blind that covered the back wall. Pinned to a cork board that had been concealed by the blind were a series of blown-up photographs taken just after the three victims had been uncovered, but before they were removed from their unorthodox graves.

'The burial sites,' Mulcahy said drily. 'Please, take a look at the victims' positions for yourself. As to their graves in relation to the grounds, there's the plan of the hospital and the gardens, with the sites pinpointed with red markers.' He pointed to a ground plan and aerial photograph on the opposite wall. 'All were buried in flowerbeds, all in holes that had been initially dug out by the gardeners and left unattended overnight. The last victim was laid north to south, the second north-west to south-west, and the third east to west. Personally I think the positioning has more to do with where the flowerbeds are situated than with Voodoo circles.'

'I merely wondered if you had considered all the options,' Crabbe said shortly.

'I'm inclined to think that our villain is simply a nut who doesn't want to do any more digging than absolutely necessary. In fact he could be a case who plants bodies without giving his actions much thought at all,' Peter declared cynically.

'Never underestimate your opponent,' Crabbe reprimanded sternly.

'Shall we go back to the beginning?' Dan went to a flip-chart pinned to a stand in the opposite corner of the room, and turned the pages with irritating slowness until he came to a clean new page. At the top he wrote PROFILE. 'We know he's strong because according to our witness, he *carried* the bodies to the burial sites.' He wrote "*Strong*" in smaller letters beneath the heading.

'Big as well, if Vanessa Hedley is to be believed,' Collins added.

Evans added "*Big*" to the list.

'Professor, you say he's a loner – doesn't relate to people, especially women. Is that right?' Evans pressed.

'Men and women,' the professor qualified. 'But someone like that would feel the absence of a woman in his life very keenly indeed.'

Dan wrote "*Loner*."

'And you say he's impotent?'

'Almost certainly, but even with the aid of our computer I wouldn't like to hazard whether his sexual impotence is physical or psychological in origin.'

'Either way, the results would be the same,' Collins commented as Dan added "*Impotent*" alongside the other words.

'He lives alone,' the Professor continued enthusiastically, pleased that Evans at least, was taking him seriously. 'Or with a domineering female relative.'

'One – or more than one?' Bill barked.

'I'd be inclined to stick my neck out and say *one*, although I suppose there is a slim possibility that there could be a mother *and* an older sister,' Crabbe said thoughtfully.

197

'What about a . . .'

What about what, Collins?' Mulcahy demanded sharply.

'Well how the hell would you explain . . .' Peter's voice tailed away as he followed Bill's glance towards Harry Goldman. He snapped his mouth shut like a goldfish. He'd forgotten Goldman was in the room, and he could hardly accuse the live-in companion of his most senior assistant psychiatrist of being the murderer. 'I mean . . . a relationship where a man and a woman live together on a platonic basis just to pool expenses, like pay the rent,' he finished lamely.

'Our man doesn't share a house on a rent-sharing basis unless he has his own space, his own front door, and a key for it,' John Crabbe insisted firmly.

Dan picked up the pen again and added "*Lives alone or with domineering female relative*".

'Possibly a collector,' Harry reminded sharply. He was proud of his contribution, and knew exactly who Collins had in mind when he mentioned platonic relationships.

Dan scribbled "*Collector*".

'He chooses and gets himself a mate; a female. Keeps her hidden for a while. Plays with her. Does whatever he wants with her, shows her kindness, cruelty, torture even, and all on a whim. Then when he eventually tires of the game, he buries her.' Goldman described the scenario as graphically as he could. 'The ultimate collection that is his secret, belonging to no one else, uniquely his forever,' he finished with a flourish.

'He must know this hospital inside out,' Collins commented, 'to spirit Vanessa Hedley away the way he did.'

'That's if he does have her.' Mulcahy lifted his feet from the desk. 'I thought I ordered coffee,' he grumbled.

'Even if he doesn't, he buried the others when there were security guards around, and that must mean something where this place is concerned. We know he kept his victims somewhere private, and starved them. He couldn't have brought them into this hospital on a number 10 bus.'

'No, but he could have had them tucked in the boot of his car.'

'Either way, I think it's safe to assume he has a reasonable knowledge of the layout of this hospital,' Crabbe pressed, anxious to move the proceedings forward.

Evans unscrewed the cap of his pen.

'And you can add *"Knowledge of, and access to drugs"*, Peter muttered.

'He would have suffered mood swings at or about the time of each disappearance and murder. You've nothing more accurate to give us on dates of the first two murders?' Crabbe asked.

'We've had to rely on the pathologist, and the only thing we can be certain of is that the latest victim was buried on a cloudy night when there was an intermittent full moon.'

'You've forgotten to list his low socio-economic grouping,' Goldman reminded, as he left his seat. 'I'm sorry, gentlemen, but I must leave you. I have an appointment with a patient, with Sergeant Joseph in fact.'

'If you sign him out, fit for duty, let me be the first to know,' Mulcahy said, not entirely humorously. 'I need every man I can get.'

A knock at the door interrupted them. Harry Goldman opened it no more than a crack.

'Coffee, sir,' a female voice floated in.

'Take the coffee from her Collins,' Bill ordered brusquely. 'The last thing we need is a woman passing out at the sight of this little lot.' He indicated the photographs Dan had uncovered.

Blocking her view into the room, Collins opened the door a bit wider and removed the tray from the constable's hands. She was a blonde, one he hadn't seen around the Station before, about twenty-five years old by the look of her – older than the latest influx of rookie constables by about five years. He winked at her and she kicked him sharply and painfully on the shin.

'So sorry Sergeant Collins,' she apologised, smiling sweetly. 'My foot slipped.'

As he carried the tray inside, Goldman took the opportunity to sidle out. Collins slammed the door by putting his back to it. He dumped the tray on top of the papers spread on the table, much to the disgust of Crabbe, who made a great show of extracting his file from beneath it. All four men stared at the words on the flip-chart while they helped themselves to coffee, milk and sugar.

Big. Strong. Loner. Impotent. No friends or visible woman in life apart from domineering mother or older sister. Possible collector. Knowledge of hospital layout, drugs, and has access to drugs. From the lower echelons of socio-economic grouping. Had noticeable mood swings at times of victims' disappearance and murder.

'Anything else, Professor?' Mulcahy asked.

'Twenty-five to thirty-five years old – possibly forty at the outside.'

Dan obediently amended the list, and stood with his pen poised next to the chart.

'He's also neat, tidy and careful,' Dan said slowly.

'What makes you say that?' Crabbe asked.

'Absence of hairs and fibres in those graves. The pathologist found nothing there that didn't belong to the victims.'

'He's certainly careful,' the psychologist agreed tentatively.

'Bloody careful.' Collins parried the psychologist's stare. 'Well, we haven't caught him. And let's be totally honest here, are we any further forward after this little episode?' He stared at the list.

'Suppose we try to match our suspects to this profile,' Mulcahy suggested. He agreed with Peter's sentiments, but Crabbe was Home Office after all.

'Start with the patients?'

'Staff,' Collins suggested, still smarting from his realisation that Mulcahy and Evans had regarded Trevor as a potential suspect.

'The gardener Jimmy Herne is too old. The administrative officer Tony Waters is married . . .' Evans began.

'To a woman who's so cold I wonder if she's flesh or ice,' Collins broke in.

'For all you know, she could be a veritable volcano in private.' Mulcahy smiled wryly.

'I seriously doubt it.'

'What's the matter? Didn't she fancy you, Collins?' Bill asked, forgetting the presence of Crabbe for a moment. He was stiff, aching, tired of these proceedings – and just plain tired. All he wanted was bed, preferably alone, and the sooner the better.

'If you're going to do this properly,' Crabbe interrupted, 'you're going to have to consider everyone – from the top down.'

'Harry Goldman?' Peter smiled at Mulcahy.

'Single. Lives alone,' Bill entered into the spirit of the session.

'Wrong socio-economic grouping.' Evans finished his coffee and replaced his empty cup on the tray.

'Look at all the variables. Remember, I warned you about discrepancies,' Crabbe lectured again.

'Right on knowledge of drugs, and hospital, but wrong on size.' Collins pulled a cigar from his pocket. 'He weighs what? Seven stone at the outside, and two of those represent his glasses. Can you really see him trotting across the lawns with a twelve-stone woman slung across his shoulders?'

'OK. What about Jimmy Herne the gardener? He didn't seem to like us digging,' Dan mused.

'Too old, at sixty. And he's married with six children. Three of them are still at home,' Bill revealed.

'Spencer Jordan?' Dan returned to his chair and flicked through his notebook.

'Now there's a name to conjure with,' Collins exhaled twin streams of smoke from his nostrils. 'Right age bracket at thirty-eight, tall, strong, loner, no visible women, or friends, knowledge of hospital both as a patient and staff member, I dare say he could organise access to drugs, and after three years spent in psychiatric hospitals he should know how to use them.'

'Collector?' Crabbe asked.

'He has lots of pictures on the walls of his room,' Peter commented.

'It is an art therapy room,' Dan chipped in. 'And he's the wrong socio grouping; he's not a low achiever.'

'That depends on where you're starting from. A few years ago he was a mile higher than he is now,' Peter pointed out. 'He fulfils a lot of the other criteria. Lives alone in a hospital flat. I'd say, after visiting his workroom, that he's neat, tidy, careful, and he has a past that could have turned his psyche upside-down.'

'Put him down as number one on an interview list.' Mulcahy tapped a cigarette out of a new packet. 'Next one!'

'Adam Hayter.' Collins sat forward.

'Big, but not strong,' Dan murmured. 'He's flabby.'

'Coming from you, that's rich.' Peter smiled. 'And flabby or not, he could manage a twelve-stone woman. After all he must manage Dotty Clyne.'

'What about no visible woman in his life?' Evans asked

'You call Dotty a woman?' Collins sneered.

'Other criteria,' Mulcahy snapped.

'Collector?' Dan suggested.

'I don't know about collector, but have you been in his kitchen?' Collins asked. 'Talk about everything in its place and spotless. He's neat, tidy and careful, right age at twenty-nine, I'd go along with impotent, and as for loner, every time I see him I'm practically trampled to death in the rush of people desperately trying to avoid contact with him.'

'Lower socio-economic group?' Crabbe reminded.

'Cooks are notoriously ill paid, he has knowledge of both hospital and drugs, and he lives with Dotty who's a domineering woman.'

'Add his name to the list, then we'll move on to the patients,' Mulcahy left his chair and paced across the room. If he didn't close his eyes soon, he'd go stark raving mad.

'Wait a minute. What about Dotty?' Collins asked.

'We're looking for a *man*,' Bill said impatiently.

'A dyke?' Collins looked inquiringly at Crabbe. 'What do you think?'

'There's only one recorded case of a lesbian serial killer to date,' Crabbe said authoritatively. 'And that's in America. One Aileen Wuornos. Working as a prostitute, she picked up, shot and killed at least seven men . . .'

'I didn't ask for a lecture,' Peter broke in. 'Only an opinion as to whether or not it's a possibility worth considering in this case?'

'It could be, but on the other hand you could be barking up the wrong tree,' Crabbe replied huffily, annoyed by Peter's interruption. 'The only data we have is related to the Wuornos case, and as I said it's American. A British lesbian serial killer would be a first for us psychiatrists, and psychologists, as well as yourselves. But I admit, in this case, I'm a little confused. I thought you said that Dotty was living with a therapist – this Adam Hayter. Am I right?'

'You're right,' Peter agreed.

'In my experience, lesbians rarely live with men.'

'Precisely. She's living with Hayter.'

'Let's move on,' Dan said evenly. 'She's big, strong—'

'Impotent,' Peter interrupted.

'And a psychiatrist which puts her out of the socio-economic grouping,' Bill said.

'But that's the only variable,' Peter pointed out. 'She has a knowledge of the hospital, and drugs. She's the right age at thirty-six. She's certainly impotent in male sexual terms,' he repeated drily. 'She has to be worth thinking about.'

'Add her to your list,' Bill ordered Dan Evans.

'If we're going to look at one woman, we'd better look at them all. Jean Marshall, Lyn Sullivan, Carol Ashford . . .' Collins recited.

'Carol Ashford's married,' Evans said.

'Happily?' Mulcahy asked.

'You tell us,' Collins ventured. 'She's married to Tony Waters. They live together on a farm.'

'Then it's a safe bet it's neither of them,' Crabbe pronounced decisively.

'Jean Marshall's divorced, but outgoing and friendly.'

'Peter, you've known her longer than any of us.' Mulcahy stubbed his cigarette out on a saucer and lit another.

'I'd say she's more the "Looking for Mr Goodbar" type than a murderer.'

'Lyn Sullivan's only just twenty-one, and has a boyfriend; that nurse, Karl Lane,' Dan said.

'I think it's safe to leave the women,' Mulcahy snapped. 'Let's start on the patients.'

'Roland Williams is too old.'

'He's lecherous,' Peter observed.

'Not impotent, from what I've heard.'

'Likes to touch up females every chance he gets.'

Mulcahy looked over at Crabbe. 'Our man?'

'Is neither a toucher nor a lecher. In fact he's probably a prude. Wouldn't stand for public mention of sex.'

'A prude!' Collins exclaimed.

'Outwardly he probably sees sex as something dirty. Remember the domineering woman.'

'Roland out,' Collins murmured reluctantly. 'Michael Carpenter?'

'Pyromaniac only – not impotent from what his girlfriend said at trial. In fact whatever the opposite is, that's him.'

'On to the women.'

'Vanessa's disappeared. Lucy is too scared to say boo to a goose. She's young and believes herself married to Jason Donovan,' Collins explained to a bewildered Crabbe.

'In that case she's an extremely unlikely candidate.'

'And Ali Bevan is fixated on men.' Collins sighed as he crunched his cigar to powder against the side of a metal bin. 'Which means we're left with Spencer Jordan, Adam Hayter, Dotty Clyne, or any one of the fifty-two porters split between day and night shifts. Not to mention the nurses, male and female, or the security guards . . .'

'Maintenance men, gardeners—'

'And uncle Tom Cobley and all,' Collins broke in. 'God help us. For all of this,' he waved his hand at the flip-chart as he turned his back on it, 'it could be just one stray nut. And, as I've said before, what chance do we have of finding one screwed-up nut in a full bloody orchard that's ripe and ready for harvesting. Now, if you gentlemen can possibly spare me from this interesting exercise, I'll go and see if my team has turned anything up. Superintending a search that'll probably turn out futile isn't exactly mind-blowing hard work, but it'll make me happy,' he added cynically. 'And it will give me the opportunity to cling to the illusion that I'm doing something constructive towards finding Vanessa Hedley. Wherever that poor soul is.'

Chapter Fourteen

'I heard you went out yesterday.'

'Can't keep anything secret in this place, can you?'

'Tell me, how did you find the world after your absence from it?' Harry Goldman, hands clasped together on his lap, sat back in his chair and waited patiently for Trevor's response.

'It didn't appear to have suffered unduly by my absence,' Trevor replied shortly. Goldman's voice, which during his previous visits had droned on, just like so much background noise, now seemed incredibly condescending. He wondered if all psychiatrists treated their patients like recalcitrant children incapable of understanding even the most simple ideas unless broken down into words of single syllables.

'I see.' Goldman thoughtfully rested his chin on the tips of his fingers. Trevor was left with the uncomfortable feeling that he was frantically searching his mind for something else to say. 'Please, let's be honest with one another here,' the psychiatrist suggested eventually. 'Do you consider yourself ready to leave your ward?'

'You were right all along,' Trevor replied abruptly. 'I was fit to leave weeks ago. In fact, looking back, I should probably have gone home as soon as I left the General.'

'You really think you're ready to leave right away? Today?'

'I *know* I'm ready, but I'd like to talk to you about that.' Trevor left his chair and paced uneasily to the window. 'It's just that . . .'

'Everyone has doubts before taking such a monumental step forward. This place has been your sanctum, your second womb . . .'

'I don't have any doubts left,' Trevor interrupted, cutting

impatiently through Harry's professional jargon. 'But thank you for taking care of me when I did,' he conceded, not wishing to sound ungrateful. 'I intend to visit my flat today, and sort out a few things. But then there's the question of work.'

'Work!' Goldman stared at him in stunned amazement. 'Surely you can't be considering a return to such a stressful job so soon. Quite aside from your traumatic physical injuries, there's the question of pressure. You are only just starting out again. After an experience like yours that will be akin to re-learning how to cope with the day-to-day living process all over again. I don't doubt you genuinely believe yourself ready to face up to it, but I must warn you, the balance of your mind is still very delicate. The slightest upset may well cause a relapse. In my professional opinion, you should take a rest, relax, see some friends or perhaps visit somewhere entirely new. It really would be most unwise to contemplate returning to work for at least six months.'

Trevor smiled; now it was his turn to patronise. 'I don't think you know the police force, Dr Goldman,' he said quietly.

'Perhaps not, but I think you'll grant that I am *beginning* to learn something about the way it works.'

'When I spoke to Superintendent Mulcahy,' Trevor revealed, 'he suggested that I stay here, on the inside, for a few more days, to see if I could help them with their inquiries.'

'Into the murders?'

Trevor nodded.

'As your physician I must warn you that I think it a most unwise suggestion. As I said, the slightest stress or strain could . . .'

'They're pushed,' bored with Goldman's constant repetitions, Trevor cut him short. 'They need all the help they can get.'

'I'm sure it's very laudable to see such dedication in a public servant, but you have to realise that my first duty is to Trevor Joseph the patient, not Trevor Joseph the policeman.'

'I'm really grateful to you for getting me this far,' Trevor turned and smiled at Harry Goldman. 'Could I impose on your good nature for just a little longer. Would you write me a pass which would enable me to continue living here, and also to come and go as I please during the day.'

206

'It would be most unorthodox.'

'Not really. You have other patients who work.'

'Train – on sheltered government schemes,' Goldman corrected.

'Consider this one of those.'

'A murder inquiry?'

'It'll only be for a week or so.'

Goldman looked at Trevor for a moment before reluctantly picking up his pen. 'I'll give you a pass, on two conditions. First, you see me here every morning at eight-thirty for half an hour, so I can check on your progress, or lack thereof.'

'And?' Trevor demanded.

'And you limit your working time to no more than two hours a day,' Goldman finished firmly.

'I think I can agree to that.' Trevor smiled thinly. Most police work meant talking to people, interviewing, so it would be very difficult for anyone else to determine when he was and wasn't working, let alone the actual hours.

'And you will have to be back in your ward every night by ten o'clock.'

'I intend to be,' Trevor agreed, remembering the timing of the last burial.

'This is however most unorthodox,' Goldman demurred, as he finally signed his name to the pass.

Trevor went directly from the psychiatrist's office to the therapy unit in the old Victorian block. Everywhere he saw evidence of intense police activity. The fleet of cars and vans abandoned in every vacant nook around the building. The team of rookies combing the shrubberies, advancing inch by inch on hands and knees. The cracked voices that bounced back and forth on the radios of the team that were now searching the floors above him. Shuffling along, relying heavily on his stick, he made his way purposefully towards Spencer Jordan's room.

His timing was impeccable; the coffee break had just begun, and he found Spencer sitting alone on a stool pulled close to one of the clay-covered work tables, a couple of slices of carrot cake and a cup of decaffeinated coffee laid out on a sheet of newspaper in front of him.

207

'Coffee?' Spencer offered, pointing to the kettle.

'Thanks,' Trevor went to it and poured himself a coffee, without bothering to reheat the water.

'You look better today,' Spencer complimented.

'Everyone's saying that. It's just the clothes and the haircut.'

'And something else. You look . . .' Spencer put his head on one side and studied Trevor carefully, 'quietly confident.' He smiled, pushing a piece of cake to the edge of the newspaper facing Trevor.

'Thanks to you.' Trevor took the cake and bit into it. 'I stayed in town all afternoon yesterday, as you can see.' He smoothed down the back of his shorn neck. 'Today I'm going to look at my flat.'

'Leaving us?'

'Sort of, for the day at least.'

'Harry breaking you in gently?'

'Something like that.' Trevor was grateful to Spencer, liked him even, but breaking the glass on the fire alarm last night had been a watershed. It was something he wouldn't have thought twice about doing before he'd been injured, and the action had served as a timely reminder of what exactly being a policeman meant – and the restrictions that came with the job. He'd been warned as a rookie that policemen couldn't afford the luxury of too many friends outside the force. Particularly those who might be villains in disguise. And how well did one person ever really get to know another?

At any moment Spencer too could become a suspect. As Mulcahy constantly drummed into all the officers on his team, "Friendships cloud judgements." There were plenty of coppers who'd made mistakes on that score, and some of them had even ended up in the slammer.

Spencer stood looking out of the window at the officers combing the grounds. 'You part of the team again now?' he enquired shrewdly.

'Me, I'm on the sick.'

'My old grandfather used to say "Once a copper, always a copper".'

'Yesterday I was hoping to prove the maxim wrong.'

'And today?'

Trevor finished his coffee. 'I need to do some more thinking on the subject. That's why I want to go back to my flat.'

'Scared?'

'A little. I haven't seen it in four months, and I've begun to wonder about the rest of my life. I've recalled a few aspects of it that I didn't like, even at the time.'

'Worried in case you may want more than's on offer if you merely pick up where you left off?'

'Before . . . before I was injured, I never had time to think, really think about me, my life or where I was headed. I'd roll out of bed dog-tired in the morning, wake myself up by standing under a jet of cold water, work ten, twelve, on occasions twenty hours a day, eat lousy luke-warm takeaway food in the Station before going out again. No time to spend on anything important, like creating a home or a relationship that mattered.'

'And now you're going to look for that?'

'You've probably heard it all before,' Trevor smiled wryly, 'but if there's one thing I've learnt during the past four months, it's that once you're dead, that's it. You stay dead for one hell of a long time. No one's going to come round to the crematorium, pat you on the head, and say, "Well, you were a nice hardworking conscientious fellow last time round, so we'll give you another crack of the whip." So now,' Trevor rinsed his cup under the tap in the paint-spattered sink, 'I'm determined to make as much as I can of whatever time I've got left.'

'I wish you luck,' Spencer said quietly.

'In fact, at this moment I'm probably in very great danger of turning into a right selfish swine. I intend to make time, not only to put together a real home, but build relationships. Are you married?'

'I was,' Spencer said in a voice that dared him to press further. He crumpled the newspaper that had been under the cake, and threw it into the bin.

'I'm sorry,' Trevor murmured. 'Breaking up with someone is always hard.'

'It is,' Spencer replied shortly.

Trevor made his way back to his ward. He opened his wardrobe door, intending to dig out his new coat. He paused for a moment, staring at the row of clothes Collins had hung up for him when he'd first been admitted. The only reasonable item there, was the jacket he'd bought yesterday. The rest of his new clothes were still folded in the carrier bags that he hadn't yet had time to unpack. He lifted those from the floor and on to the bed, and tossed his new jacket on top of them, before flicking through his old clothes. Taking one of the black bags Collins had brought in for his laundry, he removed everything from the hangers and threw the entire contents of the wardrobe into the sack. He tied a knot firmly on the top.

'Spring cleaning?' Sister Marshall asked, pausing outside the open door.

'And tidying up before I leave,' he answered briefly. 'Harry Goldman's just given me a free pass for a week. After that I'll be out of here, and on my own.'

'You going out now?'

'To take a look at my flat. Thought I'd see if it's still standing.'

She looked him squarely in the eye. 'How would you like to have dinner with me tonight?'

'If I'm allowed to buy it, fine.' His pulse raced at the thought of taking even the first tentative step towards establishing a relationship with a woman. 'How about that pub on the Marina?'

'Eat in the same restaurant two nights running, and you're in danger of falling into a rut. Have you tried the Greek restaurant in Argyle Street?'

'There's nothing down there except offices.'

'It's new, it opened three months ago.'

'There you have me,' he smiled. 'Turn my back for a couple of months and the whole town changes. Shall I meet you there?'

'Seven o'clock,' she whispered as approaching footsteps echoed down the corridor. 'That'll give us time for a drink afterwards.'

Trevor slipped on his jacket, and deliberately tested himself by walking down the tunnel to the old block. Both his legs were aching, a nagging toothache type pain that had its origins in the unaccustomed exertions of yesterday. Forced to rely on his stick, he paused several times before reaching the far exit. Ordinary, everyday sounds fell strangely on his ears, eerily transformed and muted by the perspex sheeting. The roar of car engines became the dull, distant cries of large animals in pain. The crashing of pots of pans in the kitchen, became the clashes of a swordfight, the rattle of a trolley travelling over hard floors was the staccato report of machine gun-fire.

He pulled himself together sharply. The other thing a policeman couldn't afford, along with close civilian friends, was an over-active imagination. He hurried as purposefully out of the tunnel as his legs would allow, and into the main hall. Bypassing the milling crowd of blue-coated searchers, he turned back on himself and walked out of the rear door and up to the mobile headquarters. He knocked on the door just once before entering.

'Sergeant Joseph.' Sarah Merchant beamed at him, as he climbed awkwardly up the short flight of steps. 'You look a lot better today.'

'I feel a lot better ' He smiled at her and the other two girls manning the telephones. 'Busy?' he enquired lightly.

'Wish we were busier,' one of them grumbled. 'If we were, it might mean that all of this sitting around, waiting for something to happen, would soon be over and done with.'

'Rookies always get given the worst jobs,' he commiserated. 'But don't worry, it doesn't last forever. There'll be another batch of recruits coming in, and when they do, you'll be kicked upstairs to more interesting things, and then,' he grinned, 'you'll wish yourselves back here.'

Before either had a chance to reply, he spoke to Sarah.

'Any of the heavies in?'

'The Super and Inspector Evans.'

'They on their own?'

She nodded, and he went to the door.

After he'd disappeared into the inner sanctum, one of the other girls turned to Sarah. 'Who is that?'

'Sergeant Joseph. He was on the Drug Squad.'

'He's the one who almost got killed?'

'Almost.' Sarah swivelled round and stared at her computer screen. Trevor Joseph *had* almost got himself killed on his last case, but her own man hadn't been quite so lucky. Murdered during the investigation, they hadn't even found enough of him to fill a small box, let alone a coffin.

'He treats us as though we're human beings,' the girl chattered. 'Like we're police officers first, and women second.'

'Hasn't he heard about the force's official attitude to women recruits?' the other demanded.

'Perhaps it was the bang on the head,' the first one giggled. 'Perhaps a similar thump could do the same for the Super and Sergeant Collins.'

'Sergeant Joseph has always behaved the same,' Sarah Merchant replied. 'He's a thoroughly nice guy, but don't let his appearance deceive you. He used to be a damned good policeman,' she continued vehemently, 'and he also knew how to get tough when he had to.'

Mulcahy eyed Trevor warily as he entered the office.

'How are you?' he asked meaningfully.

'Fine.' Trevor propped his stick in a corner and sat down without waiting to be asked. 'Dr Goldman's just told me I'm fit enough to leave the hospital.'

'And you came here to tell us that?' Mulcahy failed to keep the irritation from his voice.

'No. I thought I'd let you know that I've decided to take you up on your offer. Goldman knows about it, and he's given me a pass for the next week. I'll be sleeping here, but I'll also be able to move freely in and out of the grounds during the day. I was hoping you'd be able to brief me on what exactly you want me to do.'

'Move around and mix with the natives. Pick up the vibrations. You know how much it helps to have someone on the inside.'

'This is hardly undercover,' Trevor warned. 'In this place I'm well known as a policeman.'

'Then you do intend to rejoin the force?' Bill murmured significantly.

'You agreed to reinstate me.'

'From the day you return to work. Is today soon enough?'

'One day too soon.' Trevor rose clumsily from the chair. 'Could you make it tomorrow? I'd like to go and look at my flat today, and there's not much I can do with the search going on. I'll be back tonight.'

'Want a ride into town?' Dan Evans asked.

Mulcahy glared thunderously at him. 'You're supposed to be running a murder investigation, not playing chauffeur.'

'O'Kelly rang. He wants to discuss the results of the tests he ran on the victims' blood samples.'

'Keep me posted, I'll be in the station.'

Trevor and Dan heard him barking at the girls in the outer office after he slammed the door behind him.

'Things aren't going too well at the moment,' Dan offered by way of an explanation. 'It's good to have you on board.'

'I'm not sure I'll be able to contribute that much. And to be quite honest I don't exactly relish the idea of staying on in this place when I don't need to.'

Evans opened the door of the office and led the way out. 'The car's around the corner,' he remarked, as he watched Trevor limping awkwardly along. 'Would you like me to bring it to the door?'

'No thanks. Sorry if I'm slowing you up,' Trevor said touchily.

'You're not,' Dan replied easily, without taking offence. 'Sometimes I think that's what's the matter with all our investigations. Everyone rushing around like a load of crazed ants out to build a nest at all costs, no one taking a second to stop and think, and overlooking the obvious even when it's right in front of them.'

'And what's the obvious in this case?'

'I just wish to God I knew,' Evans muttered, looking around at all the police activity. 'But it's there somewhere, waiting for us to spot it. Take my word.'

Lyn Sullivan tossed restlessly on her bed in the nurses' hostel. She had never slept well when she'd been on night shifts, and it seemed worse at the beginning and the end of a run of shifts. Her body-clock simply refused to move itself around to conform to hospital requirements. She turned over, stretched out on her back, and pulled the pillow over her head.

A minute ticked by on the clock, then another. Absolutely no good. It was simply no use at all. She lifted her pillow and stared at the electronic alarm clock on her bedside table. Ten-fifteen. She was due back on duty at seven-thirty, only eight hours away, and she'd promised to meet her friend Miriam for tea at five. Miriam had been in school with her, and had recently taken the post of junior mortgage advisor to the largest bank in town. Being Miriam, she hated it all. Her job, the town, the people she worked with, she saw every condition of her life as part of a conspiracy to make her miserable. She had never settled, and Lyn was beginning to wonder if Miriam's sole joy in life was moaning about her lot, over tea and cream cakes in the most expensive patisserie the town had to offer.

Lyn closed her eyes again and cursed the daylight filtering into the room despite the thick curtains. All she could now hope for was six hours' sleep, and she hadn't slept for twenty-four hours as it was.

Thoughts raced disquietingly through her mind. Vanessa Hedley? Where was she now, this minute? She was fond of Vanessa, despite all the upset she inevitably caused. She was a character and, unlike one or two of the other patients, not an unpleasant one. What was it her father always said? "A product of circumstances." That was it; Vanessa was a product of circumstances. If her husband hadn't fooled around, if she hadn't decided to follow him that night, her whole life would have turned out very differently. She'd probably still be queening it in that hotel on the beach front.

Lyn continued to toss restlessly in the narrow bed, listening to the revving engines of the police cars as they queued impatiently at the gates. How much longer before Vanessa would be found? And when she was, would it be at the bottom of a pit like all the others? Choked and suffocated by a ton or more of earth shovelled on top of her.

The buzz of a police helicopter hovering overhead reminded her of the heat-seeking cameras used to find the others. Was Vanessa already out there in the earth? Decay raising the

214

temperature of her cold flesh? Lyn turned violently on to her stomach, pulling the pillow down over her ears. It was useless. What would help? A warm shower? She'd had one just an hour ago. Hot chocolate? Cocoa? She'd drunk two cups already that morning; any more and she'd spend half the day going back and forth to the bathroom at the end of the corridor.

The radio? A book? A boring, boring book. Had to be a nursing textbook! She left the bed and went to her bookshelf, standing momentarily in front of the washbasin and the mirror that hung above it, naked except for a thin strand of red ribbon that pulled her hair back, away from her face.

She was standing there poised, holding the book in mid-air, when she heard a soft whispering noise outside her door. A cleaner pushing a polishing mop over the floor perhaps? She stood stock still. The noise was overlaid by the quiet hiss of breathing; she was certain of it. Or was she listening to her own intermittent intake of air. She held her breath, just to be sure.

A thud sent her scurrying back to the safety of her bed. The key which had been nesting securely in the lock of the door, had fallen, pushed out on to the doormat. She stared at it for a split second. Then she screamed.

Nerves ragged with fear, she recalled the gruesome details of the murders rumoured around the hospital, and she continued to scream as she grabbed her long green and purple silk dressing-gown from the foot of her bed. She tried to pull it over her shoulders, but only succeeded in getting it hopelessly tangled.

'Lyn! Lyn! Are you all right?' Above the hammering on her door she heard the voice of Alan, one of the charge nurses who had a room down the hall.

'Someone was at my door. The key . . .' she finally managed to get her gown on properly and tied the belt, then with shaking hands she picked up the key from the mat. Keeping the chain fixed across the door, she tentatively opened it. Three nurses were standing outside, all in dressing gowns too. 'I'm sorry I woke you . . .'

'What happened?' Alan demanded. 'You're shaking like a leaf.' She unfastened the chain and he walked into the room, looking around to check that everything was in its place.

'I was lying in bed and I heard a noise. When I looked up the key was being pushed out of the lock. Someone was at the door . . .'

'Richard, go downstairs and dial 999,' Alan ordered, his thoughts turning, like everyone else's to the murders.

'With all the police we've got hanging around the building?' Richard replied. 'I'll walk over to the main block and find one.' Without stopping for shoes or slippers, he ran off down the stairs. A door banged outside, somewhere above them.

'The fire escape.' Alan rushed out through the door.

'For God's sake be careful,' Mary, a second-year student nurse, called out after him.

'Wait for Richard to fetch the police,' Lyn shouted.

Both pleas fell on deaf ears.

Mary looked nervously at Lyn. 'Do you really think someone was there,' she whispered.

Lyn went to her window and opened her curtains.

Arms outstretched like a crucifixion, face squashed and distorted against the glass, the thin figure of a man stared back at her, dark eyes gleaming in puddles of white. He looked almost like a spider, a black venomous spider. His fingers clawed at the eaves above him, his toes retaining a tenuous grip on the window ledge. His open mouth leered, its breath fogging his features as he pitched alarmingly close to Lyn.

This time Mary screamed. The figure hovered for what seemed like an eternity, then he swayed. His face jerked backwards, giving the impression that his body terminated at his neck.

Then he fell. A cry echoed, lingering in the sweet spring air until the moment he landed with a dull thud on the flowerbed three floors below.

Chapter Fifteen

The woman in the wheelchair sat hunched forward, a shawl draped over her rounded shoulders, her forehead practically resting in her lap, her blonde hair curtaining her face and obscuring her features.

'Out for count,' shouted Mark Manners, a brash young porter, as he pushed past, wheeling his own chair that contained the emaciated, shrivelled figure of a geriatric. 'Isn't she just the lucky one?'

He received only a curt nod from the white-coated, baseball-capped figure that pushed the other chair. Someone new, Mark thought to himself. The meagre wages porters earned ensured a large and rapid turnover of staff. He no sooner got to know a bloke than the man moved on; but then, hopefully one day he'd be doing the same. He continued propelling his chair down the slope that led towards the old hospital. Whenever Mark got to this point, he had to fight the urge to let go of any chair or trolley he was pushing. He would love to watch his load roll down the hill towards the therapy units under its own steam.

'Soon be there now, love,' he murmured reassuringly to the elderly patient in the chair.

'I want to go home!' she yelled. 'Want to go home . . . Want to go to home,' she continued chanting. '*Now*! I know my rights. You can't keep me here against my will.'

'I am taking you home, love,' he promised rashly. As he was dumping the old dear off on Adam Hayter, no porter's favourite staff member, the problem would soon no longer be his. And that suited him just fine. Five minutes more and he could take a break, steal a cup of tea, and chat up Mandy in the kitchen. He whistled as he went on his way, wondering how much longer he would need to talk Mandy into letting him take her out, and, what was more to the point, into dropping her knickers. One week? Two? Or was his lucky star shining right now, making tonight the night?

The wheelchair rolled into a deserted ward. It was always the same on Observation and Depression; everyone who was physically able went out each morning to therapy; or if they were astute enough to know, and demand, their rights, they could go into the garden for an unsupervised walk.

High-pitched laughter rang out from the ward kitchen. The clock pointed to ten forty-five. Coffee break had just begun.

Head down, the figure pushed the wheelchair swiftly on down the corridor. At the end of the passage, close to the fire-escape door, was a single room. This was usually the last bed allocated for use on any ward. The authorities, aided and abetted by the nurses, tried to keep it for emergencies or those privileged enough to warrant a private room to themselves.

Quietly, ever so quietly and slowly, the door closed behind both the wheelchair and the figure that pushed it. The curtains at the window? They had to be left open, rather than risk attracting attention by closing them. It was broad daylight. The chance of being noticed, had to be taken. But busy mornings weren't like the nights, when others had time to stop and stare, and when people's outlines and features could be clearly seen against the harsh glow of artificial light.

A swift intake of breath. Relief! No not yet. Easy . . . take it easy. Take it slowly, calmly. No noise. No undue haste, lest mistakes be made. Steady, deliberate, determined action, that was what was needed.

Wheel the chair next to the bed. Pull back the pristine sheet, single blanket and beige cotton bedcover. Ease the limbs forward. Hands locked around a slim, cold waistline; warm breathing face next to chill, leaden, dead one. A lift, a push . . . tuck the small stiffening figure between the sheets. On its side lest the knees remain upright with the onset of rigor. Raise the blonde head on to the pillow. Gently brush the ruffled hair forward, to hide the face.

A shudder, a tremor of apprehension as a lifeless arm rolled out and dangled, the fingers swinging from side to side, inches above the floor. Pick-it up, push it firmly beneath the sheets, between the knees to hold it fast.

Look around – the chair! Fold it. Place it next to the bed, against the wall. Then a quick glance in the mirror. Pull the baseball cap down lower. Open the door. Listen! Voices still chattering in the kitchen. Slip out, open the fire door, rubber-gloved hand over the bar lest its click be heard. Head down. Outside . . . fresh air. A tearing-off of rubber gloves. Pass one block, then another, and another. Easy. So easy. And done!

'Do you know him?'

Lyn Sullivan nodded her head, and sank teeth into her lower lip in an effort to stop herself from crying out. Peter Collins saw the shock beginning to register on her face, and accorded her grudging respect. Shaken, clearly upset by her ordeal, her slender and – as he lustfully noticed – very shapely body trembling beneath her thin dressing-gown, she hadn't even protested mildly at his request that she follow him outside to see if she could identify the body. But then again, he decided, she was a nurse, and sooner or later all nurses had to get used to looking at people with broken necks. In which case, by making that sooner, he was probably doing her a favour.

'Lyn, are you all right?' Karl Lane, dark hair combed back away from his face, jumped over the fence and strode purposefully towards them, over the flowerbeds that sur-rounded the hostel. 'I've only just heard. Are you all right?' he repeated, looking her over keenly.

'Perfectly,' she snapped.

'Sergeant, don't you think this is a little insensitive? Questioning Nurse Sullivan straight after an ordeal.' He looked down at the body stretched out on its back about six foot away. Mary's hysterical sobs made conversation almost impossible, until the soft murmur of Alan's voice managed to quieten her a little.

'The best time to question a witness is when events are still fresh in the mind, Mr . . .'

'Lane,' Karl said abruptly. 'Senior Nurse Lane.'

'Karl, you're not helping matters. Please go away.' Lyn

concentrated her feelings, transferring fear into an irrational anger directed at Karl, simply because he was there when she didn't want him near her. 'This is Michael Carpenter, Sergeant Collins.' She deliberately turned her back on Lane and faced Peter. 'He is – was – a patient in the ward I work on.'

Peter nodded to a constable who hovered at his elbow. 'Is the pathologist on his way?' he asked.

'Yes, sir.'

'Good. Keep everyone, and I mean absolutely everyone, at bay until he arrives. And make sure no one else puts their big flat feet on those flowerbeds. There's a couple of prints there that look interesting.'

'Sir.' The constable stood smartly to attention.

'You,' Collins called to another constable standing nearby. 'Put out calls to Inspector Evans and the Super.'

The constable retraced his steps up the drive towards headquarters.

'Shall we go inside,' Collins turned to Lyn. 'I'm sorry, but I have to ask you a few more questions, and we may as well continue in comfort.'

Lyn led the way inside the building, just as Michelle Grady arrived breathlessly at the front door.

'I came as quick as I could, Sergeant Collins,' she said enthusiastically. 'Thought you might need a woman.'

'You offering?' he enquired crudely.

'Only in one sense,' she responded smartly. He looked at her with a new light in his eyes.

Lyn showed them into a large square lounge which was every bit as bleak and soulless as the day-rooms in the hospitals. A blank television screen stared, like a sightless eye, from the corner of the room; the carpet was a vivid, clashing combination of orange and purple swirls on which islands of hard, very upright gold-vinyl upholstered chairs stood uninvitingly. Peter wondered if they'd been chosen and bought with this appalling room deliberately in mind, or if they'd been donated as left-over goods when the hospital had last been furnished.

Alan and Mary sat side by side, with their backs to the television. Richard sat alongside them, and, after draping her dressing-gown carefully around her naked legs, Lyn Sullivan sat in-between Collins and Michelle. Karl Lane perched on the window-sill and faced the room, keeping them all well within his sights. Collins noted this drily, wondering if Karl had been sent over as Tony Waters' deputy until he could get away from whatever meeting was claiming his attention.

Collins pulled out his notebook, and removed the pencil wedged inside.

'I'm Constable Grady.' Michelle rose like a clumsy gazelle from her chair and introduced herself, knowing full well she could wait forever before it occurred to Collins to carry out the common courtesy. Half the time he didn't even bother to introduce himself to potential witnesses, let alone anyone else.

'Pleased to meet you,' Alan replied.

'I wish I could say the same, given the circumstances,' Lyn murmured in a feeble attempt at a joke.

'Now, let me see if I've got this right.' Collins eyed Lyn as he held his pencil poised over his notebook. 'I've already heard part of the story from your colleagues here.' He indicated Richard and Alan. 'You were lying down in your room and you suddenly screamed. Hearing you, these people came running to investigate, and that would have been about a quarter past ten. Am I right?'

'About that time, yes.' She plucked nervously at the hem of her dressing-gown. 'I couldn't sleep, and I was looking at the clock every few minutes . . .'

'Watching the clock is no good,' Michelle interrupted knowledgeably. 'The only thing when you can't sleep is to go for a good brisk jog,' she assured Lyn gravely.

'I thought we were interviewing witnesses here, not running Auntie Michelle's advice column,' Collins cut in scathingly, instantly losing that fraction of ground he'd gained earlier in Michelle's estimation.

Lyn gave the policewoman a sympathetic glance. 'Thank you for your advice,' she murmured. 'I'll try that next time.'

'Works wonders with me,' Michelle said in defiance of Peter's mounting exasperation.

'We were at where you couldn't sleep,' Collins reminded Lyn testily.

'I got up to fetch a book,' she continued.

'You left your bed?'

'Yes. And just as I reached the bookcase, I heard a noise at my door.'

'What kind of a noise.'

'A soft scuffling. At first I thought it was one of the cleaners with a polishing mop. Then I heard breathing . . .'

'Heavy breathing?' he interrupted.

'Yes. When I turned around, I saw the key fall out of the lock on to the carpet.'

'Do you always leave your key in the door?'

'Yes.'

'And I take it the door was locked?'

'I always lock my door and leave the key in it, when I'm sleeping. Day or night it makes no difference. I know it's not the best thing, when you consider what could happen if fire broke out, but I feel safer that way. There've been a few prowlers around.'

'First I've heard of this.' Collins stopped writing.

'There are always prowlers around nurses' hostels. You of all people should know that, Sergeant Collins.' Tony Waters strode into the room. 'Sorry I couldn't get away any earlier, but we had an important meeting arranged.'

'The Health Authority thinking of closing this place any sooner, in view of what's happening?' Collins enquired undiplomatically.

'If they are, they haven't told me about it.'

'These prowlers?' Peter sat back in his chair. 'Have any of them been reported to us?'

Waters sat in a chair opposite Collins. Resting an ankle on one knee, he ran his hand through his thick, white-blond hair.

'Not recently as far as I can remember,' he said thoughtfully. 'The last incident was about a year ago, but I'd have to check to make sure. He was caught and tried for indecent assault.'

'Convicted?' Peter asked.

'I assume so. I really can't remember all the details.'

'And when was the last reported sighting of a prowler around these premises?'

Waters shook his head. 'I really couldn't tell you off the top of my head. Alan?' He turned to the charge nurse. 'Do you know where the incident book is kept here?'

Alan tried to leave his chair, but Mary clung to him, refusing to let him go.

'I'll get it,' Richard offered.

Lyn pulled her dressing-gown closer to her shivering figure. She was very conscious of her nakedness beneath the thin robe, and every time she looked up and her eyes met Waters' or Collins', she was left with the uncomfortable feeling that both men were mentally undressing her.

'Nurse Sullivan here identified the Peeping Tom outside as one Michael Carpenter, a patient in this hospital. Can you explain how he could have gained access to this building?' Peter demanded of Waters.

'I'm afraid I can't, Sergeant Collins. Not before checking with his ward sister, and even then you'd have to understand that the whole emphasis of modern psychiatric treatment is on rehabilitation within the community. The old notions of incarcerating the mentally ill in secure wards, out of sight and out of mind of the general public, are no longer in vogue. If this young man was indeed one of our patients, it could well be that he was here voluntarily, of his own free will, in which case he would have been at liberty to come and go as he pleased, and not only within the hospital and its grounds.'

'This "young man" as you call him, was convicted of arson, attempted murder and using threatening behaviour towards a young girl and her new boyfriend,' Collins said, trying to remember details of a case tried over two years before. 'In short, Mr Waters, he had been convicted of crimes which clearly marked him out as a danger to the public.'

'Sergeant Collins, if, and at this stage it has to be an if, he is the man you think he is, his doctors could have long since considered him cured and of no further risk . . .'

'No further risk! He died prowling round a nurses' hostel. God alone knows what damage he would have done, if he hadn't been surprised when he was!'

'Surely I don't need to remind you that nothing is proved yet.'

'Nothing proved! The bastard is lying out there with his neck broken!' Collins exclaimed. 'If – and unfortunately for all of us, it is still an *if* – ' he deliberately echoed Waters' words, 'he is our killer, I'd say he was pretty close to securing victim number five.'

'We can't be sure that there's a *fourth* victim yet.'

'Our only witness to a murder disappears, and you're not sure she's a victim?'

'How can we be sure. Nothing's been found or proved.'

Collins left his chair. 'You,' he jabbed his finger at Waters' chest, 'and all the bloody, namby-pamby, do-gooding clowns like you disgust me,' he spat out angrily. 'What's the hell is the point of us working around the clock to catch the rapists, sadists, killers and villains of this world if all you'll do is continually give them the benefit of the doubt, until there's a dead girl dumped right in front of your eyes. And even then,' he backed off, 'all you give their killers by way of punishment is a couple of years' holiday in a camp like this, under the name of rehabilitation. Before patting them on the head, and telling them to carry on in their own sweet way, out through the door to do it all over again.'

'Sergeant, may I remind you who you're speaking to.'

'I know exactly who you are.' Collins turned on his heel, and pulled a cigar out of his pocket. 'That's why I'm so bloody angry.' He bit the end from his cigar and spat it out on to the carpet. 'If I were in your shoes, I'd be doing a head count of your nurses right now, Mr Waters.'

'But the whole point is he didn't get inside the hostel,' Karl countered.

'Someone here eased Nurse Sullivan's key out of its lock.'

'But you can't say for certain whether that someone was Michael Carpenter,' Waters insisted.

'No, we can't, but as he wasn't wearing any gloves, we'll soon find out. And the only alternative to it not being him, is that there were *two* prowlers creeping around your buildings this morning. Which option would you prefer, Mr Waters?' Peter asked caustically as he walked across the room to where Richard was waiting with the incident book.

'Lyn?' Karl Lane followed her up the stairs towards her room. 'If you're at all nervous about being on your own, I can stay with you until your next shift starts.'

'If you don't mind, Karl,' she replied heavily, 'I'm going to take a shower and dress.'

'Look . . .'

'Look nothing,' she bit back. 'I said I was going to get dressed.'

'I've watched you dress before.' He smiled.

'Cling to your memories, Karl. It's not something you're likely to see again.' She ran up the stairs away from him.

'I actually caught a bus last night, first time in years but I can't honestly say that it was a wonderful experience,' Trevor said to Dan Evans as he drove him out of the suburbs and into the town. Dan, like most policemen, drove too fast, but he was a more careful and considerate driver than Collins, Trevor noted gratefully.

'So you're going to take a look at your car and put it back on the road?' Dan suggested.

'Peter found a garage in the alleyway at the back of Frank's place. When I saw the rent he'd signed up for, on my account, I did wonder if the car itself was worth it.'

'With all the back pay you've accumulated over the past few months, you can afford to treat yourself to a new one.'

'I probably could,' Trevor agreed.

'So what happens when this case is wrapped up? Back to the Drug Squad?'

'Or wherever else Bill wants to put me,' Trevor said carelessly.

'You don't mind where you go?'

'No.'

'You returning to the force because you can't think what else to do?' Dan asked shrewdly.

'I like the company,' Trevor said drily. 'And the pension.'

'You do have a sense of humour after all. That explains a lot.'

'What in particular?' Trevor asked warily.

'How you've put up with working with Collins all these years. But, then, I must admit I've found the man a great deal better than his reputation,' Dan said honestly.

'Peter's all right,' Trevor murmured. When he thought of

everything that his colleague had done for him since he'd been injured, he realised that 'all right' was miserly of him. 'He's a good friend, and a good copper,' he continued more generously. 'Just needs someone to keep his temper in check now and again.'

'I'll try to remember that,' Dan drew his car to a halt outside a small minimarket with boarded-up windows in the run-down dock area of the town. 'This where you live?' he asked.

'It is.' Trevor reached for his stick.

'Place looks derelict.'

'Only way to stop the locals vandalising it even more.'

'Good luck. I hope today goes well for you.'

Trevor left the car. Supporting himself on his stick, he pulled his keys out of his jacket pocket and went to the side door, but he didn't manage to escape being seen. Frank spotted him from inside the shop, and came rushing out.

'You're back. You look great,' he said, as he shook Trevor's hand vigorously. 'Collins said it could take months . . .'

'I'm only back for the day, Frank,' Trevor interrupted. 'I have to return to the hospital tonight.'

'But you'll soon be out for good.'

'I hope so.' Trevor limped towards the door set in the side wall beyond the shop. He stood poised on the step for a moment.

'I've things to do inside,' Frank said tactfully, sensing Trevor's need to be alone. 'You'll come down and see me before you go?'

'I will .'

As Frank disappeared back inside, Trevor inserted his key in the lock. He pushed open the door and, balancing himself with a steadying hand on the wall, he negotiated the narrow flight of stairs that led up to the first floor. He then inserted a key in the only door facing him at the top, and opened it. The room was lighter than he remembered, larger and not so cluttered. The three-piece gold dralon suite, stained and shiny with wear, had been moved closer to the small, double-bar electric fire that filled a fake mahogany fireplace. The bent-wire magazine rack, which usually overflowed with old newspapers that he always meant to clear out, was now empty. He went over to the imitation teak sideboard and ran his finger over the bare top. A thick layer of grey dust stood proud on his fingertip. It was obvious that no one had cleaned the place in weeks, if not months, and yet it was tidy.

Propping his stick against the couch, he sat down and faced the stained and scarred surface of the coffee table, bare except for the telephone and directories. Then he remembered that his mother and brother had stayed here during those traumatic weeks when he had hovered somewhere between life and death on the intensive care ward. He pictured his mother, small, grey-haired, duster in hand, tut-tutting as she rubbed these battered, secondhand, comfortless sticks of furniture.

Leaving the couch he limped into the kitchen. It was strange; everything was familiar, yet all the time he had been away he hadn't given the place a single thought. The kitchen table, formica-topped, rickety legs, stood proud in the centre of the room. The same strip of ugly, torn wallpaper dangled low over the skirting-board in the corner, as it had done since the day he'd moved in. Plain blue tiles, chipped, cracked but sparkling clean, framed the sink top. His mother had obviously given the place a good going-over in his absence. He looked out of the window at the high, moss-covered brick wall that hemmed in the back yard. He'd seen better views out of a prison cell.

He walked into the bathroom, its decor every bit as worn and depressing as the kitchen's; saw the clean folded towels hanging over the bath in the absence of a rail. The new bar of soap laid out on the cracked washbasin, the shine on the enamel, worn thin in places, on the old cast-iron bath. He went into his bedroom, lay down on the bed made up with clean sheets, blankets and an old candlewick bedspread.

He recalled the luxurious decor of Jean Marshall's apartment, and looked around. This flat was past redecoration, at least the kind of redecorating he was prepared to do in a place that wasn't, and would never be his own. It was ugly, horrid, the sort of transient stop-gap that students, and young people who lived more out than in, could put up with for a while. It was no place for a man of his age. He had to do something with himself – with his life. Spencer had been right: what had been enough before, wasn't any longer. And to think that his mother had actually expended time and effort cleaning here ... His mother! He suddenly realised that he hadn't spoken to her in weeks. He rose stiffly from the bed and walked into the living-room. He sat down, picked up the telephone and dialled her number.

'Do you think he could be our man?' Dan Evans asked O'Kelly as they watched Michael Carpenter's body lifted out from the flowerbed, zipped into a body-bag, and loaded into the back of an ambulance for its short journey down to the mortuary.

'Difficult to say.' Patrick pulled off his rubber gloves and threw them into a plastic bin-bag he was holding. 'If you asked me, I'd have said that our man there wasn't the kind to go scaling three storeys of a nurses' hostel in broad daylight. But then, the one thing I've learnt with murder cases is that there's no accounting for people's actions, especially where the insane are concerned. He could have started off with this lark at night, but become over-confident until he believed himself invisible.'

'What I can't understand,' Collins murmured, 'is why a killer should turn Peeping Tom?'

'The two aren't usually synonymous,' O'Kelly agreed.

'And even supposing he had wanted to go beyond peeping, into kidnap, and if he had got hold of Lyn, how did he think he was going to spirit her out of the hostel? There were other people close by. He couldn't have done it quietly or unseen. Not down all those corridors and stairs, and in daylight. And even if he had by some miracle managed it – then what was he going to do with her?'

Bill Mulcahy stood back and studied the hostel and its surroundings. 'One of the joys of hospitals is the way they always landscape their grounds,' he muttered derisively. 'Half the poor buggers inside can't even raise themselves high enough in their beds to see out of the windows, but there it is. Look at all those trees and shrubs.' He pointed to a screen of thick, high greenery that fringed the back of the hostel and swept along the perimeter of the grounds towards the old hospital. 'You could hide the whole nursing staff in there. Supposing he did get her out, he could . . .' Bill followed the path and contemplated the side of the building facing the shrubbery '. . . have gone out through that fire door. There's only a narrow gap between there and the shrubbery bushes.'

228

'We've fought our way through every bloody inch of that shrubbery,' Collins snapped vehemently. 'And we found nothing. Absolutely bloody nothing.'

'No buried boxes?' O'Kelly asked suddenly.

'What?' Mulcahy looked at him through narrowed eyes.

'Buried boxes,' Patrick repeated. 'A few years back, in America, there was a spate of kidnappers burying people alive in boxes, with just enough air and rations to keep them going until their ransom was paid.'

'If this character tried that, his victims would have been picked up by the heat-seeking cameras,' Mulcahy said shortly. 'We've had our helicopter hovering over this whole area every day since this case started.'

'Now what?' Collins asked wearily.

'Now we go back to HQ and sift through files,' Mulcahy announced.

'Wouldn't it be a darned sight easier just to arrest everyone here, put the whole bloody lot in the cells and watch to see who turns killer,' Collins grumbled.

'We haven't enough cells,' Bill smiled coldly. 'And we have to face the possibility that our villain could be an outsider. Someone who doesn't even work here.'

'But the knowledge of the hospital,' Peter broke in.

'A lot of people have inside knowledge of this hospital. Over four hundred staff have been made redundant in the last five years. Nursing – office – catering – cleaning.' He smiled tightly. 'That's why you are going to rake through every single one of their files with a fine-tooth comb.'

Chapter Sixteen

'That was a good meal.'

'A very good meal,' Trevor agreed, screwing his paper napkin into a ball and throwing it on to his plate. 'Dessert?'

'After all I've eaten, you must be joking,' Jean Marshall smiled.

He picked up the bottle of wine they'd shared and poured the last few drops into her glass. 'More wine, then?' he asked.

'I don't think so,' she drained her glass. 'But I do know what would go down a treat. Coffee and brandy?'

Trevor raised his finger to the waiter.

'The bill, please,' Jean said quickly, before Trevor had a chance to speak. 'We'll indulge ourselves in my flat,' she added firmly. 'That way I can drink as much as I like without worrying about driving home.'

'If you're sure,' Trevor said diffidently. He'd been looking forward to returning to her flat, but now that the prospect was in imminent danger of becoming reality, doubts insisted on stealing into his mind. What could he, battered, bruised and steeped in an overwhelming feeling of worthlessness, have to offer a mature, attractive and confident woman like Jean Marshall?

'I'm sure,' she said briskly. 'I'll get my coat.'

Trevor handed his credit card to the waiter, then flicked through his wallet looking for a low denomination note for a tip. His fingers fumbled and he dropped the wallet. The waiter picked it up for him as he returned. Trevor signed the chit and laid the tip he'd extracted on to the waiter's tray. He reached for the stick he'd left propped against an empty chair, and waited impatiently for Jean to reappear. It was ridiculous; here he was, a grown man of over thirty nervous as a schoolboy

231

because a woman had invited him home for a drink. But then it had been a long time since he'd even tried to ask a woman out, and the last time hadn't exactly been successful. He could almost hear the brush-off again, *"Thank you, Sergeant Joseph, but I've more men in my life than I can cope with right now . . ."* Always another man, never him.

Even with Mags. *"Not tonight, Trevor, if you don't mind. I'm not feeling up to the mark."* One woman in six years, and none at all for the last two, only a pathetic hopeless crush that hadn't, and never could have, led anywhere.

'Ready then?' Jean tapped his arm. Using his stick he propelled himself forward, and followed her out through the door towards her car.

Lyn Sullivan didn't return from town until six-thirty. She'd deliberately left herself barely enough time to take a shower, change her clothes, and walk over to the ward. The last thing she wanted was idle minutes in which to brood on the traumatic events of the day. She needed to keep busy, keep working, get on with her job. But her limbs ached and her eyes hurt from staying awake for so many hours. She knew from past experience that, however dreadful she felt now, she'd feel a hundred times worse tomorrow night, even if she did catch up with her sleep. And, after the happenings of the morning, that was doubtful.

Not usually nervous, she took care to lock the shower-room door securely. Even that wasn't enough; she jammed her slippers beneath it, and hung her wash-bag on the door handle, so she would hear the rattle of her soap dish if someone attempted to force the lock. Lyn showered quickly, dividing her glances between the translucent shower curtain and the patterned glass in the window. Nerves at breaking point, she turned off the water and dried herself in the tub. When she attempted to dust herself with talcum powder, her hand trembled so much she succeeded in shaking most of it over the floor.

She knew she was behaving absurdly. Michael Carpenter was dead – and the dead couldn't walk. There was no reason for her to be nervous. But then she remembered Michael. He'd been so young and, apart from his obsessive behaviour over his ex-girlfriend, incredibly naive, childlike and trusting. Could he really have been a murderer? Had he taken those women and planted them in a hole in the ground, watched while they slowly – ever so slowly – suffocated, fighting for each and every breath, as the blood vessels burst in their eyes.

She shuddered, expelling the graphic images of lingering death from her mind, and forced herself to concentrate on cleaning up the powder from the floor. Tying her dressing-gown cord securely around her waist, she threw back the bolt on the door and stepped into the corridor.

'All right now, Lyn?'

She jumped as though scalded, dropping her wash-bag.

'Sorry, didn't mean to scare you,' Richard murmured sheepishly as he left the adjoining bathroom.

'I'm a bit edgy,' she confessed as she bent to retrieve her bag. 'You still on night shift?'

'Yes.'

'So am I. I'll walk up the drive with you, if you like.'

'There's no need. I'll be fine,' she said hurriedly, remembering everything that Peter Collins had said that morning. If Michael Carpenter hadn't been the murderer, then it could be anyone . . . anyone else in the hospital. She looked at Richard's brown hair, his pleasant nondescript features, his brown eyes – could it even be him?

'Don't be silly,' he said, dismissing her protests. 'I'd welcome the company. See you downstairs in ten minutes.' He added in a quieter tone, 'Mary will be walking up with us. Alan isn't working tonight, and the poor girl is set for a nervous breakdown.'

'I'll see you downstairs then,' she agreed, feeling faintly ridiculous. How on earth could she suspect Richard, of all people?

She went back into her room and sorted through the clothes she intended wearing, hanging her dressing-gown away in her wardrobe, putting everything neatly and meticulously in its allotted place. If someone entered her room during the night and disturbed anything, she wanted to know about it.

She found Mary and Richard waiting for her in the foyer. It was picking with rain, so Lyn pulled the hood of her anorak over her head before following them out on to the drive. They walked quickly and in silence, all three of them glancing uneasily at the twilight shadows that were gathering thickly in-between the bushes and trees around them.

'Sit down, I'll get us a drink.' Jean Marshall left Trevor in her living-room and went to the kitchen to fetch ice. He walked over to the window and looked out over the Marina, watching as the pale, soft lights of early evening flickered on, one by one, across the bay.

'You really do like that view, don't you?' she said, as she returned with two glasses of brandy and ice.

He held up his glass. 'Is this wise after half a bottle of wine?'

'You only drank about a quarter of a bottle, and we've been cutting down your drugs for the last three weeks. A brandy isn't going to do you much harm. But as I warned you earlier, I won't be able to drive you back after this.'

'I wouldn't expect you to.' He took a tentative sip of the brandy – his first in over four months. 'If I can use your phone, I'll call a taxi. I don't think I'm up to facing a bus again, and that's nothing to do with my rehabilitation. More self-preservation. After months of hot-house hospital temperatures, freezing night winds whistling through open bus shelters are likely to bring on pneumonia.'

'Don't I know it. My car had to be serviced last week. It was easy enough getting a taxi from here to the hospital, but hopeless trying to arrange one the other way.'

'They probably thought you were a patient playing a practical joke.' He continued to sip at his brandy, while he contemplated the mix of Victorian, Edwardian and modern housing that fringed the shoreline below him. 'I hope I'll not offend you by asking, but what do these apartments sell for?'

'Less than they did when my husband was talked into buying one. As you've probably noticed, half this block is up for sale.'

'That's why I asked.'

'Are you thinking of moving here?'

'Not particularly. Just to somewhere better than where I live at the moment.'

'Do you see that short terrace down there?' She pointed to a dozen bay-windowed houses directly below them, that faced the sea. The whole row was painted white, with Grecian columns set on either side of their front doors, supporting a continuous strip of balconies that ran the whole length of the terrace.

'I see them.' He noticed their new roofs, and the long thin gardens that ran down to the beach.

'I wanted to buy one of those, but my dear ex-husband insisted on buying this place.' She fetched the brandy bottle to top up their glasses. 'This place has a superb view, but it also has very little privacy. If I sit out in my conservatory, or even in here, with my curtains open I'm on view to the entire Marina.' She moved over to the couch and sat down. 'No matter how hard you try, you can't see into those houses. Something to do with their small-paned Georgian windows.'

'Their gardens are well overlooked,' he commented.

'You can always build a patio and grow vines on an overhanging trellis.'

'At least four of those are for sale,' he observed.

'Eight actually, and they're all going cheap.'

'Why?' he asked suspiciously.

'The builder who renovated the entire terrace is now on the verge of bankruptcy. He bought high, before the last slump, did a no-expense-spared conversion, and is now absolutely desperate for money.' She looked across at Trevor. He'd pulled a receipt out of his wallet and was patting his pockets.

'Here,' she handed him a pen. 'I take it you want to make a note of the estate agent's name?'

'Thank you.' He took the pen from her.

'It would be nice to have a policeman for a neighbour.' She smiled. 'I'd feel safe knowing that you could look up here any time and check on me.'

'You make me sound like a Peeping Tom.'

'That analogy runs a bit too close to the bone at the moment.'

'What do you mean?'

'Well, after what happened in the nurses' hostel this morning.'

Trevor stared at her blankly.

'Good God, you don't know, do you?'

'Know what? I've been in town all day.'

235

'Michael Carpenter climbed up the outside wall of the nurses' hostel, this morning. Apparently Lyn Sullivan heard him, opened her curtains, and disturbed him trying to peer through her window.'

'Poor kid,' Trevor said sympathetically. 'She must have been frightened out of her wits.'

'Not as frightened as Michael. He lost his hold, and fell and broke his neck.'

'Dead?'

'Very,' Jean assured him dryly. 'But more to the point, rumour has it that your lot have now stopped hunting for the killer.'

Trevor tried to think coherently, but the brandy on top of the wine blurred his thoughts.

'Michael was a nice enough kid,' he protested. 'Just a bit mixed up.'

'You never can tell with obsessives,' Jean said knowledgeably. 'They sometimes get quite peculiar notions totally unconnected with their original fixations.'

'You nursed him for long enough. Do you think he could be the one?' Trevor asked bluntly.

'I'm the one who's been looking at everyone sideways since they dug up the first body,' said Jean without a trace of humour. 'Including the poor old gardener, who's sixty if he's a day. I couldn't tell you if Michael was the one, but on the other hand I'm not ready to bet my life on it. I'll still be carrying this.' She reached for her handbag and tipped its contents out on to the couch. She picked up a can of cheap body-spray. 'Better than mace,' she assured him gravely. 'And it's not classed an offensive weapon. Then there's this.' She rummaged through the mess and pulled out a rape alarm.

'Just make sure that you don't get caught out anywhere alone,' Trevor warned seriously. 'And by *anywhere* I include the hospital corridors. Especially the hospital corridors.'

'No one's going to have a go at me,' she dismissed his fears lightly. 'I've read up on the psychology of victims. Most of them announce their vulnerability to all and sundry in the way they walk, the way they . . .'

'Don't you believe it,' Trevor contradicted. 'Not in this case.

One of our victims was a nurse. And everyone remembers her as being a very efficient, together sort of person.'

'Including me,' Jean said thoughtfully. 'That's if the rumours flying round the wards have any truth in them. Her name was Elizabeth Moore wasn't it?'

'No formal identifications had been made by the time I left the hospital this morning.' He drank the remaining brandy in his glass. 'Do you mind if I call a taxi now?' he asked.

'Now! But we haven't had coffee.' Jean looked at him, saw the hard edge of excitement in his eyes.

'You're working, aren't you?' she said flatly. 'Undercover I mean, in the hospital.'

'No,' Trevor shook his head.

'Yes, you are.'

'For pity's sake,' he said irritably, 'Do you think I got myself into this mess,' he looked down at his battered legs, 'just to go undercover inside a hospital?'

'Did you?'

'I was there before they found the first body, remember?'

'Yes, but Harry Goldman wanted to release you a week ago.'

'A week ago there was no murder hunt, and I wasn't ready to be released,' he protested.

'And you are now?'

'I will be by the end of the week.'

He left the window and hobbled over to the sofa she was sitting on. 'If I've made a rapid recovery, it's because a kind nurse befriended me in a pub, took me home with her and reminded me that you can have such a thing as a social life,' he glanced appreciatively around the room. 'And good living, comfort, luxury and beauty,' he concluded.

She smiled and moved closer. 'It's kind of you to say so,' she said softly. Wrapping her arms around his neck, she pulled his face down to hers and kissed him.

His senses reeled as he was drawn in, engulfed in the warm, moist sensual feel of her mouth caressing his. He closed his eyes, and attempted to kiss her back, fighting to make the embrace an equal effort trying to give her something of himself, before his senses were totally lost, overwhelmed, asphyxiated by her rich musky perfume, the urgency and sheer blatant sexuality of her caresses.

She pulled back, away from him for a moment. Seconds later, her naked arm brushed against his cheek as her hands closed once more around his neck. He looked down and realised with a start that she had shed the silk blouse she'd been wearing. He found himself staring at the half globes of her tanned breasts, the nipples hardening as she thrust herself against him.

'We could go into the bedroom,' she murmured as she nuzzled his ear.

'Jean, I . . .' he faltered, embarrassed and ashamed of the injuries that had drained his strength – and with it his masculinity. For the first time since Mags had left him, a woman had undressed for him, yet he felt nothing. No more than a flicker of transient lust that could just as well have had its origin in a five-minute flick through one of the men's magazines that littered the Station.

Jean disregarded his stammerings, and leant past him to press a button on the coffee table. The lights dimmed and the drapes swished together. Before she embraced him again, she sloughed off the remainder of her clothes. Her fingers busied themselves with the buttons on his shirt and fly, and he stood helplessly, allowing her to undress him, feeling more than a little lost and bewildered. He felt as though he was back on the ward at the General. The nurses there had dressed and undressed him because he'd been too weak to do so himself, but when Jean's hand slipped down between his naked thighs he realised that he was well and truly out of hospital. That she had succeeded in arousing passions within him that he had almost believed dead.

He bore her down on to the sofa beneath him, but even as she lay on her back and opened her legs to receive him, he felt that it was not he who was making love to Jean, but Jean who was swallowing him whole. He felt cannibalised, consumed by her greed and hunger, a hunger he realised – as he rose to meet her thrusts with his own – that could have been satisfied by any one of a number of other men. Most of whom would surely have proved themselves far more acceptable to her than himself in his present, weakened state.

'It's just too damned neat, having our murderer fall three

storeys and break his neck.' Peter Collins walked over to the chart that Dan had drawn up that morning. 'Besides, he doesn't fit our profile.'

'I thought you didn't pay any credence to profiles,' Mulcahy said.

'That was this morning,' Peter replied with an artificial smile. 'Just look at it. The age is wrong for a start. Michael was nineteen, not twenty-five to thirty-five. His father's a bank manager, his mother a solicitor, so that leaves out the working-class, blue-collar hypothesis . . .'

'What job did he do?' Dan interrupted.

'Bank clerk,' Collins answered quickly. 'I checked. But he wasn't showing anywhere near the same promise Daddy did at his age. In fact he probably wouldn't have got into the bank at all if it hadn't been for his father's influence. Far from living alone with a domineering female relative, he lived with both parents, and three brothers before he was admitted here.'

'But he did try to kidnap his girlfriend and burn down her house while her entire family was asleep inside,' Mulcahy said flatly.

'Only when she went off with another fellow. There's a world of difference between desperately trying to hang on to one particular girl and picking up anyone who comes along and burying them alive.'

'Where are we on dates?' Bill demanded.

'He was held on remand in the hospital wing of the local prison for four months. After sentencing he was transferred here and that was . . . a year ago,' Evans declared, after glancing at his notebook.

'Well there you are, then. He's been here ever since the murders started, he had the opportunity, the personality, and he was caught red-handed. I say we've got our man.' Mulcahy felt so tired he was prepared to wrap up the case at almost any cost. If the profile didn't fit the suspect, then that was the fault of the psychiatrists who'd drawn it up. They'd got it wrong before, so obviously they'd got it wrong again.

'Until two months ago, Michael Carpenter was locked into a secure ward for twenty-four hours a day,' Dan remarked, still studying his notes.

'Secure secure – or secure Compton Castle style?' Mulcahy queried cuttingly.

'Your guess is as good as mine.'

'Then for Christ's sake stop guessing and find out the facts!' Bill exploded.

'As we've never been allowed into that hallowed unit, it's a fair assumption that the inmates would find as many difficulties getting out as we do trying to get in,' Collins remarked testily.

'Who says?' Bill shouted angrily. 'The bloody authorities in this place think we're running this show just to annoy them, and for my money . . .

The telephone buzzed intrusively.

'I said I wanted no interruptions,' Bill barked, knowing that his voice would carry through the thin partition wall.

'It's Mr O'Kelly, sir. You did say that you wanted us to put him through,' the constable's tone held a theatrical subservience that bordered on insolence.

Mulcahy snatched up the receiver and took a deep breath. 'Patrick?'

'Just finished Michael Carpenter.'

'And?'

'Died instantly. Clean break at top of spinal column, which severed spinal cord. In your terms, that's a broken neck. Otherwise fairly clean. I've opened the cranium and sliced a few frozen brain sections, but so far there's nothing. Not a single abnormality to be seen. Some barbiturate and tranquillisers in the bloodstream, but no more than you'd expect to find in a patient in a psychiatric hospital . . .'

'What I need to know is, could Michael Carpenter possibly be our man?' Bill demanded irritably.

'He didn't have *murderer* tattooed on his forehead, if that's what you mean,' O'Kelly replied caustically.

'Look, I really need to know . . .' Bill pressed.

'I'm a pathologist not a fortune-teller. If you want to know any more, you can look at the results when you come down here this evening.'

'This evening?' Mulcahy repeated blankly.

'Relatives are coming to identify three of the bodies. You're

240

creating quite a corpse jam down here,' O'Kelly said tactlessly as he hung up.

'Anything?' Dan dared to ask.

'Bloody nothing,' Bill spat, crumpling the inevitable poly-styrene takeaway container in his large, capable hands.

'It looks like we're back to square one,' Collins said irritatingly. 'We haven't a clue as to whether Carpenter was our man, and after wasting the entire force's morning on a futile search, we still don't know where Vanessa Hedley is. In fact,' he said brightly, 'we know sod all.'

Trevor always felt faintly ridiculous and embarrassed after sex, and more so with Jean Marshall than he had with Mags. As Jean eased herself out from under him and they both reached for their clothes, physically close, but mentally estranged, each engrossed in their own thoughts, he wondered if it was that way with everyone. It had been easier while he was living with Mags; at least their lovemaking had generally taken place under sheets, in the dark. And usually both of them had been so worn out at the end of it there was no time or energy to do anything other than roll over and fall asleep.

'I'll call that taxi for you.' Jean had finished dressing and was now sitting next to the telephone.

He buckled his belt and pulled his pullover over his head. Picking up his stick he limped towards her, and kissed her gently on the cheek. 'Thank you,' he murmured.

'For calling a taxi.'

'No,' he smiled.

'Then for what?'

'Being there when I needed someone, and being understand-ing when I most needed sympathy, and . . .' he coloured, too embarrassed to refer to the experience they had just shared.

'All part of the nursing service,' she said in a brittle voice. 'Just count it as a NHS extra.'

Ten minutes after Trevor left Jean Marshall's flat to meet the taxi, the telephone rang. She reached out and picked up the receiver.

'All right if I come over?'

241

She knew the voice. She didn't have to ask the name.

'I thought you wouldn't be able to get away for days . . .'

'I can get away now.' The voice was curt, impatient.

'When will you be here?' she asked, knowing it would be useless to protest, but grateful that Trevor Joseph had gone, for her lover, who was so offhand and neglectful most of the time, could be uncontrollably jealous when the mood struck.

'Twenty minutes.'

She remembered the champagne she'd put in the fridge to cool, the sheets she'd changed early that morning in the hope of enticing Trevor to stay the night. Strange that the ten minutes of intense physical grappling on the sofa had killed all urge for conversation between them, and stifled any desire she might have felt to keep him with her longer.

'I'll tell the porter to expect you,' she answered. 'You can use your key.'

'Want me to check inside for you, miss?' One of the constables detailed to watch the hospital grounds walked over as Nurse Ashford inserted her car key into the lock. 'The light isn't good here, and I have a torch.' He switched on the powerful police-issue torch as though he felt he had to justify his words.

'Thank you,' she said lightly. 'I'm afraid we're all a little on edge.'

'Not surprising, when you consider what's been happening in there.' The constable gestured towards the silhouette of the Gothic pile behind them as he took the keys from her fingers and opened the car door. He shone his torch inside and looked around. 'No bodies alive or dead lurking in there,' he said, attempting a joke that sounded both flat and tasteless. 'But I'll check the boot for you as well, if you like.'

'Please,' she said quickly, and the constable noticed that she was trembling. He swung the torch high as he closed the boot, taking the opportunity to scrutinise her. She really was rather beautiful. Cool shining bob of smooth blonde hair, mesmerizing deep blue eyes, full luscious lips . . .

'Thank you Constable.'

'Glad to be of assistance, Nurse,' he said quickly, realising that he was still staring at her. Once she was seated in her car, he closed the door on her, watching as she locked herself in. He wondered if she was married or not, but he didn't have time to mull over that. Four other nurses were walking into the car park, and as they'd seen him do a check of Nurse Ashford's car, they now all demanded the same service. But he didn't regret this new procedure until later when Adam Hayter also insisted on the same privilege.

'Everything quiet Tom?'

He looked up from investigating the interior of Hayter's car, pushing aside the owner who was hovering too close to his back for comfort. 'Yes Sergeant Joseph,' he said, automatically addressing him by his working rank. Old habits died hard and, after all, Joseph had never worn uniform in the Drug Squad.

'Anyone in HQ?'

'I think Inspector Evans might be. Sergeant Collins and the Super have gone down to the mortuary.'

Trevor nodded and walked on towards the main drive. He was glad in a way that Collins wasn't around. Dan Evans was a much calmer, easier man to deal with than either the Super or his ex-partner. And yet he sensed that Dan, for all his relaxed ways and leisurely way of speaking, reaped the same results, if not better ones than the Super and Peter put together. Peculiar to think that he had found the man's Welsh accent slow and irritating at first. Now it was so obvious that he spoke that way to give himself extra time in which to think. And Trevor had little doubt that Evans was generally one step ahead of most of his colleagues when it came to deduction.

A scream, soft and muffled, came from the bushes to his right. He stopped and peered into the darkness, wondering if it was a cat or even a fox. Squeezed out by the suburbs encroaching on their old habitat, whole packs of them had taken to living in and around the town, scrounging out of bins and raising their litters in burrows on waste ground. And the hospital gardens, though sadly depleted in size from what they had once been, were still vast by the tablecloth standards of the "executive homes" outside the walls. Trevor waited, then saw a bush move, heard a rustle of leaves.

He swung his stick forward on to the lawn. It sank into the soft earth as he stepped forward. He saw a flash of white cloth, a pair of gleaming white naked legs stretching out from beneath the covering shadow of a bush. He took another step ... then a burst of crimson exploded in his head, darkening the grey evening shadows into unrelieved black, and bringing in its wake a sickening tide of nausea, pain and, eventually, blissful, numbing unconsciousness.

Chapter Seventeen

Jean stretched out in the bed, searching for a fresh, untouched stretch of satin sheet on which to cool her unpleasantly warm body. Her companion's slow, rhythmic breathing rose and fell lightly in the still air of the bedroom, and she found herself envying her lover the unconsciousness that came with sleep. She tossed on the bed restlessly, wishing she too could be borne into the land of blissful nothingness, but her body burned from exertion cut abruptly short, and from aroused, unsatisfied sexual urges.

She couldn't remember ever feeling like this when she had been younger. Was frustration something that came with maturity? Maturity or old age, she debated scornfully, feeling every one of her forty-six years weighing heavily around her neck. It was so unfair. Her companion could sleep the sleep of the contented; why not her? Had she become more demanding, or had her appetite increased with her years to the point where it could no longer be alleviated by anyone, even her beloved lover?

She moved slightly but, reluctant to move too far from the naked body stretched out alongside her own, she kept her hand resting lightly on the smooth, soft skin of the abdomen. She moved it tantalisingly downwards, her fingers brushing the pubic hair with feather-light strokes that she hoped would provoke a response; but her calculated caresses only served to intensify the fire that burned within her own body. She elicited no reaction; the same slow, small, steady sounds of breathing continued to fill the room, neither varying nor intensifying in pattern.

She turned over and stared at the face that lay on the pillows alongside her own. The blond hair shone like cold moonlight in the darkness, highlighting chiselled features. The stern, firm lines of the mouth, softened by relaxation and sleep, curved upwards into a full-lipped smile that she'd never witnessed when the same face was animated by consciousness.

There had been a time, and not that long ago, when she would have given almost everything she owned to be able to spend an entire night of passion – and sleep – with the love of her life; but three years of secrecy, of being constantly on guard to keep her feelings hidden in public, of being always alone during long solitary nights and holiday weekends, continually aware of and jealous of the 'bliss' her lover shared with another and therefore denied her, all these had worn some of the gilding from the first flush of all-consuming love.

Three years ago she wouldn't have dreamt of eating dinner with Trevor, let alone taking him, if not into her bed, then on to her sofa. But now – now she realised that she'd used Trevor as she'd used so many others during the past year; as a stopgap, a filler with which to while away empty hours. He wasn't the first with whom she'd been unfaithful to her lover, nor was he likely to be the last. But, she smiled sourly, she could probably accord him the title of being the least successful.

Greed and loneliness had honed her sexual appetite into a demanding one that made no allowances for failings – or weakness – and prolonged sickness had made Trevor weak. If anyone had needed tenderness, gentleness and understanding that night, it was Trevor. She should have realised it would be no good with him from the start. That she should have left well alone. Now, if only she had succeeded with Peter Collins . . . she pictured his hard, firm-muscled body, his grim set mouth, eyes that never betrayed weakness or his inner thoughts . . .

The figure lying next to her moved slightly, and mumbled in the depths of sleep. It was then she realised the heinousness of what she was doing; lying next to the person she professed to love most in the world, while thinking of another. Perhaps she was no longer in love?

After all what was '*love*' anyway? As a schoolgirl she could have answered the question with complete and absolute certainty. Love was the all-consuming, wonderful emotion that incited men and women to heroic, unselfish deeds, and inspired

246

poets such as Byron to pen their immortal lines. After her marriage she had known different. If she had been asked to define love then, she would have called it "a transitory madness that causes women to fling aside every ounce of independence and thought they possess." And now . . . now it had finally come into its own, teaching her that alongside wonder, passion and indescribable pleasure and happiness, it also brought into being the existence of uglier feelings such as envy and rage.

Perhaps it was time to make a clean break. Free herself from the bonds that came with the dubious, second-class status of 'mistress'. To say *no* when the telephone rang, to re-build a life outside of this relationship that only existed in snatched, borrowed moments of time. But then . . . she looked again at the face next to her own, and knew that once those eyes re-opened she would not be capable of thinking of anyone or anything else except that same person who looked at her.

She had been far freer, and certainly more lighthearted, when still married to her husband. He had demanded so little of her time and, keeping busy with her child and her friends, she had not pined for his attention. In retrospect she realised, that he had always been off with one woman or another. If she'd cared, really cared about his philandering, she would have taken the trouble to notice it then, but his doings had not seemed important to her at the time. Now she had no child to take care of and, for some obscure reason that she had never really fathomed, far fewer real friends, time often hung heavy on her hands. Even her demanding job did not always fully satisfy her need to be needed. More than anything else she craved the constant presence of a lover in her life. And that was something she could not entirely forgive, even the person who lay next to her, for.

A whistle blew loudly, hurting Trevor's eardrums as he swam upwards into uncomfortable, aching consciousness. The explosion in his head had left in its wake a residue of thumping pain that intensified the moment he tried to move. He attempted to speak, only to find that his mouth was filled with something damp, unpleasant and foul-tasting. He choked, coughed, and spat out a clump of heavily manured bedding soil. He realised

that he was lying on something soft and yielding like . . .
like . . .

'Sergeant Joseph?'

He heard shock and dismay in the voice. It was a voice he recognised.

'Murphy?' he mumbled. Pushing himself up on his hands, he slumped forwards, one arm sinking into cold damp earth, the other into . . . into . . . He suddenly realised what he was leaning on.

'Here, sir. I'll give you a hand.'

The first thought that came to mind was that Andrew Murphy was being ridiculously, ludicrously formal considering that they had both been constables together. He couldn't remember Murphy calling anyone, not even Bill Mulcahy "sir" before. Then the ground beneath him reverberated with the pounding of feet as he was helped off the body he lay on.

'Oh, my God!' The voice was young. A rookie's?

'What the hell . . .'

Trevor heard a stream of swear words in what sounded like Dan Evans' voice being played at the wrong speed. He struggled to open his eyes.

'Steady there. Prop him against that tree.' Dan's voice again, shocked as Murphy's had been, but more urgent. Trevor finally succeeded in opening his eyes. He was surrounded by a ring of torches and Dan Evans was peering down at him, while shouting orders over his shoulder.

'Call an ambulance.'

'Sir,' came an answer from a tall figure indistinguishable from the rest behind the blaze of lights.

'The Super . . .'

Another dark-uniformed figure ran off towards the brilliantly lit windows of the main building.

Trevor groaned again, and put his hand to the back of his head. When he withdrew it, his fingers were wet, sticky with dark clotted blood. Dan's attention was still fixed on the huddled heap on the ground.

'What happened?' he asked, without looking at Trevor.

'I was walking down the drive and I heard a noise . . .' Trevor looked over to the tarmac shining in the moonlight twenty yards to his left. Had he really walked that far across the lawn? He struggled to focus both his mind and his eyes. The blurred clumps of rags he saw lying partly beneath a bush, and partly on the flowerbed, sluggishly but surely merged into one. He ran his hands down his front and realised that the blood wasn't just on his head. The front of his jacket was soaked with it.

'What happened?' Dan Evans pressed.

'I was walking down the drive . . .' Trevor repeated, more hesitantly.

'Where had you been until this time of night, man?'

Trevor didn't need to look up into Dan's anxious face to know what he was thinking.

'To town,' he answered weakly.

'Until now? It's nine-thirty.'

'I had dinner with a friend. Sister Marshall if you must know,' Trevor revealed testily. His head hurt, he was in pain, and he was angry that those two factors didn't appear to concern anyone other than himself. We went to a restaurant. Greek I think,' Trevor mumbled. He was seeing three of everything, including Dan. He turned his head, painfully skinning his ear on the tree trunk he was leaning against. Bile rose into his mouth, and he barely had time to turn away from Dan before he began to vomit.

'Sergeant Joseph came in by taxi.' Chris Brooke volunteered the information.

'How long ago was that?' Dan looked from Trevor, blood-stained, vomiting and obviously dazed, to the pathetically slashed and mutilated body lying on the flowerbed behind him.

'No more than ten minutes or quarter of an hour ago, sir.'

'Which was it, Constable? Ten minutes or quarter of an hour?' Evans interrogated harshly.

'I . . . I'm not sure,' Brooke stammered. 'I think . . .'

'Who is it?' Trevor's voice was quiet, detached and remote, but it cut across the night air like a whiplash. Brooke fell silent.

'Who is it?' Trevor reiterated.

'I don't know. It could be one of the patients,' Evans replied. 'There's something familiar about her. I think I saw her on the geriatric ward.'

'Is she . . .'

'She's dead all right,' Dan answered firmly. 'Very dead.'

'How?'

'Cut up – with a broken bottle by the look of it. There's shards of brown glass protruding from her windpipe and jugular.'

'Has she been dead long?' Trevor persisted. Even in his dazed and disorientated state, he knew he had to clear himself of all suspicion.

'Difficult to say. She feels cold, and it's odd, but there's very little blood on the body . . .'

'It's all over me,' Trevor said ruefully.

Dan shone the torch over him again, and took a closer look. 'There's a piece of glass embedded in your chest, man. Whatever you do, don't move.'

'It's my head that's hurting,' Trevor complained.

'Look, I don't know what the hell went on here,' Evans whispered, bending his head close to Trevor's ear, under the pretext of examining the wound in his chest. 'But,' he glanced over his shoulder at the gathering circle of constables, 'it's vital you tell us everything you remember now, before the ambulance arrives.'

Trevor turned his back on him once again and vomited up the last of Jean's brandy and the Greek meal on to the grass.

Collins hated accompanying relatives of the dead into the mortuary for two reasons. The first was that the moment they appeared to claim their kin, the mortuary lost its impersonal, laboratory feel, and took on an atmosphere that was half chapel of rest and half graveyard; secondly, because murder victims were just that, *victims*, no more and no less important than any other piece of evidence in an inquiry. That is, until weeping mothers, fathers, sisters, brothers, boyfriends and husbands appeared on the scene to turn them into per-sonalities, lovable or otherwise, who had breathed, loved, laughed, fought, argued, worked and played, and not that long ago.

Like hospitals and cemeteries, mortuaries with relatives around reminded him of his own mortality; and he hated any reminder of his own human weakness. So he'd managed to delay his response to Mulcahy's urgent summons by continuing with a succession of routine interviews. It was a task he would normally have delegated to the likes of Michelle Grady.

Collins finally arrived in the car park just in time to see a red-eyed Constable Grady lead a plump, wild-eyed, fair-haired middle-aged woman out of the mortuary. Her resemblance to their photograph of the first victim discovered was self-evident, and he knew he was looking at Rosie Twyford's mother. A man, preceded by a large beer paunch, walked slowly behind them, misery etched into every line of his bloated face.

'Mr and Mrs Moore and Mr and Mrs Moon are still waiting,' Michelle Grady whispered to him as she walked past. Collins nodded, but stood in the foyer for an instant before pushing open the door to the bleak, comfortless waiting room.

'Sergeant Collins, this is Mr and Mrs Moon.'

Peter nodded to the couple Mulcahy had introduced. Mr Moon looked every inch the successful businessman in his extremely expensive hand-tailored suit. Mrs Moon was attractive, suntanned and also well-dressed, but behind their fine clothes he saw a look of nervous misery and expectancy on both faces that he recognised at once. They still hoped. Despite the overwhelming evidence of the suitcase, and the dental records that the lab boys had slaved to match up, they still hoped.

'I'm taking Mr and Mrs Moore in now,' Mulcahy said abruptly. 'Patrick will send for you as soon as he's ready. Shouldn't be more than ten minutes.'

Collins nodded. Given a choice, he wasn't sure which he would prefer to superintend; the identification of the badly decomposed body or that of the skeleton. Perhaps it was just as well that O'Kelly had made the decision for him. He sat across the room from Mr and Mrs Moon and studied them.

'If you'd like a cup of coffee, I'm sure I could rustle up something,' he offered abruptly, suddenly feeling a little of their absolute misery. The three foot that physically separated the Moons' two chairs somehow also bore testimony to their mental estrangement. They'd borne a child together, yet both were facing the loss alone, without even the dubious comfort of one another's touch. Collins had never had a child, or even the

251

desire for one, but even his under-active imagination could grasp that to lose a son or daughter before your own death must be one of the greatest hells on earth for a parent.

'Thank you for the thought, Sergeant Collins, but I'd prefer not,' Mr Moon said stiffly. Mrs Moon merely shook her head. A painful silence fell uneasily over the room.

'I'd like to extend my sympathies and those of everyone on the police force,' Collins continued, now regretting his tardiness in answering Bill's summons. If this was bad for him, he should have realised how much worse it would be for the parents.

'Thank you, Sergeant Collins,' Mr Moon replied mechanically.

'What I can't understand' – Mrs Moon pulled out a handkerchief and held it to her nose; it obscured half her face, but the signs of grief were still there, harrowing and unmistakeable – 'is why she wrote to both of us and said that she was going away with a friend. That last letter was so . . . so . . .' Sobs choked her, and for a moment or two she failed to say anything. 'So happy,' she finished at last. 'It was full of plans for the future. I thought . . . I thought.' She looked at her husband and there was such a wealth of bitterness in his return glance that Peter was taken aback. But not so taken aback as to forget his job.

'Where *did* you think she was, Mrs Moon?' he prompted gently.

'On a round-the-world trip. She asked her father for money for the ticket, and we . . . I,' she corrected rapidly, 'sent her some spending money. She knew that if she ran out, she could always have more . . .' She dabbed at her eyes with her handkerchief again. There was something far more touching and pathetic in the sight of her trying to keep a grip on herself than there would have been in a wild bout of hysteria.

'I don't suppose you still have that letter she wrote?' Collins asked hopefully.

'Here with me.' She opened her handbag and pulled out a tattered and creased envelope. She offered it to him with a shaking hand.

'You don't mind?' he asked, taking it.

252

'We don't mind, Sergeant Collins.' Mr Moon left his seat and walked to the window. He looked out through the slats of the Venetian blinds at the unprepossessing vista of car-park and the blank, box-like facade of the General Hospital. 'But I don't think you'll find it any more illuminating than we do. Belinda and I must have read it a hundred times since we discovered Claire was missing.'

'And when exactly was that?' Peter asked.

'About two months after she left here. Belinda' – he turned and acknowledged his ex-wife's presence for the first time since Peter had entered the room – 'contacted me, and asked if I'd heard from her. Then I realised that the last contact either of us had with her was about the money for her trip, so I reported my daughter missing. Not that I got much help from you fellows,' he added curtly. 'I was told that youngsters go missing every day, and that sooner or later the majority turn up again, none the worse for wear. Of course, we all know different now, don't we, Sergeant Collins?'

'I'm sorry sir.' The words sounded totally inadequate, even to his own ears, but Collins didn't know what else to say. He looked down at the letter in his hands, and removed it from the envelope. It was written in bright blue ink, fountain pen or felt, not biro, and the letters were large, rounded, those of a child. Another facet that removed Claire further away from the bundle of green, mildewed bones and ragged remnants of tissue and hair that he had seen stretched out on Patrick's slab, and closer to living, breathing humanity. He unfolded the single sheet of paper, and trying to close his mind to the misery of the other two occupants of the room, began to read.

Dear Mummy,

Just a brief note to thank you for the money, and to let you know that I am still well and truly fit. The doctors were right, now that I am out of the hospital for part of every day I am getting better and better.

I went into town today and bought a lot of cool summery things. We have decided to stop off at Hong Kong and Sri Lanka on our way to Australia, from there it is anyone's guess as to where we'll go, so you mustn't worry if you don't hear from me for a while, I'm sure that the postal service in those out of the way backwaters must be dreadful.

As well as being fit I am also very, very happy. That's Happy with a capital H. You were right Mummy when you said that there is someone special for everyone. As soon as I am absolutely sure that this time it's the right person I'll come home and tell you all about it. Until then I want to keep it to myself. Hug it close to me like a secret. But it feels good, knowing that there's someone special who cares for me every bit as much as I care for them.

Take care of yourself Mummy darling. Love to everyone in Spain, especially Sebastian. I'll write again when I know that I'll be settled for a while.

Love and Kisses
your Claire

Peter refolded the letter and replaced it in the envelope. 'Would you mind if we took a copy of this?' he asked Mrs Moon.

'Not if it would help in any way,' she murmured.

'Sergeant Collins?' the pathologist's assistant was standing in the doorway. 'Mr O'Kelly is ready for you now.'

As Peter rose to his feet, he saw Bill Mulcahy talking to Mr Moore out in the car park. Mrs Moore was every bit as hysterical as Rosie Twyford's mother had been. He glanced at Claire Moon's mother, and felt that he hadn't drawn the short straw after all. He might be landed with the skeleton, but he was also landed with a mother who seemed made of sterner stuff than the common breed.

Collins' pager bleeped as O'Kelly was showing the Moons the contents of their daughter's suitcase and, more poignantly, the personal jewellery and remnants of clothing that had been stripped from her corpse. Peter switched off his pager, deciding that whoever and whatever it was would just have to wait. Mrs Moon kept her mouth and nose covered with her handkerchief as she looked at the pathetic display that O'Kelly's assistant had laid out on the slab. All she could do was nod. Mr Moon, however, was more forthcoming.

'That's the Rolex I gave her last Christmas.'

'I'm sorry to have to tell you this,' O'Kelly mumbled uncomfortably, 'but there really isn't very much left for you to recognise your daughter by. However, as Sergeant Collins here would tell you, the formalities have to be observed.'

'Am I right in thinking it will suffice for just one of us to identify the remains?' Mr Moon asked.

'That's correct,' Collins assured him, holding open the door for Mrs Moon to leave. She hesitated at the head of the slab, fingering a ring. A cheap silver ring decorated with an enamelled masked head. Peter looked to O'Kelly who nodded. 'You can take that with you if you like, Mrs Moon,' Peter assured her sympathetically.

'I can?' She lifted her head, and Peter thought that he had never seen such anguish in a fellow human being's eyes.

'You can. The rest will be given to you later.' He looked around for Michelle Grady, but she was nowhere to be seen. O'Kelly led Mr Moon purposefully down the long narrow mortuary towards the three shrouded slabs at the far end of the room. Collins knew he should be there too, but he could hardly leave Mrs Moon on her own. He signalled frantically to O'Kelly's assistant, but by the time he had seen Mrs Moon escorted back into the waiting-room the remains had been uncovered.

To O'Kelly's credit, he had kept most of the skeleton covered up, revealing just the skull. The hair, long, luxuriant and golden brown, clung to the cranium, held in place only by a cap of dried skin. The sightless eyes stared blankly upwards at the ceiling, the nose had fallen in on itself. Threads of gum clung to the teeth, now yellowed and stained by earth.

'It's Claire's hair.' Mr Moon's voice sounded strained, inhuman.

'Thank you sir,' O'Kelly swiftly re-covered the skull.

'I want . . . I demand to know how it happened,' Mr Moon shouted angrily. 'How – how did she die?'

O'Kelly looked helplessly over at Collins.

'We think she suffocated,' he divulged, twisting the truth.

'You don't know for sure?'

'The other bodies we found buried nearby definitely bore signs of suffocation,' O'Kelly intervened quickly. 'And from what little we have been able to glean from examining your daughter's body, we assume . . .'

'Assume? Assume!'

'Clive?' Moon's ex-wife was standing in the doorway, flanked by O'Kelly's assistant and Constable Grady. 'We have a lot of arrangements to make.'

'Yes, of course.'

Her calm matter-of-factness restored him to his senses. 'Thank you gentlemen.' He might have been thanking a shopkeeper for his assistance.

Collins watched the Moons walk out of the door, in company with Michelle. When the door finally swung shut on them, he turned to O'Kelly. 'Mind if I use your telephone?'

'Help yourself,' Patrick opened one of the drawers and removed two glasses filled with amber liquid; each glass and its contents were frosted, chilled by the refrigeration temperature inside.

'Drink?' He handed one to Collins.

Peter didn't refuse. As he tossed the contents back, he found to his pleasant surprise that it was remarkably good whisky.

'I've left yours in the drawer – didn't know how long you'd be,' O'Kelly shouted to his assistant, who now returned through the door. He followed Collins into the office and sank down into a chair. Before Peter had time to pick up the receiver, the instrument rang. O'Kelly stretched out his hand and took the call. Two seconds later he was shouting for his emergency kit.

'Not another one?' Collins groaned, still feeling emotionally shattered.

'At Compton Castle,' O'Kelly said flatly.

Vanessa Hedley?' Peter asked.

'Your guess is as good as mine. You coming?'

Peter remembered his pager, but dismissed it from mind. 'We can take my car,' he said, as he followed O'Kelly out of the door.

Chapter Eighteen

Collins drove through the gates of Compton Castle and, following a constable's directions, over the lawns to the area where Dan Evans had already arranged floodlights. Patrick O'Kelly went directly to the site to make his initial inspection, while Peter looked around for Evans or Mulcahy. He didn't have to look far, as they both made a beeline for him as soon as they spotted his car.

'Another burial?' He could see newly-dug earth in the flowerbed.

'No,' Mulcahy replied tersely. 'Seems we got to this one before he had a chance to start digging.'

'Vanessa Hedley?'

'No.'

'In God's name not another one?'

'Elderly woman stabbed with a broken bottle, and it looks like rape.' Bill began.

'Not much doubt about rape this time.' O'Kelly left the corpse and came to join them. 'First impressions lead me to think you should be looking for a necrophiliac. This one's been dead some time. At least two days – if not longer. I'm going to need my kit from the car,' he shouted his assistant. He looked at Collins. 'The keys?'

'It's open,' Peter said abruptly.

'This time we thought we'd caught the bastard red-handed,' Mulcahy shouted angrily; frustrated and furious because, yet again not one of the proliferation of guards in the grounds had seen anything suspicious before the event. 'Lying on top of the victim, blood all over him.'

Something in the tone of Bill's voice struck Peter as ominous. He looked from the Super to Dan Evans and back.

'Who?' he asked, afraid he wasn't going to like what he was about to hear.

'Trevor Joseph. He was unconscious . . .'

Turning his back on his colleagues, Collins walked swiftly over to the figure stretched out on its back beneath the bush. O'Kelly was already hard at work, so he tried to ignore the pathologist's distasteful procedures and concentrate on the victim's face. The features were contorted, slashed to ribbons, the nose and ears hanging by threads of skin. But the first thing that struck him was the age of the corpse. The wrinkled skin was parchment yellow in the strong glare of the floodlights; it could have been Methuselah lying there.

'She was a sweet old lady from the geriatric ward?'

Collins whirled around; Mulcahy was at his elbow. 'You can't possibly believe that Trevor had a hand in this. Not after all the years you've known him,' he protested vehemently.

'I'm not sure. The man's gone nuts.' Bill was too exhausted to consider what he was saying.

'You didn't think so this morning when you asked him to start work again.'

'Maybe no sane man would agree to going undercover in this place.'

'No sane man would bloody well want to work with you, but we do,' Collins retorted bitterly. 'Just look at the marks on her. Those blows were inflicted with a hell of a lot of strength behind them. Trevor's been sick, he's severely weakened . . .'

'We found him covered in blood, with a lump of glass stuck in him. Maybe the poor old biddy fought back.' Refusing to look beyond the bare facts, Mulcahy wasn't making sense, least of all to himself; but Collins' righteous anger coming at the fag end of an interminably long, draining day was proving more than he could take.

'A two-day-old corpse fought back!'

'We can't be sure of the time of death until O'Kelly puts in his full report!' All Bill knew was that he had to postpone investigating – or even thinking about this one crime too many – until after he'd slept.

'Where is Trevor?' Collins demanded.

'I sent him to the Hospital,' Evans offered. 'He had glass embedded in his chest and a cut on his head.'

'Is anyone there with him?'

'A couple of constables.'

'Is he under arrest?'

'As soon as the doctors have finished we'll start questioning him,' Bill snapped. 'Then we'll see.'

Peter turned to Dan Evans. 'You can't think Trevor did this too?' It was more heartfelt plea than question.

Dan looked at Mulcahy. His boss was swaying on his feet, his face grey with fatigue. He knew that if he expressed an opinion either way, he'd only succeed in provoking a head-on confrontation. 'As soon as Patrick's given us the basics we'll talk to Trevor,' he hedged evasively, 'then ...' He was speaking to thin air. Collins was running across the lawn at a brisk pace, heading directly for the old hospital. He tried the front door, and found it locked. He slammed his knuckles against it out of sheer frustration. But of course, he wasn't thinking straight. There were no medical facilities here. They would have taken Joseph to the General.

He tore back across the lawns and, ignoring his colleagues' shouts, dived into the driving seat of his car, and hit the accelerator hard. And he didn't slow down until he was outside the casualty ward of the General Hospital.

'Trevor Joseph? Sergeant Trevor Joseph?' he asked a nurse carrying a tray set out with sterile packs.

'I'm sorry. The public aren't allowed back here.'

'I'm not public. I'm police.' Collins pulled out his identification card and waved it at her.

'He's with a doctor at the moment.'

'I need to see him immediately.' He pushed past the nurse and spotted Chris Brooke standing guard at the end of the corridor behind her.

'This way, sir,' Brooke called out, assuming that Collins had come to interview Trevor officially.

Andrew Murphy was standing outside the open door of the treatment room. Trevor was sitting in a chair next to an examination couch. A doctor was washing her hands in the sink, and a nurse was swabbing Trevor's head with cottonwool balls and antiseptic.

'Those stitches will need to come out in a couple of days. Don't worry, we've shaved off very little of your hair. But it's so thick it hardly shows,' the nurse murmured reassuringly.

'If you experience any of these symptoms,' the doctor handed Trevor the standard *Signs of concussion* card, 'or if you're concerned in any way, come back immediately.'

Trevor winced as the antiseptic being dabbed on his wound touched raw flesh.

'The cut on your chest is deep, but fortunately for you, the wound's clean and nothing vital has been affected. Your X-ray's are clear – who are you?' The doctor whirled around as she noticed Collins moving into the doorway.

Peter again produced his ID card. 'I need to talk to this man. Alone.'

'I'll be finished in a few moments, but I think he should return to Compton Castle to rest.'

'That's all right, doctor.' Trevor looked around for his stick, so he could leave the chair. 'I want to talk to him.'

'Here,' Collins offered Trevor his arm. 'Bill and Dan have kept your stick. Apparently it's evidence,' he added cynically.

'Don't forget to come back in four days, so we can take those stitches out,' the nurse reminded. 'You can make an appointment in reception.'

'Fine,' Trevor murmured absently, wondering how effective the staff in Compton Castle were at taking out stitches. The last thing he wanted to do, was return here to waste another hour sitting around waiting to be treated.

'I'm taking Sergeant Joseph back with me to Compton Castle,' Collins announced to Brooke and Murphy as he helped Trevor limp along the corridor.

'But, Superintendent Mulcahy . . .'

'That's all right son.' Andrew Murphy elbowed the rookie out of the way. 'We'll see you back there, sir?'

'So what the hell happened?' Collins demanded as soon as they were alone.

'I wish I knew,' Trevor mumbled sinking his head into his

hands. 'I'd been out in the town, then I got a taxi back to the main gate. While I was walking up the drive, I saw something like a pair of feet lying on the grass. I walked towards them – and that's the last I remember.'

'You think someone hit you?' Collins studied him carefully. He could smell strong drink on Trevor's breath. And Trevor had never had a head for spirits. 'Sure you didn't just fall over and hit your head?'

Trevor put a hand to his head and winced as his fingers touched the sensitive area that had just been treated. 'I think that's pretty impossible, up on the crown unless I did a head dive. And I've no memory of attempting one.'

Collins leant over to inspect the wound. There was an enormous, split lump on Trevor's crown, blood clots matting the thick black hair around the area that had been stitched.

'So Dan and Bill think I killed her!' Trevor might have been feeling pleasantly merry earlier as he'd walked up the drive, but he was stone-cold sober now. A combination of cold night air, vomiting, and painful medical treatment had cleared his stomach, if not his breath, of any remaining alcohol, and the serious expression on Peter's face, was enough to lift the fog of concussion from his brain. 'For God's sake . . .'

'Don't waste your breath. It's not me you've got to convince, mate,' Peter murmured as he turned the key in the ignition.

'Well?' Bill asked O'Kelly, as he rose stiffly to his feet.

'I'm not sure how she died, but I'd suggest natural causes. She's been dead for at least two days, and that's official. All the injuries you can see, including the rape, were inflicted after death.'

'You sure?'

'No localised bleeding. Those cuts were definitely made after death.'

'But the blood on the site . . .'

'I've taken swabs. It looks a lot, but it's spread thinly. I'd say it was all Joseph's.'

'But she was raped?' Evans said slowly.

'The corpse was interfered with. Yes.'

'You'll type the blood and the semen?'

'Don't I always.' O'Kelly snapped his case shut.

'Trevor Joseph . . .'

'If you're going to caution me, Bill, take it as done,' Trevor sank wearily into a chair in the day-room of his own ward. 'I understand my rights,' he added bitterly. 'So what do you want me to say?'

'No one's accusing you of anything,' Mulcahy glowered.

'Yet,' Peter added scathingly. He turned to O'Kelly. 'As you're here, take a look at the cut on his head.'

'Nasty,' said Patrick probing the stitches with his finger.

'I hope you've washed your hands after you played around with corpses,' Trevor reprimanded coldly.

He sat back in the chair and closed his eyes. Peter had asked endless questions on the journey from the General. His head was throbbing like a drum, and Bill hadn't helped by meeting him at the door and asking him to change out of his bloodstained anorak and sweater so Patrick could examine them. He hadn't even been able to snatch enough time to wash, and he felt hot and sticky and desperately in need of a bath. His mouth was dry, foul with the aftertaste of spicy food, too much beer, brandy and vomit.

'You should be in bed getting some rest,' O'Kelly folded the anorak into a plastic carrier bag.

'He can rest as soon as we've cleared a few things up.' Irrational with fatigue, Mulcahy was incapable of conducting a proper investigation, and too stubborn to walk away for the night.

'Look, I've already talked to Trevor,' Collins said quickly, 'and we've established the timing to a point that proves Trevor's innocence. It'll be easy enough to check as taxi drivers keep logs.'

'Not all of them,' Mulcahy said scornfully. 'And certainly not the ones who go moonlighting.'

'Look I'll find the guy,' Peter broke in furiously. 'And even without him, Trevor tells me he spoke to Constable Brooke in the car park. That at least can be verified.'

Mulcahy and Evans watched as Trevor slid slowly to the floor.

'Now can he go to bed?' Peter demanded belligerently.

'So you've found Vanessa Hedley, Inspector?' Tony Waters joined Dan Evans in the drive just as the police ambulance drove away.

'I'm afraid not, Mr Waters.'

'Not more problems?' Tony frowned.

Dan muttered enigmatically, 'You turning up like this is quite fortuitous. It saves me having to send for you.'

'It's not in the least fortuitous,' Waters said firmly. 'The DMO sent for me when she saw all the new activity.'

'DMO?'

'Duty medical officer. In this case Dotty Clyne. She telephoned to see if I knew what was happening. We were all rather hoping that you'd found Vanessa Hedley.'

'I'm afraid not, Mr Waters, but we have found another body. And we have reason to believe that it's another of your patients.'

'Who?'

'The body hasn't been identified yet,' Dan answered, waving on the car that was carrying Mulcahy home. 'May I ask where you've been all evening?'

'In my office until eight-thirty. Then at home. Why do you want to know, Inspector?'

'Just trying to get a picture of everyone's movements.'

'Was it murder?'

'What else in this place, Mr Waters,' Dan said as he turned his back. 'What else?'

'Taxi driver confirms the time he dropped Trevor off as nine-thirty.' Collins who'd left Trevor in the care of Lyn Sullivan, with Chris Brooke standing guard outside his door, slumped down in a chair next to Dan Evans in the mobile headquarters.

'You did well to get it verified so quickly.'

'Connections,' Peter said mysteriously.

'Brooke called me on his radio at nine forty-five,' Dan poured out coffee for both of them.

Peter picked up the plastic coffee cup. 'It takes, what, ten minutes to walk from the front gate to where Trevor was found?'

'Five,' Dan corrected.

'Ten in his present state,' Peter argued insistently. 'Which leaves him only five minutes to discover, mutilate and rape a corpse which just happened to be lying there. I don't buy that. Just mutilating that corpse would be a tall order for someone in Trevor's state. And where do you find one anyway?'

'In a mortuary,' Dan replied without thinking.

'Of course. The mortuary here.'

'Where are you going?' Evans called after him. The door banged behind Peter, as he left the room. Evans picked up the telephone and dialled the number for Compton Castle's administration.

Collins saw lights on in the hospital mortuary as he approached, and he blessed O'Kelly's conscientiousness. He hadn't known for sure, but he'd guessed that Patrick wouldn't leave this postmortem until the morning. He had to bang the door before the assistant, tired and bleary eyed, opened it to let him in. O'Kelly was working down at the far end of the room, a dictaphone tucked into his top pocket.

'Sergeant Collins, what a pleasant, unexpected surprise,' he said caustically. 'And how is Sergeant Joseph?' he tossed a heavily stained rag into a bin positioned at the top of the slab.

'Sleeping I hope.'

'Tell him what he's come here to hear.' O'Kelly nodded to his assistant, who was fiddling with a row of test-tubes on a side bench.

'We found only one blood grouping.' The man held up one of the test tubes. 'Sergeant Joseph's.'

'His blood was on his sweater, the anorak, and the sheet that covered the victim.'

'She wasn't dressed?'

'Just wrapped in a sheet and a shroud. As I said, she'd been dead for at least two days. And Trevor's blood grouping doesn't match the semen I found in the corpse's vagina,' he added. 'So, whoever our necrophiliac is, it most certainly isn't Joseph.'

Lyn Sullivan felt uneasy; she couldn't have said with any certainty why. But she spent the greater part of the night

264

checking and double-checking her patients, pausing first at Vanessa's empty bed, then at Michael Carpenter's, and finally outside Trevor Joseph's door, which was still guarded by a policeman. Mercifully her other patients slept peacefully, unperturbed by the two empty beds in their ward. She wondered what had happened. Inspector Evans had told her nothing except that another corpse had been found. He wouldn't even confirm that it was another murder, but if it was, that would mean Michael Carpenter had not been the killer. And then there was the question of Trevor's injuries. Sergeant Collins had been so angry when she'd asked about them, but then, she reflected dismally, Sergeant Collins always seemed angry.

The trainee made coffee for the nurses working on the ward at four-thirty, and Lyn took hers into the office. She didn't bother to switch on the light, but instead, opened the blinds and stood in darkness looking out over the hospital grounds. The police were patrolling the area, shining lights, presumably watching and waiting for . . . what? For Michael Carpenter's ghost to appear? Or someone else? Someone who still prowled free.

If Michael wasn't the one, was the murderer here in the hospital, now, tonight? Were the police hoping that the killer would be insane enough to run the gauntlet of guards in an attempt to bury Vanessa the same way he'd buried the others?

Lyn wished with every fibre of her being that Michael was the one, but even as she pictured him, spade in hand shovelling earth, she knew he wasn't a killer. She only wanted him to be, because then it would all be over. Over and done with. But Michael . . . she pictured his boyish grin, his shy diffident manner whenever he spoke of anything other than his beloved girlfriend, and she knew it couldn't possibly have been him. As a sly Peeping Tom, she could believe, but not a cold blooded murderer who shovelled earth on top of living, breathing beings. And if it wasn't Michael, it was who?

She gazed out again at the floodlit lawns, shrubberies and high walls that hemmed in the grounds. Above the line of brickwork she could discern the top storey of one of the halfway houses. Its curtains were open, the lights on, and she clearly saw the tall, dark silhouette of Spencer Jordan as he paced back and forth between his two rooms. She wondered what was keeping *him* awake. Indigestion, or something more sinister? She looked to the left, towards the old hospital. There were lights on in the administration block, and she wondered if Tony Waters was there. Was something more than pressure of work keeping him awake? A guilty conscience perhaps? Shuddering, she finished her coffee, trying to convince herself that she was being foolish. Seeing bogeymen under every bed, as she had never done even as a child. Was there anyone she didn't suspect in this hospital. Tony Waters? Spencer? Karl? Adam Hayter . . .

'Why the dark?' The lights were switched on behind her, and she closed her eyes against the sudden brightness. Karl moved over to join her at the window.

'I just wanted some peace and quiet,' she said abruptly.

'And I need to apologise for last night,' he said contritely. That was partly true. Hauled over the coals early that morning for not reporting Vanessa's absence at once, he'd subsequently felt low and miserable. Particularly at Tony's threat to demote him. But then he'd remembered Lyn, how angry she'd been, and how his life, and not only his sex-life, had improved since she'd been around, so he'd decided to make an effort to reinstate their relationship. 'I'm sorry. You were right and I was wrong.' Confident that his apology would be accepted as soon as it was made, he slid his arm around her waist. The feel of his warm fingers clamped against her cool flesh irked her, and she moved away. 'Didn't you hear? I said I'm sorry.' He struggled to suppress a note of exasperation in his voice.

'I heard you,' she replied shortly.

'Lyn, we've all been under a terrible strain for the past few days. All this upset with police, and bodies, and then two patients on your ward involved . . .'

'And now another one,' she said coldly. He looked at her blankly. 'Haven't you heard?' she asked. 'Another corpse was found in the grounds tonight.'

'I didn't know. How . . . ?' he asked.

'The police won't elaborate on the how or the why. They'd only tell me that they'd found another corpse. Apparently

266

Trevor Joseph arrived at the scene before anyone else. He was hurt . . .'

'I haven't heard any of this. I've been working on Drugs and Alcohol. Roland went wild tonight. It took four of us to calm him down and get him to bed, even with a tranquilliser.'

She was still staring out of the window, although all she could see now was his reflection in the glass.

'Lyn, please. I thought we had something good going between us . . .'

'So did I,' she interrupted coldly.

'Don't let a stupid row end something as special as us. I was hoping that we could . . .' His voice tailed off as she turned and stared at him.

'We could what, Karl?'

'Move in together,' he suggested. 'I . . .'

'That "I" is the reason why I could never move in with you, Karl. There will only ever be one "I" in any relationship you're involved in.'

'That's unfair!'

'Is it?' Her grey eyes blazed with a fire he'd never dreamt of existing as she turned on him. 'What about yesterday? You think an apology is enough for the way you put me down?'

'Lyn, please. I'm the senior nursing officer here. I have to make decisions. I can't let personal considerations interfere with the running of this hospital.'

'Personal considerations? All I asked you to do was report that someone was missing from my ward.'

'She *was* reported missing.'

'But not until a fire broke out.'

'A fire that someone deliberately set.' His snide tone voiced suspicions that hadn't been brought up until now.

'I was on break.'

'Of course you were. Very convenient . . .'

'If you've just come here for another row, I'm leaving, Nurse Lane.' She tried to pass him, but he reached out and grabbed her arm.

'Lyn, please, let's not quarrel.' He refused to believe that she was really going to leave him, even now.

'Let me go!'

'Lyn . . .'

'Let me go.'

'You're getting hysterical.'

'I'm not.'

'Just listen to yourself. Lyn, it's all right. I understand. You're safe with me. No one's going to hurt you.' He wrapped an arm around her shoulders, and she screamed as though he'd hit her. The door burst open and Dan Evans barged in.

'I'm sorry.' Embarrassed at breaking in on what appeared to be a lovers' tiff, he mumbled something about seeing how Trevor Joseph was doing.

'I'll check for you now, Inspector Evans,' Lyn brushed past him on her way through the door.

'This murder business is stretching everyone's nerves to breaking point,' Karl complained bitterly.

Chapter Nineteen

Edith Jenkins hummed the latest coffee advert ditty to herself as she whirled the electric polisher back and forth across the vinyl tiles that floored the corridor.

'Happy today, Edith?' Jean Marshall called out as she rattled down the ward with a loaded drugs trolley.

'Got to make the effort, haven't you?' the cleaner called back, taking the time to put an extra shine over a dull stain where something had been mopped up by an abrasive cleaner.

'Could you give that four-bed ward at the end a good going over for us, please,' Jean asked. 'It's empty and ready for you.'

'Empty?' The cleaner looked at her in surprise. 'Been kicking the guests out?'

'Something like that,' the Sister hedged evasively. 'We've had a bit of a reshuffle; moved everyone out of there and into other wards. She didn't elaborate on the reasons. They had included a bout of total hysteria from Lucy Craig when she had woken up that morning to find out that Michael Carpenter had disappeared from the ward permanently. 'The beds have been stripped down and washed, so the rest of the room's ready for a good clean,' Jean added briskly.

Edith pushed her polisher to the end of the corridor and entered the four-bed ward. With no patients or belongings underfoot, she finished its whole floor in a quarter of an hour. She changed from the coffee jingle to a few bars of a chocolate advert's background music. She was ahead of herself this morning. The corridor and one room done, and it wasn't even half past eight. But she wouldn't be able to press ahead with the rest of the rooms for at least another ten minutes – until everyone was at breakfast and out of her way. There was still that empty room at the end. She hadn't been in there for over a week, there being no call for her to clean it, not with the ward being run down, but she didn't have anything else to do for the next five minutes . . . and the polisher was in her hand. Wheeling it in front of her, she backtracked, passing Sister Marshall who was dishing out painkillers to that nice young sergeant in the first room. Putting her back against the door, she depressed the handle and swung around to enter.

The first thing she noticed was the smell, a dead, rotting kind of stink. Just like when a mouse had once died behind the skirting boards of her flat and her husband practically had to rip the place apart to find it. She scanned the floor for the offending object. Whatever it was, maintenance could deal with it. Her job description was cleaner, and cleaners cleaned; they didn't carry dead animals out of rooms.

The floor was empty, so coughing and spluttering she went to the window and opened it wide. Edith didn't see the body in the bed until she turned around. Then she screamed, long and loud enough to terrify every patient who hadn't already set off for the dining-room.

Andrew Murphy who'd been detailed to stay with Trevor until Mulcahy could interview him later that day, reached the room the same time as Sister Marshall. Trevor followed more slowly, hobbling along behind them, leaning heavily on a new stick Jean had found for him. The cap bandage that Lyn Sullivan had wrapped around his head in the early hours of the morning, gradually slipped, until it fell sideways over one ear.

'Bloody hell!' Murphy caught the hysterical cleaner in his arms, and stepped back into the corridor, overwhelmed by the stench of decay.

'A body?' Trevor asked, though he already knew the answer. One of the first things he had come to recognise after joining the force had been the smell of death.

'And a bloody ripe one,' Murphy said vehemently, bringing on a fresh fit of hysterics from Edith Jenkins.

'It looks like . . . like . . .' Jean Marshall stepped back into the corridor, a hand over her mouth.

'Vanessa?' Trevor asked.

She nodded.

270

'Phone HQ,' Trevor ordered Murphy, automatically assuming command, despite his present battered and bruised state. 'Go on, man! I'll stay and keep everyone away until Patrick comes.'

He limped past the Sister and looked into the room. The polisher with its lead trailing stood incongruously in the middle of the room. The curtains and window were wide open. Careful not to step any further than Murphy had done, he looked from behind the door at the bed. All he could see was a small section of black, bloated face beneath a mop of blonde hair. 'Have you got a handkerchief?' he asked Jean abruptly.

She handed him the one she was holding over her nose. Wrapping it around his fingers, he gingerly pulled the door closed.

The cleaner, left to her own devices after Murphy had gone to telephone, began to wail again.

Jean gazed at him, shock etched in her round, staring eyes.

'We shouldn't do anything until the forensic team get here,' he said firmly. 'Tell me, when was this room last used?'

'Edith?' Jean looked over at the white-faced cleaner, who was swaying on her feet. 'Edith,' Jean yelled sharply. 'Take my arm.' She helped the stricken woman across the corridor and into the sluice. There the cleaner crumpled gratefully on to a chair, while Jean pressed a buzzer to summon help. 'There's never anyone around this place when you need an extra body,' she grumbled bitterly.

'I gave that room a good going over only last week,' Edith began as soon as she'd recovered enough to speak. 'It's not used that often,' she added.

'No one's criticising you,' Trevor said weakly. He'd left his bed so quickly that his legs were beginning to give way beneath him.

'Bring a chair down here,' Sister Marshall shouted to the auxiliary who'd come to answer her buzz for help. 'Quickly, before Mr Joseph keels over.'

The young woman ran off into the day-room and dragged out an unwieldy armchair. Jean pushed it in front of the door leading into the single room, and helped Trevor settle into it.

'Just look at those marks you've made all down my nice clean floor,' Edith wailed. 'Just look . . .'

'It doesn't matter, Edith,' Jean countered. 'No one will ask you to do it again.' She turned to the auxiliary. 'Can you fetch a brandy for Edith. Here take my keys. The bottle's in the medicine cupboard in my office.'

'Brandy?' Edith perked up.

'You've had a nasty shock,' Jean said wryly, amazed at the signs of recovery the mention of brandy had precipitated. She turned to Trevor. 'You all right?'

'Apart from a thumping headache, fine.'

'Those pain-killers I gave you should start working soon.'

'That's good to know.' He looked impatiently down the corridor. 'Where the hell is Murphy?' he asked no one in particular.

'He'll be along soon,' she muttered, not really knowing what she was saying. The auxiliary returned with the brandy, and Jean left Edith in her care. 'We all hoped Vanessa'd be found,' she murmured as she continued to stand alongside Trevor in the corridor. 'But not like this . . .'

At that moment Collins strode into the corridor, Andrew Murphy at his heels. 'I presume it's Vanessa Hedley?'

'Looks like,' Trevor answered.

'Well he's made us look a right load of Charlies this time,' Collins said coldly. 'While we're all playing detective, creeping around the grounds and searching the old hospital, he calmly walks in here to dispose of his latest victim.'

The staff canteen was full to bursting twenty minutes before the meeting that Bill Mulcahy had called was due to start. Every chair was taken except the four ranged at a table placed on a dais at the far end of the room. The heat, with so many bodies packed into a limited space, was already overpowering, as was the din of conversation. Tony Waters paused in the doorway and stared in amazement.

'I didn't expect to see all the night-shift here,' he murmured. 'I thought they'd come to tonight's meeting.'

'They're scared,' Collins commented baldly, as he pushed his way through to join the row of police officers at the back of the

272

hall. 'And they're hoping to find out something that will make them less scared.'

'Safety in numbers,' Harry Goldman added, as he joined them. 'One of their neighbours might be a murderer, but the chances are it won't be more than one.'

'I think we may as well start,' Bill Mulcahy said impatiently.

'I did tell everyone ten-thirty,' Waters said sharply.

'It seems crazy to wait another ten minutes when the room is full to bursting.' Bill turned his back on Goldman and Waters and pushed his way through the throng of staff who'd been forced to stand because of the shortage of chairs. Dan Evans was already up at the table, setting out pens, pencils and sheets of paper. Mulcahy took one of the centre seats, Dan sat on his right, leaving Waters and Harry Goldman to take the other two.

'Would you like to begin the proceedings?' Bill smiled coldly at Tony who'd taken the chair next to him.

Waters stood up and tapped the microphone that had been specially set up. A hollow boom echoed around the packed room. 'I called this meeting . . .' he began authoritatively. He had to repeat himself three times before the noise subsided to a level at which he could make himself heard. 'I called this meeting,' he said finally, as soon as he was confident he had everyone's attention, 'because I want to put an end to the wild rumours that are sweeping this hospital. I'm sure I don't need to tell you people just how unsettling the present atmosphere of this hospital is for our patients. It negates everything that we are trying to accomplish here.'

He glared at his audience as a whole, but unfortunately his eyes settled on poor Mary who became semi-hysterical as she clutched Alan's arm tightly in the front row.

'There is, I repeat, there is no need for panic,' he lectured. 'All we need do is take simple precautions to ensure our personal safety and the safety of the patients who depend on us; and of course to assist the police in every way we can,' he acknowledged Mulcahy and Evans with a curt nod, 'so they can resolve this unpleasant situation as quickly as possible. Inspector Evans?'

He poured a glass of water from the carafe and took a sip before sitting down.

In the event it was Bill not Dan who rose to his feet. Collins standing next to the chair that someone had scrounged for Trevor, and placed close to the door, shook his head in disgust at Waters' speech.

'If he calls murder unpleasant, what would he call a massacre?'

'Offensive,' Murphy suggested from behind him.

'Don't panic – the man's a total prat,' Collins continued. 'Four dead bodies, five if you count the dog, and the man tells his staff not to panic. How many more does this idiot want?'

'Ssh,' Trevor said sharply, conscious of heads turning in their direction.

'You've all heard the rumours.' Mulcahy pulled the microphone towards him. Unlike Waters he didn't relish or enjoy public speaking, and he elected to remain seated while he spoke to the sea of faces. 'I have no intention of elaborating on rumour. What I intend now, is give you the bare facts of this case, or at least as many as I can without jeopardising our investigation. You all know that four women have been murdered, and that yet another corpse was found in the grounds last night. Well I can allay any fears you might have had about last night's happenings. The corpse did belong to one of the patients here, but she died of natural causes two nights ago. Apparently her body was removed from the mortuary here and, from what I understand' – he looked pointedly at Waters – 'the authorities are already investigating its disappearance. If any of you can shed any light on this macabre theft, Mr Waters would be glad to hear from you.'

His words fell into stony silence. Dan Evans left his seat and wheeled a large board around. The side that had been concealed up until now was covered with photographs of the victims, all of them taken from hospital records.

'Rosie Twyford, was the first victim found, but not the first to be murdered.' Bill pointed to her photograph with a sheet of paper rolled into a cylinder. 'We have reason to believe that she was abducted only last week, probably some time Monday afternoon, after she had kept her last appointment at the out-patient clinic of this hospital. We also have reason to believe

274

that she was kept hidden somewhere until Saturday night – when she was murdered.'

The silence greeting his revelation was broken by a small animal-like whimper. Terrified, Mary now clutched at Alan's neck instead of his arm.

'She was buried alive,' Mulcahy continued harshly, 'but like all the other victims she had been drugged with tranquillisers and barbiturates, probably for several days rather than hours. After we disinterred the body of Rosie Twyford, we made a through search of the hospital grounds, and two further bodies were found. One, which we believe to be the first murder victim, was probably killed sometime in the region of four to five months ago, and she again was an ex-patient and out-patient, Claire Moon.' He waved his roll of paper in front of the photograph of Claire. Everyone's attention focused on the smiling image of the pretty girl with twin rows of even white teeth, and long dark hair. 'Approximately two months after Claire Moon was murdered, the killer picked on Elizabeth Moore.'

A gasp tore through the air like a gust of wind. The staff of Compton Castle wasn't so large that the name went unrecognised, even three months after she'd left them.

'Claire Moon and Rosie Twyford were both patients here,' Mulcahy continued evenly. 'Both had suffered from depression, and both had previously attempted suicide. Elizabeth Moore was different; she was a nurse. One of the most alarming things about the disappearance of all of these victims is that none of them was missed. At least not immediately enough for any connection to be made between their disappearance and this hospital. In fact Claire Moon was the only one of the three ever to be reported missing, and even her parents believed that she'd disappeared some time *after* leaving Compton Castle. No doubt Rosie Twyford's parents would have reported her missing in due course, but probably they, like Claire Moon's parents, would have assumed she had disappeared after leaving the hospital. Elizabeth Moore wasn't even missed. Recently divorced, her friends and family, believed that she was too busy living it up in America to bother to contact them. Which means ladies, and gentlemen,' Mulcahy again surveyed

275

the faces in front of him, 'that we are dealing with an extremely calculating, cold-blooded killer who chooses his victims with great care. But that's before we come to the latest victim, Vanessa Hedley, whose body we found only just over an hour ago.'

Everyone's attention again turned to the board as Evans removed the "missing" sticker from above Vanessa's photograph.

'All of you have probably heard by now that she claimed to have seen the killer burying Rosie Twyford, and we can only presume that her witnessing of that act led to her own abduction and murder.'

'If you knew she was a witness, why didn't you try to protect her?' a burly porter demanded furiously.

'We tried,' Mulcahy insisted, but his words sounded lame and pathetic even to his own ears.

'Perhaps you didn't try hard enough,' shouted an angry voice.

'She disappeared from her ward during the late afternoon, when the day-room was full of patients, and the ward was staffed with the half-hour overlap of shift change,' Mulcahy explained tersely. 'The question I'd like you all to consider, is where she could have been held captive for the past week. Either it was somewhere outside the hospital, in which case I'd like to know exactly how she was spirited in and out of the grounds through our security barriers . . .'

'Which weren't erected until nearly twelve hours after she disappeared – and we all know why,' Peter muttered, staring at Tony Waters.

'Or she was held somewhere within this hospital complex. And I find it difficult to believe that anyone could conceal a fully-grown woman without someone here knowing something about it. I want all of you,' he thumped the table hard, 'to think. Really *think* about everything you've seen and done in this whole place during the last week. Did any of you see Vanessa, perhaps, on one of the other wards? Did you pass her in a corridor? Was she being pushed along on a trolley or in a wheelchair by someone you didn't recognise? Or by someone you did? Because one thing is certain ladies and gentlemen, it wasn't a phantom that spirited her away. A living, breathing body took her, hid her and then returned her to the room where she was discovered. Someone put her in the bed we found her in. And I assure you we're doing all we can to trace that person or persons—'

'You think there could be more than one person involved?' Tony Waters interrupted.

'Let's say we're keeping an open mind,' Bill said coldly. 'And while you cast your minds back to last week, can I ask any of you who feels that you might have seen something to report to one of the tables at the back of the room, where we have constables ready to take your statements. Please remember, no matter how small and insignificant, your contribution just might be the vital piece of evidence we need to bring this case to a swift conclusion.'

'Shouldn't we close the hospital?' one of the domestic staff shouted. 'Surely none of us are safe with this murderer . . .'

'Inspector Evans can reassure you on that point.' Taking the coward's way out, Mulcahy handed the audience over to Dan.

Evans walked around in front of the table, and soon his slow Welsh drawl could be heard in every corner of the room. Unlike Mulcahy and Waters, he didn't use the microphone; he didn't need to. He reached his audience by voice projection, yet in a tone that didn't even seem unduly loud.

'It would be pointless to close the hospital, simply because we'd have to find alternative accommodation for everyone here, and if the killer is either a patient or a staff member, then all we'd be doing is transferring our troubles to another place – not solving them.'

'That makes sense,' a voice drifted up from the front row.

'You all must be aware by now of the intense police presence in the hospital,' Dan continued drily. 'We have officers stationed permanently alongside your own security guards both at the gates and in the car park. And I must ask all of you to please co-operate fully with the routine searches of all vehicles that enter and leave these premises. I apologise in advance for any delays, and I would like to thank all of you now for your co-operation and patience.' He turned and smiled at Tony Waters.

'I would also like to add these words of advice; walk to and from your wards in threes and fours if you can, not in pairs. If you must drive to the hospital, then try to arrange a car rota so all of you drive in a full car. Threes are good, fours are better. If you have to drive into the car park alone, do not, I repeat do *not* walk to your ward alone, no matter what time of day. Wait until the duty police officer assigns you to a group. While working on your ward, stay in constant touch with the others working with you . . .'

'What happens if there's only one of us on a ward, like at night,' Sister Marshall, less diffident than some of the younger nurses, asked the question for them.

'We have a minimum of four staff members working on a ward at any given time,' Waters insisted testily.

'Only in theory,' Alan retorted angrily. 'Even in the daytime, we can easily drop to just one if two of the staff take a meal break together and another one has to take a patient over to therapy. And at night, if someone's sick we're often down to only one.'

'In cases of problems get on the phone to me, and I'll get an agency nurse over right away,' Tony replied abruptly.

'And at night?' Alan insisted.

'I'll look at the staffing ratios straight after this meeting. If there's a shortage I'll book extra agency nurses from tonight onwards.'

'Alleluia!' Jean Marshall said loudly.

'There'll now be a police presence in every nurses' hostel, in every ward, throughout the grounds, and in the old hospital building. In fact, for the next few days you won't be able to *move* for police personnel,' Dan Evans said firmly. 'And also the Health Authority announced this morning that they are issuing every member of staff, male as well as female with a personal alarm. If you see anything at all suspicious, use it. I'd rather see a red-faced person who's tripped up and accidentally set it off than another dead body.'

'What about the patients?' Alan asked.

'Mr Waters is arranging for head counts to be carried out every two hours.'

A series of groans greeted his words.

'I know it'll be a bind.' Dan held his hands up for silence. 'But Dr Goldman convinced us that it isn't practical to issue the patients with alarms.' A burst of raucous laughter rocked the room. 'Right, if you could make your way to one of the tables at the back, where you can pick up your alarm, or make a statement to one of the constables . . .'

'And a good time was had by all,' Collins muttered, as he watched the queues forming.

One woman, alarm in hand, hesitated for a moment in front of the door. Trevor, who was hanging back because he dreaded trying to move his stiff and awkward limbs through the crowd, noticed her hesitation.

'Can I help you?' he asked quietly.

She stopped and stared at him. 'You're Sergeant Joseph, aren't you? I'm Angela Morgan, Tony Waters' secretary.' She glanced over her shoulder to check that her boss was still engrossed in his discussion with Mulcahy and Evans. 'Could you give Inspector Evans a message for me?' she continued nervously. 'Tell him I'll meet him after work today – but not in the Green Monkey, in . . . in the . . .'

'Where do you live?' Trevor interrupted.

'The Marina.'

'Then how about I suggest to him the pub on the Marina at six?'

'Fine.' Clutching her personal alarm she hurried out of the door.

'That all?' Evans asked.

'That's all she said,' Trevor repeated. 'What do you think it's about?'

Dan looked up at the ceiling and reached for the inevitable peppermint. 'Maybe the lady wants to tell me something about her boss.'

Dan took Collins along to the pub with him. They reached the Marina at a quarter to six, and the pub five minuter later. Collins looked wistfully at the menu.

'We're working,' Dan told him sternly.

'And I'm starving. There's no rule that says a copper can't

eat during an interview,' he said dolefully.

'All right,' Evans capitulated. 'If they do something quick and easy like sandwiches, I'll have one too.'

As Collins ordered two twelve-ounce steaks, with chips and peas, and also two pints of beer, Dan Evans looked around the almost deserted pub for a secluded seat. Eventually he settled on a small alcove to the side of the bar.

'What's the cutlery for?' he asked suspiciously.

'Open sandwiches,' Collins lied, pushing a napkin wrapped knife and fork towards him.

They'd almost finished their first pints when Angela Morgan turned up at ten minutes past six, with her husband in tow. She stood in the middle of the room, staring at the empty tables, attracting the attention of the few customers. Collins left his pint on the table, and walked over to greet her.

'Sorry I'm late, Sergeant . . .'

'Peter,' he corrected swiftly, recognising a press reporter in the far corner of the room. 'Dan's waiting for you over there.' He indicated the alcove. 'What are you drinking?'

'I hope you don't mind me bringing my husband,' she gabbled nervously. 'It's just that—'

'Not at all,' Collins interrupted swiftly, wishing that the woman would shut up before she attracted any more attention. 'What are you drinking?' he repeated.

'I'll have a . . .' she gazed blankly at the rows of bottles behind the bar.

'A sweet white wine and a beer,' her husband volunteered for both of them.

'If you'd like to join Dan there, I'll fetch the drinks over.'

'I hope you don't mind me bringing my husband, Inspector Evans.'

Collins could hear her piercing voice, as he ordered for them.

'I brought him along, because . . . well because I felt I needed some moral support . . . and then again, I wasn't sure what I should tell you. It's not as if I have any hard proof, if you know what I mean. It's just that . . . well I didn't know what you'd make of it all,' she began to whisper after her husband gestured for her to keep her voice down.

'What exactly is it that you want to tell us, Mrs Morgan?' Dan Evans pressed, valiantly trying to steer her conversation on to an even course.

'Well, it's all those girls, isn't it.'

'The victims?' Dan asked astutely.

'Yes, well. He knew them all, didn't he? I think . . .' She lowered her voice again so they all had to bend their heads forward to catch what she was saying. 'I think they were all special to him in some way or another. Every one of them. And if you want my opinion,' her voice was now so low that they all found it a strain to follow, 'he was having affairs with all three of them. At different times of course.'

Chapter Twenty

Even Angela fell silent as the waitress returned to their table carrying two large oval plates overflowing with steaks and chips.

'Sauce, vinegar, salt?' the girl enquired pleasantly.

'Nothing, thank you.' Dan Evans was anxious to resume his conversation with Angela. But Peter's attention was now riveted on the food; the first decent meal he'd seen since this case had started, and certainly the first laid out on a china plate.

'I'll have some English mustard if you've got it, love.' He winked at the waitress. 'And some salt and vinegar.'

Dan tapped the table impatiently with the end of his fork, while Peter arranged these condiments over his meal to his satisfaction. Once he'd finished, he thanked the waitress and smiled at the Morgans.

'Would you like to order something?' he asked, the food in front of him making him feel uncharacteristically generous.

'I put a casserole in the oven,' Angela said distractedly.

'You were telling us about Mr Waters, 'Dan Evans prompted as he pushed three fat chips on to a fork, then into his mouth.

'Well, Mr Waters has always had a roving eye, as I told you last time.'

'You did,' he agreed, simply because she seemed to be expecting him to say something.

'And it's such a pity – for the girls who get involved with him, I mean.' She wrapped her fingers around the glass holding a double measure of wine that Peter had bought her. 'It's not as if there's only the one, or that he cared, really cared, for any of them. Well, I mean he couldn't, could he?'

'Why?' Collins asked, between chewing mouthfuls of the best steak he'd ever tasted.

'Well, they all telephoned him a lot . . .'

Did you ever listen in on their conversations?' Dan asked astutely.

'No, that would hardly be proper!' she exclaimed, affronted by the suggestion.

'Never inadvertently overheard anything?' Peter pressed.

'Not really,' she stammered.

'Yet you're sure he was having affairs with all three women?' Evans persisted.

'Well, there was the staff party last Christmas, when some of the nurses caught him and . . .'

'And who?' Peter asked bluntly.

'Well, no one would say, but everyone had their suspicions. He was caught in *flagrante* as it were – stark naked in one of the rooms at the top of the old building . . . and . . .' She blushed crimson as the two policemen stared at her.

'And?' Peter pumped mercilessly.

'Well, everyone who saw them said they were lying on the floor, and neither had any clothes on. It was all round the hospital the next day.'

'*Who* was it that saw them?' Dan asked.

'I can't remember all of them, but one was that pretty nurse who works on the ward your friend's on.'

'Jean Marshall?' Dan queried, a bit surprised by the adjective 'pretty'.

'No, the young one.'

'Lyn Sullivan?' Peter suggested.

'That's her.'

Dan took out his notebook and wrote down the name.

'Sounds pretty damning evidence of adultery to me,' Collins stopped eating just long enough to polish off half a pint of beer.

'It's his wife I feel sorry for.' Angela shook her head, until her brown curls bounced against her wrinkled neck. 'She's such a pretty thing. They've got everything you know. Beautiful house – you wouldn't believe how beautiful. Not that I've been inside, of course, but I've seen pictures, and heard what other people say about it.'

'You've told us about what might just be a brief fling. What makes you think he's had affairs with the three victims?' Evans asked pointedly.

'Well, there's that first one for a start. Rosie Twyford, he used to take her home. You see I was sick for four months. I had a hysterectomy. I was ever so poorly . . .'

'And Rosie?' Dan prompted, keeping the conversation firmly on course.

'Well, Rosie Twyford was personal assistant to Mr Chalmers, and he was made redundant about the same time as I had my operation. So she was sent down to cover for me. I wasn't around then, but the girls who came to visit me in hospital said that she and Mr Waters were getting pretty thick. He used to take her home after they both worked late.'

'There's a lot of late-night working is there?' Collins intervened.

'Not now,' Angela informed him. 'Not with all the cutbacks, but there was then. It was just after we, the department I mean, moved out of County Hall. I think that's why I had to have the hysterectomy. It was all that heavy lifting of boxes and everything.'

'And Rosie Twyford used to work late along with Mr Waters?'

'She told the girls that they were just trying to straighten out the office – but then she would, wouldn't she? When I came back to work and she had to return to her desk in the typing pool upstairs, well that was when she had her nervous breakdown. Rumour had it that was because he'd lost interest in her. But when she was ill, he sent her flowers . . .'

'Wouldn't any boss do that?' Evans asked carefully.

'I suppose so,' she agreed doubtfully.

'Did he send you flowers when you were ill?' Peter asked.

'Yes,' she admitted. 'But, then, it's not just Rosie Twyford. There was Claire Moon. Her father was someone important, and when that Sunday newspaper came to do that article on her, Mr Waters took a great deal of interest in it.'

'Wouldn't that be because he was interested in what the papers might print about the hospital?' Dan suggested blandly.

'That's what I said.' Mr Morgan spoke for the first time since they'd sat down at Dan's table. 'I told her that's what most people would think.'

'But he used to go walking around the grounds with her every chance he got,' Angela remonstrated. 'And that's without Elizabeth Moore.' She'd kept her trump card until last. 'A lot of people said she was the one he was caught with at the staff party.'

'I thought you said no one knew who it was?' Dan murmured.

'Not for certain,' Angela conceded. 'But there were rumours.'

'Ah, rumours,' Collins scraped the last of the steak on to his fork.

'Whoever she was, she had auburn hair,' she defended her opinion vehemently.

'So you believe he did have links with all three victims.' Dan looked thoughtful.

'When I noticed all three photographs up there, side by side, I had to talk to you,' Angela asserted. 'Warning bells rang in my head if you know what I mean. Well, Mrs Waters . . .'

'Is she the jealous sort?' Peter finally and reluctantly retired his cutlery.

'I wouldn't say that,' Angela shook her head.

'Does she often visit your offices to see Mr Waters?' Dan asked.

'Hardly ever. If she does, it's only because of work.'

'Do you think she knows about her husband's philandering?' Peter picked up his beer glass.

'Well, I presume she does. When you think about it, she must do, mustn't she? After all, it's common gossip around the hospital. Everyone else knows about him, so I don't see how she can escape knowing.'

'Would you tell her yourself?' Dan asked shrewdly.

Angela looked at him vacantly.

'Not many people would be prepared to tell a wife when her husband strays,' Peter elaborated.

'I suppose not,' she conceded.

'Is there anything else that you can think of? Anything that you've seen, or heard?' Dan persisted, set on gleaning as much hard fact from her embellishing as he could.

286

'You promise that what I say will be treated with confidence?'

'Of course,' they chorused together.

'Well, there is one thing,' she murmured. 'When Mrs Hedley first went missing, he wouldn't let anyone go into the electricity sub station in the cellar. I heard him have a real set-to with the engineer from the Electricity people about it. But he still wouldn't let him in.'

'What do you think?' Dan asked Peter after Angela Morgan and her husband had gone home for their casserole and a scintillating night of television. The two officers were sitting back with their second pints, rejoicing in the comforting feel of full stomachs.

'I think *she's* genuinely concerned,' Peter asserted, handing Dan one of his cigars. 'That's why she wanted this meeting.'

'Concerned and agitated enough to put two and two together and make eight?' Dan appealed.

'Probably. But if I were you I'd get the forensic team to look over that sub station all the same.'

'Look, I wouldn't ask if we weren't really stretched. And I'll get one of our men patrolling the grounds to call in every hour and check that you're coping.'

'It's all right. I'll do it,' Trevor assured Bill Mulcahy quietly. He was vaguely amused to think that Bill, who last night had been prepared to believe he was a rapist and murderer, was now asking him to sit up all night to keep an eye on the ward.

'Everyone's screaming down our necks on this one,' Mulcahy insisted on justifying his request, although Trevor had neither asked for, nor expected an explanation. 'In fact it might be helpful if you came to the briefing. Nine thirty, in the mobile HQ.'

'What about the ward, when I'm at the briefing?'

'I've got two extra bodies assigned to every shift. I'll see that one of them is here to take over.'

'In that case I'll be there.'

Mulcahy left Trevor's room and headed down the tunnel towards the old part of the hospital.

287

'So you *are* working?'

Trevor turned to see Lyn Sullivan standing in the corridor outside his room. 'What makes you say that?'

'Senior policemen in the middle of murder investigations don't have time to make social calls to the sick and ailing.'

'If it was anything other than a case, on the doorstep, I wouldn't have been drafted. But after Vanessa's reappearance this morning, it's all hands to the pumps.'

'In case he strikes again?'

Trevor didn't answer.

'You think he will strike again?'

'I don't know.' He tried to smile reassuringly, but she looked past him, staring blankly out of the window. 'It's all right to be scared,' he murmured. 'If I was a woman working in this place, I would be too. Scared witless.'

'I'm sorry. I'm not usually jumpy like this. It's just that since Michael climbed up on to my window . . . and that meeting when I realised . . .'

'When you realised that all four victims spent some time on this ward. Believe me, you're entitled to be upset.'

'Finding a corpse out in the garden last night didn't help.'

'It didn't help anyone,' he agreed drily, instinctively putting a hand to his head.

'Was that the murderer?'

'We don't think so, but then we don't really know,' he said honestly. 'No one saw anything except me, and I only spotted the body after it had been laid out on the ground. But don't worry. From now on you're going to be fine,' he assured her, reaching for his stick and leaving his chair. 'You have me and my trusty weapon completely at your disposal.' He lifted his walking-stick. 'I give you my most solemn and absolute promise, Nurse Sullivan, that I won't allow anything to happen to you. Is that a good enough guarantee?'

This time she found no difficulty in returning his smile.

'As no one has offered me anything better, I'll accept it, Sergeant Joseph ' She walked across his room and closed the blinds against the thickening twilight. 'How about I make both of us a cup of coffee?'

* * *

'It just might work,' Bill Mulcahy suggested.

'It's the most harebrained suggestion I've heard of yet,' Collins snorted in disapproval. He and Dan Evans had been in the mobile headquarters for exactly ten minutes, and already two of the girls in the outer office had gone off to take an early teabreak. Of choice Dan would have gone with them, but he felt duty-bound to stay and mediate in the hope of restoring harmony between his two colleagues.

'All right. All right,' Mulcahy folded his arms across his chest. 'Let's see you come up with something better, Collins,' he snapped.

'When has a killer ever been caught by a ruse as basic as that outside of a cinema screen?' Collins persisted. 'The only way we're going to nail this villain is with police work. Dull, boring, routine police work.'

'Our psychiatrist says . . .'

'I might have known that one of your bloody Home Office shrinks dreamt up this one. Has he ever left his snug office and taken a short holiday in the real world?'

'Shut up and listen for once in your life,' Bill roared furiously. 'We've all been talking this over . . .'

'Who's we?' Peter demanded. 'Dan and I certainly weren't consulted in any of this.'

'The "we" being our superiors, Collins,' Bill informed him icily. 'Yours and mine,' he added. 'This case has developed a press profile almost as high as your bloody ego. We have to be seen to be doing something.'

'By the press?' Peter sneered. 'That's bloody marvellous. You put someone undercover in the hope of flushing out a killer, then you call a press conference?'

'Not the press,' Bill bellowed, his face now coronary-coloured. 'By the men upstairs, and by the Health Authority . . .'

'Great. They sit on their backsides in some upholstered office, while we send some poor bloody sod out as bait to catch a killer. Well just remember Harries while you update those suits on our progress or lack of it. He proved great bloody bait, didn't he? We didn't even find enough of him to bury.'

289

'That was unfortunate . . .'

'Unfortunate?' Collins sneered with an anger in his eyes that took the older man's breath away. 'You're talking to the officer who had to scrape what was left of Harries off his shoes.' He took a cigar out of his top pocket, and pushed it between his lips. 'All right, I know when I'm talking to the mentally deficient and the deaf . . .'

'One day you'll go too damned far, Collins, even for me!'

'Just tell me. Who's won the lucky draw this time?'

'We decided on more than one,' Bill divulged coldly. 'We thought we'd try a member of the hospital staff as well as a patient.' He looked at Collins, expecting another outburst. When none came, he continued in a quieter vein. 'We went through all the staff profiles, looking for someone we could eliminate completely from our suspects.'

'And?'

'It wasn't easy. But then we realised that Sister Jean Marshall was with Joseph at the exact time of Vanessa Hedley's disappearance.'

'Pity you didn't remember that last night,' Peter said frostily. 'If you had, you might have saved Trevor some heartache.'

'We called her in earlier,' Mulcahy continued, valiantly ignoring Peter's barbs. 'We explained what we're trying to do, then we asked if she'd hand in her resignation, to take effect from a week today.'

'Does anyone else in the hospital have a clue as to what you're up to?' Peter asked ominously.

'No one besides Jean Marshall and these four walls has any idea.'

'Not Dr Goldman? Not Tony Waters?'

'No one,' Bill repeated. 'The story is that she's decided to go to Canada, to spend a year with her married sister who lives out there.'

'*Does* she have a married sister in Canada?'

'Oh, yes. There's also another reason. Her son's just been offered a place in Harvard for a year's postgraduate work, so she'll be closer to him as well.'

'I see. And you expect everyone to swallow that?'

290

'Everyone already has.'

'Who's shadowing Jean? There is a shadow, I take it?'

'Michelle Grady.'

'For pity's sake, she's not even out of kindergarten. That girl's worse than useless. She thinks in terms of Brownie badges.'

'There'll be other back-up.'

'Of the same kind that Harries had?'

It was one crack too many. 'If I were you I'd be looking to my stripes, Sergeant.' Mulcahy's voice and temper rose precariously.

'You said that there was going to be more?'

'Yes,' Bill replied shortly. 'We're putting someone else in the same ward as Joseph, and letting it be known that she's only a short term stay.'

'Who?'

Bill took a deep breath. 'Sarah Merchant.' He added, 'she volunteered,' hoping to pre-empt Peter's objections.

'You do know that she was Harries' girlfriend?'

'I didn't, as it happens,' Bill admitted gruffly. 'But does that make any difference?'

'In my book, yes. She could have offered her services because she's feeling suicidal – have you thought of that?'

'She passed the psychological profiles . . .'

'A bloody child of two could run rings around those. The test questions are so damned obvious, they're farcical. Isn't it enough that her boyfriend died last year, without you trying to kill her too?'

'No one is going to die.' Mulcahy closed his hands into fists, and leant across the table towards Collins. 'We've three people inside the ward; Jean, Sarah, and Trevor, who's a trained detective . . .'

'A sick, physically frail and unfit detective, who yesterday you believed was your number-one suspect,' Collins broke in.

'We have men everywhere, ready to provide back-up at a split second's notice. In the grounds, in the old hospital, outside the ward.'

'For how long?'

'Two weeks,' Bill admitted reluctantly. 'If nothing happens

by the end of that time, we have orders to run down the manpower working on this case.'

'Great.' Peter slumped down on the bench seat, and propped his feet on a metal waste-bin. 'So if our villain gets frightened off by all this activity, all he has to do is go to ground for a fortnight. Afterwards he can go back to burying the entire remaining complement of patients and staff if he feels like it. I think I've got another theory for you,' he added sardonically. '*He*, whoever he is, could well be an undercover agent for the Health Authority. His mission being to save them a bloody fortune in redundancy pay for the staff, and relocation expenses for the patients. They'll probably pay him a massive bonus and still be quids-in, when he finally buries the last inmate of this nut house. Then all the Health Authority need do is warn the re-developer not to dig down deeper than six foot when he starts on the upmarket housing estate that'll replace this place. And, bingo, the new residents on this site will get an added bonus of well fertilised gardens.'

'You're sick, Collins. Sick and twisted. As soon as this case is over, I'm putting you up for transfer.'

'Promises,' Peter folded his arms and glared. 'Bloody promises, that's all I ever get.'

'One day you're going to push him too far,' Dan Evans cautioned as Mulcahy left the room.

'I doubt it,' Peter murmured as he struck a match to light his cigar. 'Ten years of trying, and I still haven't pushed him far enough to get near commonsense. Have you phoned forensic about that sub-station?' Dan shook his head and reached for the telephone. Mulcahy had been right about Peter. He was good, but he was also hell to work with.

'Your people have already been over every inch of this cellar three times in the past week.' Arnold Massey, titular head of a maintenance staff that had shrunk from a formidable fifteen, to just two over the past five years, was complaining irritably.

'We need one more quick look,' Collins said casually. 'Just between me and you, we've had a tip-off. And you know what it is. If we don't act on our tip-offs from the public, everyone starts breathing down our necks. Press, politicians, higher ups, Joe public, and all.'

'I can imagine,' the man agreed, slightly mollified by this confidence.

Dan Evans who was following behind Massey and Collins along with the forensic expert, wondered why Peter never bothered to soft-soap the brass the way he did the public. A tenth of the patience and explanations he expended on others could do wonders for his relationship with Mulcahy. But then, Evans had long since decided that Collins was a genuine Jekyll-and-Hyde personality, and, as his temporary partner, he should be grateful for the times when Jekyll surfaced – like now.

'This cellar goes on forever,' the forensic expert grumbled as he shifted his heavy case from one hand to the other.

'Over half a mile long from end to end,' Arnold informed him knowledgeably. 'Counting all the passages that is.' He ducked his head beneath a bridge of grimy, dusty central-heating pipes. 'Here we are,' he announced. 'This is your sub-station.' They halted in front of a securely locked iron door set in a solid brick partition wall. 'By rights I suppose I should have called the Electricity people first . . .'

'There's no need,' Peter said lightly. 'The less people involved, the less dirt is carried through. That's supposing you know enough to tell us what's safe or unsafe for us to touch.'

'Oh, ay, I know that much,' Massey replied defensively. 'Besides most of the dangerous stuff is labelled.' He pulled an enormous bunch of keys out of his pocket and threaded through them, looking for the right one.

Collins stepped forward expectantly, only to see him unlock just one of several locks on the door. It took Arnold another two minutes of searching and sighing to produce the key needed to unfasten the second lock. Finding the third was slower still. Only then did the door swing open. The maintenance man put his hand inside and fumbled for the light switch.

'There you are, gentlemen. All yours,' he said grandly.

They all peered inside. The lighting was considerably brighter within the sub-station than it was outside in the general area of the cellar. They found themselves staring at an impressive array of dials, switches, and gleaming black paraphernalia that meant nothing to any of them.

'It's all right to go inside,' Arnold assured them. 'Just be careful with anything that's labelled in red. And don't pull any switches, or you'll black out the wards.'

Collins stepped gingerly inside and looked around. Charles, the forensics expert, followed him.

'Who else has keys to this place?' Dan asked Arnold, as he examined the locks on the door.

'Electricity people, of course. But they haven't access to the rest of the building, so they can't get down here without one of us along.'

'One of "us" being maintenance?' Dan asked.

'Or administration. Mr Waters keeps keys to the entire building in his office safe.'

'Including this sub-station?'

'Of course. He'd need them, wouldn't he, in case of emergency.'

'I suppose so,' Dan said slowly, beginning to think that, just as all roads lead to Rome, all clues on this case seemed to lead back to Tony Waters.

'Where do you want to start?' Charles called to Dan, from inside the sub-station.

'Your opinion on that subject might be a lot more valid than mine,' Dan replied.

'Floor up, or ceiling down?' the forensic expert elaborated. 'Front to back, or back to front?'

'How about ceiling down, back to front,' Collins suggested walking to the far end of the sub-station.

The area above ground level was easy. Nothing larger than a shoe-box could have been hidden there with any ease, but when they examined the floor, Dan's eyes lit up. It was covered with heavy metal plates, each a foot wide and three feet long. It took the combined strength of both Evans and Collins to move the first of them. Underneath the plates lay a gap more than a foot deep.

'Hide a corpse in there?' Dan looked to the others.

'As long as it wasn't a fat one,' Collins agreed. He looked across at the forensics expert. 'What do you think?'

'I think I'll get out my kit.'

Gradually Dan and Peter removed all the plates, carrying them outside and propping them out of the way, against the cellar wall, while Charles arranged his kit as best he could in the poor lighting of the main cellar. When he'd finally finished unstoppering bottles, and arranging rows of test tubes ready to hold any specimens he might find, he opened all the compartments of his case so everything would be ready to hand. Then he donned his rubber gloves, slipped rubber socks over his shoes, and stepped out on to the narrow cement band surrounding the newly opened floor of the sub-station. Crouching on hands and knees he began to check the area, centimetre by centimetre, with his magnifying glass.

'Cigar?' Collins pulled three from the top pocket of his shirt and offered them to Arnold and Dan.

'Don't mind if I do.' Arnold took one, and held it in his mouth as Peter lit it. 'Do you think you'll strike lucky?' he asked.

'We can hope,' Dan murmured, leaning against the wall.

'If I were you I'd take a closer look at the therapists,' Arnold nodded wisely.

'Therapists?' Peter's attention pricked up like a dog's ears.

'If I were you, I'd want to know why that big man . . . you know the one who's only got one eye.'

'Spencer Jordan?' Peter asked.

'I'd want to know why he's taken to carrying women's clothes around with him.'

'Women's clothes. Are you sure?'

'Saw him plain as I can see you here. Sitting in his room, lunchtime, playing with a woman's pink scarf and a blouse. Crying like a baby, he was. Sobbing his heart out.'

Collins looked over at Dan, and Dan nodded wearily. He didn't want or need any more clues. He was beginning to feel as though they were caught on an endless treadmill leading absolutely nowhere.

Chapter Twenty-One

'Trevor, I'd be obliged if you'd stay for a moment,' Bill Mulcahy murmured to him as the officers who'd attended the briefing filed out of the cramped mobile headquarters.

'Shouldn't I be getting back to my ward?' Trevor asked.

'I told Andrew Murphy to stay put until you get back. He's capable enough.' Bill waited until only himself, Evans, Collins and Trevor were left in the room, then he kicked the door shut. 'I won't keep you long,' he said as he took his customary seat at the head of the long table. 'We've all got things to do, and a long night ahead. I just wanted to see if we could cut the workload by pooling our knowledge in the light of the new evidence. Then, instead of sitting around guarding bait, perhaps we can catch our villain by watching the sharks.'

'Can we eat while we talk?' Collins walked to the door and leant on the handle.

'Dan?' Bill looked inquiringly at the Inspector.

'Make mine fish and chips.'

'Twice,' Bill said.

'Trevor?' Peter asked.

'Nothing, thanks. I ate earlier.'

'Hospital food,' Peter scoffed. 'I'll order some for you, too,' he countered arbitrarily, opening the door and shouting to the girl manning the reception desk outside. 'Phone down to the gate, love, and order four cod and chips from up the road, please.'

'Right, now can we start?' Mulcahy asked as Collins shut the door.

'Start away,' Collins reached for the plastic cups and poured out four coffees.

'As I mentioned during the briefing, I've had all the

interview reports in.' Bill reached over and lifted a pile of blue-jacketed files from the shelf behind him, and dumped them on to the table. 'What I didn't say earlier, Collins, was that they came along loaded with some pretty hefty criticism from Dr Goldman on your interviewing techniques.'

'You win some, you lose some.' Peter shrugged his shoulders as he poured long-life milk into his coffee.

'Just tread a little more carefully in future,' Bill snarled testily. 'I'm tired of apologising for you. In fact I think it's high time you did some of that for yourself – and not only to the hospital staff.'

'So, we here to pool ideas, or what?' Peter asked blandly.

'Yes,' Bill snapped. 'Starting with . . .' He looked around. Trevor looked as exhausted as he still felt, even after half a night's sleep, Collins was obviously heading towards belligerence again, Evans – he settled on him as the most innocuous choice. 'Dan?'

'It looks like take your pick,' Dan said slowly. 'As I said in the briefing, Angela Morgan's convinced that it's Tony Waters, but when Forensics went over the sub-station nothing was found that shouldn't have been there. Not as much as a fibre, or a stray hair.'

'Only traces of mud,' Peter said flatly. 'Probably carried in on people's shoes. But they're going to sift it, and test it just the same, to see if it's surface or subsoil.'

'Because if it's subsoil, it could have been carried back by the killer?' Mulcahy's tired mind groped with the possibilities.

'It's difficult to see why he'd want to go back to the cellar *after* he'd buried the victims,' Collins chipped in.

'To hide something there?'

'We found nothing,' Evans interposed.

'He could have taken it away later,' Bill said sourly. He looked up at Evans. 'You were saying something about Arnold Massey, the maintenance man.'

'Oh yes,' Dan replied with that slowness of speech that sometimes irritated Mulcahy. 'He said he'd seen Spencer Jordan fondling women's clothing. Something made of pink silk.'

'When did he see this?' Bill asked suspiciously.

'He claims every lunch-hour for the past week. The storeroom where he eats his sandwiches overlooks Jordan's room.'

'Shall we start with Jordan as a potential suspect,' Dan suggested.

'He cracked up. He's odd . . .'

Bill gave Collins a hard look

'He knits, for pity's sake!' Peter exploded.

'You're accusing a man of multiple murder because he knits?'

They all turned and stared at Trevor, more surprised by the unaccustomed sound of his voice than because of what he'd actually said.

'Start again.' Bill dragged his chair over to the flip-chart and flicked the sheets over until he came to a clean page. He wrote SPENCER JORDAN at the top.

'He's been here long enough to commit all the murders, so that fits. He's familiar with the place, both as a patient and as one of the therapy staff. He probably knows enough to administer drugs, he's certainly intelligent, and he's known to have flipped his lid when he saw his wife and three children carved up by a group of nutcases.'

'He what?' Trevor stared round-eyed at Collins.

'Sorry. Forgot you didn't know that little titbit.' Peter reached for the boxfiles stored behind the table, and extracted the one containing the press cuttings he'd brought in. He took out an envelope marked *Spencer Jordan*. 'Read for yourself,' he said.

'What about keeping the victims hidden?' Mulcahy asked.

'He lives in a halfway house just outside the wall,' Collins explained. 'And he works in the old building, so he must have a reasonable knowledge of the layout . . .'

'But *where* did he keep them?' Bill demanded short-temperedly.

'For my money, somewhere in the old hospital.'

'Why so?' Bill badgered.

'The newer buildings and the wards are always too frantic. Too much coming and going; too many people around. He'd run a greater risk of discovery there. Besides there's no nooks and crannies, only straight corridors, square rooms . . .'

'Our man chose to hide Vanessa there. And she stayed hidden for far too bloody long,' Bill said irascibly.

'Lyn Sullivan said . . . said . . .' Trevor lost the thread of what he was trying to convey as he stared, horrorstruck at the photographs and headlines detailing the murder of Spencer Jordan's family. Sickened, he slammed the file shut.

'Said what?' Dan Evans prompted gently.

'Said that if she wanted to hide someone in this place, she'd drug them, wrap shawls and blankets around their shoulders, and put them on one of the wards, preferably geriatric.'

'The lady's got a point,' Collins mused. 'Does anyone know if they hold regular head-counts here?'

'Not often, judging by the number of people they seem to lose,' Mulcahy commented.

'We were talking about Spencer Jordan,' Dan broke in, still hoping for a short meeting. 'We're all agreed that he has the knowledge of this place, and the means . . .'

'But no motive,' Trevor protested.

'He's nuts,' Peter announced flippantly.

'*Was* nuts,' Trevor corrected.

Collins stared at Trevor, saw a firmness around his jawline not evident since his accident, and backed down. 'OK, I'll go along with that. So Jordan didn't have a motive, but you tell me, what motive does anyone have for kidnapping women, drugging them, and then burying them alive as a grand finale?'

'Why would anyone want to do that to a helpless woman?' Dan asked.

'First rule of a murder investigation; you can't apply logic to insane motives,' Collins said coldly.

'The psychiatrist suggested simply power.' Bill finished his coffee and crumpled his cup.

Trevor looked at the men around him. 'Have you considered that those women might not have been chosen at random?'

'They were all on the point of leaving or had just left the hospital,' Dan protested.

'Exactly,' Trevor said. 'Has anyone here considered asking why?'

300

'The patients were leaving because they'd just been discharged.'

'Then why weren't they reported missing?'

'He's got a point,' Peter said thoughtfully. 'Claire Moon told her mother that she planned to travel extensively with a friend. We found her passport, foreign money . . .'

'So whoever he is, he isn't a thief.' Trevor pushed his cold coffee aside.

'Rosie Twyford told her mother that she was taking a holiday in Scotland. And Elizabeth Moore was leaving for a job in America.'

'Why America?' Bill asked.

'Tony Waters said higher wages, and better working conditions. She'd recently been divorced.'

'And there's a rumour going around that she was having an affair,' Collins interrupted Dan.

'Do we know who with?' Bill asked.

'According to Angela Morgan, with Waters. But in her opinion he was having affairs with virtually every female in the hospital.'

'Why didn't you mention this at the briefing?' Mulcahy demanded.

'Hearsay,' Dan said baldly.

'All sour grapes and no facts,' Peter supported Dan. 'Nothing you can really get your teeth into; only a middle-aged woman who's probably griping because her boss has made a pass at everyone working here except her.'

'And Vanessa Hedley?' Bill asked.

'She's got to be the wild card in the pack.' Collins reached in his pocket for a cigar but found it empty. 'She saw him doing away with the others, and got done herself because she could identify him.'

'But she couldn't,' Trevor remonstrated. 'That's just the point.'

'Murderer obviously thought so.'

'Even if he did have affairs with all three women,' Trevor continued, 'that still doesn't explain why he'd want to kill them.'

301

'You live like them, you grow like them. He works in a nut-house, doesn't he,' Peter quipped. He saw pain flash across Trevor's face and instantly regretted his words. But he realised that if he tried to apologise or retract, he'd only make matters worse.

'I've interviewed both Tony Waters and his wife,' Mulcahy murmured. 'It's easy to see who wears the trousers in that household.'

'His secretary agrees that he's the dominant partner,' Evans agreed drily.

'Right, we've gone now from one suspect to two.' Mulcahy turned the page, and wrote TONY WATERS in large capitals on the top of the next sheet. 'Like Spencer, he's been here long enough to have carried out all four murders. And he has close knowledge of the hospital.'

'Actually he knows this place better than anyone.' Collins paced to the window and looked outside for any sign of their fish and chips arriving.

'What about medical knowledge?' Bill asked.

'He was a medical student for two years before he switched to a business studies course.'

'I didn't know that,' Peter muttered, as he answered a knock at the door. Chris Brooke was standing outside with four bundles wrapped in white paper. Collins fumbled in his pocket, and handed him a note. 'Thanks, mate, I owe you one.' He shut the door in Chris's face before the constable could hand over the change. He tossed the parcels across the table, and as Trevor caught his, he had a real sense of being caught in a time-warp. He'd been in a room with Peter, Bill and fish and chips before, and it had led to . . . he pulled himself up sharply, reminding himself that this time it was different. It was the spring of a new year, and this time Dan was working with them.

Mulcahy turned to Trevor. 'Did Spencer Jordan actually know Vanessa Hedley?'

'She attended his art therapy classes.'

'So he could have overheard her bragging about seeing the murderer?'

'Him along with half of the other staff and patients,' Trevor lifted the corner of the paper wrapped around his fish and chips.

302

Dan and Peter were already both engrossed in breaking off large lumps of battered cod.

'What about the other victims?' Mulcahy ferried the first long, greasy chip to his mouth.

'Claire Moon and Rosie Twyford also attended his classes.' A piece of cod fell back on to the paper, leaving Collins snapping at thin air.

'And Elizabeth Moore was a nurse on the depression ward, when he was a patient there,' Dan continued.

'So Jordan knew all of the victims.' Having finished his chips, Mulcahy wrapped his cod in the greaseproof bag and bit into it. 'Right that's Jordan, and Waters,' he mumbled through a full mouth. 'Any other ideas?'

'Adam Hayter,' Collins offered quickly.

'Why?' Bill demanded.

'Because he's obviously a pervert, because I don't like him, because he's been here for two years, and because he has the relevant knowledge.'

'Medical knowledge? He teaches needlework and cookery,' Bill demurred.

'All the therapists are competent first aiders, and all of them have practical knowledge of intravenous injection techniques.' Dan pushed the last piece of fish into his bulging mouth, and crumpled his papers into a ball. 'It was part of a cost-cutting package brought in by Waters. They were all issued with tranquillisers to be used in emergencies, taught how to administer them, and, in return all nursing cover was withdrawn from therapy groups.'

'So he has the medical knowledge as well as the knowledge of the hospital,' Mulcahy conceded.

'Look at his profile,' Collins threw his chip papers into the bin. 'Obsessively neat, lives with a domineering woman, impotent . . .'

'I thought you didn't like profiles,' Bill said coldly.

'I still don't think he's the right one,' Dan said.

'Why?' Peter pressed.

'I can't give you a reason. I just feel it in my bones.'

'Look, he's got enough to put on the list. Let's keep going. Anyone else?' Mulcahy asked.

'Harry Goldman, fits all the criteria on the profile. Separated from his wife after six months of marriage. Divorced after two years. Now lives alone. Collects trains . . .'

'Collects what?'

'Trains,' Peter rummaged through the press file until he came up with an envelope marked "Dr Goldman". He passed it to Bill. 'Toy trains, like train sets.'

'Is there anyone we shouldn't be watching?' Bill asked caustically.

'No one's mentioned the patients?' Trevor pushed aside the chips and cod that he'd barely touched.

'Michael Carpenter is dead. O'Kelly's checking Vanessa's body for time of death. But he doesn't fit the profile.'

'All right, forget about Michael for the moment. What about Roland Williams?' Trevor suggested.

'Lechers aren't impotent. Psychiatrist threw him out,' Mulcahy announced.

'For my money he's a far more likely candidate than Spencer Jordan.'

'Trevor, just because you like a guy . . .' Collins began.

'He's no killer,' Trevor said firmly.

'On what basis?'

'He's too damned sensitive to be a killer.' Trevor handed back the envelope on Spencer Jordan. He'd seen all he wanted to.

'Now you're saying killers can't be sensitive? What about all those concentration camp guards who used to weep when they heard Beethoven and Mozart?'

'Sensitive to music isn't sensitive to people. Psychopaths are often charming, cultured, but cold, dispassionate . . .'

'So now you've decided our villain is a psychopath.'

'Not necessarily.' Trevor fell silent. He sensed the others looking at him; he knew that he was still on probation as far as they were concerned.

'So what it boils down to, is that we have reason to watch half the men in this hospital, but not enough factual evidence to hand one of them a parking ticket,' Bill concluded wearily.

* * *

'You've got to learn not to take everything so much to heart,' Peter lectured, as he slowed his pace to Trevor's limp on their way across the lawns towards the ward blocks.

'You really do think it's Spencer Jordan, don't you?'

'I don't know.' Peter sounded curt with exasperation. 'What I do know is that my head hurts from thinking about it. You know what it's like on the Squad. A junkie goes down, we pick up a cache, and we start looking. And we always know exactly where to look, give or take there's only four major dealers in this town anyway. Even a normal murder case would cough up one or two obvious suspects, but this one . . .' He stopped and stared at the looming shadows of the buildings that surrounded them. 'This one has to have about . . . how many staff did you say worked here?'

'I didn't,' Trevor murmured.

'One week on this case, and I feel as though I've been thinking about nothing else for years. Do you know, I'd give a week's leave for a night off right now. Right this minute. I'd have a couple of jars down the pub . . .'

'I still think there has to be a connection between the victims,' Trevor cut in.

'They're not all women. There's also the dog,' Peter reminded him.

'I forgot about the dog.'

'How could you. The dog that Angela Morgan wept over, when it disappeared.'

'It was a stray?'

'Most definitely a stray.'

'What do you think? It attacked the murderer as he was burying one of the victims?'

'We'll probably never know,' Peter growled.

They paused outside the ward block. Trevor looked up into the clear, star-studded night sky.

'You coming back to join us, then?' Collins asked suddenly.

'I am back,' Trevor reminded him curtly.

'So you are,' Peter smiled. 'How long do you think it's going to be before you're back to normal?'

'What's normal?'

'You snapping back at me like now,' Peter grinned. 'I suppose if nothing more happens here in the next two weeks, you can pack and leave – go back to your flat.'

Trevor recalled the empty, grubby, dismal rooms, the lonely workaholic life he'd led before he'd been injured. And knew with a sudden and unequivocal clarity that he didn't want his life to continue like that. Not any more. He resolved to plan the changes he would make, now while he was still in hospital. He had a mental image of Jean Marshall's apartment, and suddenly knew that he didn't want that either. Then he remembered a woman with long dark hair and sad eyes . . .

'Trevor!' Peter shook his head in despair. 'You can't even stay awake when someone's talking to you.'

'Sorry, just thinking again.'

'Save it until the morning, will you,' Peter headed off in the direction of the old hospital, wondering if his partner would ever totally recover from having his head bashed in.

Tony Waters was sitting in the ward office with Lyn Sullivan and an auxiliary nurse. Trevor could see them through the glass window between the office and the corridor. Lyn's dark head was bent close to Waters' fair one, as both studied a sheaf of papers he was holding.

'New security arrangements for the wards that the hospital authorities have come up with.' Andrew Murphy waylaid Trevor before he had a chance to reach his own room, and handed him a thick file.

'Any good?' Trevor asked.

'How should a mere constable know?' Murphy replied flatly.

'I suppose anything has to be an improvement,' Trevor said drily.

'This is the ward that live women are spirited out of, and dead ones spirited back in, isn't it?'

'It's the one.'

'Sergeant Joseph, I take it you're back on duty?' Waters walked out of the office to greet him.

'Not really,' Trevor demurred. 'I'm just being used as an extra pair of eyes.'

'Well, I've arranged for another nurse to work on this ward. Day and night.'

'That's good,' Trevor murmured absently, as he gazed at Lyn Sullivan through the glass. She certainly had more colour in her cheeks than earlier.

'The Health Authority held a committee meeting this afternoon. They decided that all outside doors will be kept locked during the night – all qualified nurses to hold keys of course, in case of emergency – and a head-count of patients must be carried out every two hours.'

A woman's high-pitched screaming pierced the air.

'Lucy Craig again,' Nurse Sullivan said, as she ran off down the corridor.

'That's our main problem at the moment,' Waters added. 'Keeping the security low-key, so it doesn't upset our patients.'

'Better an upset patient than a dead one, like Vanessa Hedley.' It was the sort of cheap remark Collins would have tossed off without a second thought, but the hostile glare that Waters sent his way lingered afterwards in Trevor's mind.

'This is ridiculous,' Jean Marshall complained. She poured herself a glass of brandy after handing Michelle Grady a cup of coffee.

'What's ridiculous?' Michelle was perched uncomfortably on the edge of her chair, completely overawed by the opulence of Jean's flat. Brought up by a house-proud mother, she deliberately set out to touch as few items as possible, lest she damage or stain them.

'You being here,' Jean replied shortly, beginning to realise just how much this female bodyguard was going to cramp her style. 'I mean there's a porter on permanent duty downstairs, electronically-activated doors and safety devices, so there's no way anyone could get up here without my permission or the doorman knowing.' She conveniently omitted mention of the fire escape as she turned her resentful face to the window and its magnificent view. While Michelle Grady was dogging her every movement, there was no way that she'd find the privacy to telephone, let alone see her lover.

Michelle bristled indignantly. 'Just remember what happened to Vanessa Hedley and all the others.'

'They were taken from the hospital.'

307

'Vanessa certainly, but we can't be too sure of the others.'

'No . . . I suppose you can't,' Jean agreed. 'Well, take your pick of the spare bedrooms. There's clean towels and soap in all the bathrooms, so help yourself to whatever you want. I think I'll go to bed with this,' she lifted the brandy bottle, 'so, if you don't mind, I'll say goodnight.'

'You have your alarm to hand?' Michelle asked.

'Never go anywhere without it.' She held up her hand so Michelle could see it dangling from her wrist.

'The first all-night shift I worked, I learned that it can stay dark forever,' Lyn Sullivan complained as she went into the kitchen. Trevor was standing next to the near boiling kettle.

'The first night I worked,' Trevor smiled, ' I learned that a new day always dawns, no matter what happens during the night, and whether you want it to or not.' He held up a jar of instant coffee.

'Yes please. It's a way of killing another ten minutes. I've just checked everyone, extra staff as well as patients. And all's quiet, sir. God, I hate nights. Roll on tomorrow.'

'Back on days?'

'Not for two whole weeks.'

'Holiday?' he asked.

'My parents have a house in Brittany.'

'Lucky you.'

'It's not very luxurious, just a cottage on the beach, but we had some super times there when I was a kid. Beachcombing, finding mussels, crabs and winkles for tea, learning to speak French.' She laughed. 'And learning how to drink wine.' She took the coffee he handed her. 'When I get back, you'll probably be gone from here, won't you?'

'Probably. I don't suppose I'll be able to spin out my stay any longer, although I may still be on this case. The problem is,' – he looked through the black square of uncurtained window – 'that with all this activity, our people in the grounds, and the corridors, extra staff drafted on to the wards, he's likely to be frightened off. For a time, anyway.'

'So he could stop for a while, then start up again?'

'We'll get him in the end,' Trevor said, with more confidence than he felt. 'Maybe not immediately, but we'll get him.' But all he could think, as he looked into her frightened eyes, was; before or after another murder?

Chapter Twenty-Two

'You were right, Sergeant Joseph. The dawn did come after all.' Lyn put a cup of coffee on the desk in front of Trevor. He opened his eyes, blinked and tried to focus, but he was totally disorientated. 'Don't worry I won't tell anyone you slept,' she whispered, laughing at the confused expression on his face as he rubbed his hands through his hair.

'Oh God, I'm . . .'

'In the ward office, and everyone's safe. I've just counted them; staff and patients.' She put her own coffee next to his and sat in the office chair behind the desk. She turned and snapped back the blind, and he saw the cold, clear light of a new day stealing through the ragged border of trees that fringed the lawns.

'Did anyone come round to check after half-past four?' he murmured, his voice still thick with sleep. Half-past four was the last thing he remembered, and it was now – he glanced at his watch – seven o'clock.

'Only Constable Murphy, and I saw him at the door. Told him you were interviewing the night staff.'

'Bless you,' he said gratefully, knowing that Andrew wouldn't take the matter any further. 'Just as well it wasn't Bill, he'd have put me back on the sick, sharpish.'

'Where you should be, considering the state of your head and legs. Who's Bill?' she asked as an afterthought.

'The super who thought I'd be OK for sitting up all night.' Trevor wrapped his fingers around his coffee cup. 'I don't think I'm going to be much use to the force for a while.' He smiled wryly. 'Too used to getting my eight hours every night.'

'And two hours in the afternoon?' she teased.

'And two hours in the afternoon,' he echoed. 'Thanks for the

311

coffee.' He rose stiffly from his chair, walked to the window and stretched his arms as far as he could, given the small space.

'I don't envy you trying to sleep today.' She picked up both their cups. 'Not with all the extra bodies and activity there's going to be on this ward.'

'If extra bodies come in, I think I'll go . . .' he faltered. He'd almost said "home". His flat wasn't home. 'To my place,' he continued abruptly. 'I'll get the car out of the garage. It might come in useful now that I'm working again.'

'If you do bring it up here, leave it in the staff not the visitors' car park,' she warned. 'Neither are really safe, but you're more likely to find your car jacked up on bricks in the visitors' car park.'

'Thanks for the tip, but no car thief would want to take mine, and even the joyriders would give it a wide berth.'

'You haven't seen some of the cars that have disappeared from here.'

'No, I haven't.' He turned and smiled at her. 'Right, I'm for a shower and then, if you've finished your shift I'll walk you to your hostel, madam.'

'Is that really necessary, with half the town's police force lining the garden.'

'Call it a thank-you for not snitching on me last night.'

'What's snitching?' she asked.

'A word that was probably in vogue before you were born.'

'You sound like a grandfather.'

'At the moment' – he picked up his stick and hobbled to the door – 'I feel like one.'

'Nothing, bloody nothing,' Peter Collins complained as he swung his feet down from the bench seat and reached for the coffee pot.

'Did you really expect anything to happen?' Dan asked, pushing two plastic cups towards him.

'I'm the one who believed in Santa Claus until I was ten.'

Peter raised his eyebrows as they both heard a banging and scuffling at the door between the inner and outer offices, but neither of them was energetic or interested enough to move out of their seats and investigate what was happening.

'It's me,' Trevor knocked at the door, and walked in.

'You look like I feel.' Peter moved along the bench so Trevor could sit down. Trevor parked his stick in the corner of the room and hobbled next to him.

'Nothing?' Trevor asked, looking from Peter to Dan.

'Sweet nothing,' Dan repeated. 'And as the day-shift is about to take over, I'm for home and bath.'

'Be careful,' Trevor warned. 'You look tired enough to fall asleep and drown.'

'There might be baths big enough, but I don't possess one,' Dan said. 'I have a choice of either soaking my legs or my back. It's not big enough for both.'

'Have you ever thought it's not the bath that's the wrong size?' Peter pushed a cup towards Trevor. 'Coffee?' he asked.

'No thanks. I came to see if I could beg a lift back to my place. I've decided to bring my car back here.'

'Tell a man he can crawl, and he tries to run the marathon. Sure you're up to driving with that leg of yours? Peter asked solicitously.

'I can but try. How about it?'

'You're on,' Peter agreed. 'But only if you buy me breakfast in that transport cafe down on the docks.'

'All you ever think about is your stomach,' Trevor complained. He reached for his stick and followed Collins out of the van.

With Peter's help, Trevor managed to extricate his car from the garage. Leaving the battery on charge in the back room of Frank's shop, he then went upstairs and lay down on his bed, intending to catnap for an hour or two. Nothing was going to happen in daylight; not with every building, every ward, and every inch of the hospital grounds under surveillance by the largest force that Bill had ever assembled to work on a single case. He took off his jacket and stretched out, but found himself too restless to sleep. A line of suspects paraded in his mind's eye. Spencer Jordan – Tony Waters – Harry Goldman – Adam Hayter – he visualised each and every one of them, and tried to match them to Vanessa's description of a big man with evil eyes. But no matter how he tried, he couldn't make any of them fit the profile of a serial killer who buried his victims alive. His active imagination went into overdrive as he pictured the girls in the pit; lying conscious and helpless while someone slowly, infinitely slowly, shovelled earth on top of them, painstakingly covering every visible inch. He heard the dry patter of dust as it fell, the dull thuds of damp, sticky clods. He saw the small rectangle of night sky as they must have seen it. The face of the moon shining behind the silhouette of their killer.

Did he take time to study his victims' features as he covered them? Had they known who he was before they died?

Trevor closed his eyes, but the images wouldn't go away. He saw a victim, only this time it was Jean Marshall, her auburn hair spread out as it had lain on the cushion of the sofa the night he'd made love to her. Her eyes round, terrified, the irises bright red with bursting blood vessels . . .

He woke up in a sweat, realising that he must have slept. He went into the bathroom and, running the cold tap, splashed water over his head. The battery should be charged by now. He'd get Frank to help him lift it back into his car, and then perhaps they'd sit down and talk for a while. He looked around his flat one last time before he locked the door. It was a talk that was long overdue.

'I was wondering where you'd got to,' Jean Marshall said as Trevor walked into the ward around midday. 'Can't cope with the food outside so you've come back for a delicious hospital lunch?'

'Brought sandwiches.' Trevor tossed a plastic carrier bag on to his bed.

'As you can see, everything's quiet, and I'm well protected. Constable Grady is in the kitchen making coffee.'

Trevor walked over to the door and closed it behind her.

'Why, Sergeant Joseph.' She batted her eyelashes theatrically.

'Do you have any idea of the risk you're running?' he asked, still on edge after his nightmare.

'Someone had to do something,' she said earnestly. 'Besides, what on earth can happen to me? I've got a round-the-clock female dogging my every step, which is a lot more of a bind than I thought it would be, and a man outside the door of every building I'm in, whether it's here, the canteen, or my flat. Really, I don't think as much as a mouse could creep near me, but thank you for your concern.' She finished on a less exasperated note. 'It's nice to know that someone cares enough to worry about me.'

'I'm worried about the whole hospital!'

'You really are concerned, aren't you?'

'There's a killer on the loose, and you ask if I'm concerned?'

With the memory of their evening's lovemaking lying between them, he couldn't meet the searching look in her eyes. He picked up the carrier bag, and removed the sandwiches he'd scrounged off Frank. A burst of laughter resounded through the open window, and he looked outside. A group of policemen were standing there, smoking, drinking coffee from disposable cups, and chatting on the path right in front of the ward.

He didn't have to say any more. Jean was sensitive enough to read acute embarrassment in his sudden preoccupation with his sandwiches. She too remembered the evening they'd spent together; how his clumsy, selfconscious fumbling compared with the rapturous physical pleasure of the subsequent night she had spent in her lover's arms.

'About the other night,' she said briskly. 'It was a one-off – you do know that, don't you?' She forced a laugh. 'Call it spring madness.'

The relief was evident in his eyes.

'I'd still like to thank you for it,' he said quietly. 'You showed me that there was life outside these four walls.'

'Call it part of the recovery process.' She managed to keep an unaccountable bitterness from her voice.

'Lyn?' Dressed in his bathrobe, and clutching his washbag, Alan peered through the open door of her room on his way from the bathroom. 'You leaving us?' he asked, wondering if events had finally got to her.

'Holiday,' she replied. 'I booked these two weeks last Christmas.

'Lucky, lucky you. Want a hand to carry your case downstairs?'

'It's not as heavy as it looks, but thanks anyway.' She lifted her case into the corridor, picked up her handbag, and locked the door behind her. 'It's mainly washing,' she explained, as she picked up the case again. 'I never got out of the habit of keeping most of my things at home.'

'It must be nice to have a real home in the same town you work in.'

'As opposed to travelling all of fifty miles away.'

'Well have a good time, and don't go drinking too much wine.'

She gave him a sideways look.

'Stupid thing to say. Do drink too much wine.'

'There won't be anything else to do. I'll send you a postcard if I can find one rude enough.'

'Rotten sod,' he grinned as he went into his own bedroom. 'Bet you will, and all.'

Lyn heard Mary's high-pitched giggle from behind Alan's closed door, and she smiled. It was good to know that someone was still in love and happy in Compton Castle.

After Jean left Trevor's room, he rummaged in the bottom of his wardrobe for the cans of beer that Peter Collins had brought in. He found half a dozen, all luke-warm. But at least they were wet, he reflected, as he took his first sip before stretching out on the bed. He picked up a book from his bedside locker to read as he ate his sandwiches. The hands on the bedside clock pointed to two-thirty. All around he could hear the usual hum of hospital noises, interspersed with sharp masculine voices that he remembered from the force. Strange how little he'd thought of work all the time he'd been ill, yet how easily he'd slipped back into the routine of take-aways, working long hours, and caustic exchanges with his colleagues.

When he woke again, the first thing he realised was that he hadn't managed to read a single page, but the hands on his clock had somehow moved around to five o'clock. Then he heard it again, the crashing thud that had woken him. He was up and off his bed in a matter of seconds. He wrenched open the door and dashed into the corridor. A white-faced Michelle Grady was standing helplessly outside the ward office, watching as

Jean Marshall grappled with a large, dark-suited figure behind the glass.

'He's locked the door,' she wailed hysterically.

'Call for help!' he shouted. Picking up a lightweight stacking chair from the corridor, he threw it hard at the glass window. It bounced back, the legs falling away from the moulded plastic seat. 'Use your radio, you stupid woman. Now!'

While Michelle pulled herself together enough to radio for help, he picked up the chair legs again. Hitting the window hard on its corner, he succeeded in cracking the glass, but not shattering it.

'Where?' shouted Andrew Murphy as he dashed through the door, closely followed by Chris Brooke. Before Michelle had time to answer, they'd both sized up the situation, and put the full weight of their shoulders to the office door at the same instant. There was a sharp, snapping, splintering sound as the lock gave way.

Jean was pinned up against the back wall, facing them, her face bright red, her eyes bulging. Roland Williams stood in front of her, one hand around her throat, the other wielding a syringe perilously close to her eyes. Andrew nodded to Chris. They both went for an arm each, and dragged him backwards out of the office. Out in the corridor, Andrew kneed him in the back, and pinned him to the floor.

'Cuffs!' he shouted. Chris pulled a pair out of his pocket.

The door at the end of the corridor flew open. Dan and Peter Collins burst into the corridor, closely followed by Tony Waters.

'Who is it?' Peter shouted, as Trevor fought his way past the huddle on the floor and into the office.

Jean panted, as Trevor helped her on to a chair. 'I was in here when Roland came in. He slammed the door and pulled out a syringe,' she whispered hoarsely.

'Where did he get that from?' Tony Waters demanded coldly.

'You tell me?' Jean sagged against the back of the chair. 'This isn't even his damned ward.'

'They've put him in a room in the secure ward,' Peter announced as he walked into Trevor's room. Trevor and Dan were sitting drinking warm beer straight from the can. 'That's my beer,' he protested.

'You gave it to me,' Trevor retorted tossing him a can.

'For you to drink, not hoard.'

'We're drinking it now.' Trevor raised his own can as Collins ripped off the ring-pull.

'Well, is he the one?' Dan voiced the question uppermost in all of their minds.

'I checked over his record with Bill.'

'And?' Dan pressed. 'Do I have to drag it out of you?'

'He's an alcoholic, he's been here six months . . .'

'Long enough to have carried out all four murders.'

'And he's a private patient. His family, his doting aged parents that is, have money. Enough to pay his somewhat considerable bills here. If they didn't, something tells me that he would have been out of this place long ago.'

'Which explains why the staff around here are prepared to put up with his drinking and his leching.' Trevor sat forward on the edge of his seat. 'But I didn't realise there were private patients here.'

'*Your* room is paid for by medical insurance,' Peter said pointedly.

'Is it?' Trevor asked in surprise.

'Tell that man what time of day it is.' Peter took a long pull at his can and wiped the froth from his mouth, as he sat on the bed next to Dan.

'So we can say that he had the time, the knowledge . . .' Dan began to mull it over.

'What was in the syringe?' Trevor asked.

'Initial diagnosis is water, but they're checking that now, along with all the places where syringes are usually stored, to look for signs of theft or tampering. I managed to talk to him briefly, but then Tony Waters took over. Damned man has sent for a lawyer, and won't let us question Roland until he comes.'

'Accused's legal right,' Dan commented.

'Waters is just covering his backside against the flak that's beginning to fly?'

The room in the secure unit was warm – unpleasantly so. There were thick iron bars on the windows, and as if these weren't enough in themselves, they were fronted by closely-woven wire-mesh screens that blocked out most of the light. Roland was sitting across a narrow table from Dan, flanked on his right by the solicitor. Both table and chairs were chained to the floor. Karl Lane, Carol Ashford and Dotty Clyne sat in a row at the far end of the room. Collins hovered in the corner, clenching and unclenching his fists in anger at his present impotence.

'Come on, Roland,' Dan pleaded. 'Tell us, where you got the syringe from?'

Roland lifted his bleary face from his arms, and stared at Dan unseeingly.

'Why did you attack Sister Marshall?' Dan tried another tack.

'We have yet to establish that an attack took place, Inspector Evans,' the solicitor reprimanded sternly.

'There are four witnesses to the attack,' Peter interrupted. 'All of them police officers.'

'But can they identify Mr Williams?'

'Oh, yes.' Peter shifted slightly towards the table. 'I assure you that they can. All of them.'

Dan faced Roland again. 'Did you attack Sister Marshall?' Roland remained obdurately silent.

'All right, Roland, let's move on. You were holding a syringe. Where did you get it?'

'Rubbish.'

The single word was enough to galvanise Dan's attention. 'What rubbish, where?' he pressed.

'In the sacks.'

'Where are the sacks kept, Roland?' Dan persisted.

'In the corridor.'

'Which corridor?' Dan was beginning to feel as though he were caught up in that irritating children's nursery verse, "In a dark dark wood, there's a dark dark place, and in the dark dark place there's a dark dark house" – and that sooner rather than later he was going to end up back where he started. Possibly even a great deal further back.

'The corridor where the rubbish sacks are kept,' Roland revealed unhelpfully.

'They're kept in a room in the old hospital,' Collins chipped in, unable to stand another moment of this repetitive questioning.

'Right, Roland, did you go into the old hospital?' Dan pushed the questioning one step further.

Roland sank his head back on to his arms again, and closed his eyes.

'I'm afraid you're not going to get much more out of him Inspector.' Carol Ashford rose from her chair in the corner. 'He was so upset we had to tranquillise him.'

'Perhaps you could try again later, Inspector?' Karl Lane suggested, as Roland began to snore noisily.

'How much did you give him?'

'Standard dose, Sergeant Collins,' Carol Ashford replied disarmingly. 'I'm sorry it had to be done, but he was so upset . . .'

'And violent,' Karl reinforced.

'We're aware that he can be violent,' Peter said tersely. He watched as she gently shook Roland awake, while Karl brought in a wheelchair.

'We'll let you know when he wakes up, Inspector.'

'Thanks. Thanks a lot,' Peter retorted sarcastically, as he and Dan walked away.

'His profile and records don't give any indication of him being a potential murderer,' Harry Goldman assured them. 'I've looked at his case history, and I've asked Miss Clyne to call in as soon as she's free. He's one of hers – patients I mean.'

'What *does* the profile of a murderer look like?' Bill Mulcahy enquired innocently.

'In my opinion there'd be a great deal more previous evidence of psychopathic or sociopathic tendencies,' Goldman retorted brusquely, resenting Bill's apparent condescension. 'You asked for my opinion, Superintendent Mulcahy, and I'm giving it to you. I don't believe that Roland Williams is your man.'

'But you can't say for sure?' Bill replied. 'Well I suppose we have enough to book him for the present.'

'Only if Sister Marshall presses charges,' Tony Waters interposed.

'It was aggravated assault, grievous bodily harm, and he also tried to attack two police officers.' Bill stared Waters coolly in the eye.

'I assure you, it won't help matters if you arrest him – unless you're prepared to leave him here, of course,' Goldman continued. 'If you move him, it would undoubtedly upset him, and then he would regress. Lose all the ground that he's made under Dotty's supervision during the past six months.'

'He could,' Bill agreed drily. 'But given the nature of his crime, and the nature of this case, that's a risk I'm prepared to take. We'll charge him as soon as he wakes up, then we'll transfer him to the Station.'

'I really must protest. You'll be destroying a great deal of hard work on the part of the staff of this hospital.'

'Hard work?' Bill looked at Goldman. 'Have you any idea how much he drinks? My men have seen him several times in the shrubbery.'

'Do you have any evidence of this?'

'Evidence. Every time I've spoken to the man I've smelled spirits on his breath.' Bill left his seat. 'We'll give him two hours to sleep it off. After that, Sergeant Collins will go along and charge him. Then we'll hold him in our cells. That's if you manage to contain him securely in yours until then,' he added scathingly as he left the room.

'Anything on Spencer Jordan?' Bill demanded, as he stormed into the back room of the mobile headquarters.

'Nothing,' Dan sensed his mood and trod warily.

'The pink silk thing?'

'Sarah saw it earlier . . .'

'Sarah?' Bill glared at Dan as though he'd taken leave of his senses.

'Constable Sarah Merchant. She joined his therapy class today. She's moving, undercover, into the ward tonight.'

'Oh yes. I'd forgotten about her. Well, get on with it man. 'What did she see?'

'It's a woman's headscarf, sir.'

'Judging by his taste in knitwear, his own,' Collins broke in sardonically.

'There's nothing else to report?'

'Nothing. He left the lights burning in the bedroom and living-room of his flat for most of the night . . .'

'Guilty conscience?' Bill bounced the idea off them.

'Possibly, but then again it might be indigestion.' Peter reached for the coffee pot and a box of biscuits that someone had brought in. 'He cooked himself breakfast this morning, then he left for his therapy room, and that's where he's been all day.'

'Playing with the silk scarf,' Bill snapped.

'And working with his art groups.'

'Does he ever leave the hospital?'

'Not so anyone's noticed.'

'Keep him under surveillance, but put someone on Harry Goldman as well,' Bill barked.

'Yes, sir. And Adam Hayter?' Peter suggested artfully.

'If we've a man spare for the job.'

'Then you don't think it is Roland Williams?' Dan asked.

'I don't bloody well know,' Bill swore fiercely. 'A full week into the case, and no one has come up with any evidence pointing in any particular direction. What am I leading here?' he demanded indignantly. 'A police investigation or a game of bloody Cluedo?'

'We'd stand a better chance with a game of Cluedo,' Peter quipped, as he stepped smartly out of the door. 'Less suspects.'

'What's the problem here?' At the beginning of the second leg of a split shift, Andrew Murphy, was tired, irritable, and ready to bite the head off the security guard on gate duty, who was arguing with a rather good-looking, tall, slim, dark-haired man.

'He wants to see someone in the nurses' hostel,' the guard explained. 'I've had orders to ring through the name of every visitor, and the girl he's asked for left this morning to go on holiday.'

'Then you'll just have to give him the date she gets back, won't you?' Murphy said impatiently.

'That's just it, Constable.' The young man pushed his way into the booth. 'It's my sister and we were supposed to travel together to my parents' house in France. We arranged to meet at home, but she didn't turn up.'

'You probably missed her on the road,' Andrew looked at the queue of traffic building up on the road leading out of town. 'It *is* the rush hour.'

'You don't understand.' The young man's voice was pitched high in temper and something else. Something Andrew recognised at once as fear. 'It's nearly six o'clock, and she was supposed to meet me at ten this morning.'

Chapter Twenty-Three

A ghastly sick, empty feeling rose from the pit of Trevor's stomach as he stepped into the mobile HQ.

'What did you say?' he asked, his voice hoarse with dread.

'We think Lyn Sullivan is missing,' Dan repeated slowly.

'Are you sure?' Trevor's voice fell hollowly into the still office. 'She was going on holiday to France . . .' His voice dried to a whisper as he recalled the stench in the ward when they had found Vanessa Hedley.

'Peter's over with her brother in the hostel now. They've emptied the place by ringing the fire alarm, and they're checking with everyone to pinpoint the last sighting of her.'

'Any idea how long she's been missing?'

'We might know more when he's finished.'

Trevor fumbled his way blindly towards a seat. All the time he'd been having nightmares about Jean, the killer had actually been stalking and watching Lyn. He imagined her fresh young, unlined face, pale with terror, her eyes staring upwards, as she lay on damp earth at the bottom of a cold pit. Earth shovelled spadeful by spadeful, covering her arms, her legs, finally her face . . .

'No matter what we do, this bastard is always one step ahead of us,' Andrew Murphy cursed as he stepped inside the van. He handed one of the girls a sheet of paper.

'Found her car?' Dan Evans asked urgently.

'It's still in the car park. Lab boys are springing the locks on it now.'

'Ever get the impression that someone is goading you, laughing in your face?' Dan asked the room in general.

'We sew this place up tighter than a monkey's bum, and he still gets himself another girl.' Andrew helped himself to a cigarette from a packet lying on top of the computer. For once, none of the girls manning the desk objected.

'You all right?' Dan turned to Trevor.

'I will be in a moment.' Trevor lifted his head out of his hands.

'We will find her, you know.'

'Like we found Vanessa?' Trevor asked. No one dared answer him.

'I want this place sealed off now – this minute,' Bill's voice reverberated through the thin walls of the van, sending shudders of instant activity through the assembled constables. 'From this moment on, not so much as a moth flies in or out of this place without giving us its name and address and being searched.'

'We sealed off the place when Vanessa Hedley was taken,' Trevor commented flatly, as the Super stepped heavily inside the van.

'And we'll do it again,' Bill said harshly. 'We'll search every inch of the buildings and the grounds. Once a room or an area is evacuated, it's searched, it's sealed, and a man is then put on surveillance until we've finished the whole complex.'

'And the personnel?' Dan asked.

'Those working the wards can go back to them, but the administrative staff will be searched and eliminated from our enquiries before they will be allowed out. If they're driving cars, we'll strip them back to the chassis. Right?'

'You want me to tell Tony Waters that we're closing down the Health Authority side?'

'Until further notice,' Mulcahy snapped.

'And the grounds?' Dan asked patiently.

'Same principle; area searched, tagged, wrapped in tape, and men covering the grounds at intervals. Every bloody inch!' Bill shouted, pushed to the end of his patience by frustration and weariness. 'Dog handlers are already in the girl's room, being primed with her bedclothes.'

'Oh God, do I have a sense of walking this way before,' Peter Collins grumbled, as he negotiated the last few steps up to the top of the old building. He stopped on the small landing and looked down at the twenty men following him. 'Right, let's start again, room by room, ransacking every cupboard, every nook, every cranny, every box and every file, tapping every wall, every stair, every ceiling, sealing off everything as we go. Take it slowly, floor by floor. Right let's go to it, five starting that end,' he pointed to his left, 'and five this end,' he indicated right. He looked at Trevor. 'We'd do this quicker, Joseph, if you make a start in the cellar and we meet in the middle.'

'It might save time,' Trevor agreed.

'Meet on floor two, and we'd better double-check that one to make sure we've covered everything.'

Trevor turned, leaning heavily on the bannister rail, he called down to Chris Brooke. 'You heard the man. Let's go.' They walked silently down the stairs until they reached the cellar at the boiler-room end. There they began by checking the incinerators, the men following behind the dog-handler. They checked every sack, every crack in the solid cement floor, every inlet and outlet of heating pipes, then the ceiling. And even after the whole area had been thoroughly sniffed over a second time by the dogs, and he'd seen the emptiness with his own eyes, Trevor still found himself wondering if they'd missed something.

It was a long and tedious job that progressed all the more slowly when Tony Waters appeared and insisted on dogging their footsteps. After much wrangling he grudgingly presented Trevor with a full set of keys, and Trevor, who'd heard about the sub-station from Collins, supervised the lifting of every iron plate out of the place.

'Nothing, sir,' Chris Brooke said flatly.

'Nothing sir,' the dog-handler repeated.

They checked, searched and double-checked. Knocked every wall, shone torches over every inch of the floor, every inch of wall, every inch of cellar.

'If there's a bleeding mouse that we haven't tagged and tailed down here,' Andrew Murphy complained bitterly at the end of two hours of searching. 'I'd like to know about it.'

'Steps and corridor to next floor,' Trevor ordered abruptly.

'Half floor,' Tony Waters corrected.

'Half floor,' Trevor barked. In his eyes Waters seemed too cool, too collected for an administrator who had just lost another nurse to the same serial killer who had done away with a nurse and three patients already. He looked back into the empty cellar as he posted a seal on to the wall. 'You,' he called out to the last man. 'Stand here. And you,' he called back another one. 'Stand at the far entrance in front of the locked door. Use your radios. Every ten minutes to main control, and every five to each other.'

Trevor couldn't resist the temptation to look back as he walked away. Were there secret passages beneath the floor, dating back to the days when a Norman castle had dominated the site? Was Lyn hidden down there, half dead if not dead already? Was she still conscious and suffering? Hoping for a rescue that might never come?

'My wife—' it was the first time Trevor had heard Waters use the word. 'My wife will show you over this floor.' He folded the note Carol had brought him into his pocket. 'I'm sorry to have to leave you, Sergeant Joseph. It appears I have to attend an emergency meeting of the hospital committee.'

'I'm sure Sister Ashford will look after us,' Trevor said mechanically. As Waters walked away, Carol Ashford drew closer, and the dogs went wild, pulling at their leashes.

'I'm sorry, Sister,' the handler apologised.

'It's all right.' She patted one dog on the head. 'I keep two Dobermans.'

'You also use the same perfume as Nurse Sullivan, and half the other females working in this hospital.' The handler made a face. 'Dogs have gone berserk over seven nurses already, sir.'

'I'm afraid Laura has a lot of customers.' Carol smiled wryly.

'The staff here all shop together?' Trevor looked puzzled.

'No time for shopping, so we grab what we can. Laura Stafford, the staff nurse in Alcohol and Drug Abuse, is married to a pharmacist. We give her our orders, she gives us discount, and this I'm afraid' – she fingered her lapel – 'was last month's special.'

'All of which makes our job bloody impossible – begging your pardon, Sister,' the handler apologised.

Carol smiled absently at him. 'You do know this floor is scarcely used now, Sergeant Joseph?'

Trevor referred to the notes that Collins had thrust into his hand as they'd separated. 'Except for the rooms opposite the old padded cells,' he observed. 'The hospital stores rubbish in them that's destined for the incinerator.'

Carol nodded.

They ascended the narrow staircase, one dog and its handler preceding them, another bringing up the rear. The men regularly tapped the walls, but there was no point in testing the concrete steps. The stairwell beneath them was an empty void.

'Make a note that we haven't looked at the outside steps,' Trevor said sharply, studying the plan to match it to the surroundings and ensure that there were no oversights. He headed forward down the grey, echoing emptiness of the corridor that was floored and walled in concrete. A row of bare lightbulbs overheard cast a weak, pale, yellow light, but that was completely drowned by the powerful torch-beams the team swept over dusty corners. As Trevor tagged off the areas and locked partition doors, they moved on to the rooms where the rubbish was stored. The handlers allowed the dogs to sniff each bag before they were slit open. Foul-smelling waste tumbled out, carpeting the concrete as the constables spread it thinly, poking, prodding, and turning it over with long canes that the team who had preceded them had fortunately left stacked in a corner. All that surfaced were used syringes, stained balls of cottonwool, and clumps of damp, dirty paper towels.

'Does this job come with a free Aids test?' Andrew Murphy muttered drily.

'The end of the corridor now,' Trevor ordered, as he watched the last of the rubbish being scraped off the floor into fresh bags. Murphy and Brooke were wearing thick rubber gloves, providentially borrowed from the kitchen.

'Mortuaries first?' Carol Ashford halted before the male mortuary. 'Do you have a key?'

'You lock them?' Trevor pulled the ring of keys out of his jeans pocket.

'Always when there's bodies in them. That's why we can't understand how the body of Mrs Hope appeared out in the grounds.'

'Mrs Hope was the corpse I landed on?' Trevor asked.

329

'She was,' Carol acknowledged. 'We've had two more deaths on geriatric earlier today. Both straightforward; one senile dementia, ninety-two, and one heart attack, eighty-four.'

'It must be soul-destroying work.'

'I beg your pardon?' She looked at Trevor.

'Working on geriatric,' he explained.

'Sometimes.'

Trevor opened the door and allowed the dogs in first, but they still persisted in showing more interest in Carol's perfume until they reached the bank of body drawers.

'There's no need to stay. We'll check those out,' Trevor said to the handlers.

When they had finally led their dogs further up the corridor, Trevor walked in with Andrew Murphy, gratefully noting how little furniture there was. Sinks, large, stone and open, without fittings beneath them. Plain wooden tables covered by sheets of zinc, and a large bank of a dozen body drawers, four wide and three high, propped against the back wall. Andrew jerked out the top left-hand drawer, and he jumped back, visibly shaken as a pair of greyish white feet twitched towards him, the gnarled and yellow toenails pointing dramatically upwards.

'The 92-year-old senile dementia,' Carol said coolly, walking towards him and heaving the drawer out further. She folded back the sheet that was wrapped around the slight, emaciated body, and uncovered the face of an elderly man Trevor last remembered seeing sitting and shaking on one of the benches in the gardens.

'Will you transfer him to the General?' Trevor asked.

'No. We only transfer the ones who need a postmortem to the General, Sergeant Joseph.'

'If you'd like to wrap up again, Sister?' Andrew was staring at the corpse. It wasn't a sight he particularly wanted to study, but he couldn't seem to get his eyes to look in any other direction while the drawer remained open. She rewrapped the body gently, and Andrew pushed the stiff drawer back in. Then he and Trevor began to pull out one drawer after another.

'Careful!' Carol shouted, as the whole bank leant dangerously forward. Chris Brooke ran towards them and threw his weight alongside Andrew's, while Trevor and the nurse tried to close one rusty drawer after another. By the time they'd succeeded in setting the unit on to an even keel again, they were all exhausted.

'At least we now know there's nothing behind those drawers,' Murphy said, as he mopped his brow.

'Check the floor under the sink,' Trevor ordered Chris Brooke, as he walked to the window and examined the mesh covering them.

'Nothing, sir.'

Trevor was beginning to hate that word more than any other in the English language.

'Nothing sir,' Andrew echoed, as he managed to force the last drawer home.

'Tab it and we'll move on to the female mortuary.' Trevor waited until everyone had moved on down the corridor. In the second cold, comfortless, clinically ancient room, he paced the floor uneasily while Chris Brooke and Andrew Murphy fought with another set of rusted body drawers, this time they were careful to open no more than two at a time.

Clenching and unclenching his fists he stared at the joins between walls and ceiling. If only he could think harder, the way the murderer did. There had to be a body sized gap somewhere! People simply didn't vanish into thin air.

Dogs and men sniffed round the huge tubs, sinks and old dry linen cupboards of the laundry.

'Nothing,' Chris Brooke repeated dully.

The word echoed from the floor above where Collins' team was already working. He imagined Lyn's face, so lively and animated in life, now frozen lifelessly in death.

'Shall we move on to the kitchen, sir?' Chris Brooke had to repeat himself before Trevor heard. There was nothing left to do but follow his suggestion and move on.

The staff lined up in the dining area while his search team opened stoves and refrigerators, emptied freezers, pantries, even the microwaves and food processors.

'Nothing – nothing – nothing—' Trevor felt as though he were going to go mad if he heard that one more time.

Collins was at his side.

Trevor held up his hand. 'Don't say it. Where to now?'

331

'Interview Roland Williams. I've just had word he's awake. Bill wants him given the third degree.'

Peter Collins dumped a stack of papers on to the table before he sat down and faced Roland Williams. Trevor closed the door then took the only vacant chair, next to Dotty Clyne in the corner.

'Did you see Nurse Sullivan this morning?' Peter asked bluntly, without any preamble.

Roland shook his head so vigorously that his fat cheeks and chin wobbled.

'Did you see Nurse Lyn Sullivan at any time this morning?' Peter repeated.

'No.' Roland's voice was so low Trevor had to strain his ears to catch what he was saying.

'Where were you all this morning?'

'In therapy.'

Peter looked at Trevor.

'Which therapy?' Trevor asked.

'Art,' Roland was so terrified he was almost gibbering.

Trevor got up and opened the door. He nodded to Michelle Grady who was standing outside in the corridor. She hesitated, then walked into the room. He pointed to his chair, before closing the door behind her.

'Why did you attack Sister Marshall?'

Trevor could hear the question, but not Roland's answer, as he made his way down the corridor towards the therapy rooms. It was only when he reached the other end that he remembered the old block had been evacuated for the search. He nodded to the Constable stationed there and took a right turn into the garden.

Mulcahy was standing in the centre of the drive, directing the outdoor search operation and talking to Tony Waters at the same time. Trevor limped towards them.

'Do either of you know where I can find Spencer Jordan?' he asked.

'We moved his class into the day room of the drug and alcohol abuse ward,' Tony replied. Trevor moved on, anxious not to get involved with Bill in his present vitriolic mood .

As he approached, he saw Spencer's tall, lean figure through the window, bending over Lucy Craig's chair, pencil poised over her sketchbook.

'Come to join our class, Sergeant?' Spencer asked when he saw him standing in the doorway. It was the first time Spencer had addressed him by his title, and Trevor detected a condemnatory note in Spencer's voice, as though he didn't approve of his transition from patient to police officer.

'Not at the moment,' Trevor said quietly. 'But could I have a word with you outside?'

Spencer dropped his pencil on to a table, and followed him into the corridor.

'I'm sorry to interrupt . . .'

'I bet you are,' Spencer said bitterly.

'Look, we're all having a hard time . . .' Trevor was taken aback by his vehemence.

'Some harder than most. Have you any idea what it's like being interrogated by that man?' Spencer demanded.

'Who?' Trevor asked.

'Your bloody Superintendent Mulcahy.'

'Oh yes.' Trevor lifted his eyes to meet Spencer's. 'I know. And . . . and I also know what happened to your family. I'm sorry.'

'You're sorry?' Spencer stared at him incredulously.

Trevor was suddenly conscious of the passage of time, how important that was for Lyn wherever she was. 'If we're riding roughshod over people, I apologise, but we're trying to save Lyn Sullivan's life. And we don't believe that we have too much time to do it in. You, more than anyone here, knows what it's like to lose someone you love to senseless violence. Her brother is sitting frantic in the hostel now. Her mother and father are hurrying back from France.'

'I'll help in any way I can,' Spencer replied. 'Just tell me how?'

'Roland Williams. Was he in your therapy class this morning?'

'Yes. Surely to God you don't think it's Roland now?' he demanded wearily.

'We simply don't know. He attacked Sister Marshall.'

'I heard about that. But attacking Jean Marshall isn't quite the same thing as kidnapping and burying women alive.'

'We're fumbling in the dark, and hoping our fumbling doesn't cost Lyn her life,' Trevor replied honestly.

Spencer stood in thought for a moment. 'He came in this morning at half past nine, along with everyone else. I remembered him tripping over Alison Bevan's easel.'

'And afterwards?'

'He stayed with me all morning, even through break. They all did. Lucy Craig and Alison were particularly upset. They just wanted to sit and talk.'

'Did Roland join in the conversation?'

'I don't have to tell you what he's like.'

'When did he leave?'

'He went with the others at lunchtime.'

'It was just after lunch he attacked Sister Marshall,' Trevor reflected. 'Did he leave the therapy room at any time?'

'He might have gone to the toilet. I don't clock people in and out, you know that.'

'But he *could* have left the room?'

'If he did, and I'm not saying he did, I doubt that it was for longer than five or ten minutes. He and Alison were making papier-mache models at the sink in front of the window, and I seem to remember non-stop conversation in that area. You could check with Alison Bevan and Lucy Craig.'

'I will. And thanks.'

Trevor went first to the dayroom and checked with Lucy, then over to his ward to talk to Alison Bevan. Finally he went to HQ to find out which constable had been posted closest to the therapy room. Reached on the radio, the man corroborated Spencer's story. No one had walked in or out of the door he'd been manning all morning.

The last sighting of Lyn had been that by Alan in the hostel at ten. And as she was already carrying her suitcase out of her room, and on her way home, the chances were she'd been waylaid shortly after that time. Otherwise her car wouldn't have been left in the car park . . . unless that is, someone had called her back into the hospital on some pretext or other.

Trevor returned to the secure unit to find Roland slumped in a torpor, while Collins was fending off a verbal attack from Dotty Clyne.

'You cannot intimidate my patient in this fashion, Sergeant. You have no idea of the long-term damage you are causing . . .'

'I do have a fair idea of the damage *he* has already caused,' Peter retorted icily.

'Sergeant, as a patient in this institution, Mr Williams is entitled to certain rights . . .'

Her voice droned on as Peter turned and saw Trevor standing in front of the door.

'Roland?' Trevor spoke softly, pitching his voice below Dotty's ranting in an effort to gain Roland's attention. 'Where were you all morning?'

'Therapy,' Roland murmured.

'And afterwards?'

'Went to eat lunch.'

'And after that?'

'In the office with . . .'

Trevor turned to Collins and shook his head.

'Corroborated?' Collins demanded.

'Every which way, by staff, patients and our own people.'

'You see, Sergeant Collins,' Dotty crowed triumphantly.

'There's still the little matter of the assault charge,' he replied as he gathered his papers together.

'Sister Marshall won't press charges,' she announced firmly.

'Do I take that to mean that she won't have a job here for very much longer if she does?' Collins enquired drily, as he and Trevor left the room.

Chapter Twenty-Four

Mulcahy was calm, too calm, Trevor thought as he stepped into the crowded back room of headquarters. Experience had taught him that whenever Bill was this composed, it was generally the still before hurricane gale force-ten struck.

'Now we start interviewing,' he began to speak even before the last of those entering had time to find a seat. He went straight to the point. 'There'll be four teams. Sarah Merchant is already splitting up the staff that are still on the premises. Dan, you take one team; Peter, another; Trevor a third. I'll lead the fourth myself. Your priority is to establish everyone's movements and whereabouts between the hours of nine-thirty and twelve this morning.'

'And if it's an outsider, like the milkman or the laundry-man?' Collins was playing Devil's Advocate.

'We've searched and double-checked everyone and every-thing entering the gates since Vanessa Hedley's dis-appearance.' A frown creased Mulcahy's forehead, as his glare settled on the hospital security chief and the policeman he'd put in charge of traffic flowing in and out of the hospital, who were, unfortunately sitting side by side. 'There's been no let up in security since then, has there?'

'None,' the security chief assured him hastily. 'Nurse Sullivan couldn't have been taken out of this place this morning, without us knowing about it. I'm willing to stake my reputation on it.'

'You just did, mate,' Peter murmured as he walked to the door. 'You just did.'

Trevor watched the dietician as she left the corner of the dining-room where he was conducting his interviews along

337

with Sarah Merchant. In the opposite corner Collins was working in uneasy tandem with Michelle Grady. He waited while Sarah keyed the essential information from their latest interview on to her laptop computer.

'Name – age – position held in Compton Castle?'

'Herne, Jimmy Herne. Fifty-eight years old. Head gardener.'

'Where were you this morning between ten and twelve?' Trevor was bored with the endless tedium of repeating the same questions. He wanted to do something – anything more constructive – towards finding Lyn Sullivan.

'Let me see now . . .' Herne scratched his bald head thoughtfully, further trying Trevor's frayed patience. 'I cut the lawn first thing. I never trust the boys to make the early cuts, when the grass is still tender like . . .'

'What time did you finish cutting the grass?' Trevor interrupted, thinking of the fifty-two other people still waiting to be interviewed.

'About ten, I think.'

'And what did you do then?'

'Had second breakfast with the maintenance men, like I always do.' Jimmy sounded indignant, as though Trevor should be well acquainted with his movements.

'What time did you finish this second breakfast?

'Half past ten, same as always.'

'And after?'

'Worked on the flowerbeds down by the front gates, with those two damned useless boys who can't tell a . . .'

'Until what time?' Trevor cut him short again.

'Until dinner time. Half past one.'

'Those boys you were with – did they eat second breakfast with you?'

Trevor only wished that he could rid himself of the feeling that all of this was a worthless waste of time, that they weren't making any real headway with the case, that none of this – the people, the computers, the interrogations – had anything to do with Lyn or her disappearance. He looked at his watch. Nearly six o'clock. Lyn had last been seen eight hours ago, and they were still no closer to finding her.

'Is there any truth in the stories you told Sister Marshall and

Nurse Sullivan about secret tunnels in the grounds – leading out from the cellars to the folly?'

'Yes, there's truth in them,' Herne snapped, piqued at the implication that he'd been spinning yarns.

'Could you lead me to them?' Trevor asked.

'Well, I could . . .' Jimmy mused, 'Then again I couldn't . . . not exactly, that is.'

'Explain.' Trevor ordered shortly, loathe to waste potentially valuable time on extraneous words.

'Well, they were all blocked off years ago,' Jimmy admitted reluctantly 'When the therapy blocks were first built.'

'Exactly how long ago was that?' Trevor pressed.

'Let me see . . . it must have been sometime back in the sixties. Builders came in here, and they went round the grounds and the old block, plugging all the old tunnel entrances and exits.'

'With temporary shuttering?' Trevor asked hopefully.

'Nothing temporary about what they did. They had cement mixers in, and concreted up the holes. Tons of cement and rubble they poured in. Tons and tons,' Jimmy emphasised heartily.

'But you could show me where they poured it?'

'Now, let me, see . . .' The irritating scratch of his head again. 'Oh yes, I think I could find the spot, if you wanted.'

'Take the rest of Mr Herne's statement.' Trevor turned to Sarah. 'I'll be back after I've found a plan of this place.'

'There has to be someone who can take over from me,' Trevor begged.

'You know how important these interrogation sessions are. It could well be our only real chance of getting Lyn Sullivan back alive.' Bill Mulcahy looked up at Trevor and saw that he remained unconvinced. 'How often have you said yourself that the only way to catch this villain is with routine police work?'

'Never!'

'Then it must have been Collins.' Bill seemed totally nonplussed by his mistake.

'While we're sitting here talking, she could be dying by inches, suffocating . . .'

Mulcahy stared blankly at Trevor for a moment, while his mind worked overtime. 'All right,' he said finally. 'Get Murphy to take over from you, then go and check out the bloody tunnels, if you're really convinced they exist. And while you're about it, find out if those rookies have come up from Police College. If they have, get someone to deploy them in the grounds.

'I'll do that, sir.' Trevor walked away jubilant, hoping against hope that this was the first step towards discovering the killer's hiding place. Even if the tunnels had been sealed off as solidly as Jimmy Herne had said, there was the possibility that a gap might have inadvertently been left. It would only take a small one – a loose side brick that gave way long after the seal had been put in place – a plug that had worked loose and fallen out – Possibilities writhed and wormed through his mind. A small gap, that's all he needed. One just big enough to take a crawling man, dragging an inert, drugged, lifeless body behind him.

'Here you are. Sealed off, just like I told you.' Jimmy Herne pulled back a clump of hydrangea bush that had spread its lower branches wide within the decaying walls of the folly, and exposed a bare concrete plinth set well below the original floor level. Balancing on his stick, Trevor leant over awkwardly and inspected the solid concrete. He ran his hands around the edges. Encountering flakes of bark, he picked up a fistful and allowed them to run through his fingers.

'We use that to keep the weeds down,' Jimmy informed him.

Trevor signalled to the raw recruit behind him. The girl hadn't even finished college, but with experienced police so thin on the ground, he hadn't felt justified in taking anyone else with him on what could turn out to be a wild-goose chase.

'See if you can find any gaps around the perimeter of that,' he ordered her.

The girl dived forward and ran her hands around the smooth edges of the plug.

'It's set in solid Georgian brickwork, that one,' Jimmy said dishearteningly. 'There'll be no moving it. I watched them fix it; took six of them nearly two days just to set this plug off alone. The tunnel was still open at both ends before then. That

340

was the problem; people kept trying to walk through. Student nurses out for a lark on staff do nights, you know the sort of thing.'

'I can imagine,' Trevor said drily.

'Well, one of the nurses got caught in a fall of earth. Halloween it was. Lucky they pulled her out in time. After that the Hospital Authorities paid to have the tunnel sealed up both ends.'

'Where was the other end?'

'The cellar of course.'

'It seems solid enough, sir,' the rookie ventured tentatively.

'Right then, let's go.' Trevor used his stick to propel himself swiftly forward.

'Where to?' Herne protested. 'I can't hang about with you lot all day. I've a garden to run, and this is the busiest time . . .'

'Your work is going to have to wait,' Trevor said firmly. 'I need you down in the cellar.'

Trevor nodded to the constable who was still standing on the cellar steps, in exactly the same position he had left him.

'All quiet, sir,' the man commented.

Trevor handed Herne and the rookie a torch each from the pile heaped at the foot of the stone steps. He took two for himself.

'Right, where was this entrance?' he asked Jimmy.

'Well, bearing in mind that I only walked down that tunnel once – and that was when I was a boy, when I first started here. Did it for a bet,' he wandered off on yet another digression. 'The older lads were always egging us youngsters on. Well, there was a lot more of us in those days. Twenty experienced gardeners and fifteen boys . . .'

'But *can* you find the tunnel end?' Trevor broke in. He stepped forward and snapped a switch. A single row of dim-wattage lightbulbs flickered on overheard, shedding a leprous glow over the grimy concrete floors and the dusty pipes that snaked around the cellar walls.

'I think it was over here.' Herne made his way uncertainly through the cellar until he came to the electricity sub-station. 'Yes, this is it, alongside here.' He patted a large cement patch on the wall that hadn't gone unnoticed by the search teams

341

earlier. But, after tapping it to make sure that it was both firm and solid, they had ignored it, not realising that there had once been anything behind it.

Trevor ran his hands around the edges and knocked at it again. It certainly looked solid enough, but what if there was something else they'd missed. A side-tunnel, perhaps, that opened out somewhere else?

'Constable?' Trevor shouted back to the man on duty.

'Sir?' The boy leapt forward, bright-eyed and eager.

'Go upstairs and fetch a pickaxe. And' —Trevor looked at the fragile, blonde, petite rookie who stood next to him – 'another man,' he murmured. 'A dog-handler if you can find one.'

Fortunately both the constable himself and the dog-handler he commandeered, were in better physical shape than Trevor. They took it in turns to wield the pickaxe, and within twenty minutes of hard, banging graft that shook the cellar, they broke through the thick covering skin of concrete to reveal a gap.

The first hole was barely two inches wide, but it was a start. It enabled Trevor to guess the thickness of the concrete plug at about a foot. With Trevor's chivvying, both men managed to enlarge the hole to a rough three-foot square, all within another ten minutes.

'That's the beginning of the tunnel you remember?' Trevor turned to Jimmy Herne.

'Yes, but you can't be thinking of going in there. It was sealed up because of earth falls. No one's been down there in more years than I care to remember. It's dangerous. You could get killed . . .'

'Did you ever hear of any side-tunnels? Anything leading off from this end or the other?' Trevor persisted.

'Plenty,' Jimmy said flatly. 'The usual sort of buried treasure nonsense. These tunnels were supposed to have been built as secret passages leading out from the dungeons of the old castle. There's stories that a medieval king stashed his gold here once, an Edward, or perhaps it was a William. I can't remember the details . . .'

'But there *were* rumours of side-tunnels?' Trevor repeated.

342

'Legends, yes. But nothing that I ever saw.'

'Give me a hand to get in here.' Trevor beckoned the constable, as he propped his stick against the wall.

'Sir?' The constable looked at Trevor's leg as he stood awkwardly in front of the hole. 'You can't be thinking of going in there?'

'Why not?' Trevor asked sharply.

'It's not my place to be saying this, sir,' the lad ventured diffidently, 'but . . .'

'You're quite right,' Trevor interrupted, stripping off his jacket. 'It's not your place. You're out of order.'

The tunnel was damp, icy-cold, and crumbling. After the constable had helped him in, Trevor inched forward on his stomach, propelling himself on his elbows. He pushed the two torches in front of him, one lit, the other held in reserve. Every time he slithered forward, gobs of soaking wet earth fell on to the thin shirt that covered his back, and into his hair and ears. After ten feet of painstakingly slow crawling, the tunnel opened out. He pushed himself forward . . . forward . . . then fell, in a clatter of torches and a shower of earth and rubble, on to a hard stone floor. The torch went out and he fumbled blindly in total, terrifying darkness – for five panic-stricken, agonizing minutes.

As he fought for breath, his fingers finally closed on a hard, smooth object. He wrapped both hands around it, fumbling frantically for the switch. He pressed it downwards, and a blessed warm glow of light dispersed the darkness, and his fear.

'You all right, sir?' the constable's voice echoed towards him down the tunnel. Trevor turned and shone his torch back at the hole from which he'd tumbled.

'Fine, Constable,' he shouted, as he rubbed his legs. 'I've broken through into an area that's high enough to stand in.'

'Do you want me to follow you up, sir?'

'Not much point until I've had a look around,' Trevor answered as he shone his torch upwards. What he saw made his heart miss a beat. A bulge of earth, held precariously in place by a network of tree roots, loomed a bare inch above his head.

343

He looked away, desperately trying to ignore it, and concentrate on studying the walls for signs of any continuation of the tunnel. They were little different from the ceiling, although here and there he could see a few large stones, presumably put there at some time to contain the earthfalls that had covered the outer edges of the stone floor with a thick layer of mud. He squelched forward, looking for another outlet, but he could find none. Dark, crumbling walls of earth, met his torch beam at every turn. Starting at the point at which he'd entered, he walked slowly around the open area, thrusting his hands against banks of, now solid, now crumbling dirt.

He'd worked his way virtually around the whole of the chamber, when he thrust his hand against the wall, lost his balance and plunged headlong into it. He tried to cry out, but dirt clogged his eyes, his nose, his mouth. He fell even deeper, downwards, ever downwards, unable to stop himself. Again he tried to shout out, but couldn't even breathe, let alone speak.

This time he'd been careful to keep a tight grip on his torch. He tried to lift it into view, but there was too much earth between his hands and his face. Choking, coughing, spluttering, he remembered the way in which three victims had died, and wondered, in an oddly calm way, if that was going to be his fate too. Because help would come too late unless – unless he tried to help himself.

He struggled with every ounce of energy left to him, using violent swimming motions in an effort to propel himself upwards, and out of the dirt. Pushing up with his hands, he finally managed to create some space around his face.

After a choking, coughing eternity, he collapsed on the floor, in inches of freezing, sticky wet mud. He was filthy, soaked to the skin, icy cold. But he was alive. And as his scalded lungs heaved in yet another breath of stale air, he formulated a silent, grateful prayer that fortune had been kind to him.

An enormous fat worm slithered its way across the freshly fallen earth that coated his legs. Then he realised, the air was chill only because of the deep layers of insulating soil above and around him. He could feel no fresh draughts. The earth he'd tumbled into had obviously fallen and blocked the continuation of the tunnel. If there had ever been any side shafts, any networks of secret passages spreading out down here, they were no longer serviceable or accessible.

He rose slowly and with great difficulty, to his feet, trying to support himself by clasping his hands on his knees, too wary to reach out and touch the sides again.

'I'm coming back,' he called out, turning to where he thought the tunnel should be. Staring at the fall of earth, he realised he'd got it wrong, so he spun the beam of his torch around. All he could see now was blank walls of earth. He breathed in deeply, forced himself to remain calm. If he took it slowly, inch by inch, he was bound to find his entrance point. It had to still be there. Even if it was covered, that covering wouldn't be very deep. It couldn't be . . .

Slowly, painstakingly, he inched his way around the walls. Studying every clump, every pile of earth until he thought his eyes would fall from his head with the effort.

'He what?' Peter Collins bellowed down the radio.

'He went into the tunnel fifteen minutes ago, sir, and we can't see or reach him. We can't even see a light. The tunnel is in total darkness . . .'

'Where are you?' Collins shouted down the radio.

'Cellar, sir. Close to the sub station.'

'Stay there. Don't move. Don't do anything. I'm on my way.' He left his seat and broke into a run.

'Where's *he* going?' Bill Mulcahy bellowed as he watched Peter's back disappear out through the door.

'Over here, sir,' the constable called out, as soon as he saw Collins charging down the cellar steps.

'What the hell happened?' Peter demanded.

'Sergeant Joseph ordered us to break through that cement plug into an old tunnel . . .'

'He went in there?' Peter stared at the square that they had hacked in the concrete plug. 'And you didn't try to stop him?'

'He did try, sir,' a young girl piped up.

Peter squinted at the girl wearing a rookie's uniform.

'He would, the bloody hero,' he muttered under his breath.

'Sir?' she questioned brightly.

345

'Nothing.' He stripped off his jacket and thrust his radio into his shirt pocket. Was he getting old, or was the force picking up recruits from junior comprehensives these days? She looked about fifteen years old. 'Right, I'm going in,' he said sharply.

'You'll get caught in a fall, too,' Jimmy Herne crowed. 'I'm warning you.'

'Get some rope,' Peter ordered the dog-handler. 'I'll tie it around my waist. If there's any problems, I'll shout out and you can pull me back.'

Unlike Trevor, Collins didn't need any help to climb into the tunnel. He pushed himself forward, stretched out full-length with a torch carefully poised in front of him, dug his toes into the soft earth beneath him, and propelled himself into the inky blackness ahead. It took him only ten minutes of hard, and despite the temperature, sweating work to reach the earth wall at the end of the tunnel. As he prodded his finger gingerly into it, a shower of earth fell over him. He sheltered his face in his arms as it continued to fall for five full minutes. Even after he dared to raise his eyes again, he could still hear the soft thud of damp clods falling a little too close for comfort.

He shone his torch around the top and sides of the tunnel in front of him, looking for an exit that he might have missed. Seeing nothing, he yelled at the top of his voice.

He then held his breath, and waited a few moments. Had he heard an answering cry – or only a manifestation of wishful thinking? He called out again. This time he didn't wait. Shielding his head with his arms, he dug his toes in and charged.

Trevor still sat on the floor, thinking what a complete and utter ass he'd made of himself, by rushing in, playing Sir Galahad, and incidentally going against all his training. How often had he been told that it was inevitably the simple, boring, routine everyday police legwork that caught the villains – not heroics. Not racing blindly up secret passages . . .

A black mass hurtled out of the wall, and fell on top of him. Choking clouds of dirt filled the air.

'Joseph, you bloody idiot, are you there?'

346

It was a voice Trevor would recognise anywhere. Too shocked to be grateful, it was as much as he could do to whisper a subdued; 'Yes.'

'Here, you fool. Grab hold of me. I'll rope us together, so they can heave us out of this unholy mess.'

Chapter Twenty-Five

'Well?' Peter Collins demanded, as soon as he and Trevor were dragged head-first out into the cellar.

Trevor shook his head. He coughed violently in an attempt to clear his lungs.

'Nothing?' Peter pressed.

'No one's been down there in years,' Trevor managed to croak.

'I told you so,' Jimmy Herne chanted.

'Haven't you got some gardening to do?' Peter enquired frostily, as he bent down to help Trevor to his feet. 'Go on, off you go.'

As Jimmy Herne moved unwillingly towards the door, Peter looked down ruefully at his torn, filthy shirt and muddy trousers.

'Right bloody predicament you got us into this time, Joseph,' he swore irritably.

'Thought I was on to something,' Trevor muttered, as he groped for his stick.

'You.' Peter turned to the rookie 'Report to the duty officer on the gate. They need every single body they can lay their hands on. Even one as small as yours.'

Like all the new female recruits, she had been well primed about the male chauvinism that flourished on the local force, despite equal opportunities and discrimination acts. Suppressing any urge to answer back, she disappeared smartly up the cellar steps.

'If you can manage without me now, sir, I'll show her the way,' the dog-handler murmured.

'Always got to play the cowboy in the white hat, haven't you, Joseph?' Collins complained as soon as they were alone.

'I suppose now, you expect me to help you back to your room?'

'Thanks,' Trevor murmured, as he limped forward.

He glanced at Peter and for a single blissful moment they both forgot the urgency of the search and the tensions of the case, and burst out laughing.

Despite Peter's pleadings, Trevor refused to stay in his room for a minute longer than it took him to strip off his filthy clothes, shower and change. Collins wasn't so lucky, and had to make do with wiping off his muddy trousers as best he could, then showering and borrowing a clean shirt and sweater off Trevor.

When they finally returned to the dining-room, they found it deserted except for the inevitable constable on duty.

'Everyone's back in mobile HQ, sir,' he explained.

The outer office was ominously quiet as they entered the van. Sarah Merchant sat in front of the main computer, loading discs and pressing keys.

'My God, the wanderers return,' Mulcahy said, as they pushed open the door. 'Been for a mud bath, Collins.'

'Something like that, sir.'

'Tell me?' Bill glared at Trevor.

'We didn't find anything, if that's what you mean.'

Trevor stumbled towards a chair. He felt suddenly drained, incredibly weak and exhausted. And there was no prospect of rest in the near future. Not with Lyn Sullivan still missing. 'We found the tunnels, sir,' he admitted. 'But it doesn't look as though they've been used in years.'

'So your little trip was a complete and utter waste of police time . . .'

'Not really.' Collins came to his colleague's defence. 'Now we know for certain that the tunnels do exist, and there's nothing in them, we can forget about them.'

'Something coming up on screen now, sir,' Sarah Merchant interrupted, as the VDU began to flash.

'What's it up to?' Mulcahy barked.

'Cross-checking and cross-referencing all the alibis. Any that don't match up with the others will come up on screen.'

'What time-scan have you programmed it to?'

'Ten to twelve o'clock this morning, sir. Any absences of ten minutes or more should show up. Starting with the longest.'

'What do we do if all the alibis match up,' Collins asked drily.

'There's bound to be some discrepancies,' Mulcahy commented. 'If only in the way people remember things.'

'You do realise there's no patients on this list?'

'Obviously not, since we haven't interviewed any,' Bill retorted brusquely.

'And, for my money, our villain has to be a patient.'

'One thing at a time, Collins. One thing at a time . . .' The first name flashed up on to the screen.

'Angela Morgan?' Dan read disbelievingly.

Sarah pressed the return key on the computer, and the bare bones of Angela Morgan's statement flashed up on to the screen.

'Worked alone in her office between ten and eleven, then went for break eleven to eleven-twenty in canteen. Returned to office, where worked alone until twelve.'

'You can't think for one minute that it's Angela Morgan!' Peter exclaimed in disgust.

'No,' Bill said flatly.

'But if she was alone, where was Tony Waters?' Dan asked quietly.

'Can you check his alibi without waiting for this machine to go through all its rigmarole again?' Mulcahy asked Sarah.

Sarah entered a search mode. She keyed in Tony Waters' name, and sat back. A few seconds later the information was on the screen.

'Slept alone at home until twelve. Entered hospital at twelve forty-five. Saw no one. Alibi unsubstantiated.'

Bill left his chair and tapped Dan on the shoulder. 'Bring him in.'

Before either Dan or Peter had time to respond, Michelle Grady knocked and opened the outer door.

'Mr Waters to see you, sir?'

'Superintendent, I've only just found out that two policemen, have knocked a hole in the wall of the cellar. I'm surprised that

I have to remind you of our previous conversations regarding the age and condition of this building. They could have seriously undermined the foundations . . .'

'Please,' Bill smiled, as he opened the door to the inner office. 'Wouldn't it be better to discuss this in private. Inspector Evans?'

Dan followed him into the room, and closed the door behind him.

'Is there an intercom in here?' Peter asked.

'There is, but they'd hear if I switched it on,' Sarah replied.

'Got a glass?'

'Peter,' Trevor protested. 'If there's anything in it, we'll find out soon enough. How about you carry on running that programme.' He pulled his chair alongside Sarah's.

'You weren't in the hospital this morning?' Bill asked Waters.

'No, but I've come here now to . . .'

'Complain? We know. And we'll get around to your complaints later. Right now we'd like to verify your movements this morning.'

'As I said to Constable Grady,' Tony continued testily. 'I was at home asleep until twelve o'clock.'

'Because you worked late last night?' Bill suggested.

'Because I've been working late for several nights. What is this?'

'This is an interrogation of every member of the hospital staff who cannot account for their movements during the time when Nurse Lyn Sullivan was snatched.'

'That's ridiculous. You can't suspect me . . .'

'We suspect everyone Mr Waters. That is why we're here,' Mulcahy said calmly. 'Let's start at the beginning? What time did you get home last night? What time did you go to bed? Would any of your neighbours have seen your car . . . ?'

Trevor and Peter Collins, were staring intently at the screen, watching while the computer worked to match and cross-match alibis. Suddenly Dan Evans walked into the outer office.

'Can't break his story at all. Can't budge him.'

'Try booking him?' Peter suggested.

'On what charge?'

'Make one up?'

'This isn't some dropout that we've picked up with a pocketful of hash. He's educated, he has connections, and we haven't got enough to pin a parking ticket on him. And, unfortunately for us, he knows it. He's already shouting for his lawyer.'

'Does any part of his alibi check out?'

'No one to check it with. When he got home last night his wife was asleep. She left before he woke this morning. Man even has an alarm clock instead of a wake up call. No one telephoned him. He has no neighbours near enough to see his car either coming or going. This morning he saw no milkman, no postman, no nothing. Even his daily cleaner called in sick last night so she didn't work this morning.'

'So where in hell do we go from here?' Trevor said angrily.

'I was wondering if it's worth tackling this from a different angle?'

'Such as?' Peter asked.

'How about you and Trevor having a chat with his wife? Chances are, if there is any funny business, she'd know about it.'

'You know what they say about wives?' Peter grimaced as he left his chair. His trousers were sticky with congealed mud. 'They're always the last to know when the husband goes a wandering.'

'It's all too damned neat,' Trevor said as he and Collins walked towards the ward blocks. 'Waters being the only one who can't verify his alibi.'

Peter grabbed his arm and pulled him back behind a bush. 'Ssh! Look!'

'Where?' Trevor hissed.

'End room in the geriatric block. Is that, or is that not, Sister Ashford comforting Sister Marshall after her frightening experience?'

Trevor stared blankly at the building bathed in red and gold light from the last rays of the sinking sun.

'Third window from the left,' Collins hissed.

Confused, Trevor peered at the slatted blinds. After a minute he noticed the shapes behind them. Two people drew together, hugged, their figures merging into one, as the taller of the two bent slightly and kissed the other passionately on the lips.

'Is that, or is that not Carol Ashford offering Sister Marshall sisterly comfort?' Peter asked.

'You've got a foul mind . . .'

'Possibly. But then unlike you, I'm prepared to believe the evidence of my own eyes. That's why I became a policeman. Where are you going?' he demanded as Trevor walked away.

'To knock on the front door,' Trevor said shortly. 'Are you coming or not?'

'We'd like to talk to Sister Ashford,' Trevor said curtly to the trainee nurse who opened the door to them.

The girl looked at her watch. 'She's just about to finish her shift.'

'It won't take a moment.' Peter stepped past the nurse, and Trevor followed.

'I think she's just gone to the end room to check that Sister Marshall is all right,' the girl continued, 'I'll get her, if you'd like to wait.'

Collins walked into the ward office. He looked through the glass window that gave an interrupted view into the corridor, and pulled down a roller-blind set above it, effectively screening off the room from the rest of the ward. The click of high heels on vinyl tiles echoed down the corridor. A door opened and shut.

'Sister Ashford repairing her lipstick,' he gibed.

'Knock it off,' Trevor said vehemently. 'Everyone's entitled to a private life. What Jean Marshall and Carol Ashford do in their own time has no bearing on this case.'

'No?' Peter murmured doubtfully. 'Tell me, do you consider this their own time? And then again, does having a lesbian for a wife make a man impotent?'

'Sergeant Collins, Sergeant Joseph.' Carol Ashford entered the office and closed the door behind her. 'The nurse said you wished to speak to me?'

'We do,' Peter answered.

'Then you won't mind if I sit down. I've been on my feet all day.' She laid claim to the chair behind the desk, and sat waiting for them to begin. The very essence of cool self-possession.

'Carol?' Jean Marshall knocked on the door and opened it, stepping back quickly when she saw the two men. 'I'm sorry. I didn't realise you had anyone with you,' she apologised, colouring.

'That's quite all right,' Carol said stiffly. 'We haven't really begun.'

'I just wanted to say that I was going back to my own ward.'

'I thought you were advised to take the rest of the day off, Sister Marshall?' Collins said evenly.

'I've been resting in one of the empty rooms, now I feel fine. With . . . with Lyn away,' she said brokenly, failing miserably to camouflage her emotions. 'There's a new staff on the ward. It's not easy to take over an unfamiliar ward, and I'd sleep easier tonight if I could see to the formalities myself.'

'If you'll wait, I'll telephone Constable Grady?' Peter laid his hand on the telephone.

'Help yourself, Sergeant Collins,' Carol Ashford said, with a trace of irony in her voice.

'There's no need,' Jean protested. 'I arranged to meet her in my ward.'

'There's no way we can allow any nurse to walk around the grounds of this hospital alone at the moment – not even from one ward block to the next,' Peter said firmly, as he picked up the telephone.

'I'll wait for her in the foyer,' Jean Marshall withdrew, closing the door behind her.

'How can I help you, sergeants?' Sister Ashford asked, as soon as Peter had replaced the receiver.

'By answering a few questions about your husband.'

'Tony?' She glanced at each of them in turn – and Trevor felt as though a veil had been drawn over her eyes.

'Could you tell us what time you left your house this morning?' Peter began.

'Six forty-five, the same as usual.'

'And your husband?'

'He was in bed asleep.'

'What time did he come home last night?'

'Some time after I fell asleep. Could you give me some indication as to what this is all about, Sergeant Collins?'

'We're just trying to establish his movements over the past two days.'

'Are you saying you suspect Tony had something to do with those murders?'

'Did he?' Peter asked bluntly. When she didn't reply, he continued. 'He's the *only* member of staff who can't account for his movements between the hours of ten and twelve this morning.'

'The time when Nurse Sullivan disappeared?' She sank her face into her hands. 'Where did he say he was?' she murmured faintly.

'Sister Ashford, is there anything you want to tell us about your husband?' Peter probed.

When she didn't answer, Trevor pressed on. 'If you know anything, anything at all, about Lyn Sullivan's disappearance, please tell us,' he implored. 'Otherwise we'll almost certainly have another corpse on our hands. Please, you knew Lyn . . .'

She raised her eyes until they were on a level with his. 'I'll tell you everything I know, Sergeant Joseph. I only hope that it will be enough.'

Patients on geriatric wards are routinely bedded down earlier than those on other wards. In the intervals when Sister Ashford wasn't speaking, the silence was filled with small, soft noises; the quiet whirr of the electric clock on the office wall, the last tentative notes of evening birdsong in the garden, the murmur of the constable who was stationed in the foyer making radio contact with headquarters.

'You must understand, Sergeant.' Carol was speaking to Peter, but she was looking at Trevor. 'My husband was utterly charming when I first met him. I thought he possessed every quality I'd ever looked for and wanted in a man. He was handsome, courteous, considerate. He had a marvellous sense of humour. His parents adored me, and they were wealthy on a scale I'd only dreamt about. They'd given Tony everything; the best schools, the best university, the confidence to talk to people – important people that is. He had influential, and glamorous friends, he took me to all the right places . . . You can have no idea how overwhelming that can be to someone like myself who was . . .'

'What?' Peter demanded brutally.

'Brought up on a slum of a council estate, Sergeant Collins,' she finished eventually. 'When I first met Tony . . .'

'In this hospital?' Collins interrupted her, much to Trevor's chagrin.

'No, not this hospital. Greenways in Kent. He seemed so sophisticated, so wonderful, I couldn't believe my luck. That he'd actually chosen me to be his girlfriend.' She lowered her long, thick eyelashes. 'The first time I went out with him, I was swept off my feet. Quite literally. He really knows how to treat a woman,' she added bitterly. 'Flowers, chocolates, cards, presents. I married him only eight months after I met him, and by then we were both working here in Compton Castle. He comes from this area, you know. We moved down here soon after his mother was diagnosed as having cancer. A week after her death, his father shot himself. It was . . .' Tears filled her beautiful navy-blue eyes, but their advent didn't affect the clarity of her voice. 'It was then that I think he became unhinged. You see, he absolutely adored his parents. He was an only child.' She added as an afterthought, 'or perhaps he'd been unhinged all along, and I'd simply chosen to ignore his mental state because I didn't want to confront his problems, or see anything unpleasant that might have flawed my Prince Charming.'

'Exactly what are his problems?' Peter asked.

'His cruelty,' she admitted reluctantly. 'He has a sadistic streak. It all started when I didn't get pregnant straight after our wedding. Our sex life changed,' she whispered the words prudishly. 'He started to beat me.' She rolled up the sleeve of the sweater she was wearing, and uncovered a series of enormous black and purple spreading bruises that encircled her upper and lower arms. Pulling down the roll-neck collar, she disclosed multicoloured contusions on her neck. 'And his demands on me increased with his brutality. Nothing I did was ever good enough for him. In the kitchen, in our home, in bed, in work – you must have seen what a perfectionist he is. I have never managed to keep a domestic help for more than three months, although I pay double the going rate. He'd begin to criticise their work, and then they'd leave.'

'Do you know of any links between your husband and the missing girls?' Collins asked.

'Yes with all the girls that were found dead, except for Vanessa Hedley, that is . . .'

'Go on,' Peter ordered abruptly.

'Well I have no proof, no real proof except a couple of letters and intercepted telephone calls. But I know, Sergeant Collins,' she looked Peter straight in the eye. 'Believe me, I know. He had affairs with all three of them, and when Lyn disappeared this morning I feared the worst.'

'Why?' Trevor interrupted swiftly.

'Because I saw him talking to her yesterday afternoon in the ward office. Saw the way he was looking at her . . .'

Trevor had a sudden flash of memory. Tony Waters' chair pulled close to Lyn's. White-blond and black hair touching as their two heads bent over the notebook in her lap.

'I'm afraid, Sergeant. Afraid for Lyn. You see, I think he took her. You know Lyn Sullivan, Sergeant Joseph,' she appealed to Trevor. 'I can't imagine her *agreeing* to go out with him, not so soon after she broke up with Karl Lane. And if he asked, and she refused . . .' tears poured down her cheeks and she struggled to suppress them. 'I believe he's quite capable of abducting her.'

'Where do you think he's hidden her?' Trevor asked urgently.

'If I knew, I'd tell you. There have been nights, so many nights, when he hasn't come home at all. And there's one more thing; he's impotent.'

'You mean he can't make love?' Collins asked bluntly.

'Oh, he's capable of performing the physical act, after a fashion,' she commented scathingly. 'If that's what you call "making love". But he can't have children. And since he's found out, he's resorted to . . . to . . .' She burst into a paroxysm of weeping that made further questioning impossible.

Peter smiled coldly at Trevor. 'Got the bastard.'

'But not Lyn,' Trevor murmured. 'We're still no nearer to finding her.'

Collins put a call out for a woman police constable to take care of Carol Ashford.

'I really would like to go home,' Carol pleaded, having made a partial recovery from her hysteria. 'I'd like to shower, change my clothes.'

'We may need you again,' Peter said firmly. 'I'm reluctant to let you go until we've finished questioning your husband. There may be something else you know . . .' The telephone rang and he picked it up. 'That was Michelle,' he turned to Trevor. 'Bill's suggesting that Sister Ashford could join Jean Marshall and Michelle in a hospital flat for the time being. Spencer Jordan has volunteered his. It will only be for a few hours,' he said casually.

'How long is a few hours, Sergeant?' Carol Ashford demanded.

'Just as long as it takes to get your husband to tell us where he's hidden Lyn Sullivan.'

'Superintendent, the whole idea is bizarre, the fabrications of an insane mind. You simply can't believe . . .'

'The mind is your wife's,' Bill Mulcahy said flatly. 'The evidence is there for all to see. You had the means, the opportunity. On your own admission, you know this place inside out.'

'Where have you hidden Lyn Sullivan?' Collins demanded, looming threateningly over the table.

'Nowhere!' Waters retorted furiously. 'I haven't even seen the girl.' He suddenly burst out laughing; a high-pitched, frenzied laugh. 'Oh, I see what you're doing,' he said suddenly. 'You're making up stories in the hope that I'll confess. I want to make a telephone call *now*. To my lawyer.'

'Fine,' Mulcahy picked up the telephone, and slammed it down in front of him. 'But I warn you; you make that call and we're charging you.'

'With what?'

'Four counts of murder and five of kidnapping.'

'That's absurd. You have no proof. If you did, you'd have taken me to the police station.'

'To all intents and purposes this *is* a police station. And the reason we haven't moved you is a six-foot-tall, slim, attractive black-haired nurse that you've hidden somewhere on these premises. Tell me, Mr Waters, is she still alive?'

'I wish I could help you, Superintendent. But I know nothing.'

'Nothing?' Collins produced the statement he'd got Carol Ashford to sign before Michelle Grady had taken her over to Spencer's apartment. 'Do you deny having affairs with Claire Moon, Elizabeth Moore, and Rosie Twyford – and receiving phone-calls from them at your home?'

'I might have received one or two calls from them, but . . .'

'Go on!'

'Receiving phone-calls is hardly a crime. And even if they did call me, the chances are that those calls were connected with business.'

'Like the affairs you had with them?'

'Affairs, like phone-calls, are hardly crimes.'

'And the bruises you inflicted on your wife?'

'Carol enjoys rough lovemaking.'

'Lovemaking?' Collins sneered. 'From an impotent man?'

'What the devil do you mean?' Waters turned crimson and Peter knew that he'd finally hit a raw nerve. He was too good a policeman not to keep on hitting at it.

'Impotent as in can't have children.'

'Whether I can father children or not is none of your damned business!' Tony Waters' face turned from red to purple with rage.

'Where is she?' Peter demanded, thrusting his face close to Waters'. 'Where is she?'

'I swear to you, I haven't seen her since yesterday.'

'You trying to tell us that you didn't take her? That you didn't grab her from the hostel because you can't make love to a woman properly?'

'I might not be able to father a child, but in every other way I'm a normal man,' Waters countered furiously, too angered to realise that he hadn't denied the accusation Peter was making.

360

'That's not the story your wife's told us.'

'Carol? But she knows . . . she . . .'

'She made a statement,' Peter waved it in front of him again. 'She confirms that you had affairs with all three women.'

'Even if I did, that doesn't make me a murderer.'

'No, but it doesn't mean you're able to engage in normal lovemaking either.' He was really stabbing at the man's Achilles' heel.

'For pity's sake, I'm normal I tell you. If you want to know how normal, just ask Jean Marshall.'

An eerie silence fell over the room. Trevor Joseph rose abruptly from his chair and slammed his way out through the door.

Chapter Twenty-Six

Trevor stumbled as he flung himself down the steps. Peter, who was running close on his heels, reached out and steadied him.

'You're going to see Jean Marshall?'

'You thinking what I'm thinking?' Trevor asked.

'Either our esteemed administrator or his wife is lying,' Collins replied. 'The question is which one. Taxi?' he shouted to the driver of a police car, who was standing nearby, chatting to the constable on duty. 'To the halfway houses, and step on it.' He dived into the back of the car.

'You've been on duty since Constable Grady escorted the two women inside?'

'Yes, sir.'

'Looks like our little bird is still cooped up then,' Collins murmured to Trevor.

'If this little bird proves to be the one I think it is, I'm not counting on buying any birdseed until I see her for myself.' Trevor led the way into the building.

The health authorities had gone to a great deal of trouble to ensure that the ground floor of the halfway house resembled a private home, but to Trevor, the atmosphere in the bleak, bare, white-walled rooms retained the distinct air of an institution. The coat rack in the hallway was bare, as though no one dared to use it. All the adjoining doors were open, including one into the cupboard under the stairs, which held an improbably tidy display of cleaning tools; vacuum cleaner, brushes, and mops. The kitchen surfaces were bare, and the spotless stove had a disused air.

The lounge was furnished with the same lack of imagination

as the sitting-room in the nurses' hostel, and Collins saw Spencer sitting on the edge of an uncomfortable upright chair, playing chess with a slim young man Trevor recognised as a past inmate of the ward.

'You're here to see Sister Marshall and Sister Ashford?' Spencer guessed. 'I'll take you up.'

'No, don't disturb yourself,' Collins said. 'Just point us in the right direction.'

'Go up to the top floor, and it's the door facing you at the top of the stairs.'

'Thanks.' With Trevor lagging behind, Peter climbed the first flight of stairs. Five closed doors greeted him, all fitted with Yale locks. As he began on the next flight of stairs, a man rose to his feet, from the top step where he'd been sitting.

'Slacking on the job, Murphy?' Collins asked caustically.

'Resting my feet before you dump the next load on me,' Andrew snapped back.

'Anyone gone in or out of there?'

'No. Apart from a little classical music, it's been as quiet as the grave.' He pushed a dirty coffee cup into the corner behind him.

'When did they give you coffee?' Trevor asked, wincing in pain as he tried to put his right foot flat on the floor.

'Just after we got here. About . . .' he looked at his watch, 'an hour and a half ago.'

As there was no bell, Peter banged on the door. There was no response. 'Constable Grady, it's Sergeant Collins!' he shouted. 'Open up.'

The silence that fell after his frenzied banging, hung, heavy, pregnant with foreboding.

'Got a key for this lock?' Peter turned to Murphy.

'No.'

'Then go downstairs and get Spencer's,' Trevor suggested.

'No time.' Peter put his shoulder to the door and heaved. The wood splintered and the door swung inwards, its lock hanging free. He stood poised for only a moment, then barged through the door into the living-room, tripping over the inert body of Michelle Grady, who lay stretched on the floor, still holding a coffee cup in her right hand. The dregs had spilled over the orange and brown whirls of the carpet, staining the area around her head. Jean Marshall was lying sprawled on the sofa. Some coffee had tipped on to her blouse.

Trevor dived into the room and knelt down between them, his face contorting at the agony of bending his shattered knees.

'They're both breathing,' Collins said coldly. 'Probably just tranquillised. Call an ambulance,' he shouted to Murphy.

As Spencer superintended the clearing out of the hostel inmates, the ambulance teams dashed upstairs, soon returning with two loaded stretchers.

'What I can't understand,' Murphy said in a hurt tone, 'is how she could get out. I was in touch with both our man at the back and our man downstairs every ten minutes, and neither of them saw anything amiss.'

Collins opened the window wide, and leant out.

'What do you see?' Trevor asked.

'A bloody big drop . . . and the roof,' he said shortly. 'There's barely four foot between this building and the next. If she climbed up instead of down, she could have . . .'

'Stepped across?' Trevor suggested.

'Jumped,' Peter corrected. 'I don't know if you noticed, but she's an athletic-looking girl.'

'I noticed.'

'Can I come in?' Spencer hovered in front of the splintered wood that had once been his front door.

'There's no need to ask,' Peter said blandly.

'It's one of the girls from the house next-door,' Spencer said hesitantly. 'I wouldn't have bothered you, but it might be important. She says she hung her coat on the rack by the door, but now it's gone.'

'What colour was it?' Trevor asked.

'She says a silk paisley pattern, green and black. She'd only just bought it . . .'

Trevor didn't wait for the rest of the sentence. He turned to Collins.

'Car park?' he suggested.

'Let's go.'

The constable had been on duty in the car park since six o'clock,

365

and insisted that nothing out of the ordinary had occurred; only the usual staff had come and gone.

'And Sister Ashford?' Peter had pressed.

'Sister Ashford?' The man gazed at him vacantly.

'Tall, slim, blonde, blue-eyed, beautiful,' Trevor elaborated.

'The one married to the chief administrator?'

'That's her,' Peter confirmed.

'She took her husband's BMW. She said that her Peugeot was giving her trouble, so he'd offered to take it to the garage.'

'Take us up to mobile HQ,' Collins ordered the police driver.

'Why not follow her?' Trevor demanded urgently.

'Because she could be anywhere.' Peter snapped impatiently. 'And because, if we're going to find Lyn Sullivan before it's too late, we'll need all the help we can get. And in my opinion we should begin with the person who knows her best. Tony Waters!'

When Peter and Trevor returned to headquarters, Tony Waters was still sitting at the conference table, head in hands. Dan Evans was thumbing through computer printouts of the interview reports, and Bill Mulcahy was bawling out the constable who'd been manning the gate when Carol Ashford had driven out of the grounds, to the main road.

'No one warned me, sir,' the man protested. 'I didn't realise she was a suspect. She wasn't even driving her own car. She was driving her husband's BMW.'

'I know what she was bloody well driving!' Mulcahy exclaimed.

'Mr Waters?' Trevor pulled out a chair alongside Waters and tapped the administrator's hand. 'Have you any idea where your wife could have gone?'

He stared at Trevor with vacant, hollow eyes. 'I don't know,' he whispered bleakly. 'She didn't keep in contact with anyone from her past, and she didn't have many friends. Lots of acquaintances; people she met through Rotary Club, charity committees – that sort of thing. But no real friends.'

'The house. You think she might have gone back there?' Trevor demanded.

'I don't know,' Waters mumbled carelessly, as though he no longer cared.

'Do you keep any valuables there?' Peter asked. 'Money, passports, that sort of thing?' he explained impatiently to the vacant expression on Tony's face.

'I keep some money there, in the safe. Our passports are there as well.'

'She has the key to the safe?' Peter asked.

'She knows the number, it's a combination lock.'

'Senseless both of us going.' Collins already had his hand on the door handle. He shook his head as Trevor rose stiffly to his feet. 'You'd only slow me down. I'll keep in touch. Mr Waters, you'd better come. We may need you.' He nodded to Dan Evans who followed him out.

'The car your wife drove would have been searched thoroughly before she went out of the gates. That must mean that Lyn Sullivan is still hidden, somewhere in the hospital,' Trevor spoke earnestly, detaining Waters for a moment. 'Please. You know this building better than anyone. Do you have any idea where she could have hidden Lyn?'

'Do you think I didn't think of that when Vanessa Hedley disappeared?' Waters retorted acidly. 'Everywhere, absolutely everywhere has been thoroughly searched by your own people.' He followed Collins and Evans out through the door.

Although Waters gave the police driver precise directions to his farm, the driver twice missed turnings in the winding country lanes, and then they lost frantic minutes while he manoeuvred tight ten-point turns in impossibly narrow spaces, during which all of them counted off the passing seconds.

When they finally reached the farmyard, Peter Collins wondered how anyone could have missed it. It was fully floodlit, with two large Dobermans barking and circling crazily by the front door.

Peter looked hopefully at Waters who climbed out of the car and called out to the dogs. They stopped their barking and ran over to him, tongues hanging out, ready to roll over in delight. He pulled out his keys and shut them away in the conservatory. Collins walked round to the front door, which was on the same side of the building as the kitchen door. He held out his hand as Waters approached.

'Keys,' he said shortly.

'It's all right. I'll open it.' Tony seemed strangely reluctant to hand them over.

'Stand back,' Peter ordered abruptly. 'There's a strong smell of gas.'

'Then shouldn't I . . .'

He didn't have the chance to say another word. Dan Evans hooked his arm around his waist, lifted him off his feet, and yanked him right back into the yard, while Peter inserted the key gingerly into the lock. He pushed the door open tentatively with his fingertips.

'You on mains or calor gas?' Dan asked Waters. But he never heard the reply to his question.

A massive, deafening explosion ripped through the house, blasting the front door off its hinges. It caught Collins' shoulder as it hurtled back, carrying him to the centre of the yard in a hurricane of shattering glass and shooting flames, that blew windows, roof and wall outwards. For five full minutes all Dan could do was lie flat on the ground, his nose buried in the dirt, his eardrums in agony, as he watched flames lick out of the building into a strange, red unnaturally silent world.

'Peter?' he gasped, looking over to where Collins was lying, eyes wide open, half buried beneath a heap of smouldering debris.

Their driver, hit on the neck by a piece of window-sill, had staggered back to the car and was now yelling down the radio phone for the fire brigade, back-up units, and ambulances.

Tony Waters had been partly shielded by Dan's massive figure as the full force of the blast had struck, so got off lighter than the other three men. Dan could only watch as he scrambled to his feet and ran towards the house. A charred figure was crawling through the gap where part of the front wall had stood only minutes before. Blackened and shrivelled, its skeletal arms and blistering, bubbling skin were scarcely recognisable as human.

Waters took off his coat and flung it over the ragged scarecrow of baked flesh.

'I couldn't bear it,' the lipless mouth mumbled.

'Bear what darling?' Tony demanded as he cradled her in his arms.

'Anyone else living in my house. That's what I was afraid of, that you'd leave me for one of those girls. That's why I had to take them from you. I didn't want to kill them – just keep them away from you. But, you see, I had no choice. I couldn't hide them forever, and when the time came to move them I found I couldn't hurt them. I. . .' There was only white to be seen in her eyes. Blind, staring white. 'So in the end I buried them. It was easier that way . . . just to bury them . . . even the dog. It was always in your office . . . I thought,' she gasped painfully. 'I began to think you preferred it to me . . .'

Where's Lyn?' Dan Evans asked urgently, crawling over the littered yard towards them. 'Where have you hidden Lyn?'

'Vanessa. She saw me. I didn't want to harm her. But I had to, don't you see. She kept talking about it all the time. I injected her with air. It had to be quick. It's a quick way to go . . . You see, I couldn't bear it.' She mumbled faintly through blackened gums. 'I couldn't . . .'

'Where did you put Lyn?' Dan demanded again.

'She's dead,' Tony Waters announced in a voice devoid of all emotion.

'She'd rigged a piece of flint under the door.' Collins stumbled towards them leaning heavily on the driver. His left arm was cradled at a peculiar angle in his right. 'I heard it striking. But I'd already pulled the door back, and it was too late. There was nothing I could do.'

'She was expecting *me*,' Tony said bitterly.

Collins sank weakly to the ground.

'Hospital for you,' Dan Evans muttered.

'We still don't know where Lyn Sullivan is,' Peter complained faintly, eyelids drooping.

'That's someone else's problem now,' Dan said firmly, putting his hand on Peter's shoulder. He turned his back on Tony who was still cradling the obscenely mutilated body of his wife. He could find no words of comfort to offer the man, but he could and did offer privacy – of a kind. 'From now on, Sergeant

369

Collins, you're well and truly out of this race,' Dan continued as he heard the first siren in the distance.

'Peter's in the hospital?'

'He's all right,' Dan Evans reassured a shocked Trevor Joseph. 'Carol Ashford had turned on all the gas appliances in her house, and then rigged a flint under the front door so the place would go up the minute it was opened. Peter got caught in the blast; his back and arms are a bit scorched, and his collarbone is broken, but a couple of days in hospital, a couple of weeks' rest, and he'll be back to normal.'

'And you?' Bill Mulcahy asked.

'Slightly deaf . . .'

'Slightly pitted,' Bill commented looking at the burn holes in Dan's sweater.

'They kept the driver in, with a burn on his neck. Tony Waters is in severe shock. They sedated him, so he'll be in overnight.'

Trevor glanced across to Harry Goldman and Dotty Clyne. 'Damn Carol Ashford for dying,' he said savagely. 'We still haven't a clue where Lyn Sullivan is . . .'

'No. And I've a feeling that if we don't find her soon, we may as well stop looking.' Mulcahy rose from his chair and paced uneasily across the room. 'We have to be missing something. All of you have to think,' he ordered. If sheer forcefulness could have conjured Lyn's presence, she would have materialised in the room that moment. Bill thumbed through the search reports and tossed them across the table, then he stared at the team leaders sitting around the table. 'Every single man jack of you, close your eyes and think back to our last search. Relive it in your mind. Crawl through it, step by step . . .'

Step by step, Trevor mentally inched his way around the cellar. He shuddered when he remembered the tunnel. He limped over the flagstoned floor, Tony Waters at his side, telling him stories about the history of the place . . . then Carol Ashford taking over . . . the bare, open, padded cells which didn't offer enough shelter to conceal a fly . . . the room where the rubbish was kept . . . the mortuary . . . Carol Ashford in the mortuary. The corpse! The geriatric corpse with the yellowed skin and thick horny toenails of the elderly . . . the corpse in the garden . . . Roland had taken it . . . Roland who had found the mortuary unlocked . . . Why had it been unlocked? Because someone had been too busy to lock it. Someone who had removed a body. A body that shouldn't have been there . . . a body that had to be hidden in a room rarely used . . . Vanessa's body.

White-faced he left his chair.

'Where you off to, Joseph?' Bill demanded.

'The mortuary.'

Both Harry Goldman and Dan Evans stared at him.

'The mortuary,' he repeated as he picked up his stick. He hobbled as fast as he could through the door, down the outside steps, towards the rear of the building. Once he reached the level, he positively raced along the corridor, with Dan and Harry Goldman lapping at his heels. Switching on lights as he went, he hurried to the male mortuary, and heaved at the door.

'Damn, it's locked.'

'Of course it is.' Goldman was close behind him.

'Do you have the key.'

'A master key, but I'm not sure it fits these old locks.' The two minutes it took Harry Goldman to open the door dragged by longer than years. As soon as the room was open, Trevor burst in. He paused to stare at the bank of drawers. Which one first? The top left hand?'

He heaved on the handle. It grated sluggishly. He tugged at it again. The same corpse was still inside. He recognised those feet that looked as though they'd been wrapped in yellow parchment. The face was covered by a sheet. Peeling it back he uncovered the body of the old man. Thrusting his hands beneath the light corpse, he lifted it out and laid it quickly on one of the zinc-covered tables. Beneath was another sheet; thick, lumpy. Scarcely daring to breathe, Trevor drew it aside.

The white face of Lyn Sullivan stared up at him, eyes wide open, muscles immobile. He could hear Dan calling down his radio, for a doctor. Trevor laid his hand on her sweater, felt her heart beat. Slow, but definite.

'She's alive,' he whispered, as he leant back against the table. The hand of the corpse rolled aside and hit his back, but he was immune to the dead man's touch. 'She's still alive,' he repeated gratefully, only just beginning to believe it.

Epilogue

'Thanks Trevor. That was a good film and a good meal.'

'The film was good,' Trevor agreed. 'I have my doubts about the fish and chips.'

'Perhaps it was the company.' Spencer pushed his bicycle clips on to his trouser legs and proceeded down the empty echoing passage of Trevor's new home, towards the front door.

'We'll do the same next week?' Trevor suggested.

Spencer managed a tight smile as he turned to face him. 'Yes, I'd like that.'

Trevor opened the door, and stood on the doorstep, watching as Spencer rode away. He passed Peter Collins who, arm in sling, was walking up the path.

'Came to see if you'd like to go out for a drink after all the hassle of moving.'

'I don't think so, if you don't mind.' Trevor led him back through the house, past the lounge and dining-room both carpeted in plain grey Wilton but completely devoid of furniture, and into the kitchen. 'There's still one or two things I need to do.'

'*One* drink?'

The telephone interrupted them. Trevor picked up the receiver of the wall phone fixed next to the door. Peter leant against the fridge, and listened to the one-sided conversation.

'Yes . . . yes . . . fine . . . yes . . . I'd like that . . . yes . . . see you a week Monday, then. Yes . . . look forward to working with you. Fine. Goodbye.'

'You took it, then?' Peter watched him replace the receiver.

'What?' Trevor asked blankly.

'The job Dan offered.'

'You already knew about it?'

'There's been talk of nothing else down the station. Special Crimes Sergeant. You won't forget us poor sloggers in the Drug Squad when you're lording it in your new office, bored out of your mind, waiting for a murder to happen, will you?'

'Would you let me?'

Peter followed Trevor into the kitchen, and stared at the pile of dirty dishes in the sink. 'Want me to tackle those?'

'With one arm? I was just about to load the dish washer.'

Collins studied the shining antiseptic surfaces of the gleaming blue-and-white kitchen. 'You've done well for yourself here, Joseph. Tell me, do you think you'll survive such uncluttered cleanliness?'

'I can but try.'

'Must have cost a bomb.'

'A small one,' Trevor agreed wryly 'And, then again I couldn't have done it if the sitting tenants hadn't bought my old flat.'

'I don't suppose you could,' Peter said a little wistfully remembering the house he had handed over lock, stock and barrel to his undeserving ex-wife. 'Come on, just one quick one,' he pleaded.

'Tomorrow night,' Trevor compromised.

'We could all be dead by then. I know you and your tomorrows.'

'I'm busy right now,' Trevor said impatiently. 'Tomorrow night.'

'You'll slide right back into a depression if you're not careful. Staying indoors, moping around . . . Tell me, what did you do in Cornwall?'

'Eat, sleep . . . play with my brother's kids.'

'That's my point. Now look at you. You may have bought a wonderful house, but what's the point in hanging another millstone around your neck, if all it means is that you're going to lock yourself up here and concentrate your every waking minute on furniture and fittings, instead of having a good time. I keep telling you it's what you *do* that's important.'

'And I'm very grateful for your advice,' Trevor said firmly. 'But tonight I'm tired. I'll go for a drink with you tomorrow. All right.' He deliberately led the way down the passage towards the front door. 'Believe me I appreciate your concern, but right now I want a bath and an early night.'

'I can take a hint.' Peter dumped a bottle he'd been carrying on to the kitchen work-surface. 'Tomorrow then. I won't forget.'

'Neither will I. Around nine?'

'I'll be here.'

Peter turned back as he stepped on to the garden path. 'They're not prosecuting Roland Williams for mishandling that corpse.'

'Well, it's not surprising, is it. There isn't much you can do to a man who steals a corpse from a mortuary, carries it out to a garden and attacks it, except lock him up in an institution. And as he's already there, there seems little point in wasting taxpayers' money on holding a trial.'

'He's locked up safely for now,' Peter said grimly. 'But what will happen to him next year when they close down Compton Castle?'

'The same thing that is going to happen to all the others,' Trevor said flatly. 'He'll be out in the community again.'

'Think we should apply for doubling of manpower now?'

'Either that or a new prison. See you.'

After he shut the door, Trevor made sure that all the downstairs windows were locked. He loaded the dishwasher and tidied around, switching off the lights after he took one last look at the empty lounge and dining-room. Tomorrow morning he'd go and choose some furniture – perhaps start off in the antique shops. If he couldn't find anything there, he'd visit one or two of the better-class furniture shops. There was no hurry though. He was going to be in this house a long time, so he could afford to take a few months to find the right pieces. He'd already sorted the master bedroom; it was large enough to take the television, video and chaise-longue he'd bought, as well as the king-size bed. The builder had turned the fourth bedroom into a walk-in dressing room and wardrobe. That had made all the difference to the upstairs and still left two guest-rooms. More than enough for any likely visitors.

He opened the fridge, and took out the bottle of wine that had been cooling all day. He walked slowly up the stairs, concentrating on putting one foot carefully in front of the other.

It wasn't easy without his stick, but he was getting there. Another two to three months, the physiotherapist had said, then he'd be walking properly again.

Switching on the small lamps at either side of the bed, he opened the french doors that looked out over the sea, and went outside. He'd put up screening at both ends of the long balcony that ran the full length of his house. Sitting here he could only be overlooked from the beach, and at this time of night it was deserted.

He set the bottle and glasses on the wrought-iron pub table he had bought in a secondhand shop in Cornwall, then sat down on one of the matching chairs. He took his time over opening the wine, screwing the cork firmly on to the opener, while he stared out thoughtfully, drinking in the beauty of the glittering path painted by the moon on the shimmering surface of the sea. Listening to the quiet hiss of the waves, as they glided back and forth on the pebble-strewn shore.

'I might have known I'd find you out here.' Lyn suddenly stood behind him, her hair wrapped in a towel, another wrapped around her slim inviting body.

'Wine?' he asked.

'If I didn't know you better, I'd think you were trying to get me drunk.'

He poured her a glass and she reached for it.

'If we're going to sit out here, I suppose I'd better put on something more substantial than this.' She stepped back into the bedroom, and he followed her. Reaching out he held her close for a moment, revelling in the warm, sensual feel of her and the rhythm of her heart beating against his. As she raised her face, he kissed her on the lips; slowly, deeply, and infinitely satisfying.

'You're not sorry I moved in with you?' she teased.

'Someone has to make sure that you stay in one piece, and if you continue like today, you could save me a fortune in cleaning bills.'

'I won't cramp your style, then?' As she wrapped her arms around his neck, the towel she was wearing fell to the floor.

'I'm not sure I even had a style before I met you,' he whispered thickly, kissing the hollow above her collarbone.

'The wine's going to get warm,' she murmured.

'There's a cool breeze blowing.'

'That's all right, then.' She pulled him back on to the bed.

'Lyn?' He looked into her deep dark eyes as she unfastened the buttons on his shirt.

'Yes,' she answered.

He smiled at her. 'Nothing.' He kissed her again, and then there was no need for any more words between them for a long time.

Lyn was a miracle which had transformed his life. And experience had taught him that miracles shouldn't be analysed or questioned. For once he'd struck lucky, but it wouldn't last – it never did, and in this case it couldn't. There were thirteen years between them; a wealth of bitter experience on his side, and youth and beauty on hers. But for now at least, she was his. He had learned a hard lesson in Compton Castle, but he had learned it well. *Now* was all anyone ever really had. And this *now* was more than he deserved.